First Published by Fuzz Publishing 2012.

Copyright © Fuzz Enterprizes Pty Ltd (ACN 127 510 169)

Cover designed by Brendan Sanders.

www.sevenstonesofpower.com

THE JADE DAGGER

ANDY STONE

Prologue: An Enemy Revealed

"We've been sitting here for over a week now, there's nothing to eat here. That snake is not coming back," the creature that sat around the camp fire spoke with a deep, rasping voice.

There were five of them, their features all similar, leathery dark skin with only dirty loin cloths covering their bodies. They all stood hunched over, unable to stand up straight. Their long fingers ending in sharp claws capable of ripping flesh straight from the bone. Sharp teeth protruded from their mouths.

"I sick of this place," barked another one in agreement. "I say we move now. Find some meat to eat."

Suddenly a man dressed in black armour loomed over them. None of the orglin heard his approach. His breast plate glowed in the fire light. His black helmet, with the visor down, covered his face. His presence was enough of an announcement and even though there was not a breath of wind the shadows flickered around him. They were visibly afraid. He had been gone for so long the orglin had hoped he wasn't going to return.

"We have our instructions to wait. If you want to go, then go and see how far you get." His voice was as cool and as calm as his stance. "No one disobeys our master. Not unless you want to suffer for a thousand years." There was nothing but confidence in the man standing before them. At least he had once been a man, but now he was something else, something more. He was the Dark Knight Argoz and one of the chosen few of the Great Lord.

To emphasize his point he reached out his arm and clenched his fist. Although he was a good pace away from the nearest orglin the creature grabbed at its throat, gasping for air. If anyone else had the power in them they would have felt his magic, but since there were none there was no point in masking it. With a final convulsion the orglin went still, its lifeless eyes staring towards the night sky.

Death made Argoz feel better. He despised the lowly creatures. They were not fit to share the same campsite of someone in such high standing as himself, but even he had to accept orders. A small grin appeared on his face under the visor as he savoured the death.

"We didn't mean anything by it." The one who made the original comment started to grovel.

Before anyone else could move there was a shimmer in the air. A robed figure appeared with seven soldiers on horseback and two prisoners on foot behind them.

The leader stood at the front of the group, his face covered by his hood. His mount stood nervously behind him and there was an even stronger feeling of dread emanating from the new arrival. The orglin shrunk back, away from the fire, trying to hide in the shadows.

Argoz was disgusted with the simple trick. It was completely unnecessary as they were leagues away from anyone who would recognise the prisoners. He was sure the serpentant was purely trying to show off. He wanted nothing more than to crush the creature, but that would anger the Great Lord.

"I thought you were supposed to bring them undamaged?" said Argoz. To accentuate his point he looked at the two prisoners. The male prisoner had a lot more bruises on his face than the female. The She-Elf looked as though she laboured more as she walked. Both had received some rough treatment. "What do you have to say for yourself?" he spoke with complete distaste.

The robed figure walked towards him. He waited until they were face to face before he said anything. "I do not follow orders from you," he spoke with a hiss and nearly spat the words.

It took all Argoz's will power not to draw in the energy around him and crush the serpentant who stood with complete confidence. There was no fear in his demeanour.

"Well what do you have to report Viper? Tell me some good news. I've be coming here for over a month now and I'm sick of these cretins." He spat at the orglin sitting around the fire and they all flinched away.

Viper hissed before turning to face his prisoners. Both of them kept their eyes low. They had learnt early on not to stare at the serpentant. If they didn't show respect then Viper would make them learn it. The first lesson was to not look him in the eyes and to be meek and humble. Eldred and Alena were far from breaking, but if they could avoid another beating they certainly would. Although Viper really didn't need any excuse he always seemed to have one. It had taken them a week since they left Nostiria to reach the camp site. The first day they were strapped to the spare horselings, but with each day Viper's temper became more severe. Even the seven soldiers accompanying him were shocked. He could push things, but not too far, for if he delivered the packages to Nyrra too damaged then his life wouldn't be worth living.

Viper made a point to avoid striking Alena's face. Her blonde hair was a scraggly mess covered with dust and dirt. Her once creamy soft skin was burnt and cracked from the sun. Dirt covered her face and arms and her ragged clothes were filthy.

Eldred had not fared any better. His grey hair was knotted and dirty, his skin seemed somewhat unaffected from the sun, although his face seemed more aged that normal. Old bruises were fading from his face and arms and on first glances it seemed that he had received the worst of the beatings.

"Everything is going to plan, Argoz," Viper hissed, still facing his hostages. "By now the Great Lord should have finished the first stage of his plan and Alaric should be on his way." Even though he could not see for himself Argoz was sure there was a smile on Viper's face.

"What of Morgoz?" his patience was starting to wear thin at Viper's short answers. He was one of the chosen seven and deserved respect from the... reptile.

"He left to chase after Alaric. My guess would be he is floating in the void by now. I think he is one that you don't have to worry too much about any more." Viper seemed pleased to speak of Morgoz's demise. "Otherwise he has helped the Great Lord to defeat Alaric and he is even now sitting on his right hand side, either way I don't know." Although he did not believe the second explanation, Viper added it just to agitate him.

"So it is true, I thought I felt a shift in the world. Morgoz is dead." Argoz ignored Viper's last comment. "One less that I have to contend with," Argoz mumbled the last to himself. When he realised what he had said he looked up with a start, to see if anyone had heard him. No one seemed to, but he couldn't be sure without seeing Viper's face.

"You leave for Jarrat tonight and I shall return to my other life," Argoz commanded as he regained his composure. "Shkerlok," he called to one of the Orglin. "Ready the camp. We leave within the hour."

With a soft shriek the orglin started to move. They knew not to rouse the wrath of Argoz. The Dark Knight took great pleasure in torturing the pitiful creatures. He believed they didn't deserve to live. They did, however, make up to bulk of Nyrra's army and he would be in great disfavour if he started randomly killing them for fun.

"Stay where you are Shkerlok." Viper's face did not leave the prisoners. "We have travelled far in the last week to get here. If you want the prisoners to die before we reach Jarrat we can leave tonight, though I'm sure you wouldn't get a very pleasant reception once we get there. Unless Alaric has learned the forgotten art of travelling then he is at least a month behind us."

It was all Argoz could do to hold his temper. He wanted nothing more than to draw his sword and cut the snake down. Viper was deliberately trying to bait him. He knew that there was nothing he could do; he had to keep the serpentant alive. The Great Lord had been quite specific.

"Fine then, you will camp tonight and move out at first light." The command sent a groan throughout the camp. Orglin hated the sun-light. They preferred to sleep during the day.

Argoz could have killed them all without thinking. He had enough of his soldiers to guard the prisoners and make sure their journey was safe and hidden. The dozen or so orglin were only a liability. The savages were only going to give their position away. The excuses raced through his mind. He could always make up a reason why the orglin had died before they reached Jarrat. Viper could waste in the void if he tried to stop him.

With that thought in mind Argoz drew his sword and beheaded the nearest orglin. As if reading their commander's thoughts the soldiers drew their swords and started to slaughter the rest. The battle was short and bloody.

"Make sure the prisoners make it to Jarrat undamaged." Argoz said as he turned away. "I have to return to my true task."

Viper sneered as Argoz disappeared. Everything was falling into place for him. It wouldn't be long before he was free of Nyrra's yoke and he would look forward to gutting Argoz, of all the Dark Knights Argoz disgusted him the most.

***

The streets were dark in Jarrat as Jerome made his way home. His shift in the guard went later than usual as there was trouble at one of the taverns near the castle walls. It was two in the morning but his shift was supposed to finish at eleven. He knew he was going to get a stern talking to from his wife. She had never liked him taking a job with the city watch but he had no choice after his butchers shop had burned to the ground.

With one hand he wiped the sweat from his brow. The heat from the day had been kept in by a thick cover of cloud. His short brown hair was stuck to his head and filled with sweat. His years of working as a butcher had been the perfect work-out for becoming a city guard. If anything his thick set body and strong muscles had improved with his new line of work. It definitely helped him keep control of those who felt the need to brawl.

The afternoon and evening shift had increased in danger over the last month. Once it had been the easiest shift, but there were ever increasing fights. The troubles had started about a year ago, slowly at first, a burglary here and a murder there. It was so subtle that no one really noticed, but it was undeniable. At least that's what Jerome thought, but his concerns weren't shared by everyone.

Rumours filled the streets during the day, not that he normally believed in such idle chatter, but when you heard the same thing more than a dozen times you had no choice but to take it seriously. The stories of strange creatures roaming the woods could not possibly be true, but that was just the beginning. There were rumours that the Queen had been put under a spell by some wicked sorcerer and the most disturbing of all was that the Evil One himself taking up residence in the castle. The last rumour he knew could not be true. The Evil One was safely trapped in the Northern Wastelands and he would for the rest of his life, no matter what the people said.

Jerome laughed to himself as he walked home. He was beginning to sound like old man Boan, believing ridiculous stories. He knew the extra fighting in the taverns were mainly due to the downturn in the Kingdom's economy. It had been a very bad year in the fields and more and more supplies were being brought in from across the border. It wouldn't last forever, but more people were losing their jobs and that led to the drinking and fighting, not fantasy tales of orglin stealing babies in the night.

A light could be seen through the front window of his house. That was not a good sign. His wife was still up and was going to give him a piece of her mind. At least his son would be in bed and not awake to hear him being berated. He didn't like his son seeing him being scorned by his wife.

Taking a deep breath Jerome turned the handle on the door. Instead of the usual click the door simply swung open. The light from a still burning kerosene lamp streamed out of the front door and even without the sudden feeling of dread, Jerome knew that something wasn't right. Drawing his short sword he stepped into his front room.

The sight that met him made his legs go weak and his flesh go cold. Sinking desperately to his knees the tears had already started running down his cheeks, he looked at his wife sitting as she always did, so peaceful and beautiful, only she had a long deep red gash across her neck. She had been there for a while as the blood had already congealed. He held his head in his hands before he remembered his son.

Suddenly he sprung to his feet. His heart raced and Jerome hoped beyond anything else in the world that his child was still alive. Racing towards the back of his house he flung the door open to his son's bedroom. There was no light, but the pungent smell was enough to tell him that his son had suffered the same fate.

Jerome did not have the heart to light the room. If he saw the look on his son's face he knew he would throw himself onto his sword. His knuckles had gone white from gripping its hilt and with a strained effort he let the sword drop to the ground. He would not rest until he had found who had done such a thing and make them pay.

The sun was starting to creep over the horizon when the horse and cart left his house. He was not the only one on the evening shift to suffer the same fate. Five others of the same guard also had their families slaughtered. He did not have the heart to speak to them. There would be enough time for conversation after he had some sleep.

Sinking in his chair at the kitchen table Jerome let his head droop. It had been the longest night of his life. It was all he could do to keep from collapsing on the floor. After a while he took a deep breath and finally raised his head. He opened his eyes and saw a small letter sitting in the middle of his table.

The red wax seal on the back was one that he had never seen before. A stallion reared on its back legs was not a crest of anyone he knew. He studied the mark before sliding a knife under the seal. The letter was written in a rough scrawl, as if done in a hurry.

Jerome,

If you are reading this letter then it means that we are too late and your family is dead. We are terribly sorry, but unfortunately we cannot save them all.

More to the point you are reading this letter because you are one of the Queen's loyal guards. This letter is a warning that you and others like you are being eliminated. If you stay where you are you will not last the week. The city is in turmoil and things are about to get worse. A small rebellion is starting outside of the city. Leave as soon as you read this note. Time is short. Take the Northern Highway until you reach the town of Dural. Do not tell anyone where you are going. Once you are there get a room at the Lazy Man Inn. You do not need to bring anything except what you are wearing. You will be given everything you need when you arrive at your destination. Burn the letter when you have finished reading it.

Signed
Duke X

Jermone placed the letter into the flame of the kerosene lamp. When it was firmly alight he let the paper drop onto the floor. If he was going to make a clean start then he was not going to leave anything behind. He had to steel himself if he was going to get revenge on those who murdered his family. Now that he had a purpose he couldn't think of sleep. He could sleep once he arrived in Dural. All he wanted to do was get as far away as possible. A tear formed in his right eye as he left his house. Wiping it away he took a firm grip on the hilt of his sword. Revenge would be his.

***

Orric sat in his private meeting room and viewed the missive he had received. If the old elf thought about the worst news in the world, it would not have come close to what was in front of him. He called his council together for an emergency meeting.

The letter had arrived five days prior and he sent messages out immediately and he was only waiting for one more arrival, Valen, his son, who had been escorting King Faxon, the King of Remidia, back to his palace.

Around the table sat two men and four elves. His main council had been reduced in size over the years, especially since he could only take council with those he trusted implicitly. A tall elf who sat to Orric's left was named Kyril. He and Orric had grown up together and had been best of friends, but since Orric had taken over the house their friendship had dwindled as business took over. Orric kept Kyril as his first advisor and the elf had well earned his position over the years. Next to him was Towen, head of the guard. His skin was a lot darker than the other elves due to spending a lot of time in the fields training the new recruits. Even as the Captain Commander he liked to spend time with the cadets. The other two elves were part of Orric's spy network. Lalo and Lamar were twins who also grew up with Orric. They were both very good at what they did.

The two men were left by King Faxon as ambassadors. Brawly and Nesbit were high ranking nobles in Faxon's court and Orric had begrudgingly agreed to keep them on and keep Faxon up to date via messenger pigeon.

Just before Orric was about to speak the door opened and his son entered. Sweat poured from Valen's face. He had ridden hard all day to make it back for the meeting, there wasn't a lot of time left and as it was he who sent the message he knew the grave importance.

Orric was glad to see his son return. He had shoulder length, straight blonde hair. His skin had darkened slightly over the years and his slender frame was solid muscle. It never ceased to amaze him how much his children looked alike and how much they reminded him of their mother. He wished she was still alive.

"I am sorry that it has taken me so long to return. I hope you have not been waiting too long," the statement was just formality and Valen panted as he spoke. "Father," he put in as an afterthought as he took the seat next to him.

"Your letter was brief, Valen, and also very disturbing. Could you please tell us more of what you saw?" The tension in Orric's voice could not be hidden.

"Yes. When we were on the way back to Remidia there was a flash that lit up the entire sky. I later learned that on the same night Nyrra and his army broke free and supposedly started moving east. We knew that he had agents all over the Seven Kingdoms, but we didn't know how many. It seems that the information we had collected on Nyrra making an attempt to reach his stronghold was all misinformation." Murmurs began around the table. "On my way back when I was passing through Zenza I noticed a lot of used campsites throughout the forest. I did a little tracking and to cut a long story short I found Nyrra moving an army south through Remidia. It didn't look like his entire army. In fact it was only a small group and Nyrra was not amongst them. I think he has taken quite a few of the smaller towns in northern Remidia. Not enough for the cities to take notice, but enough to start a hold. Something is very wrong about the situation. Nothing seemed to make any sense." It was clear that there was more to the story than Valen had told them.

"This is indeed disturbing news," Brawly was the first to comment. "Did you also send word to King Faxon?"

"I didn't have the resources to send two messages," Valen did not like the man's accusations.

Brawly whispered quickly to Nesbit and he came to his feet.

"Sit, Nesbit," Orric spoke. "As soon as we get all the information I will send word to your King. There is time yet. A few more minutes isn't going to change anything

"It's not your land that the enemy has invaded. Over half our army is on the move to the east. We were assured that Nyrra would strike out with his entire army in Avalon. Now we find out that his force is a direct threat to Remidia and we do not have the soldiers to defend it. I think a few minutes is well worth saving," Brawly rebuked. "Time is our worst enemy now and you want me to wait!"

"Nyrra didn't seem as though he had any real interest in Remidia. It seemed to me that his attention was on somewhere further south," Valen interrupted.

"Everyone calm down," Orric's voice was strained. The last thing he needed was a riot inside his own council. "Let's think about it for a minute. If you were moving an army south through Remidia where would you be headed? And why?"

"I know where I would be avoiding and that is Castalia," started Towen.

"We've had some strange reports coming out of Castalia. The High Chancellor has been behaving very strangely," Lamar interrupted.

"Regardless I don't think Nyrra would risk open warfare with the High Chancellor. It would be one thing to meet his army on the battlefield, but even with that there are problems. Nyrra is moving his army in secret, I am reasonably confident. If he was going to gather them outside Castalia then the High Chancellor would know well before he was in place and annihilate his army before they were fully assembled. Not even Nyrra would be silly enough to think that he could assail the city." Towen thought carefully as he spoke.

"Good, now we are getting somewhere," Orric said as Towen finished his first theory.

"If he was going to attack Remidia he would have done it by now. Either he doesn't know that half the Remidian army is in Avalon or he doesn't care about Remidia. I find the later hard to believe, I think that maybe his intelligence isn't that good," Nesbit added.

"I wouldn't be too sure about that," Orric commented. "He has planned this very well and I wouldn't say that there is anything that he doesn't know. He tricked us into thinking he was heading east. Let's not assume that he is doing anything except what he wants."

The two Remidian men didn't like what the elf was insinuating. The tension in the room was growing by the minute. Not knowing what Nyrra was planning made them all very nervous.

Orric offered his opinion. "The first problem is trying to figure out where he is going. There are two options left as I see. I would say he is either going to Kiarome or Jarrat. If he is looking to fortify a position on the main land then they are the two cities he would most likely attack. I believe that he will want to stay as far away from the Northern Wasteland as possible."

"What about Lel Dinion or even here. How can we discount any number of options," Brawly wasn't happy with Orric's assumptions.

"I think if he was coming here then he would have made his move by now. Most of my army is on the fields in Avalon with the Alliance. He could blow through here without a second thought. Lel Dinion is too far out of the way. By the time he worked all his army towards Lel Dinion the Alliance army would realise his ruse and be able to meet him and defeat him," Orric tried to refute him in the least offensive way, but by the reaction of the two men it didn't work.

"I think we can discount Kiarome as well." Lalo added. "It is too close to the Alliance army in Avalon. It wouldn't take the army long to counter any attack made there."

"So that leaves us with Jarrat," a smile came over Orric's face. "That would have been my first guess," but the smile quickly faded. "It's far enough south that he can be sure that there will be little chance of driving him back to the north. If he holds Jarrat then the entire Kingdom of Entero will be open to him."

Nesbit wasn't convinced. "So he raids through Remidia with the objective of securing Entero. It doesn't make any sense."

"It makes perfect sense. With the raiding in Remidia it will force Faxon to pull his army out of the Alliance. With an enemy army on his borders King Unwin will surely call his soldiers back into Darvishal. In one move he will be able to settle himself on the main-land as well as disbanding the Alliance army. It's a perfect plan." Orric's face was now grim.

"So we need to send word to Queen Oriana of Entero that she is about to be attacked?" Brawly was struggling to follow the chain of events.

"We cannot be so hasty. This is still only a theory and if our guess is right we need to be very careful. The wrong words in the wrong ears and the balance will swing even more into Nyrra's favour. We must remember that Queen Oriana has a strong contingency of her army commissioned in the Alliance. We cannot spill the pot on theories," Lamar spoke for the first time; he had the most information on the situation to the South. "Nyrra has been dictating events when we thought we were in control. We assumed we knew and now we have an army camped in the middle of nowhere with no battle to fight. We can't make the same mistake again. When we move we want to make sure the army goes where Nyrra is going to strike.'

"So what do you suggest we do?" Nesbit was just as confused as Brawly.

"We have to wait for Nyrra to reveal himself," Lamar spoke as if he was teaching a child. "It means that we may have to sacrifice Jarrat before we set our army on its course."

"We must get word to the King," Nesbit stood as he spoke, followed shortly by Brawly. "He will know what is best for Remedia's soldiers."

Kyril jumped up and moved towards the door, blocking their exit.

"What is this?" Brawly demanded.

"King Faxon will not sit idly by whilst you highjack his army. We came into the deal in good faith when many others would not." Nesbit added.

"I'm sorry we have to do this, but things are more dire than you think. If we have to sacrifice every Kingdom to defeat Nyrra then we must. Empires can be rebuilt, but if Nyrra survives nothing will ever be the same again.

Nesbit turned to Kyril "There are enemy soldiers pillaging Remidian towns. Remidian families being murdered and if you expect us just to sit here quietly you are deluded. Your plan has already failed. If you hadn't noticed Nyrra is already in the Seven Kingdoms and is already making his presence felt. If we do not act now then it will all be for nothing."

Orric nodded his head towards Kyril who in turn opened the door and let in two elves armed with spears. Brawly and Nesbit knew they were trapped. Their land would continue being raped whilst they were trapped in an elven prison. If they ever escaped the two would make sure the elves would pay for their treachery.

"When the King doesn't hear from us he will know something is wrong and send men here to find out what has happened. You are making a big mistake," Brawly knew that his threat was completely useless. Unless Orric allowed it no one could enter the village.

"This is unfortunate, but we have to finish this now. You will be safe as long as you do not try to escape," Orric sounded resigned. He waited until the two men were escorted from the room before he spoke again. "Once Faxon hears what is happening in his land he will surely draw his forces out of the Alliance."

"What are we going to do?" Kyril asked.

"We wait and hope that we don't make the wrong decision," Orric shook his head as he spoke. So many lives were riding on what they decided. A mistake would cause the death of millions.

Chapter 1: Battle Ground

The sun shone brightly in the morning for the first time in a week. A cool breeze blew in from the west keeping the temperature pleasant. The clouds, over the past couple of days especially, threatened to break with rain, but none ever came. The rain would have suited the mood of the camp perfectly, dark and dreary.

It had been ten days since Nyrra's army had joined the field. On the first day a darkness had filled the entire sky. Everyone knew that it wasn't natural. Clouds were never that dark, and with the darkness came a feeling of dread

As the days passed the darkness receded until it only remained over Nyrra's army. When nothing happened over the following days the dread slowly changed to anticipation and then a morose depression set in when there was still no move to attack.

Nyrra's army remained a blur on the horizon. The darkness made it even harder to discern any of their opponents. No one, not even the scouts, could make out any movement. The move, or lack of it, made the Alliance very nervous, they had been expecting an attack once Nyrra's army had arrived. The delay, however, only strengthened their position since they were still waiting on the army to join them from Hondin Lel. Their numbers would increase any day.

When the sun set on the first day, only distinguishable when the sky turned from dark grey to pitch black, they thought the attack was going to come. The night sky seemed to absorb the camp lights and many campfires could be seen on both sides of the field. Again there seemed to be no movement from the enemy. The fires remained the only movement and they did not come any closer. By midnight it was clear that they had no intention of attacking and the Alliance had a very tense and restless night.

By morning the entire camp seemed slow and sluggish. Weary eyes could be seen throughout. Red eyes and yawns were a common sight, although the adrenaline still ran through their veins. They knew the attack was coming soon and the restless night must have been part of their plan. Wait for the Alliance to have sleep deprivation and then attack. On the second day the sky was dark, but it seemed more natural. Whatever magic had been used it was starting to wane.

Dawn came on the third day with still no sign of an attack. The enemy had not advanced from their original position and there was nothing to suggest there was anything imminent. The army had been gathered to defeat Nyrra and the waiting was making them frustrated.

It wasn't until early on the seventh day when the first serious fighting broke out. There had always been small fights between some of the men, but there had never been more than four or five. Their commanding officers had always been able to break it up before things got out of hand. There had been bad blood between elves and dwarves for a long time and whilst the war was brewing the two sides had managed to forget their animosities. Now things had relaxed the old grudges had started to resurface.

An elf simply brushed shoulders with a dwarf as they walked passed. The dwarf didn't even lose a step, but it was enough to set off both sides. The fight consisted of at least ten elves and as many dwarves. Luckily there were no deaths, and very little bloodshed. It was the only major conflict since they had arrived on the battlefield and it was disappointing that it happened within their own camp.

The next day the elves and the dwarves were moved to separate sides of the camp and ordered not to cross paths. The remainder of the Alliance had enough force to keep both sides under control. It would have been the perfect time for Nyrra's army to attack whilst the camp was in turmoil, yet there was still no movement.

Although the weather threatened to break over the passing days, it never did. The air in the Alliance's camp was thick with tension and everyone was on tenterhooks.

On the morning of the tenth day when there had still been no sign of attack, Bern was summoned to a meeting in the commanders' tent. Since the others had left, Bern had been placed in a small platoon with his fellow Remidians. He was surprised at how well he fitted into army life. His many years as a farmer had moulded him in such the same manner as his fellow soldiers. His body was strong and he was used to rising with the morning sun, if not earlier. Although he had been conscripted into the regular infantry he was given more leniencies than his fellow soldiers. Due to his connection travelling with Prince Hawthorne he was invited to the major meetings of the commanders.

On his way to the command tent Bern ran into Dorn and Hulkan. The two dwarves were also given the same respect as Bern. Although growing up on a farm in Remidia and never seeing a dwarf before in his life Bern had quickly befriended the two when they had started travelling together. Bern had found an affinity with their stalwart natural. The three had become even closer since Alaric had left to fulfil the prophecy.

Hulkan had managed to reconcile himself with some of the other dwarves. Dorn, who had also become an outcast for arriving with Hulkan, had spent most of his time trying to fit in. Hulkan's brother Gilgi, the dwarf who had usurped power of the Western Dwarven Guild, had tried to lead the army away from the battlefield, but his subordinate officer would not budge. They knew the order to join the Alliance had to come from the guild council. As much as Gilgi was now the leader of the guild the movements of the army was still that of the council. If anything the situation made the other dwarves more sympathetic to Hulkan's position. Gilgi tried to make life hard for the two dwarves, but with every attempt to break the pair there was always a group ready to help them. Gilgi would not be happy when he found out the two had been summoned to the meeting.

When they arrived the command tent was full to bursting. It was the first time that all the commanders and advisors had been called together. Bern had to wonder why he had been called at all. Surely there was nothing that he could contribute.

In the centre of the tent sat a large oval table. Normally it was enough to seat all who were involved, but an extra table and chairs had to be brought in to accommodate everyone. With the arrival of the three there were now twenty in total, twelve at the main table, four at a smaller table and the others scattered around the tent.

At the head of the table sat General Jarwe. Although Prince Hawthorne outranked him in the Remidian army, Jarwe had been chosen to lead the Alliance. Both his body and his presence were commanding. A deep scar ran down his left cheek from a battle long ago and his dark brown hair was cut almost to the scalp making his already hard face even harder. The polished silver breastplate he wore to all his meetings was purely for show. The fox head inlaid over a broadsword, the crest of the Royal Remidian Army, had never seen a day in the field. A green cape hung down from his neck to the floor featuring a white dove over a wreath of maple leaves, his family crest. There was no expression on his face to say whether the meeting was going well or not.

The tension in the room was obvious, but no more than around the rest of the camp. No one could fully relax with a hostile army half a league away. The fact that the army didn't make a move to attack or a sign that they were going to attack any time soon did nothing to help.

Sitting to Jarwe's right was Prince Hawthorne who kept his mousy blonde cut short and shaved every morning. One thing he couldn't abide was soldiers looking scruffy. His strong jaw line remained set and there was something very disturbing about his demeanour. He was dressed in a similar fashion as the General with a silver breastplate. His cape was in the design of Royal Remidia, a purple cloth with a golden lion.

On Jarwe's right was Captain Derwin of Remidia. Like his general his hair was shaved almost to the scalp. Although he showed no visible scars he had seen many a battle and there were some hiding under his clothes.

Sitting on the other side of Prince Hawthorne was Gilgi. The dwarf's face turned from pleasant to rage when he saw the other two dwarves enter the tent. His hatred for his brother Hulkan had only escalated over the past week and it had washed off onto Dorn as well. He spoke silently over his left shoulder to his advisor, a dwarf by the name of Leo. Leo only looked slightly less annoyed at their arrival and was a good ten years older than Gilgi. Hulkan wasn't completely sure, but he thought Leo was an instigator in the coup. Leo had never liked him and time had changed nothing. A heavy halberd rested against his hip and his fingers tapped the handle as he eyed Gilgi, waiting for a sign.

Seated next to Captain Derwin was Lord Pernian. The slender Elf was in charge of Orric's small army. He looked as calm as someone out on a Sunday picnic. His golden blonde hair flowed down his back and he was a picture of beauty. Despite his youthful appearance he had seen more years than anyone in the tent. A small smirk appeared on his face at the discomfort of the dwarves. There was no love lost between them, but he knew better than to start any trouble. He was the only elf in the tent.

The man sitting next to Pernian was new to the camp. He had ridden in just after dawn two days prior with almost two thousand men from Darshival. General Sorrell was the leader of the Darshivallian army. The man had a commanding presence that rivalled that of General Jarwe. Dust on his coat showed that he had not had time to have it cleaned since he had arrived. The lines on his face showed that he was the eldest man in the room. He had seen more campaigns than anyone else. His presence was a relief to the other commanders and his advice would be greatly appreciated. Seated next to him was his military advisor, Wojtek. The man was older than Sorrell. He looked old enough to be Sorrell's father. Despite being so old the man looked as though he could hold his own on the battlefield.

Next to Gilgi was another powerful looking man, Captain Aimon who came with the first conscription from Entero. Captain Aimon had taken every available man from Oldfield and the surrounding Duchies. Queen Oriana had pledged armies from four other regions before her support was suddenly cut short. Captain Aimon had been chosen as her representative at the council table. His shoulder length brown hair was typical of the Enteroite army. Unlike other armies, which kept their soldier's hair short, they preferred longer hair. His physique wasn't has thick as the General's, but he looked strong enough to hold his own in a fight. He wore a simple leather jerkin as he felt there was no need to wear armour in the command tent. His only decoration was a red cape with his family crest of two snakes poised to strike each other. He also brought along two of his advisors to the tent, one who sat next to him.

The remaining three seats at the main table were reserved for Bern and the two dwarves. They were ushered to their seats by the two pages who were servicing the tent.

"I'm glad you could join us," Jarwe started when the tent settled. "Now we can get started. It has been ten days since Nyrra's army arrived and they have not made a single move against us. Our scouts have not yet been able to get a good visual on them and it seems there is magic at play.

Our emissaries are fired upon before they get close enough to discuss terms. I don't like making decisions without all the information, but it seems as though this is all we are going to receive."

"Have we heard anything from Hadar yet?" it was Bern at the end of the table who spoke the words that they were all thinking.

"Our scouts returned earlier this morning. The army is still more than a day's ride of here. I fear that something has waylaid them and they won't make it in time." General Jarwe seemed somewhat defeated. "We cannot sit here forever, waiting for King Lisle's army to arrive."

"We can wait them out. Our purpose is to not let them pass into Nostiria," said Wojtek.

"That is not exactly true," Jarwe looked at Hawthorne, who in turn nodded. "It is true that we are to stop Nyrra and his army from proceeding any further, but we didn't think that we would have to wait this long for the confrontation. We only have enough supplies to last another week or so and once we get past that point we won't have enough food or water for the return."

"Well that's a bloody well thought out plan then," Captain Aimon almost spat the words. "We brought enough supplies for a long campaign. Now you tell me that we'll have to feed your lot as well."

"I don't think it will come to that. What I'm getting at is that we are going to have to change our plans. We currently have a fortified position ready for defence. We have trenches here and here," Jarwe pointed to the map that covered most of the table. "We have archery towers set up along this line. Anything within a hundred paces will be covered by our archers."

"My elven bowmen will be able to hit a target at that distance. Your men will be safe up to this point, but once they are passed this line they are on their own. We can shoot up to another twenty paces or so, but if we hit anything it will be pure luck," Pernian didn't want to miss a chance to talk up his elves.

"What are you trying to say?" asked Wojtek.

"I do not believe that we can sit here and wait any longer. It is clear that Nyrra is not going to make a move on us. I think that we should start drawing up plans for attack."

Leo whispered something into Gilgi's ear before taking a step back and letting him speak. "You want to plan an attack without knowing your opposition. We have not yet had visual confirmation of any of the army. How can we plan an attack against an unknown opponent? From all accounts the army could out number us by two if not three to one. Going up against those odds would be insane. Not to mention the fact we still haven't heard from the Hondin Lel army. They should be here any day now."

Captain Derwin was about to speak up against the dwarf who was verbally attacking his General, but Jarwe silenced him with a hand on his shoulder. "You would be right to say that this is not the ideal situation. I would never want to take the field against an unknown opponent. It may be that we do not have a choice. We are cut off from the world here. We are not receiving any communications. This in itself is very disturbing. We should have received word from King Lisle about the location of his army and we should have seen the start of his army arriving five days ago at least. There is something that is very wrong. Nyrra must know that we are in disarray. It would be the ideal time for him to strike. There is no reason for him to sit on the other end of this field. I want to table it now that we draw up plans for an offensive. It will take time to make plans as we had no intention on attacking. We thought Nyrra would bring the war to us. If Nyrra hasn't shown any signs of aggression by the time we are ready then I think that we should attack."

"We shall put it to a vote," Captain Derwin was about to start the vote when Gilgi stood up from the table, pushing his chair back violently.

"They do not get to vote. They have no business being here. They have no military experience. They should not be able to vote," Gilgi sounded wild.

Although his words were only directed at the other two dwarves, Bern felt that they were for him as well. In truth he believed them. He had no experience with war. Until a week ago he had never even been in an army. He didn't know what he was doing in the tent.

"They are here under my advisement," Hawthorne remained seated, but his voice boomed. "I have travelled with these three and I trust their judgement. I have the right to choose what council I bring to the table," his words bit through Gilgi and forced him back into his seat, rage filled his face.

"Now if there are no other objections I think that we should take this vote and then continue on our course of action." Derwin spoke as if nothing had happened. "All those who are for the decision to strike at the heart of our enemy raise your hands now." Derwin paused and once he had taken the count he spoke again. "All those who are against the decision raise your hand now." Although he already knew the decision he had to ask the question. "Very well then, we need to start drawing up plans for attack. This will be very difficult. We have limited information and limited time. I think we should all get to work."

"The first thing we need to do is inform the troops that we are preparing for war. I think that should sufficiently increase their moral." Jarwe's words brought instant movement from around the tent. Everyone who was not sitting around the main table quickly vacated the room.

When it was only those at the table who remained Jarwe spoke again. "We have an open field in front of us. Once we have passed our own defences the ground is open."

"Nyrra has been there for ten days. That is plenty of time for his army to dig in. We don't know what defences he could have set up by now," Wojtek spoke slowly, as if he was thinking.

"We've been here for over a month setting up our defences. Whatever he has set up I'm sure we can rely on the fact that they are not as good as ours."

"I don't think that they have set up defences," Bern didn't know where the words had come from or why he had spoken them. He did, however, know they were true.

"What are you talking about?" Gilgi scoffed.

"I will not tell you again Gilgi. Show my friends some respect or you will not be welcome in this tent again," Hawthorne's voice remained calm. "How do you know this, Bern?"

"I can't explain. I just know that he has not set up any defences. In fact I don't think that he is prepared for us to attack. I think the army plans on waiting, but I don't know what they are waiting for. Something is very wrong," Bern's words almost sounded as though they were coming from someone else.

"Who is this man and what is he talking about. Who is he to talk about the Evil One's defences," Leo said. "You say that he is your friend, but he speaks as though he is the Leader of this army and he speaks out of turn. We have proven our worth on the battlefield and deserve more respect."

Hawthorne was clearly enraged at the advisors rude words. As the Crown Prince of Remidia he did not have to take such insolence. He was about to speak his mind, but it was Jarwe who spoke first, addressing Bern.

"There must be some reason that you think this. Please explain to us your reasoning?" Jarwe words were gentle.

Bern truly didn't know how he knew, but he knew it was true. It was a feeling he had been having, like a voice inside his mind. It was almost as if he could see what was happening on the other side of the battle field. The army was still clouded by the mysterious haze, but he knew that they were not preparing to attack.

When Bern did not answer Jarwe continued to speak. "Very well, we shall send out scouts to see if what you say is true. In the meantime we must prepare for the worst. If Nyrra has dug in it will not be easy to get him out. I think that we need to build some siege weapons."

"That's all well and good, but the forest is over a week's ride from here. We would waste too much time gathering the timber, let alone the time it would take to bring it back here and build them," Captain Derwin spoke carefully, not wanting to refute his General.

"Not to mention I don't think it would be a good idea to cut down the trees from the forest. We would lose too many men collecting the required timber," Pernian added.

"Then we pull down the archer's towers. There should be enough timber to make the engines that we need. Our engineers shouldn't have any problems adapting the materials," the General didn't seem happy about having his suggestion refuted and challenged anyone to start. Unfortunately for Jarwe the table was full of strong willed, military men.

"And if our intelligence comes back with word that Nyrra is going to attack then we will be left with little defence. We cannot cut off our toes to replace our fingers. We need to keep our defences strong," Aimon spoke forcefully as the tension in the tent started to rise.

Jarwe's frustration was evident on his face. Every solution had a greater problem. He had no idea what Nyrra had planned for his army. If he made the wrong move then he would doom them all to an eternity of suffering. The world was balanced on a knife edge and could fall either way.

"Then how do we plan for this war?" The defeated sound in Jarwe's voice seemed out of place.

Again Bern answered. There was an audible noise as everyone moved to look at him. "We have to attack them head on. There is something very wrong with his lay out. His army is spread across the field, but there is no substance to it. I don't think that all is what it seems," as Bern spoke there was a glazed look in his eyes and his voice was monotone. Before he could elaborate on what he was saying he returned to normal.

"What do you mean Bern?" Hawthorne asked quickly before anyone else had a chance to speak.

"I don't know," was all Bern could reply.

"Okay I think that we have spent enough time banging our heads. We will send the scouts out and then reconvene this meeting in the morning when we have had a chance to think." Jarwe's strength returned as the emotions in the tent reached boiling point. Jarwe knew that things were only going to become worse if they continued the debate. They were not going to resolve any problems in their current state of mind. The words that Bern had spoken were disturbing and there was something about the way he said them that made Jarwe believe him.

Bern was happy to be out of the tent. Out of everyone he was most disturbed by what he had said. The two dwarves looked at him carefully when they were outside. They wanted to ask him a number of questions, but they wanted to wait until they were away from the others. They did not get far before they were stopped by Gilgi and Leo.

"I don't know what game you're playing Hulkan, but you will not succeed. Bringing this..." Gilgi spat at the word "man, to the table and telling him to spout this rubbish. You've lost your alliances. You deserve to rot in the pits for your treachery."

Hulkan returned Gilgi's icy stare and did not flinch. There was something in his eyes that made Gilgi falter slightly. When Hulkan didn't reply it added to his irritation. Leo stepped in to assist his master.

"Elves got your tongue Hulkan or are you too afraid to speak. Your life will be forfeit before the end of this war. Mark my words." Leo's threats held little strength. It was obviously a vain attempt to unsettle him.

"Come Leo. Let us not spend another moment with this traitor lest we be tainted by his filth." Gilgi's words faltered as Hulkan's stare remained.

The dwarves remained still until the others were out of earshot. Once he knew the two could not hear them Hulkan burst into laughter. Bern looked at him in horror, whilst Dorn also started laughing. As much as he had been spending most of his time with the Dwarves he still struggled to understand them.

"What are you two cackling about?" Bern sounded somewhat annoyed at not seeing the joke.

"Gilgi will be most put out by not getting a response from Hulkan," Dorn explained. "It seems you have put a wolf amongst the sheep with your little display in the tent. Gilgi was trying to bait Hulkan into giving away some vital piece of information. He will be most upset that his game didn't work."

They continued to walk through the camp still chuckling to themselves. Since being summoned to the command tent they had not been assigned any work for the day. One of the first tents to be erected was a mobile tavern and the soldiers with time off were permitted a few quiet drinks to unwind. A perfect place for two bored dwarves and a confused man.

"Why did you say what you did in the command tent?" Hulkan asked as they sat in the tavern tent with lukewarm ale.

"Yes Bern, you could have been strung up speaking like you did," Dorn added.

"Like I said in the tent, I don't know what happened. It was like I was in a trance. I knew that the words were coming out of my mouth, but I did not know where they had come from. It was if someone else was speaking through me. Even now the memories are fading from my mind. I can see the battlefield and I can see a great cloud on the far side. It's insubstantial. There is something out of place about it. Each time I see the answer it's just out of reach. I know that it's inside my head, but there is no way for me to access it. I just hope that it comes before the army moves, because I think it is information that will be vital for our success." Bern stared into his tankard as he spoke.

"You are a strange man indeed," Dorn laughed as he slapped Bern across his shoulders. "I am glad that you're on our side."

"Hulkan, what do you think the General is going to do?" Bern asked, trying to change to subject.

"He will do all that he can. He will have to wait until the scouts return. He can't launch an offensive without knowing the enemies position."

"He won't get any answers from the scouts. The dark fog covers the army. They will not get close enough to see through the mist," again there was a strange look on Bern's face.

"Then what do you suggest that we do?" Dorn watched his friend carefully.

Shaking his head Bern looked confused. "Sorry, what was the question?"

Dorn looked at Bern... "What... do... you... suggest we do?"

"I don't know. Again I know the solution is in my head, but I just can't reach it. I know something is seriously wrong, but I have no idea what it is."

The tavern tent was relatively empty and they were given the privacy that they needed. A few men sat at another table on the far side but that was it.

After their third drink the serving women spoke to them. "I'm sorry, but I cannot serve you anymore."

"What are you talking about lassie? We haven't even begun to drink," Hulkan boomed at her.

The raised voice brought the attention of the other men, though they remained in their seats. There was no aggression in Hulkan's voice, but they would let no one start trouble with their bringer of ale.

"It's the rules of the army. No one is allowed more than three ales in a day. We have limited supplies and they must last for the remainder of the campaign. There is nothing worse than an army with no ale. I have seen it before and it's not pretty. Nothing reduces moral more than a lack of alcohol," the smile remained on the woman's face.

"Well if it that is the case then we better get going for a relaxing stroll this afternoon," Hulkan's response was gruff.

The men at the other table visibly relaxed when they heard his reply. They were all glad to see the dwarves leave. Although most of the soldiers had accepted the help of the others some still held onto the old discriminations. Anyone caught being openly aggressive would be placed in the stocks, but even the threat of recriminations would not be enough to deter everyone.

There was a strange feeling in the air once they had left the tavern tent. The sky was dark, darker than it had been since they had arrived. The air was warm and there was not a breath of wind.

"If it doesn't rain now then we will know that this weather is not natural," said Hulkan as he looked up, and as if on cue a drop of rain hit Hulkan on his forehead.

"Great, you had to say something didn't you? You couldn't just let it pass could you?" Dorn scolded.

"This doesn't bode well for the General's plans. A wet battlefield will only cause havoc for our advance. I don't think that we will be moving out for a while now," Hulkan said.

"This is not the design of the Evil One. This will only aid in our attack," Bern shook his head. Even without the movement it was clear that the words were not his.

"I really wish you would give us some warning when you are going to do that," Hulkan looked at Bern as the rain started to come down. "It would be good if someone started writing these things down for prosperity."

"What are you talking about? I didn't say anything," the look on Bern's face showed he was not joking.

Hulkan watched him carefully for a moment, not sure if telling him the truth was the right idea. When he thought better of it he turned to Dorn. "Sometimes I really wish that Eldred was still with us."

Chapter 2: A Mystery Guest

The rain strengthened over the next two days making an assault on the Evil One's army impossible. Bern had remained away from the command tent, even though he had been summoned on numerous occasions. The visions he had been having had increased, although his memories of them decreased. Dorn and Hulkan took turns in watching over him and recording what he said.

The information coming from Bern didn't seem to make any sense, at least less sense than his previous messages. When asked what he had said he had no recollection. With each message Bern became more introverted and he spoke less and less when he was not in his trance like state.

"I don't know what we can do with him," Dorn spoke loudly over the rain outside. Bern was sound asleep, another thing he did regularly in between his ranting.

"I think that we have to go to the command tent and tell the General," Hulkan replied.

"And tell him what. We can't make heads or tails out of what he has been saying. Here for example: *Take them to the east or take them to the west, but it is south where you should lead, to the mouth of the cave where the beast resides. Only there shall you find victory.* Now what in God's names does that mean? There are pages and pages of this rubbish and none of it makes any sense," Dorn sounded exhausted.

It was just on dusk when the rain started to ease. The sky remained dark, but it was clear that the storm was abating. The morale amongst the soldiers had dropped with the weather and the commanders had not been able to give them any information on what was happening.

It was early in the morning when the sun returned to the sky, the warmer weather also brought with it the return of the scouts. Five had been sent out but only four had returned. They all looked bedraggled and dehydrated.

With the return of the scouts Bern and the two dwarves were again summoned to the command tent. The only difference was that this time it was not a request. A group of eight soldiers came for them to make sure they didn't protest. Bern did not look happy when he was woken, but Hulkan persuaded him to leave without a fight. There would be no advantage in killing innocent soldiers and he knew if they killed the eight then the General would only send more men.

Bern seemed to be walking in a trance, as if he hadn't slept in the past two days. Almost all Bern had been doing, when he wasn't speaking in riddles, was sleeping. His two friends were extremely worried about his condition. There was nothing natural about his ailment and they didn't know where to begin to try and heal him.

The command tent was full again when the three of them arrived. The set up was exactly the same with the only exception of the four scouts, who had not had a chance to rest or clean themselves. Gilgi did not look impressed at the arrival of the three. He spoke briefly to Leo before he shot the two dwarves an evil glare. He saved the worst of his looks for Bern, who was now also on his hate list.

"Thank you for joining us," the General greeted the newcomers. "Now we can start our meeting." The grim look on his face showed that he had already been briefed.

The first of the scouts stepped forward; he was a slender elf with the usual look of youth on his face. Even covered with filth he still looked strangely beautiful. His light brown hair was covered with mud and was slicked back. Even being out in the terrible conditions he looked as though he wasn't at all fatigued.

"We spent many hours scouting the enemy's camp. We lost Herl in the storm on the first day. It was so dark when we became separated we couldn't find each other. We can only hope that he is still alive and manages to make his way back." The elf's story didn't seem to be getting anywhere until Jarwe interrupted him.

"Please get to the point Stian, we haven't got all day!"

"Sorry," Stian seemed somewhat nervous. "There is no other way to say it... We found... nothing." There was a great murmur throughout the tent.

"How is that possible?" Pernian was the first to speak. "You are the best tracker in this camp, arguably the best in the Seven Kingdoms, and you were out there for over two days. I know that the conditions weren't the best, but you must have some idea of what the Evil One has been doing?"

"That's what I thought, but there was nothing I could do. We crossed the battlefield and reached the fog. Once we were there we all felt a great surge of horror and despair. It was as if the world was going to collapse on itself, it was terrible. So we stayed at the edge of the fog for an entire day. No matter how hard we tried we could not pass through. It was as if there was a heavy curtain blocking our path. We walked up and down, but couldn't see through it. There was no gap for us to pass or to see through. I can't explain it, but it wasn't until we were far away from the fog until we felt right again. If we stayed there any longer the melancholy would have consumed us. There can be no doubt that the fog is pure evil. It was created by evil and that is what it is made of." Stian took a step backwards when he finished, relieved to be done talking.

The General looked towards the other scouts to see if they wanted to elaborate on what Stian had told them. None of them did. The fear on their faces showed that Stian's account was true and they didn't want to relive the experience again. The sudden silence didn't last long before the murmuring started again.

Jarwe waited a few moments, but when the noise did not subside he banged his fist down on the table silencing the entire tent. All eyes were suddenly on the General. The look on his face didn't ease anyone's mind.

"The situation is worse than what we had originally thought. We now must decide what our next move is going to be. It seems as though there is no way of telling what is on the other side of the fog." General Jarwe looked around the table in turn for suggestions.

"There must be some record of Nyrra's last campaign. We can look back through the war records and see how he set up his army last time," Captain Aimon commanded.

"Unfortunately our resources are limited and I do not believe they date back that far. The only way to work out what's on the other side would be to guess and I don't think Nyrra runs by standard warfare," Jarwe rebuked.

"Then we have to wait. I'm sure that the Evil One's supplies are nowhere near as good as ours. The Northern Wastelands are not renowned for their abundance of food. I'm sure they will be forced to attack before we are," Gilgi's words sounded true, but they also held a hint of cowardice.

"I think that…" Jarwe began to speak but was interrupted by Bern.

"We shall have to attack. The opposing army will wait us out. Our men grow restless, whilst his grow strong."

"I have had enough of this rubbish." Gilgi pushed his chair out from the table and drew a menacing looking halberd. "We have sat here for the last two days and discussed our plans and now this upstart thinks he can tell us what to do."

Gilgi's sudden movement didn't startle the stalwart occupants of the table. Both Dorn and Hulkan rose and stood between him and Bern. Leo was quick to move to his leader's side, but the others were a little slower to react. They didn't believe Gilgi would start a fight in the command tent. Once he started to move toward the dwarves the others also rose and moved to block his path.

"You have been warned Gilgi!" Jarwe boomed from the head of the table. "Another outburst and you shall be removed from your position and spend some time in the stocks."

"Do you presume to command me? I am the leader of the Dwarven army and they will not stand for these insults. We shall see how you survive without my support!" Gilgi made for the exit but didn't get far before he was set upon by half a dozen guards.

Before Leo could come to his aid he was also grabbed. Gilgi thought of trying to fight his way through, but knew it would be useless. He looked over his shoulder at Jarwe as he was dragged out with his legs dangling behind him.

"You will rue the day you did this Jarwe. When my father hears of this you will have another army to contend with. The council will not sit idly by whilst you assault their leader." Gilgi believed every word of his threat, but it didn't seem to affect the General. Before he was removed from the tent he cursed at Hulkan. "I swear that I will see you dead before I leave this camp brother."

No one spoke again until the two dwarves were cleared from the tent. Once sanity had returned and everyone was seated the discussion returned. With Gilgi's outburst everyone seemed to have forgotten about Bern's words.

"Now I think to remain here is not the answer. We are doing well with our plans for attack and I think that we should carry them out." Jarwe sat up straight.

General Sorrell spoke with the voice of a true leader. "It's a risk, but I don't think we have any choice. I think we can safely assume that the army stretches for the length of the fog. How far back it goes we can only surmise."

"The fog is a ruse," Bern said. "It's there to mislead." No one had noticed that he had fallen asleep. He spoke only for a moment before returning to sleep.

"Okay, now I'm concerned. Can someone please explain to me what's happening?" Sorrell sounded angry.

"Dorn, Hulkan can you shed some light on what's been happening with Bern?" Hawthorne looked concerned.

Dorn looked around the tent wondering what they were going to think. He really didn't want to speak and took a deep breath before starting. "For the past two days he has been sleeping and talking in riddles. Nothing he has said seems to be making any sense and when he speaks he can't remember what he has said. It's as if someone else is speaking through him. We don't know if what he's saying is true, but I can't think of any other explanation," Dorn stumbled over his words.

"So do you think we should do what he says?" Jarwe seemed more concerned than ever.

"I don't think we have a choice. The only information we receive about what is behind the fog is what is coming out of Bern's mouth. I can't vouch for its validity, but I don't think that we have any other choice. We can go in blind or we can plan around the information that Bern is giving us," Dorn's words were starting to make sense.

"I think that you might have a point. We don't seem to have any choice. We shall trust in Bern's words, but remember that they might be false."

Once Jarwe had finished speaking Bern sprung to life again. "Aim your army at the centre of the fog. Ignore the wings. Press your men hard for they will falter once they reach it. It is there to repel you. You must push them hard for they will want to turn and run. Only a strong commander will prevail." With his final words he looked confused. "How did I get here? What's going on?"

The sudden change in Bern's demeanour caught everyone off guard. It was the first time in the last two days that Bern was back to his old self. All eyes in the tent were fixed on him, waiting to hear his next words. He shot Hulkan a worried look, but received no response.

"It is settled then!" Jarwe spoke after a long minute of silence. "We shall drive our forces to the centre of the fog. From there will face the other side with strength and determination. This is our time and we shall be victorious. Nothing will stand in our way. Tell the men we leave for battle first thing in the morning!" Jarwe's confidence had returned as he boomed the words.

"Yes sir!" echoed throughout the tent.

It was the first time in the past two days that there was a cheer from the tent. Their spirits were on the rise now that they had a purpose. Although Bern didn't know how he did it he knew that he was responsible for their renewed vigour.

"I think we should get out of here," Hulkan spoke softly to the other two.

The rest of the tent was already starting to leave and it wouldn't be long before the entire camp was a hive of activity.

Once they were outside they all visibly relaxed. Even after Gilgi and Leo had been dragged away the tension didn't wane inside the tent. The warm morning air seemed to lighten their spirits. The ground was still soft underfoot, but they hoped it would be dry by the afternoon; muddy ground would make the attack even more difficult.

"What do we do now?" asked Bern.

"I guess we find something to keep ourselves busy. I'm sure that won't be too hard now," Hulkan replied.

With the imprisonment of their commanding officer Hulkan and Dorn thought it would not be a good idea to join the other dwarves. Bern suggested that they join him in the Remidian army and since they had nowhere else to go they decided they should. In truth they just didn't want to leave Bern alone.

Bern had become quite a legend amongst the Remidian army. His exploits had been told many times in the tavern tent, although the truth had been distorted considerably. No one knew the true story and Bern felt uncomfortable answering their questions. It wasn't long before his commanding officer had to ask him to leave. He was causing too much of a distraction and he couldn't have that on the eve of battle.

"What a shame," said Hulkan.

"Well it was a good idea at the time," Dorn spoke as they left the training ground shortly after midday.

"What are we going to do now?" Bern asked.

"I don't think that we have much choice. I think that we should head to the tavern." Hulkan had a broad smile on his face.

"We are going to war in the morning. Do you think it is a good idea to get drunk?"

"I couldn't think of anything better to do. We go to war tomorrow. This could be the last time we get to drink," Dorn agreed.

The tavern tent was completely empty. The serving woman didn't look impressed to see them. She had heard of the impending battle and figured she would have had the remainder of the day off.

"Are you sure you should be here?" her voice was tart.

"There is nowhere else for us to be. Our friend here is thirsty and requires an ale, isn't that right Bern?" It was no accident that Dorn dropped Bern's name at the end of the sentence.

He knew the serving woman would have heard the gossip inside the tent already. Bern's story had been told many times, by many different soldiers. News travelled fast. She looked at him with a mixture of awe and fear and once she knew who they were there was no problem.

They sat at a table far enough away so the serving woman wouldn't be able to hear their conversation. They had not been seated for long before Bern had drained his first ale. The dwarves found it odd. They had been drinking many times and not once had the man finished before them.

"Are you feeling alright?" Dorn asked.

There was something not right about the way Bern was seated. Something was off with his posture and he was more confident than usual. His eyes had a glaze about them.

"You're right. This could very easily be the last time that I have the taste of ale on my tongue and I don't want to waste it." When he finished speaking he called the serving woman over. She happily served them all a fresh tankard and assured them that they could drink as much as they liked. With the war starting there would be fewer mouths to serve.

"It seems that there are perks to being your friend." Hulkan was happy to hear they would not be cut off and smiled.

"Yes, it does." Bern smiled and took another large mouthful of ale.

***

It was late in the night when Bern awoke. His head ached and his mouth tasted of vomit. The last thing he could remember was walking to the tavern tent. He tried to sit up, but his head was swimming. He had to suppress the urge to vomit again as he let his head rest. He couldn't remember what he had done or how he had made it back to his tent.

Suddenly he remembered where he was and he gasped in horror. It wouldn't be long before he would be called to duty and as soon as the sun was up they would be on the march across the battlefield. The thought of rising made his stomach churn again and he tried to hold down its contents. Making a desperate lunge for the opening of his tent Bern felt the bile rising through his throat. He just managed to poke his head out before the liquid vomit spewed from his mouth.

He fragilely returned to his bedroll. His mouth was dry and he fished around in his tent until he found a large canteen filled with water. He knew that one of the dwarves must have left for him; the thought of his new friends looking after him brought a smile to his face.

The pleasant thought was only in his head for a moment before the sound of a trumpet rang throughout the camp. Bern knew it was the call to duty. There was no way he could stay in his tent. The battle was his idea and his face was well known throughout the army. If he didn't appear when the army started to march then it would be a great blow to their morale.

Taking another draught from the canteen and a couple of deep breaths Bern prepared himself to rise, luckily he had been put to bed still dressed. The only armour he had to put on was a breastplate.

Bern stepped out into the fresh morning air, careful not to stand in his vomit. He was glad that it was still dark and no one would be able to see what he had done. His head still ached as he tried to see where he was supposed to go. The lights seemed to be so far away and the camp seemed shrouded in darkness.

Stumbling forward Bern tried to make his way towards the light. His mind was hazy and his eyesight blurred. Something wasn't right. Before he was able to take too many more steps he felt the bile rising again. Dropping to his knees Bern let the contents of his stomach pour out onto the ground. As he did so he heard the sound of footsteps behind him. He shuddered at the thought of being found in his current state, but was too committed.

"Look what we have found here?" Bern was relieved to recognise the voice of Dorn.

"It looks like someone can't handle his drink," Hulkan laughed.

Returning to his feet Bern looked at his two friends. In the dull light he could only just make out their silhouettes. He couldn't tell if they were suffering as much as him, but they sounded as though they were not.

"I have never seen you drink like that before," Hulkan started.

"You put the both of us to shame," Dorn added.

Bern thought for a moment and decided that it was best to tell them what had happened. "I can't remember anything from inside the tavern. The last thing that I remember was the captain telling us to stop distracting the real soldiers."

The two dwarves looked at each other. Both had concerned looks on their faces. It was clear to Bern something had happened that shouldn't have. His head started to swim and he took a moment to calm himself.

"What happened?" Bern wasn't sure if he wanted to know the answer.

"I must admit things didn't seem right, but you assured us that you were just letting off steam before the battle. You drank like a man on a mission. You told us that today was a day of reckoning and we needed to celebrate. It was late when you disappeared with the serving women." It seemed like Hulkan was holding something back.

It was his last words that upset Bern the most. He had always been faithful to his wife. He couldn't believe that he could have cheated on her. Something was wrong.

"What is it that you are not telling me?" Bern had decided that even if he had left with the serving women he wouldn't have done anything with her; there was something else that had the dwarves worried.

Before either of them had a chance to answer the sound of chinking armour could be heard approaching them. Two soldiers, each holding torches, looked relieved to have found them. Bern looked at the two dwarves, who now seemed relieved at the arrival of the soldiers.

"Thank the Gods we have found you. The General has ordered us to take you to the command tent. It's not long before we set off to war and he wants to see you three before we leave," the young soldier puffed as he spoke, as if he had been running.

"Well, we can't leave the General waiting can we," Hulkan spoke quickly, not giving Bern a chance to respond.

Bern waited as the others started off towards the tent. He tried to recall some memory from the previous night, but there was only darkness.

The urgent call from the soldier brought Bern out of his reverie and into action. Whatever had happened was in the past. He had a battle to fight and needed all his wits if he was going to remain alive. The adrenaline started to pump through his body and for a moment he felt normal again. However the feeling didn't last long as he followed after the others.

The soldiers kept a brisk pace through the camp, not wanting to keep the General waiting. The two dwarves were happy to push them along, anything to avoid having to speak with Bern who just dragged his feet behind him, making sure he didn't let them out of his sight.

They both waited for Bern at the mouth of the tent whilst the soldiers went about their business. The camp had become a hive of activity. As soon as the sun bridged the horizon the army would start to move.

When Bern joined them they entered the tent. Inside there were just those sitting at the oval table, except for Gilgi who was still imprisoned. They all had sombre looks on their faces which didn't change with the newcomers.

"Thank you for joining us," said General Jarwe. "In light of what has happened over the past week we voted and it was unanimous. We would like the three of you to join us at the head of the army. It seems that your antics have been well gossiped amongst the troops." A small smile crept into the corner of his mouth, but was only fleeting.

Bern was about to speak, but Hulkan jumped in before he had a chance. "We thank you for your offer, but we would not feel right. Our place is fighting side by side with our fellow dwarves. With Gilgi imprisoned I think it would be better if we were seen in the dwarven camp." Hulkan had no problem speaking for Dorn, but his statement had also included Bern. Despite the fact they had associated themselves with the Remidian army the dwarves needed to reassimilate themselves with Dwarven army.

"Very well, I think that you might be right. Bern, I think under the circumstances it would be good for you to join us. You are vastly becoming legendary and it would be a great boost for morale. The army is keen to move, but once we reach the fog it will really test the men's mettle." Bern was sure that it wasn't just the soldier's who wanted him at the lead. The thought that the leaders of the army were afraid of the fog worried him, but he knew that Jarwe was right. The fog would test everyone's strength of will. His place was at the head of the army and it was the only way they would survive.

"I will come," although he spoke the words he wasn't sure they were his. The thought made his stomach churn and it took all his will power not to vomit all over the table. He wished that he had never drunk.

"Then if you are going to ride at the head of an army then you should look the part." Hawthorne spoke before signalling towards the back of the tent.

A meek looking page boy came to Bern and in his arms was a shining gold breastplate. On the centre was engraved the crest of the royal family of Remidia. Wrapped over his shoulders was a purple cape.

The page stood behind Bern, waiting patiently for him to rise, but Bern remained seated, not sure exactly what was happening. He didn't understand the protocol of being dressed by a page. The occupants of the table laughed softly.

Bern felt silly for making the page wait. He felt even sillier when he was dressed in front of the war council. The page bowed meekly when finished before quickly returning to the back of the room. Bern stared down at his new breast plate. The gold glinted in the light. It felt lighter than the steel one he wore in practice. He wondered how much protection the gold would give him.

As if reading his mind Captain Aimon spoke to him. "It is a specially tempered gold. It is stronger than regular gold, but it has not lost any of its lustre. It's not as strong as steel, but it will still protect you. Its main purpose is to shine out as a focal point for the army."

"Won't it also make me any easy target for the enemy?" Bern ran his fingers over the breastplate.

Again the commanders started to laugh. "The role of the leader is not to fight side by side with his soldiers. We lead them onto the battlefield, but then let them do the fighting," General Sorrell laughed.

Captain Aimon continued. "Commanding an army and moving troops is not an easy job. If an army loses its commanders in the first day then there will be no second. A good army takes its lead from its commanders."

Bern knew that the commanders believed the words they spoke. He also knew that they didn't believe that it would be the case this time. They all knew that there was an unbelievable horror waiting for them on the other side of the fog and he was going to be at forefront of it all. Although he knew he should have been afraid, he wasn't. Bern knew that events were not going to play out like they thought. A calm came over him that made him forget his hangover.

"I would love to stay and chew the fat, but unfortunately we have a war to start," Jarwe's jovial words seemed out of place considering the circumstance. "Hopefully by now the first of our soldiers should be crossing our trenches. Let's hope that we get them all across before we see what Nyrra has in store for us."

Bern's cryptic words returned. "Don't worry about that. Attack is the last thing on his army's mind. They don't think we will attack them. In fact they've put a great deal into making sure that we don't."

"I hate to ask, but would you care to elaborate on your latest theory?" Jarwe had paused mid-rise from his chair.

"I would hate to ruin the ending for you. Just trust me. When we get to the fog you must do exactly what I say." There was no doubt in anyone's mind that he had changed. What they didn't know was if it was still Bern they were speaking to.

"Who are you?" Jarwe watched him carefully for any sign. The one he received was not the one he was looking for.

The strength of presence had completely left and the same confused look returned to his face as with the previous times. Looking at all the faces staring at him he knew instantly what had happened. The thought nearly made him physically sick.

"I did it again, didn't I?"

No one wanted to answer. The question remained in the air until Sorrell spoke. "I think we should move. This war isn't going to fight itself and I would hate to miss the start."

There were no arguments. It was going to be a long day and the sooner they started the sooner it would be over. The two dwarves had already left the tent when Bern started talking. The remainder of the command slowly made their way out. Bern waited for everyone to pass before he followed. His main reason for delaying was he didn't want everyone to see how poorly he was feeling. Since he returned to his normal self the nausea had returned tenfold. He wasn't sure if he was going to make it to the other side of the battlefield.

Chapter 3: Battle?

The army spread out across the battlefield. It was late morning when the last of the soldiers had crossed the trenches. Their defences, which would have given them a strong advantage if they had of been attacked, had become a huge hindrance. Moving the entire army across them had taken more time than expected.

They would have to push hard to make it across the rest of the field. If they were not back in their camp by nightfall they would be stuck and Nyrra would gain a huge advantage.

Six men sat on horses at the head of the field. They were all within talking distance. There was a strange mood amongst them; it was almost as if they didn't want to be there.

Bern, who was in the middle with General Jarwe, had chosen the layout of the army. As much as it pained the other military minds they agreed to let him make the decisions. They had no idea what they were facing and although he couldn't tell them he seemed to know more than they did. However the more they listened, the more they regretted their decision.

On the eastern side of the field Bern had assembled the entire Dwarven army. In the centre were two battalions of the Remidian infantry. On the western side of the field stood the infantry from Entero and Darshival and lined up behind them were the Elven bowmen. Bringing up the rear, and really no use at all, were the mounted knights from the various armies.

"Are you sure this is the best set up?" General Jarwe asked.

"We've been through this already. I have no recollection of setting the army. I have no military background. I couldn't tell if it's a good idea or not. All I know is that you've put me in charge and we can only hope that whatever it is inside comes out at the right time." Bern was becoming annoyed with all the questioning. He was still feeling sick from the previous night's drinking.

"I am sorry," Jarwe apologised, recognising the tone in Bern's voice. "You're right. We're putting a lot of faith in something that's very risky. Now that we have started there is no turning back. I just hope that whoever or whatever it is who knows what happens will tell us before it is too late. Now, if it is alright with you, I think we should get moving."

There was a sudden change in Bern at Jarwe's suggestion. He sat straighter in the saddle and his face was grim. If anyone had been watching they would have been prepared for what he was about to say. "We don't leave yet." Jarwe paused just as he was about to call out to his lieutenant.

"We don't have time to wait," General Sorrell offered. "If we don't leave now we won't make it back before nightfall."

"If we leave now we won't make it back at all. When we move, we move fast, but we can't start until the right time," Bern's voice was steady and sure of itself.

"What are you talking about?" Jarwe almost bit his tongue when the words came out. One thing he'd learnt is that when asked what he was saying Bern would return to normal.

As if it had already been written Bern shrugged his shoulders. He had already slumped in the saddle and all the confidence that he had shown was suddenly sucked out of his body.

"I don't think I am ever going to get used to this," Sorrell sighed.

"Well how do you think I feel?" Bern shot Sorrell a sly look.

The comment made Sorrell burst out laughing. The sound resonated around the battlefield. "Yes, I suppose you're right."

The laughter lightened the tension, but only for a moment. The sound of his boisterous laughter silenced anyone who was talking and all eyes were on the six, waiting, breathlessly for a command.

"Now!" was all that Bern said.

"Move out!" Jarwe boomed at the top of his voice.

Like a giant, slowly waking up from a dream, the army started into action. There was a creak of steel, like the cogs in an old portcullis being lifted. The leaders spread out along the front line, while Jarwe and Bern remained at the head.

The dark fog loomed in front of them and was fear incarnate. The resolve of the leaders would be important to the strength of the army. The nightmare of the fog would not compare to what awaited for them on the other side. Somewhere in the back of Bern's mind he could see the horrors that awaited them, but he didn't feel afraid. That in itself was disturbing.

Bern slumped in his saddle as he rode. The ale from the previous night was still having its affect. His head ached and his stomach churned. If he was not at the head of the army he would have let himself purge his stomach. Instead he tried his best to be strong. The entire army, commanders included, were relying on him to bring them back safely. He wondered to himself at what point did he stop being a farmer and start being the leader of one of the biggest armies in history. As much as Jarwe was still the General, Bern knew that he would defer any judgements to him. That thought alone made his head swim.

"What will we do when we reach that?" Jarwe pointed at the fog.

"I'm sure that answer will come in due course," Bern tried his best to sound confident.

The army moved slowly. With the infantry at the front the cavalry was forced to travel at their pace. The best they could do was to push up on the back line. It was exactly what Bern had intended. He knew if there was no one to hurry the army they would travel at a snail's pace. Even though most of the men were battle hardened warriors none of them were keen on reaching the fog. The further they travelled the more they dragged their feet. It was, in fact, the horses that pushed the men on. For some reason the animals weren't afraid of the impending battle and kept them moving as best they could.

The sun was high when Bern called for the army to halt for the midday meal. Although Jarwe protested he could see the look in Bern's eyes and knew to take his advice. His major quarrel was the fact that they were no more than a hundred paces from the fog.

"What if Nyrra decides to attack? If we are all lazing around having a picnic he will be able to run us down before we know what is happening," Sorrell protested when he joined the pair.

"Then you are definitely not going to like what I am going to suggest next." Bern had a smirk on his face.

No one really knew at what point they agreed to do whatever Bern suggested, but since they had started they weren't prepared to stop. The entire situation seemed insane to everyone in the command group, even Bern when he was back to normal.

"Tell the men that when they stop for lunch they must all turn around and face our camp. This is very important. Make it well known that if anyone breaks this command that they will be stripped of their rank and horsewhipped. No matter what happens no one is to face the fog until we are ready to move again." The smile quickly faded from Bern's face.

Sorrell was about to protest again, but Jarwe silence him with a wave of his hand and a look that told him to let it go. Jarwe himself wanted to ask the question, but knew that if he did whoever it was that was making the commands would disappear. He thought that if he could keep him around he might get some clues as to who he was.

"What are we doing?" Jarwe cursed loudly as the question came out of Bern's mouth.

By the time Jarwe finished cursing the remainder of the command group had arrived. The General explained the order and they all set out to see that it was done, after some convincing.

"Do you know what he meant?" Bern was even referring to himself as someone else.

"I never know what you mean. When you, change, there is no telling what's happening. There has not been a lot of sense coming out of your mouth, but we have come this far and I don't really know what we will do if we stop listening to you," Jarwe was not as comfortable referring to Bern's split personality as a separate person. The consequences of such a thing he could not fathom.

"I suppose if I said we should have lunch, then we should eat?" Bern suggested as he dismounted.

Undoing a saddle bag from the back of his horse he sat down on the ground. A small meal had been packed for him. Having not eaten breakfast he was starving. Bern wondered if his alternate persona had the entire army stop just so he could eat. It was a nice idea, but he knew that it wasn't the case. Whatever he had in mind it was not his own self preservation.

There was enough fear, already, amongst the men that there was no need for threats for them to obey any command. The tension had grown the further the army moved along the battlefield. At first the army was keen to be on the move, they started out from the campsite excited and ready for war. The closer they came to the realisation of why they had assembled in Avalon the more they started to question their own existence. Once they were eating, all with their backs to the fog, their spirits started to lift.

"It seems to be working?" Jarwe suddenly realised why Bern had told them to stop.

"I guess this is a good sign." Bern, who didn't feel the fear as intensely as everyone else, wasn't as impressed as the others. "Does this mean that the other me knows what he's doing?"

Although the question was rhetorical Jarwe felt he needed to answer it, if only for Bern's sake. "I do believe this is the best sign we've seen. I don't know whether you are leading us to our salvation or our doom, but I feel a lot better now."

Bern didn't feel so sure, but he couldn't complain. It was the first time that day that there seemed to be an air of hope amongst the commanders. He didn't want to dampen their spirits. He knew the fog would do that for him. When they started again he needed all the positive energy he could muster otherwise there would be no way they would be able to break through.

Thoughts were coming to his head and they were just as frustrating as not knowing anything. Like the others he was getting just enough information to keep him going, but nothing to tell him how it was going to end. He sensed that they were going to be victorious, but he didn't know how.

Once the command group had finished eating they all looked towards Bern. They all knew there wasn't much point in asking him a question. The information came when they least expected it.

"I'm sure we will leave soon, but the moment must be right." Bern was speaking and he knew that timing was everything. If they left too early or too late then they would all be dead. As much as he didn't want to wait for the mysterious entity to take control of his body he knew he had to wait, so they did.

"This is very important, so listen well. This will be the only opportunity we have to speak. Once we reach the fog there will be an intense feeling to run. You must all suppress this. When we reach the fog, Pernian, you must join Jarwe and myself. We shall pass through the fog, but only us." The entity had returned.

"What are we to do?" Aimon spoke and Jarwe nearly cursed him.

Despite the question he continued. "It will be your job to make sure the body of the army does not flee. Also, although I don't think that this will be a problem, you must stop anyone who tries to cross through the fog. You will know when the time is right to attack."

"What do you mean? Why can't we cross the fog? How will we know when to attack if you're covered by the fog?" the words spilt out of Aimon's mouth.

Jarwe moved to physically restrain the Captain, but the look on Bern's face showed that the entity had already left his body. There was no recognition on his face as Aimon shot the questions at him.

"Are you alright?" Hawthorne was the only one who seemed concerned with Bern's health.

"I am feeling a little better for eating. I think that it is time for us to keep moving."

Now it didn't matter who was speaking. They were completely at the mercy of Bern and the entity speaking through him, although they all knew they would be leaving, they all waited for the order to come from Jarwe. He was still the leader of the army and they all needed reassurance.

General Jarwe faltered for a moment when all eyes moved to him. He'd become so used to taking commands from Bern that he'd forgotten he was still the leader. The truth was that he wished he was no longer the General of the Army. It would be easier for him if Bern just took control.

In the time they had spent with their back to the fog the intense fear had almost completely disappeared and once they had finished eating and were on their way again the feeling only strengthened. The army moved into action as the word came down the line. The movement was quicker than expected. The effect of lunch was the exact opposite of what Jarwe had expected, the army had been revitalised and were now ready to face the unknown with a renewed vigour.

"Do you have any idea what we're going to face once we reach the fog?" The tension had finally gotten to Jarwe after they had been on the move for another hour and still hadn't reached the fog. He was sure when they stopped the fog was a lot closer than when they started again.

Bern waited before he responded. He looked to the sky as if he was looking for an answer. "There is a mystery on the other side of the fog. Things are not what they seem. I don't know exactly what is waiting for us, but I don't think it is as bad as we think."

Jarwe looked across at Bern who rode unwavering towards the fog. He stared straight ahead even as he spoke. It was clear to Jarwe that it was Bern who he was speaking to, but he wasn't sure if he knew what he was saying. There was no doubting the entity's confidence, but Bern, on the other hand, didn't have the same power in his voice. Even so, there was something in his words that made Jarwe believe him.

"Are you sure?" As much as he didn't want to push him, he didn't want to return to the eerie silence.

Bern stared at the fog as he spoke. "I'm not sure of anything anymore. There are thoughts bouncing around in my head and I'm not sure they're mine. I'm not even sure if they make any sense. I think that some of them are real and some are not."

"There is something very strange about this entire situation. I've fought many battles and this one has got to be the weirdest. Nothing is making sense." Jarwe mused.

"Whatever is waiting for us, we will find out soon enough." Bern pointed to the fog ahead of them.

Jarwe returned his attention to it. It loomed even higher above them and they were so close they could physically feel the chill coming from it. The sudden sight almost caused Jarwe to turn his horse around and gallop back towards the camp. He could only imagine how the rest of his army was feeling. He wanted to turn around to see, but if he took his eyes off the fog he knew he would run.

When they were no more than ten paces away Bern told Jarwe to instruct the army to halt. Jarwe didn't hesitate to bark the command and the army quickly stopped. It had been moving so slowly that they'd been barely moving at all.

Bern sat in his saddle, still staring straight ahead, waiting for Pernian to ride over to meet them. Jarwe stared at Bern, trying to get a feel for what he was thinking. The tension was at boiling point. The fear was radiating and he wanted nothing more than to turn tail and run. If it wasn't for his horse, standing stalwart at the head of the army, he would.

When Pernian reined his horse Bern finally spoke. "We go into the fog."

Pernian shot Jarwe a questioning look and in response Jarwe simply shook his head. There was no point in trying to explain something he still had no idea about. Pernian was just going to have to deal with it.

"You both must do exactly what I say, when I say it." The entity spoke again. "Anything else will be death for all of us," his words were as cold as ice.

Before either of them had a chance to speak Bern slowly kicked his horse into action. His slow movement looked measured, not tentative. There was no doubt that he was full of confidence. Jarwe took a deep breath as he looked up at the fog. A sudden surge of dread rushed through his body. His heart pounded and his mouth became dry.

"Come on. They won't wait all day," There was no humour in Bern's voice and he didn't even look back.

He knew the other two would be behind him. He could feel the intense fear, but it didn't seem to affect him. He rode on, determined not to falter. Everything was relying on him being strong.

The other two rode a full horse length behind Bern. His strength was the only thing that kept them going. Jarwe wondered on how he could be so calm. The three of them were about the face the largest army every gathered, by themselves.

Bern reined in his horse just before her nose touched the fog and waited for the other two to reach him. He looked to his left and then to his right. The look in his eyes was all the reassurance he was going to give them. If they weren't ready then there was nothing he could say that would make them.

The grey mare snorted once and shook her head as she waited for instructions. The fog had no effect on her, but she knew they were headed for battle. She had been bred for war and didn't like waiting. Feeling the soft kick to her flanks she knew it was time. She danced two steps backwards before plunging quickly into the fog.

The fog was no more than a thin sheet of condensed water. From the outside it looked as though it would blanket half the countryside, but in fact it was only wafer thin. Bern was the first one through followed by Jarwe and then Pernian. The sky was dark on the other side, a small red dot was the only sign the sun even existed.

Bern had only ridden two paces through the fog before he reined his horse to a stop. She seemed irritated, but knew that she had to obey her master. He sat and stared in front of him. The horror that lay before them didn't seem to be having any affect on him; it looked as though he was searching for something.

The scene before them was from the worst nightmare they had ever dreamt. Creatures of unbelievable horror filled the countryside before them, beasts with the bodies of bears and heads of deer, some with the legs of a goat, bodies of a man and the heads of a wolf, and many more stood before them. The start of the army was no more than fifty paces away. All eyes stared at the three, but no one moved.

"What are they doing?" Jarwe's breath was short and full of fear.

Bern ignored the question. "Pernian, nock one of you arrows."

"What good is one arrow…?" Bern silenced him with a raise of his hand as he continued to scour the land.

Pernian quickly did as he was told. He didn't understand anything that was happening, but he did know that Bern was their only chance for answers. There were so many targets he didn't know why Bern was even bothering. He could shoot all of his arrows and it wouldn't make a scratch. Pernian estimated there were over a hundred thousand creatures facing them on the other side of the field.

"Why aren't they attacking?" asked Pernian as he waited for the order to draw his bow.

"I don't know." Jarwe replied. "I kind of wish they would. This waiting is doing nothing for my nerves."

"I don't think you would like that very much," a smile had appeared on Bern's face. It was clear that he had found what he was looking for. "How quick can you shoot that thing?" The entity had a friendly tone, a tone that had never been in his voice before.

"I could have a third arrow in the air before the first body has dropped," a slight hint of pride entered his voice.

"Well I don't think that I will need you to shoot that quickly, but it is good to know for future reference," Bern's tone remained friendly, if not playful, and it started to make the other two uncomfortable. He was a little too flippant for the seriousness of their situation. "Don't worry. Everything is under control," he reassured them when he noticed the concern on their faces.

"I wish you would tell us what you are planning," Jarwe added.

"All in good time my friend. For now I will just ask that you trust me a little longer." It was really hard to tell if it was Bern or the entity speaking. There was no difference in their tone. The only thing that made them believe it was still the entity was the confidence in what he was saying.

"Very well. We shall do as you command," Jarwe didn't sound at all happy.

"I will do as you command," added Pernian.

"Very good. I think that we should get started." The smile remained on his face. "Now, if you look into the army, about twenty paces from the front and about there," Bern pointed to where he was directing Pernian. "There is a creature wearing a purple robe, with the hood drawn over his face. He's wearing a steel mask, which you can see glinting when he moves."

Pernian peered into the army in the direction Bern had instructed. Now that he had a mission the intense fear that he had been feeling suddenly disappeared. All he was focused on was finding his target. The more he stared into the army the more he found the horrible creatures started to fade in and out. It wasn't long before he found the creature he was looking for. He was the only creature in the area that seemed substantial.

"You now see." Bern could see the recognition on Pernian's face. "After you fire the first arrow you must fire another at the same creature."

"I don't think that you have to worry about the second shot Bern. The first arrow will fly true. That creature will not be standing when the second arrow hits," there was no fear in Pernian's voice.

"This is the last time I will say it. Trust in what I say or suffer the consequences," the playfulness was completely gone and there was nothing left but anger.

"Of course. I'm sorry!" The apology was sincere, even if it sounded out of place.

"What should I do?" asked Jarwe, who was still suffering from the intense fear.

"Stay strong General. Once Pernian's arrow has struck you must command your army to hold. The fear that they are feeling at the moment is about to be increased greatly. Some will want to flee; others will want to charge into battle. You must remain strong... You must remain strong!" Bern looked at Pernian. "Now Pernian! Shoot your arrows."

Pernian snapped into action at the briskness of the command. The first arrow flew a second after the command with the second arrow following shortly after. He thought about sending a third arrow into the fray, just in case, but thought better of it. Bern had told him to shoot two and that's as many as he would.

The first arrow flew over the heads of the hideous creatures. None of them seemed to take notice of the fatal projectile. They continued to mindlessly stare straight ahead, ignorant of the impending danger. As the arrow was no more than two paces away it burst into flames. Before the flaming arrow struck its target it completely disintegrated into ash and dropped onto the hooded head of the creature. The wicked creature didn't seem to take any notice.

The second arrow also caught on fire before it struck its target. The arrow had made a greater distance and the second after it had been lit the arrow plunged into the robed creature's chest. It instantly burst into flame and along with it came a raucous burst of laughter from Bern. The sound surprised both the General and the elf.

"You never learn!" Bern called towards the army.

It wasn't long before the fiery creature sunk to the ground and as it did there was an audible crackle from behind them. The sudden noise made Jarwe and Pernian jump in their saddle. It was obvious that Bern had been expecting it as he remained completely still.

A huge gasp came from the entire army behind them as the fog suddenly blinked out of existence. The fear that had been radiating from the fog was nothing compared with the sight that was before them. Even the most battle hardened soldiers shrunk back in horror.

"Now Jarwe, be the General!" Bern boomed the command, annoyed that yet again he had to explain the obvious.

"Stay strong!" Jarwe's gruff voice boomed throughout the battlefield. "We must hold!" Jarwe didn't know why he spoke the words that made no sense inside his head.

The General's words shook the other commanders out of their shock. They remembered they too had a part to play, even though they themselves wanted nothing more than to turn tail and run.

The other commanders echoed the General's words and the army remained calm. The smile returned to Bern's face when he heard the words and a hush came over the battlefield. The opposing army looked unperturbed at the arrival of the Alliance. The same uncaring, unresponsive look remained on the faces of the evil creatures.

"What do we do now?" asked Jarwe, unsure on how long the army would remain stationary.

There was no answer from Bern. He had returned to his scanning of the opposing army. He looked neither frightened nor worried about what lay before him. The expression on his face showed he was only concerned about finding what he was looking for. He would not be distracted by Jarwe's comment.

The silence was deafening and seemed to last for an eternity before Bern finally found what he was looking for. A smile crossed his face before he lowered in head and shook it slowly back and forth.

"You are a clever one. You nearly had me there," Bern spoke directly to the opposing army, but the other two had a feeling he was speaking to someone else.

"Please Bern. We don't have time for this." Jarwe was starting to get frustrated. The main reason because he was purely at the mercy of Bern's whim. He had no control over the army and he didn't know if they were going to be slaughtered. Either way he was just a puppet, like everyone else.

"Do not talk to me about time," the smile quickly left Bern's face and anger filled his voice. "If you listened to me in the first place and I didn't have to keep repeating myself we would have had plenty more time. Now if you don't mind?" The question hung in the air and didn't require an answer. "Thank you," Bern said when Jarwe didn't object. "Now Pernian I need to you to focus. This shot will be a lot harder than the last one. You will only get one and it needs to be on an exact trajectory. There can be no margin for error." Pernian nodded his understanding before Bern continued. "Good then we need to ride forward."

Both Jarwe and Pernian wanted to question his judgement. If they moved any closer then there would be no chance of retreating if the enemy finally decided to attack, but after his last tirade they wouldn't dare.

The smile returned to Bern's face as he slowly led the other two closer to the frontline. A quiet murmur could be heard from the army behind them. They couldn't believe their commander was going to fight the enemy with one man and an elf.

Just before they were within half a dozen paces of the frontline Bern reined in his horse. All the details of the horrendous creatures opposing them could be seen. As much as they were terrifying from the close range there seemed something insubstantial about them. Even though there wasn't a breath of wind their fur and hair seemed to ripple. Jarwe shook his head and tried to refocus on the creature he was looking at, but when he returned his gaze the creature had vanished. There was something very disturbing happening.

"Be strong Jarwe. There is nothing here that can harm you, yet," Bern's words didn't fill the General with much hope. "Now you must focus Pernian."

Pernian had already nocked another arrow. He also had another two resting across his pommel, just in case. The hairs on the back of his neck were standing up in anticipation. He knew that it was the most important shot he would ever take.

"One hundred paces into the army is what looks like a small stone statue," Bern pointed to where he was speaking. It took Pernian a long moment before he saw what Bern was pointing to. In the middle of a group of grotesque creatures was what looked like a small statue of what looked like a cross between a goblin and a bat. The statue seemed so out of place that it made Pernian laugh.

"My arrows won't pierce that stone. Maybe at close range, but from here I would be just wasting them." As soon as Pernian spoke he thought he was going to receive the full wraith of Bern, but instead he let him off with a harsh stare.

"Your arrows will be fine and you will only need the one. If you can't kill it with one shot then we are all doomed." Bern thought about not telling Pernian the consequences of missing, but in the end figured knowing would help him to concentrate. "You must hit the creature in the head…"

"That's easy," Pernian interrupted as he took aim.

"Don't presume to know everything elf," Bern spat the word elf as he scolded Pernian. His words were so harsh that Pernian lowered his bow before he could take his shot. "Are you that much of a hurry to kill us all?"

"I thought you said I should shoot it in the head?" Pernian sounded hurt at Bern's berating.

"If you didn't interrupt me I would have told you the rest. Do you think it's much of a challenge to hit that target from here?" Bern didn't wait for Pernian to respond. "You saw what happened last time and that was just for the magician who was keeping the fog up. Don't you think they would defend a sorcerer a little better?" Pernian lowered his head and nodded as he realised how wrong he'd been. "Good, now we can continue. There's only one way for you to get the arrow through and that is to aim towards the sun. If you can arc the arrow into the sun then they won't be able to stop it, but you will only get one shot. If you miss they will know what we're doing. Now do you see how hard this is?" Bern explained.

"Hard is an understatement. I would say that the shot is impossible. The odds are stacked against us." Pernian looked towards the small red dot in the sky.

"I know, but can you do it?" Bern didn't seem concerned at the immensity of the task.

Pernian had already started aiming his arrow. There was nothing but grim determination on his face. His hands remained dead calm on his bow. Jarwe was the only one who was losing control. His hands were visibly shaking as he gripped his horse's reins. Sweat had broken out on his forehead, even though the temperature had dropped dramatically. He didn't know if he was going to be able to cope with all the tension. Even if Pernian made the shot he didn't know what the result was going to be.

Bern watched the elf closely as he slowly moved his bow. His hand remained completely calm as he moved up and down, left and right until he was sure his arrow was in the right position. Taking a deep breath Pernian pulled the bow string back a fraction of an inch more before letting the arrow loose. There was a loud twang and the arrow shot out towards the sun.

All three held their breath as the arrow soared through the air. At first it moved so effortlessly as it graced towards its target but when it reached the pinnacle of its arc it started to waver. The other two quickly looked towards Bern for his reaction.

"Damn it!" Bern cursed loudly. "I think we should all prepare for the worst," his eyes didn't leave the arrow as he spoke.

"What do you mean prepare for the worst?" It was the first time fear overruled Jarwe's voice.

"Wait," there was a glimmer of hope in Bern's voice as the arrow stopped wavering as it started its downward arc.

Whatever had caused the arrow to move had stopped. A smile suddenly appeared on Bern's face as it neared its target. It was clear the arrow was going to make it to its location. The only question was whether Pernian had aimed truly.

An ear piercing scream echoed throughout the battlefield as the arrow hit true. The previously stationary statue suddenly sprung to life before dropping dead. The entire enemy army shimmered as the sorcerer died.

"Now what happens?" Jarwe was almost afraid to ask.

"Just wait. It will all come to bare." Bern's smile became broader.

Jarwe and Pernian stared out over the immense army before them. For some reason the army didn't cast the net of fear it had before, a calm settled over them, a feeling that everything was going to be alright. As the feeling grew stronger the enemy army started to waver, much the same way the arrow did. The more they watched the more they wavered. After a minute the army started to fade. Slowly at first, one of the evil creatures disappeared and then another. Soon entire patches of the opposing army disappeared.

After a couple of minutes the entire scene in front of them changed. All of the terrifying, grotesque creatures had disappeared. In their place, in clumps around the battlefield, were no more than a thousand orglin and a dozen, weary looking, robed figures.

"Charge!!" came the cry from behind them.

"Finally," Bern spoke under his breath. Finally someone had done what he had told them and the results were obvious.

Chapter 4: Decoy's Revealed

It was in the early hours when they finally returned to the campsite and it would be mid-morning before the last of the army made it across the trenches. Everyone was exhausted and wanted to crawl into their tents, but things had developed since they had returned. Earlier in the day, just when the Alliance was about to storm the field Hadar had arrived with the start of the Hondin Lel army. As soon as he realised what was happening he started to move his army across the trenches to join the battle, which put him half way across the battlefield when General Jarwe was returning.

The battle itself was short and bloody. The Alliance, especially with the sudden advantage, was hungry for war. The small group of orglin didn't hold up much of a fight. The Alliance only suffered some minor injuries. The battle took less than an hour before the opposing army was completely annihilated. They had tried to take prisoners, but the orglin would not be taken. They fought until they were all slaughtered. The robed figures were the most perplexing, they didn't even try to defend themselves, they just threw themselves onto their enemies' weapons. There was no chance to question the decoys to find out where the real army was stationed.

They were all keen to hear why Hadar was so late in arriving. Not that it really mattered, but there was a good chance it would shed some light on what Nyrra had planned.

"There was nothing apparent that slowed us down," Hadar seemed confused. It wasn't until they told him what day it was before Hadar realised what had happened. "There was something that seemed out of place. The landscape around us seemed to blur. I couldn't look at the forest without feeling sick. The only way to return to normal was when I looked out in front. The nights and days seemed to merge. Nothing seemed real, yet nothing seemed out of place," Hadar still sounded confused.

"What does it mean?" Hawthorne asked.

Jarwe had been silent since they had returned. Both he and Pernian had been changed by their experience on the other side of the fog. The others put it down to exhaustion and opened a meeting to all who wanted to speak.

"I don't know, but it seems someone had been affecting the time of our travel. Someone didn't want us to reach this battle in time, but what I don't understand is if there was never going to be a battle what was the point in delaying us?"

Everyone's eyes moved towards Bern.

"I'm sorry. At this point in time I don't have any answers," Bern replied amongst a yawn.

"So we have all the pieces, but we are yet to know what puzzle we are building," Hadar mused.

"This is true. There is a massive army somewhere and our next move has to be the right one." General Sorrell said.

A messenger suddenly rushed into the tent carrying with him the final report from the frontline. The news was not what they were hoping for. With no prisoners there was no way for them to get any information. The entity that had been controlling Bern hadn't returned since the battle had started. Bern was extremely exhausted, but nevertheless he remained in the tent. He had retained some memories of what had happened and understood the importance of the entity's advice. If the entity returned then he would have to be part of the meeting.

"This is disturbing news," Jarwe spoke for the first time. "I believe that we should sleep on it. I don't think that we are going to achieve anything now."

As much as the others still wanted to discuss their options Jarwe was still their leader and they had to obey his command, but it was clear that something was wrong with him.

"Very well then. We shall reconvene in the morning," Prince Hawthorne made the final statement.

Bern was happy to be leaving; he was no longer the passive farm owner he once was. Something inside him had died and had been replaced with whatever was speaking through him. He was afraid that he was going to lose complete control of himself. He only hoped a good night's sleep would put him right again.

"How are you Bern?" Hadar chased after him once he had finished speaking to the others.

"You don't want to know," Bern didn't want to sound rude, but he didn't want to try and explain what he didn't fully understand.

"Have you heard from Alaric at all?" amongst all the excitement of the past few days Bern had completely forgotten about his friend.

"No, we haven't heard anything since he left us."

"Hmm, okay, well I will speak to you tomorrow then." Hadar left Bern and went to speak to the other commanders.

Bern was happy to be left alone. He was glad when he heard that there had been no major injuries. He knew that his two dwarf friends would be in the forefront and was relieved to hear that they were alright. He hoped that they would be at the meeting in the morning.

The morning came around all too soon for Bern. As soon as the sun peeked over the horizon a young page came for him. There was no chance of a meeting without him being present. The page had run a bath so Bern would be able to clean himself. It was the first time he had bathed in the past week and he felt a little more revitalised for it.

The rest of the command group, which didn't include Hulkan or Dorn, had already assembled and were eating a hearty breakfast. Although the victory was hollow it was still a victory and it wouldn't be right if they didn't celebrate at least a little. A plate of food was given to Bern as soon as he was seated.

"To a great victory!" Hawthorne made the toast as Jarwe was still in his reverie.

It was clear that Jarwe had not recovered from the horror on the other side of the fog. Pernian also seemed affected. Bern was the only one of the three who seemed to have recovered after sleeping. He still felt, off, but he was ready to fight another day.

As soon as the toasts were complete it was straight down to business. The remainder of the army had nearly finished passing over the trenches and once they had rested for a day they would need to be on the move.

"We have received some disturbing news late this morning," Hawthorne spoke. "A report has come in from Remidia. I think that it is best if you hear it from it the messenger himself." He motioned for a man from the back of the tent to come forward.

"Thank you, your majesty," the messenger cleared his throat before he began. "Nyrra has started to move his troops down through central Remidia. He is looting and burning as he goes. It is believed he has taken a number of small towns and controls most of the Duchy of Zenza." Hearing the name of his homeland Bern suddenly took notice. "No one has seen Nyrra himself, but it is clear that it's his army that is sweeping through Remidia. We will send further information when it comes to hand, but for now we request immediate assistance." The messenger returned to the back of the room.

"I think that it is clear that we need to move the army back towards Remidia. We have clearly been duped and we need to move as soon as we can!" Hawthorne stood.

"No!" Every eye moved to the end of the table where Bern was sitting He couldn't believe the word came out of his mouth. All he could think about was Mary and his children.

"What do you mean... no?" Hawthorne was more shocked than anyone else to hear Bern speak. "Our homeland is under attack. We need to move the army."

Sorrell cut in before Bern had a chance to defend himself. "The report is sketchy at best and there is no positive sighting of Nyrra. He wouldn't travel without the main component of his army."

"Yes, but it is not your land that is being invaded. We know he has men in Remidia. At least that's a start. From there we can find out the rest of his plans." Hawthorne was showing too much emotion. "We said from the start that Remidia was the logical target. Now it's time for us to move."

"We cannot make any rash decisions," Captain Aimon spoke for the first time that morning. "We all have a lot at stake here. Now we know Nyrra is not sticking with the plan we can't take anything for granted. Something isn't right here. He has enough men and other creatures to take Remidia, but by the sound of it he only has a small raiding force. I don't think that his main plan is to take the Kingdom."

Hawthorne had to concede that Aimon made sense. With the bulk of the Remidian army in Avalon the Kingdom was ripe for the picking. Anyone of the four other Kingdoms could easily invade and capture the major cities, he still couldn't sit idly by whilst his Kingdom was being invaded.

"Besides, it would take over half a year to move an army this size that far," Sorrell continued.

"You both make very good points, but I still cannot sit idly by while my land is being ravaged. I have to take some of my soldiers back to defend my Kingdom." Hawthorne was torn between his Kingdom and his duty.

"This being the case, what do we do with the rest of the army? We just can't leave it here, there's not enough food and water for us to wait. Not to mention that the sanitary pits are going to start overflowing soon," said Wojtek.

"I still believe that Nyrra will try and make a move for his homeland," Captain Aimon spoke his mind. "It is just a matter of how he's going to do it."

"If he was going to make for his homeland he would have done it by now. I believe that he will try and take one of the other Kingdoms. Let's be honest. There is nothing great in Nostiria for him."

"We need to take the army south," Bern cut in.

"And what do you base this on?" Hawthorne's tone was still extremely defensive.

"Sorry," Bern looked confused at the sudden attack. It took him a moment to realise that he'd spoken. "What did I say?"

"Let's not start this rubbish again. You know full well what you said. Now give us answers or leave this tent!" Hawthorne's face had gone red with rage.

Jarwe, who had been silent for the entire morning, jumped to his feet and levelled his sword at Hawthorne. Hawthorne was so shocked he couldn't move.

"You will give him the respect he deserves. If it wasn't for Bern we would not be here," it had been the most animated he had been since his return from the battlefield. "I am still the General of this army and you will listen to what he says."

Although his words made sense, everyone in the room was concerned. There was something very strange about Jarwe's sudden reaction.

"I am relieving you of command," Hawthorne spoke somewhat nervously with the sword still levelled at him. "And I am taking the Remidian army home."

"Let's not be hasty," Hadar said as he looked at Jarwe.

"You do not have the authority. I am the leader of the Alliance and that includes the Remidian army." Jarwe didn't back off at Hawthorne's command.

"That is true. But I am the crown prince of Remidia and the army is mine to command. It will leave in the morning." Hawthorne had made up his mind and there was nothing to stop him. "Come on Captain." He said as he brushed away the sword.

Prince Hawthorne quickly left the tent with Captain Derwin in tow. Before leaving, Derwin shot the others an apologetic look. With Hawthorne gone Jarwe returned to his chair. He looked at the others with a wild glint in his eyes. Bern was the only one who was able to return his stare. Bern was sure that something had broken inside of Jarwe and he wasn't sure it could be fixed.

"Please Bern, we need to know where we have to go next," Jarwe's said.

"I wish I knew. The only thing that I know is there is a tug pulling me South. Exactly where we need to go I can't say," Bern wanted so much to give them all the answers they longed for, but he knew there was no point in trying to push.

"Let's not be rash. I don't think that we can just move the army without more direction," Aimon added.

"Well, directly south of here is Darshival. We could move the army towards Kiarome. There are plenty supplies there and it will give us some direction whilst we figure our next move," General Sorrell tried to make the suggestion sound like the logical choice.

"Entero is also south of here. Queen Oriana would welcome the extra troops in Jarrat, especially since it is the more logical choice for Nyrra to attack," Captain Aimon added.

"And why would that be?"

"I think that is clear to everyone," Aimon snapped.

"I think everyone should calm down," Hadar's voice boomed throughout the tent. "We aren't going to get anywhere unless we take our own agendas off the table. I have sent word to King Lisle. Hondin Lel troops will remain where they are until we decide our next path. As soon as we work that out they will join us. The five hundred troops I have with me will remain under your command Jarwe."

"So where do we move the army?" Sorrell re-asked the question.

"South! We must ready the army to move south. How long will it take for the army to be ready?" Bern's words were final.

"We can have some of the army ready to move by the morning, but it will take at least three days for the entire camp to be broken down." Sorrell explained.

"I think we should all leave together," Bern suggested, "and then hopefully we should have a better idea on where we need to go."

"I will have my men set up a temporary campsite. I will let them know that we will be moving in three days." Hadar looked towards Jarwe who gave no response. He had returned to his malaise. Hadar wasn't exactly sure what had happened, but he was pretty sure that unofficially it was Bern who was in charge.

"We should prepare the army to leave," Aimon spoke to Sorrell, as it was clear that neither Jarwe nor Pernian were paying any attention to what was being said. "Is there anything else we need to do Bern?"

"No. If anything comes to mind I will let you know." As the tent cleared Bern looked at Jarwe and Pernian. "What's wrong with you two?"

Neither of them answered. They simply stared into the space in front of them. It was important the two of them snap out of their reverie. Pernian would need to inform the elves they were leaving and Jarwe was still the head of the army.

There were still three days before they were to leave and Bern needed to spend some time by himself. There was nothing he could do whilst the other two were in their current state. He spoke to a page standing outside the tent to keep an eye on them before he left to wander the campsite. Even though the report said there had been no major causalities he wanted to see his friends with his own eyes. He also wanted to make sure that the dwarves were ready to leave.

The campsite was a hive of activity when he left the command tent. Weary eyed soldiers rushed around as if the Evil One himself was on their tails. Bern knew something was wrong.

"What's happening?" Bern asked a Remidian soldier.

"Haven't you heard?" The soldier seemed confused. "Remidia is under attack. Our Prince has ordered us to break camp and make for home immediately."

Bern cursed to himself after the soldier had raced away. He would have to return to the command tent and raise Jarwe. Without the General there would be no way to stop Hawthorne from removing the entire Remidian army. He didn't know why, but he knew that Nyrra's main objective was not to take Remidia.

As Bern made his way back he found Jarwe just as he was leaving the tent with Pernian. When they saw Bern moving towards them they stopped instantly. They both looked pleased to see him. There was something fanatical in their eyes that made Bern uncomfortable.

"Hawthorne has commanded the Remidian army to break camp and move towards Remidia immediately." Bern didn't know any other way to break the news. "You have to do something to stop him."

"I don't know what you expect me to do, my lord," Bern wasn't sure exactly when Jarwe had decided to make him a noble, but he didn't like it. "Hawthorne is their Prince and ultimately will make decisions for them whilst they are on this battlefield. Only his father has the power to override him

"You're the General of the Army. Everyone has agreed to give you control. You have the power to make Hawthorne stay."

"That means nothing. It didn't help on the battlefield and it won't help now. Anyone can lead their army from this battlefield at any time, they just can't lead them on the battlefield. Anyone, everyone knows that I'm not in control of this army anymore. If you want the Remidian soldiers to stay then you will have to speak to them." As much as Bern didn't want to admit it he knew Jarwe was right. If anyone was going to stop Hawthorne from his treachery then it would have to be him.

"I'll see what I can do. Have the other commanders meet back here in the morning. Whatever happens today I think we are going to need to speak again." Bern was getting no help from the entity. He was only guessing what he should do.

"Yes, sir!" There was a small spark on the General's face after hearing the command, no matter how weak it was.

Bern stood and watched the two disappear. He wished he could remember what had happened on the battlefield. The only thing he could remember was getting out of bed. He knew there had been lucid moments, but he couldn't remember them either. It was almost as if the day had never happened. Whatever had happened put him in a bad position.

As he walked back towards his tent his head had started to swim trying to process all the information. He was trying so hard to remember. If he could then he would be more comfortable trying to wrest control of the Remidian army from Hawthorne.

By the time he reached the tent his head was aching and his body was exhausted. It was not yet mid-morning, but Bern had to rest. When he entered his tent he felt a weird heat flush through his head and felt as though he was going to pass out. He lay down on his bedroll and was asleep before he even closed his eyes.

Bern had no idea what time it was when he was awoken by a fresh faced looking soldier. He assumed that he was from Hadar's army, since the other armies had seen battle. The soldier had to wait a moment for Bern to wake properly. After taking a number of deep breaths Bern rose, dressed and left the tent.

The soldier looked somewhat nervous at the sight of Bern. It was as if the soldier was afraid of him and that made Bern uncomfortable. It took Bern a moment, but suddenly he realised that it was morning. The sun was only just starting to crest the horizon. He looked around frantically, but there was no doubting it. He had slept all day and all night and he was still exhausted.

"Sir, the others will be waiting. You insisted that they assemble before dawn." The soldier looked around nervously.

"What do you…" Bern thought about asking the question, but decided that the soldier was not the right person to ask. "Lead the way, private," Bern hoped that the command in his voice didn't sound as fake as it was.

"Yes, sir!"

Bern thought they were heading for the command tent, but instead the soldier took them on a detour. There was something different about the camp. Soon they could hear the sound of a gathered crowd and the soldier led Bern to a small podium at the front of the crowd.

As he moved closer he had a feeling they were waiting for him. To his relief he saw the rest of the command group standing on either side. Once the solider had left him Bern approached General Sorrell.

"What is going on?" asked Bern who was visibly shaking.

Sorrell had a blank look on his face. Captain Aimon, who was standing next to Sorrell, quickly responded. "You don't remember what happened yesterday?"

Bern shook his head. The thought about addressing the soldiers with no idea why he had assembled them was starting to affect him. He could feel all the soldier's eyes staring at his back as he spoke to Aimon.

"Well that's not good and I don't think that we have time to bring you up to speed."

"What is the name of the God Kings' names is going on here?" They all recognised the booming voice as it came towards them.

If the tone of his voice didn't tell them then the look on his face definitely did. Prince Hawthorne came storming up from the other side of the podium. It was then Bern realised there was room for two people to address the audience. Suddenly he realised he was compelled to meet Hawthorne on the podium. One thing he noticed was that Hawthorne was not wearing his sword and he breathed a quick sigh of relief.

"I said, what is going on here? Tell me truly Bern, because from what I hear reason is off the menu," Prince Hawthorne spoke loud enough for the crowd to hear.

A hush came over the soldiers when the two of them had reached the podium. No one really knew why they had been assembled. They had been told to turn up and that's what they did. Anything was better than drilling for the morning or even worse, packing the campsite.

"What I'm trying to do is stop you making the mistake of a lifetime," there was too much confidence in Bern's voice for it to be his words. He was still in charge of his body and he could hear and see everything, but he knew it was not him speaking.

"Our Kingdom is under attack. I move to defend our people. What do you propose? We wander around the countryside on the off chance we find Nyrra's army. We know he's in Remidia and that's where we should move to. If you will not, I will do whatever I can. Remidia will be victorious," Hawthorne's words brought a cheer from the soldiers. It was clear he had the better of the crowd, which consisted mostly of Remidian infantry. Bern would need some fancy talking to sway the crowd.

"We don't know for sure that Nyrra is raiding through Remidia. In fact all reports lead us to believe that his army anywhere except Remidia." Bern was not perturbed by Hawthorne's popularity.

"And where have you been getting your reports from?" Hawthorne scoffed.

"Where were the reports on what was on the other side of the battlefield? Do not forget that it was me who brought this army to victory." None of the other commanders objected with what he was implying.

The debate continued for over an hour. Neither party would concede to the other. The soldiers swayed as each man spoke. As the morning wore on the gathered crowd slowly grew. When they had finally argued to the point where they would just be going over old points they paused and looked out over the soldiers. It was clear neither side had won.

Bern had not expected to gain the support of all the Remidian soldiers, but if he had convinced even a quarter of those in the crowd he would be happy. Hawthorne was not going to leave with the entire army.

"Remember when you make your decision on whether to leave with Prince Hawthorne or to stay with the Alliance who is in command of this army." Bern looked at Jarwe who remained motionless.

He wished the General would stand up and be heard, but he knew it wasn't going to happen. As he stepped down from the podium he could hear Hawthorne giving his final address. Although he was no more than three paces away the words seemed mumbled and confused. His head felt dizzy and he thought he was about to fall over.

"Are you okay?" Sorrell asked as Bern walked passed.

"What? Yes, sorry, I am fine," as Bern spoke he heard the crowd cheer at Hawthorne's final words. Although Bern felt deathly exhausted, the last thing he wanted to do was to sleep. After what happened the day before he was afraid of what he might do.

"You don't look okay," there was a great deal of concern in Aimon's voice. "I think you should go and lie down."

"There is too much that needs discussing. I must..." Bern's head began to swim. He didn't think he could remain on his feet a moment longer.

"I think we should get you back to your tent," Sorrell offered.

"I'll be fine..." as he spoke Bern's eyes rolled back into his head and he collapsed onto the ground.

Chapter 5: The Mystery Grows

For two days Bern remained asleep. Not even the entity rose to lead the army. It was a tense time for the rest of the command group. Word had spread amongst the soldiers that Bern was unwell and Prince Hawthorne used it to his advantage. He gained more support amongst his own men and some soldiers from the other armies. On the morning of the second day of Bern's rest Hawthorne led his army off the battlefield.

When Bern finally woke on the morning of the third day he went straight to the command tent. He felt rested and hoped beyond all hope that he had been sleeping. The last thing he wanted to do was to walk into another trap set by his alter ego.

With his rest some of his memories had returned. They came to him as dreams. He remembered standing on the other side of the fog, the great army before him. There was no fear in his heart as he searched for the magician who had created it. He knew there were many magicians involved in making the spell, but it was the one who had focused all the energy and released the magic who would have to die.

He seemed to be able to remember things that were insignificant. He couldn't remember why he had gathered the crowd of soldiers the day before and he found it hard to believe that he had debated Hawthorne in front of the Remidian army. Six months ago he would not have believed that he would ever meet the Prince of Remidia let alone argue with him in public.

The others were pleased to see Bern when he arrived. The page, who had been standing at the entrance to the tent, introduced him as Lord Bern to the rest of the group. Bern was about to protest but Sorrell shook his head. He didn't know when he had become a Lord and he didn't like it.

General Sorrell welcomed him. "You are fast becoming legendary, my friend. The page didn't feel comfortable without introducing you as a Lord. He couldn't seem to understand that you had no title or rank. I think it's better this way. If you're to lead the army then you should have a title," his tone was warm and friendly.

"What are you talking about? I can't lead this army. I wouldn't know what to do." Bern looked around, nervously, as the faces all smiled back at him.

"I hate to break it to you," said Hulkan. "But you have been leading the army for the last week. We have been doing everything you've told us to do. Whether you like it or not you are the leader." Hulkan smiled.

Bern knew what he said was true. He had been leading the army, although he didn't know what he'd been doing. He looked at the others and noticed that the chair at the head of the table was now vacant. Jarwe was sitting to the right where Hawthorne had previously been seated. He took a step forward before he stopped.

"Thank you, but I still prefer to sit in my usual seat." Bern pulled the seat out at the bottom of the table and sat.

They all looked towards Bern to see what he would say next. It had been difficult preparing without having him around. Hawthorne had not stopped and they were two days behind.

"Okay then, we should get down to business," Wojtek had taken the job as chairman since Jarwe still refrained from taking control. "Hulkan, would you start?"

"We received some bad news late last night," Hulkan started. "It seems Gilgi escaped from his prison early yesterday morning. It looks like Hawthorne had a part to play. Reports came in late last night that Gilgi has taken the bulk of the Dwarven army and followed Hawthorne. There are only maybe a hundred dwarves left. They are the ones that are loyal to the cause," there was a hint of pride in Hulkan's voice.

"Where does that leave our numbers Wojtek?" Aimon asked.

Wojtek studied a sheet of paper in front of him. "It seems that with Bern out of action Hawthorne was able to take over half the army with him. I would estimate that there is about six thousand soldiers remaining. It's hard to say exactly. We still don't know the full extent of Hawthorne's actions. If we run into Nyrra's full army we won't have enough men to stop him."

"What do we do now? The men are almost ready to leave and we can't wait here much longer?" Sorrell spoke.

All eyes moved towards Bern, who felt somewhat uncomfortable. They had missed his advice and the strength in his command. What they didn't know was that without the help of the entity speaking through him he had nothing. None of his memories gave him any answers.

"I'm afraid I can't give you any more answers than those that you already know. I'm sure if we go over what I've already said then we can work out our next move," Bern suggested.

"There's not a great deal of information to go over. The day before your debate with Hawthorne you told the soldiers you had a plan. That's why they gathered to see you and Hawthorne. I don't know if you were really convincing, but now the army is yours." Wojtek flicked through his notes as he spoke. "At some point you were pretty keen for us to go south, but unfortunately you didn't tell us where exactly."

"Well, we have some of the greatest military minds in the Seven Kingdoms here. I'm sure we can work out where Nyrra is heading and maybe we can beat him there," Bern suggested.

"What if he's already at his chosen destination?" Aimon asked.

"What if his choice is not based on military tactics?" Sorrell added.

Bern took control of the conversation. "Let's not worry about what he might be doing and let's worry about what we know. Now we know that we have to move south. We know that his army is not in Avalon and he is not making a direct run at Nostiria. We know that some of his army is raiding in Remidia, so we know he doesn't have his entire army with him. So what we have to do now is work out the best plan for the army. Hawthorne is going to take care of the threat in Remidia, so although it isn't ideal it's one less thing we have to worry about." Bern's words sounded changed, but by the look on his face it was still him speaking.

"You knew Hawthorne was going to take soldiers back to Remidia before he announced it?" There was great surprise in Sorrell's voice.

"Of course he wasn't going to let Nyrra loose in his Kingdom and nor would I expect him to. I just had to make sure that he didn't take the entire army." There was a smile of knowing on Bern's face. It was the first time that Bern was able to call upon the knowledge contained by his alter ego. "If he had stayed it would only have been a matter of time before the guilt got the better of him. It is better him leaving now, thinking he has won a small victory, than to have him stay and resent us."

Jarwe sat up and rested his hands on the table. He spoke for the first time that morning. "Remidia was the only Kingdom that sent most of its army to the battleground. It makes sense that Nyrra will try and draw its forces away. The other Kingdoms have enough forces left to stop any random raiding. A full blown attack would destroy any nation."

"Very good. Now you are starting to think." Bern seemed rather pleased with himself.

"What about Castalia?" Aimon blurted.

"What do you mean?" asked Bern

"They have the largest single army of the Seven Kingdoms, yet they offer no support against Nyrra. I know they're isolated by their desert. Besides Nyrra's capital, the City of Night, the City of Sand is the most defensible city in the world, but that doesn't mean the threat doesn't exist for them as well."

"Do you think that Nyrra has aligned himself with the High Chancellor? If this is the case then there is nothing we can do?" Wojtek seemed worried at the new revelation.

"Something isn't right in Castalia, but I do not think the High Chancellor would ever join with Nyrra. No, I think that Castalia is safely out of Nyrra's reach and for the moment and completely neutral. I think Nyrra has another agenda," Bern deduced.

"So that leaves Entero and Darshival. Both are large and sparsely populated Kingdoms. They both have many forests. If Nyrra doesn't make for either Jarrat or Kiarome then it will be impossible to find him," added Sorrell.

"Then we should make for Jarrat. If Queen Oriana is in trouble we must help her," Aimon was quick to add.

Sorrell slammed his fist on the table and everyone suddenly stopped talking. "King Unwin may also be in trouble. If Kiarome has fallen then we need to aid him."

Bern watched the two of them carefully. Each were keen to protect their homeland, but there was something different in the way the two approached the subject. Bern wasn't sure what it was, but he knew that he had to be careful.

"We know that the Evil One is being crafty. I think he would move on Kiarome and then wait for this army to leave the battlefield. From there he would be able to make directly for the City of Night unhindered. There is no military advantage for him to take Jarrat." Sorrell added the last as a slight against Aimon.

It was clear on Aimon's face that he understood the insult. His mouth opened as he was about to speak, but then he thought better of it. A look of knowing suddenly crossed his face, but was gone before anyone noticed it. When he didn't say anything all eyes slowly moved to him.

"I think that Sorrell is right," Aimon said. "The Evil One would be a fool to attack Jarrat. The city's defences are too strong for him to attack. It makes much more sense to attack Kiarome," his tone was cold.

"Okay that is enough you two. This bickering is getting us nowhere. We have to decide where to move the remainder of the army and we have to do it today!" Bern silenced the two before they could continue their argument.

"Who's to say that he's sending his entire army in one direction? We know fairly confidently at least a portion of his army is raiding through Remidia. Just because we haven't heard from the other Kingdoms it doesn't mean that he doesn't have agents in all the lands. What if he isn't trying to reclaim his land, but instead is trying to cause chaos throughout the world?" Hadar was trying to be the voice of reason.

"That's true, but there's still the question of why I said to move the army south." The words still sounded strange coming from Bern.

"We don't know for sure that's the case. It's not that I don't believe you, but understand my scepticism. I haven't been here to see the miracle of..." Hadar hadn't finished speaking, but was silenced by a loud noise towards the head of the table.

It was General Jarwe who had caused the silence. No one had paid much attention to him since the meeting had started, but there was no option. He was standing and had slammed his bare fist on the table. He glared at Hadar with such intensity that Bern thought he was going to reach over and grab him.

"Bern's integrity is not at question. If he says we are to move south then we shall move south." Jarwe was so angry he almost foamed at the mouth. "You on the other hand, Lord Hadar, have not proven yourself yet."

"My record speaks for itself…" it was Bern who interrupted Hadar.

"This bickering is getting us nowhere. We need to concentrate on what is important and that is to decide where we are we going to move the army," Bern kept his tone level. Losing his cool would not help the situation.

"I don't think that we can rule out Hondin Lel. Lel Dinion is actually south of this campsite. It might not be far south, but it cannot be ruled out." Hadar was struggling to regain his cool.

"I think that Lel Dinion is safe from attack. It would take too much effort for the Evil One to move his army through the Cloumid Mountains." Jarwe had become suddenly vocal. The vague, fanatical look on his face had disappeared. He looked clear, calm and focused. "But you're right. Just because Bern told us to go south it doesn't mean that is where the Evil One is leading his army.

"Then that just brings us back to the beginning. We don't know where to move the army." Pernian had also regained his senses.

"Not necessarily. The fact remains the same that we need to move it. The camp is almost completely packed and we'll be ready to move by first light. We'll send out scouts to the three Kingdoms in question. For now we will start for Kiarome. It is the most logical position for us to move on. It is the closest city for us to restock our supplies and from there we can move on towards the other kingdoms if need be." The command had returned to Jarwe's voice and everyone was happy that he had taken control. They had missed his leadership over the past few days and even Aimon seemed happy with what he was suggesting. It seemed that finally a decision had been made. All that was left was confirmation from Bern.

"Very good Jarwe. Don't forget that you are a General and even if you don't have an army to command you need to act like you do," there was something different about Bern's tone. It wasn't apparent that the entity was speaking, but they were all pretty sure. "We shall move the army towards Kiarome and see what we shall see."

"Agreed then!" Wojtek looked around the table to make sure that no one was going to object. "I shall have my scribes draw up the necessary documents. If Kiarome isn't under attack from the Evil One then we shall petition King Unwin for supplies. I'm sure he will be accommodating."

"We'll leave first thing in the morning. Make sure that our scouts have left before lunchtime. Their speed and a little luck is all we have at the moment." Jarwe concluded the meeting without deferring to Bern.

***

Aimon was glad to finally be alone and inside his personal tent. Things couldn't have gone much better. He would be well provided for now. His master would be well pleased with what he had to report. No one had thought their ruse would have lasted so long and the army was heading in the wrong direction. Best of all no one suspected his motives. It was all he could do to keep himself from laughing. The last thing he wanted to do was to draw attention to himself. If he was caught doing what he was about to do then there would be no saving himself.

His tent was large enough to fit his bedroom as well as a small writing desk and chair. A short, fat candle burned slowly on the centre of the table. It had been lit by his page as the sunlight failed. The candle was lit at the same time each evening and replaced each morning. Underneath the desk was a bag packed with the Captain's personal items. Under no circumstances was anyone allowed into that bag.

Slowly Aimon dragged the bag out from under the desk. Before he opened the contents he made a quick check outside. Most of the lanterns had been taken down and the campsite was dark. He peered into the gloom to see if anyone was around. A lot of the tents had been packed and loaded onto wagons. He held his breath as he listened for movement. When he was happy that there was no one nearby, he returned to the seclusion of his tent.

His heart was racing as he placed the bag gently on his desk. Fear was mixed with anticipation and as much as he believed his master was going to be proud of him he knew that there was a chance he would be angry. The last thing Aimon wanted was to be on the other end when his master was displeased. He knew firsthand how much it hurt. He knew he had done right, but sometimes his master was unreasonable and caused him to suffer terribly. The thoughts came unbidden into his mind and he berated himself for it as he knew his master would be able to read his them. Any thoughts of betrayal would cause Aimon great pain if not death.

Once he had calmed himself and emptied his mind Aimon prepared himself for what he must do. It had been a long time since he had to calm himself and it took longer usual. He was glad he was out from under his master's watchful eye. The mission he had been given proved that he was still first amongst the seven. That thought made him smile again. It was starting to get late and he needed to make contact.

Inside the bag there were a variety of clothes and cloths, but there was only one thing of any purpose to him and that was safely tucked away at the bottom. Carefully reaching in he took out a perfectly smooth orb. If he was caught with it then he would surely be killed. The orb was pure white and cool to the touch. Not many people would know what the orb was, but even so he couldn't run the risk.

Placing it on his desk he sat back. The orb sat perfectly in the middle even though its base was rounded and the desk was on a slight slant. Aimon dry washed his hands in preparation. When he was ready his placed his hands, palm down, an inch above the orb and started chanting in as low a voice he could manage. As he did he started slowly moving his hands making opposite circles over the orb.

After a minute the colour in the orb suddenly changed from white to black with purple swirls. Pure evil was radiating now and if anyone was walking past they would easily feel it. The feeling filled Aimon with a sense of elation. White foam started to drip from the side of his mouth as the spell took effect. The orb was filled with dark storm clouds and occasionally a lightning bolt lit the tent.

When the spell was complete the clouds parted and in the centre of the orb was a grotesque head. Two horns protruded from its forehead. Its skin was deep purple, blue and red and wrinkled. Its eyes were blood red and its teeth were all sharp as fangs. The face sent a shock of fear racing through Aimon's veins.

"What do you have to report?" The voice boomed throughout the tent, although anyone standing outside wouldn't have heard a word.

"Everything is going to plan, my Lord," there was a waver in Aimon's voice.

"You are two days late in contacting me. I don't think that everything is going to plan," as Nyrra spoke the inside of the tent started to shake.

Aimon could feel an intense pressure inside his head as if someone was squeezing him with all their might. Aimon knew where the pressure was coming from. He should have expected it. His master was never going to be happy with him being late. The pressure continued for a full minute before it stopped. When it was over Aimon sucked in all the air his lungs could take before collapsing towards the desk. Aimon pulled himself back before his face touched the orb. He knew what would happen if he touched it.

"Please forgive me, oh Great Lord," grovelling was the only thing he could do.

"Stop your whining you pitiful creature. Tell me what you've been doing."

"The fake army was destroyed three days ago, two days longer than what we had expected," Aimon took a great risk pointing out the obvious to Nyrra, but he had to point out his success. "The army is moving tomorrow toward Kiarome. It seems that Jarwe has regained his senses. He has ordered messengers to be sent to Kiarome, Jarrat and Lel Dinion to see if they have been attacked. I've made sure that one of my agents has gone to Jarrat. The Cursed One's friend has not had another vision since he told the army to move south. With the misinformation I will create the army will be wandering around for months. Once they realise the truth it will be too late."

"You must be careful. If they find out who you are then they will know you have been deceiving them."

"I doubt that will be a problem. The Council of Wizards are yet to send anyone to help. No one here is strong enough to recognise our little ruse," there was again a waver in Aimon's voice. The strain of speaking with Nyrra was starting to overpower him.

"You have done well, Argoz. You must make sure the army doesn't arrive at Jarrat until we are ready," the sound of Nyrra's voice made Aimon feel sick. "Do not fail me. You know the cost of failing me!" With the final threat the orb blinked back to its original form.

Aimon collapsed onto his bedroll. He didn't even realise he had been standing. The effort of summoning Nyrra and then speaking to him had almost drained all the strength from his body. If Nyrra had not broken the link when he did there was a good chance that he would not have survived.

Argoz was disappointed with the body he had been given. Despite that the Captain from Jarrat was the perfect disguise for him. Getting Queen Oriana to send him to the battlefront was an easy task. Now the wench was in the thrall of his master. Their plan was coming to fruition. It would not be long before his master would rule the Seven Kingdoms and he, out of all the seven, would sit on his master's right hand side.

He thought he felt a presence outside the tent. Fear raced through his body, if someone had heard what he had been saying then he might be in trouble. Argoz quickly ran from his tent. The night outside was silent and a soft breeze blew. He looked around, but there was no other movement. Calming down Argoz returned inside and carefully placed the Orb back in the bag.

Once he had settled back inside he was sure he could feel the presence again. He looked around nervously before stretching out with his senses to try and find who it was. Whenever he thought he was close his senses seemed to skew away. Eventually he decided that it was just his paranoia.

The Dark Knight come Captain didn't get much sleep that night. Whenever he was able to relax he had the intense feeling that someone was watching him. When his page came to wake him, an hour before dawn, he rose with a renewed vigour. The army would be on the move once the sun had risen and his plan would go into its next stage.

Chapter 6: Southward

A dragon soared through the sky. A lone figure sat high on the its back peering down below. To see the land now it would be hard to believe that it was once the most fertile place in the Seven Kingdoms. Nyrra's evil had infected and deformed the land like a plague and there were only a few places of beauty left. The oasises were the only source of food for the nomad tribes, the remainder of what was once a thriving nation. They were those who remained behind when Nyrra went to war with the other six Kingdoms.

"What is it Alaric? What's wrong?" Cain asked as he flew away from the mountain. It might have been the shock of his fall and near death, but Cain was worried about Alaric.

"I was just thinking. If Morgoz got through to the mountain then it must mean my friends are dead." There was only a hint of sadness in his voice.

Cain's silence was all the answer Alaric required. He returned his vision to the sky in front of him. He had no idea what he was going to do. The Ruby Stone was lost and he had no idea where to find it. He didn't even know where to start looking. Most of his friends were dead and he could only imagine how the others were. He had no idea how the battle had progressed, but he was assuming the worst. He felt like throwing himself from Cain's back and being done with it all.

The thought of suicide was about to overwhelm him when Cain spoke. "There is someone down there," Cain nodded his head towards the ground.

Alaric had to lean over Cain's neck to see what he was talking about and in doing so nearly fell to his death. When he regained his balance, and his breath, he could begin to see. From the height they were soaring Alaric could only see a figure resting on the back of a wagon. Around it was a pair of white horses. Even from the distance Alaric recognised them as Adelanta and Eldred's Tormenta. He was both relieved and surprised to see that Adelanta had found the others. When they had parted at the City of Night Alaric never thought he would see the white stallion again.

"Do you want to see who it is?" Cain circled above the wagon

"I think so. The white horses are ours. I think that whoever is in the wagon is known to me." Alaric remained distant.

Cain was happy with Alaric's response and gently made his way towards the ground. Even though the descent was not at Cain's usual speed Alaric still had to hold on. He thought to ask him to slow down, but instead Cain landed with a sudden jolt that sent Alaric flying into the air.

"Sorry about that." Cain sounded embarrassed. "It's been a long time since I have had anyone on my back. Are you alright?"

Alaric rubbed his back as he got to his feet. "I think so," he said. Although the fall wasn't that bad, it still hurt. However, he was quick to dismiss it when he looked towards the wagon. All he could see was a pair of feet at the back. As he walked closer he could see an elf. His eyes were closed and his breathing was laboured. There were droplets of sweat on his forehead and although it was hot under the sun Alaric had never known Palentonal to be affected by the weather.

"Palentonal..." Alaric's voice cracked. Alaric had felt very close to the elf. He had spent many nights practicing the bow with him and he had saved his life in Arsiliac. It seemed to have happened a life time ago. He knew there was no way now his life would return to what it was. "Palentonal, can you hear me?" Alaric spoke louder when there was no response.

Slowly the elf started to stir. With a great effort, more than it should have, Palentonal lifted his head and looked towards Alaric. A weak smile crossed his face when he recognised him. Palentonal lifted himself up and then dragged himself back until he rested against the front of the wagon.

"It's over then, you've destroyed the stone?" Palentonal's voice was weak, but there was a breath of hope in it.

"Not quite, but I don't think that was exactly how things were supposed to play out." Alaric looked around nervously.

"What are you talking about?" Palentonal puffed.

"Another time. What happened here, where are the others?"

"Just after you left Nyrra's soldiers were upon us. Morgoz was there, as was Viper. We fought well, but they were too strong for us. All the nomads were killed," Alaric shook his head. "Eldred and Alena were taken. The only reason I'm still alive is to tell you where they've gone. They have..." Palentonal started coughing violently. "Sorry, they are heading for Jarrat."

"Then we must hurry, they have a good head start, but if we push hard we should be able to catch them before they reach the border." Even as the words came out of Alaric's mouth he knew that would not be possible. Even if Palentonal was well enough to track the others, there was no way they would be able to make up the distance.

"If only that were possible Alaric..." Palentonal struggled for breath. "... You have to leave me behind, if you're going to catch them. There is something you need to know..." before he could explain Palentonal lost consciousness.

Alaric cursed loudly. He could send Cain looking for the others, but it would be almost impossible to see into the canyon. He looked towards the sky before he realised that his situation was getting even worse. It wouldn't be long before the sun set and the temperature would drop to below freezing. If he didn't make it to a cave then he would freeze to death. He wondered how Palentonal had managed to stay alive overnight.

Thoughts were racing through his head so fast he didn't hear the movement of Cain behind him. If it wasn't for the nervous whinnies of the horses Alaric wouldn't have noticed at all.

"What are you doing?" Alaric asked as Cain moved closer to the wagon and peered over the side. It was strange, but Alaric could swear there was concern on the creature's face.

Suddenly there was a cry of terror from the back of the wagon. Palentonal had woken to a sight that terrified him.

"It's okay Palentonal. Cain is a friend," Alaric spoke softly.

"There is dark magic at play here," Cain mused.

Alaric had been so concerned about his friends that he had not taken any notice of anything around him. Once Cain had brought it to his attention he could suddenly feel an electricity in the air. He could feel the magic that had been used only a day before.

"Please listen. I don't know how much time I have," Palentonal quickly relaxed when Alaric had informed him that Cain had no desire to eat him. "You can't just rush into Jarrat. I'm not completely sure, but I believe they've set a trap for you. Somewhere in the depth of my memories, before I lost consciousness I remember hearing something. I can't be sure exactly who said it, but I'm confident it was Morgoz. 'Let him come now. He won't survive what the Great Lord has in store for him.' I don't believe he was referring to your encounter in the City of Night."

"That doesn't make any sense Palentonal. If Morgoz knew what was going to happen then he must know that I was going to kill him."

"I don't know Alaric. I only know what I heard." Palentonal coughed once before losing consciousness again.

Alaric let his head drop. If he couldn't get them out of their current situation it was all for nothing anyway. Soon the sun would set and they would be left to freeze. He didn't think things were supposed in end in such a manner, but he couldn't see any other options.

"Don't despair Alaric. It's not over yet," Cain tried to comfort him.

"What can I do?" Alaric sounded defeated. "Palentonal is in no condition to move. Even with the aid of the wagon I doubt very much we can find shelter for the night."

"That's where I can help. I have been around for a long time Alaric and have learned a trick or two over the years. Dragons are magical creatures. Although it's been a long time since I've used this spell I think I can still do it."

Alaric had no idea what he was talking about. There was no spell, which he knew of, that would transport them to a cave for the night. Alaric should have realised that his knowledge of magic wasn't all that comprehensive.

"Bring the horses closer to the wagon. It's going to be a lot easier if you are all close together."

Alaric did as he was told. Since he had no other ideas Cain was his only hope for survival. Both Tormenta and Adelanta didn't seem keen to move any closer to the dragon. Normally the two elven stallions were stalwart in any situation, but not this time. After a couple of minutes of coaxing Alaric was able to get Adelanta to move and it didn't take long for Tormenta to follow.

"Very good! Now I suggest that you hold their reins. This can be quite disturbing. You may also want to close your eyes as well," Cain suggested.

Alaric held the reins tight, but he kept his eyes open. He wanted to see what Cain was about to do. The dragon waited a moment, but when he was sure Alaric wasn't going to close his eyes he prepared to start.

Slowly Cain moved his great body so he was standing directly in front of the group before opening his mouth. The next thing Alaric felt was a great rush of energy. He had never felt such a rush before.

Suddenly Alaric raised his arms to block his face as flame shot from Cain's mouth. He wanted to strike back against the attack, but it was too late. Before he could react they were engulfed in flame, but instead of being burned alive all Alaric felt was a warm sensation. The flames created a cocoon around the group. As it did the air around them started to ripple and Alaric felt nauseous and he wished he had listened to the dragon and closed his eyes.

The ground started to shake as the fire and the energy rushed around him. He kept his eyes open for as long as he could before finally closing them to save losing consciousness. Even with his eyes closed he could still sense the vortex swirling around him.

It took a full five minutes before the rush of energy died down and then finally finished. Alaric knew it would be safe to open his eyes again and the sight before him was not at all what he was expecting. The desolation of Nostiria had completely disappeared. They were in a large valley surrounded by hills. In fact it was more like a crater than a valley. As the sun was already starting to set he felt it was as good a place as any to camp for the night.

When the fire disappeared horses started to jump and buck. The experience had not been pleasant for them and they wanted to be as far away from the dragon as possible. They quickly skipped away to the edge of the valley. Given a chance they would have left the valley altogether.

"Where are we?" Alaric's spoke breathlessly.

Even though he knew the answer to the question he still needed to ask. He was still learning about the power in the world around him and could not believe such an act was possible.

"We are in Avalon."

"Thank you Cain!" Alaric spoke softly when he regained his senses.

"That's alright Alaric. You saved me, it was the least I could do. Now I must go."

"Wait!" Alaric cried before Cain had a chance to lift himself from the ground. "I need your help to find my friends. They have been captured by Nyrra's agents and I need to rescue them before they reach Jarrat!"

"I would if I could Alaric, but that spell has drained my energy. I need to go somewhere to rest and regain my strength. I'll be no good to anyone in my current state."

Alaric wanted to protest, but then thought better of it. When it was clear to Cain that Alaric wasn't going to speak he flapped his great wings and lifted himself from the ground. It was obvious to Alaric the strain it took to complete such a simple task. He hovered over the valley for a moment before disappearing over the hills.

Slowly Palentonal started to regain consciousness whilst Alaric looked at what supplies his enemy had left them with. To his surprise there was more than what he had expected. There was food, water, wood and some bedrolls. There wasn't a lot, but with some luck it would last them over a week.

"Where are we? What happened? How long have I been asleep?" Palentonal asked when he realised they were no longer in Nostiria.

Alaric explained to Palentonal what had happened as he made a fire. Alaric didn't think Palentonal would survive the night and as soon as it was lit Alaric helped Palentonal from the wagon and tried to make him as comfortable as possible.

"So if you didn't destroy the stone where is it?" Palentonal sounded a little better although he still didn't have enough energy to sit.

"The stone disappeared," was all Alaric said as he returned to the back of the wagon. "You need to eat and drink something." Alaric didn't want to think about the stone. He had no idea where it was and once he said it out aloud it would make it all the more real.

As much as Palentonal wanted to know what happened he knew he had to eat. He didn't have the energy to feed himself and Alaric helped him eat a small meal before eating an even smaller meal himself.

When they had settled around the small fire Palentonal asked the question again. "What happened to the stone Alaric? Please don't tell me that Nyrra has it."

Slowly Alaric started to explain what happened. When he mentioned that Nyrra had made the stone disappear, Palentonal let out a gasp of horror. "But I don't think Nyrra knows where the stone is either, so we have a chance to find it again before he does," there was little hope in Alaric's voice as much as he wanted to keep Palentonal's spirits high.

"How do you plan on finding it?" Palentonal rasped as he struggled to breathe.

"I don't know. I will have to study the prophecy and hope there are some clues in there, but first we must rescue Alena and Eldred. Now I think you should get some rest." As Alaric finished speaking he noticed that Palentonal had already lost consciousness.

During the fight in Nostiria Palentonal had been slashed with a poisoned blade. Normally the blade would have killed him in seconds, but Viper had cast a spell to slow the affect of the poison. Alaric looked at his friend and worried. He didn't know how long Palentonal would survive. His first task had to be finding the elf help.

The Prophecy of Stone, the one true prophecy, had remained in Adelanta's saddle bag when he entered the City of Night. He hadn't thought anything of it until Palentonal had asked the question about the stone. Now he was grateful he had kept it with him. He wanted to start reading, but he couldn't keep his eyes open and fell straight to sleep.

During the night the fire had burnt out and Alaric awoke early to a bitterly cold morning. He cursed himself for falling asleep without leaving enough wood on the fire. He quickly started a new one before checking on his friend.

Despite the chill of the morning air and the dew on the ground Palentonal was still sweating profusely. Alaric ripped away a piece of his shirt, poured some water onto it and dabbed it against Palentonal face. The elf's skin was deathly cold to the touch. Alaric allowed them only enough time to warm themselves by the fire before he lifted him onto the wagon.

The horses again resisted Alaric's attempt to leash them to the wagon. He pleaded with them until they finally agreed. Alaric knew that every minute they were delayed Palentonal came closer to death. If Alaric didn't get him to a physician or a healer soon there would be no hope. He didn't know exactly what was wrong, but he knew the elf would not last long. At the very least he needed a soft bed to sleep in.

The next problem was which direction they should travel. The valley they were in was a common camping ground. There was more than one charred spot on the ground where campfires had been lit. He had been taught some tracking and hunting when he was training at Elhjem, but it was not something he had been given a great amount of time. There were too many footprints leading in, around and out of the valley for him to know which one's belonged to his friend's and their captors. There were some strange tracks that Alaric didn't recognise, but again there was no definitive result.

He assumed they were still in Avalon, but he had no idea how far Cain had transported them. For all he truly knew he could be half way across the world. The thought made him dizzy. The only way he was going to be able to continue was to believe he was in Avalon. He knew Darshival was south and that would be the quickest way to find a town.

As they started to climb the southern-most hill Alaric had a strange compulsion to turn around and head north. The feeling made no sense to him. North would only take him further away from his destination. He suppressed the feeling until it was only a mild irritation. He made his decision and he had to stand by it.

Once they had crested the hill Alaric felt a lot better. To the west, no more and a league or two away was a great forest. Although he wasn't positive he thought it looked like the Great Eastern forest and that lifted his spirits. Although his study in maps was lacking he was sure he was somewhere close to the border of Avalon and Darshival, which meant they would be very close to the border city of Bellarome. If that was true he would need to travel in a southerly direction until he reached the Darshival Royal Northern Highway which joined Kiarome with Lel Dinion and from there it would only be a short ride to the city. With any luck Alaric thought he could reach the city by the end of the following day.

Alaric ate a small meal as he guided the two horses. In fact once he had set them on his course they were happy to continue on without his guidance. It seemed as though the two horses had became used to pulling the wagon and started to enjoy it. Alaric wasn't exactly sure but he thought that the two horses were talking to each other.

Once Alaric realised that he was no longer required to steer he checked on Palentonal before taking up the prophecy. The scenery didn't change much, only the forest started to thin to the west and by midday, if he had of been paying attention, he would have noticed the steady trail of footprints on the ground. It had not been long since Hadar had led his army across the ground.

Palentonal did not stir in the back of the wagon. Occasionally Alaric checked on him. The remainder of his time was with his head in the prophecy. He had skipped over it once before, but he had not remembered how difficult it was to read. He wondered how Eldred had deciphered anything. Nothing seemed to be making sense, even passages he thought he had already read.

He was so ingrained in the prophecy that he didn't notice the day slowly creeping away and it wasn't until the light was starting to fail and he could no longer see the words clearly did he stop the horses. The day had passed and only when he put the prophecy down did he realise that he had not eaten since the early hours. He also remembered that he had not checked on Palentonal since before midday.

The back of the wagon was damp with the amount of sweat that had dripped from Palentonal's body. His skin was paler than Alaric had ever seen on a living body. If it wasn't for the slow rise and fall of his chest Alaric would have thought he was dead. Time was of the essence and Alaric thought about travelling during the night, but the temperature was already starting to drop and he didn't know if Palentonal would survive a night on the road.

Sensing his mood the two horses stopped in a small hollow. It would shelter them from the gentle, but cold wind that constantly blew through the plains. No matter what Alaric did he couldn't get them to start moving again. After a few minutes he decided that it was as good as any place to camp for the night.

He helped Palentonal from the wagon before lighting a small fire. The elf didn't stir at all when Alaric moved him. Alaric was sure there was something in the back of the wagon that would help him. He found Eldred's pack of herbs and medicine, but he didn't know what they did or how he could use them. He was sure if the elf regained consciousness he would be able to tell Alaric what to do, but for now there was nothing that could be done.

Again Alaric tried to study the prophecy, but again his eyes grew heavy and he couldn't hold off the sleep that his body so desperately needed. This time he had remembered to put more wood on the fire before he slept and with the thought of the impending city Alaric was freer with their supplies. He ate and drank his fill both in the evening and morning. Since Palentonal still remained unconscious he didn't need any food. Alaric tried to pour some water down his throat, but he wasn't sure if any of it reached his stomach.

The horses moved into place without any arguments in the morning and they were soon off once the sun had risen. When Alaric was comfortable the horses knew where they were going he returned his attention again to the prophecy. He was sure the location of the Ruby Stone, or at least direction on how he was going to find it, was hidden somewhere in the text. Without it he had no idea where he would start to look and the repercussions of not finding the stone wasn't worth thinking about.

It was shortly after midday, Alaric was still firmly entrenched in his reading, when they crested the top of a large hill. The wagon slowed to a stop and the two horses both whinnied and bucked until they got Alaric's attention. Slowly he looked up from his reading to a sight that almost brought a tear to his eyes.

"Look Palentonal, we're almost there," he didn't look back as he wasn't expecting a reply.

In front of him on the horizon was the sight he had been hoping to see. No more than a dozen leagues away were the city walls of Bellarome. If they pushed hard they would be at the gates before nightfall. Things were starting to turn around.

After an hour they reached a small dirt track which made its way to the highway. Once they were on the highway the travelling became much quicker. Alaric returned the prophecy to his bag and concentrated on the road. The highway was busy with merchants and other travellers and the last thing he wanted was for them to see a wagon being led by horses only. It wouldn't take long before the rumours were all over the city and the last thing he wanted to do was to announce his arrival. There was no telling where Nyrra's agents were and his anonymity was even more paramount.

The sun was low on the horizon when they reached the city gates. Alaric estimated there was an hour left before the sun set. That was more than enough time for him to find a physician and by morning, with a little luck, Palentonal would have improved.

Two guards stood either side of the gate. The highway in front of them was empty and the guards didn't seem to be taking much notice. It wasn't until the wagon was a few feet from the gates did the guards jump into action. They moved in front of the horse and forced Alaric to stop.

"Halt! State your name and business. Give us a good reason not to take your head off," one of the guards spoke in a gruff voice as he leaned on a long pike.

"I am but a weary traveller. We were attacked by bandits and my friend was wounded. I'm desperate to find rooms and some medical assistance. We mean no trouble," Alaric thought it was better to keep the exact truth to himself. He kept his voice as meek as he could, although he thought he would be able to disarm the two guards without much trouble, he realised his sword was still in the back of the wagon. He had not seen the point of wearing it whilst they were travelling.

"Well these are troubled times and trouble seems to follow strangers these days. Where are you coming from and what business do you have in Bellarome?" As the first guard spoke the second guard walked around to the back of the wagon. He raised an eyebrow at the elf lying in the back.

"What business do you have with an elf?" the first guard spoke once the second had reported what he had found in the back of the wagon. "We don't see too many of their kind here and to have one near death makes me a little nervous."

Alaric had no chance to answer the first question and was hoping the guard had forgotten he had asked it. "He is a friend of mine. He saved my life and in return I promised I would show him the world." It wasn't a complete lie.

"Stay here!" The first guard commanded before the two of them left to have a private discussion.

It wasn't long before they returned and their composure hadn't changed. Alaric couldn't tell from their expression whether they were going to be admitted or not. He had a bad feeling he might have to fight his way in. Without immediate medical attention Palentonal would surely die.

"Do you have any travel papers?" The first guard asked, a little embarrassed he had not already asked the question.

"The bandits took them," Alaric hoped that his lie would hold.

"Then I am afraid that things aren't looking good for you. Unless you are known to someone in the city we can contact you must remain outside." The guard seemed quite firm.

"I have something," the voice was weak and came from the back of the wagon.

Sometime since they had arrived Palentonal had regained consciousness. Alaric was relieved to hear his voice. Palentonal had managed to move himself into a seated position. He held up a piece of paper weakly in his left hand. Alaric took the paper before Palentonal dropped his arm.

Before Alaric had a chance to read it the first guard snatched it out of his hand. He seemed disappointed as he read and when he finished he handed the paper to the other guard. There was a strange look on his face as he was thinking, before an evil grin crossed his face.

"So if you were friends why would the elf have papers and you don't? I think that you're the bandit and kidnapped the elf," Alaric let out a sigh of disappointment. It was clear the guard was not going to let them pass.

"Wait," the second guard spoke to the first, stopping Alaric as he started to move for his sword. "I don't think we should get involved. If this is true then we could end up in the stocks."

"Very well. There is an inn on the highway not very far from here. It's called the Wayfarer's Stop. Stay there until we can verify who you are." The guard seemed less than impressed. He knew he could not block their entrance, but he would not make life easy for them.

"Thank you," Alaric spoke his gratitude through clenched teeth. "We also require a healer."

"We will have the local physician come and see you," the second guard spoke before the first had a chance. Alaric's posture showed that he was prepared for a fight and the guard knew his partner would only exasperate the situation.

Alaric nodded at the second guard as he flicked the reins. Once he was through the gates he let out a sigh of relief. He would be able to get help for Palentonal after all. His friend would be alright. As he looked back into the wagon he realised the elf had again lost consciousness. He looked deathly pale and was covered in sweat. They had arrived just in time. Alaric doubted he would have lasted another night.

It wasn't long before they came upon the inn. The sign hanging over the front door was of a weary looking man with a pole with a bag attached to the end over one shoulder. The Wayfarer's Stop was an old looking stone building. The wooden trim around the roof and doors had been painted a deep brown giving it a homely look.

The owner of the inn was an old man by the name of Marx. His wife had passed away only a year before and both his sons had moved to the capital in search of fame and fortune. His establishment was quite large due to its location. He employed a number of pages, grooms and serving women. Due to the recent trouble in the Seven Kingdoms business had been slow and he was glad to see Alaric on his doorstep.

"Now you understand that due to the downturn in business prices are more expensive." The friendly faced man was straight down to business. It was only at that moment that Alaric realised he didn't know if there were any coins in the wagon. The look on his face must have shown his thoughts. "Now you do have money don't you?" Marx's tone was only slightly less friendly.

"Of course we do, but that is another story. Right now I need to get my friend into a warm bed. He cannot stay out here any longer." Alaric's tone was firm. He couldn't let the innkeeper get the upper hand. "There are many more inns around here, so if you aren't going to let us in we shall keep moving."

"Right you are sir," Marx's tone became obsequious. "Marlon, get off your lazy rump and help this man. Get his friend into a room and water his horses!" Marx shouted at a man who was sitting on an oak barrel at the entrance to the stables. "If you would like to wait in the tavern everything will be ready for you shortly."

"Thank you, Marx. The guards at the front gate are sending for a physician to come. Can you please get me when he arrives?" Alaric's tone had turned friendly again.

"Of course sir," Marx bowed before he moved after Marlon. "Come on, come on. You would think you have never worked a day in your life."

Once inside the tavern Alaric collapsed into one of the chairs around one of the many tables. The exhaustion suddenly hit him and he couldn't remain standing. He thought he was going to lose consciousness. Taking a number of deep breaths he regained his composure. He rubbed his head before reaching into his shirt pocket. He had not noticed before, but there was a small silver coin there.

"Can I help you sir?" The serving woman was quite well spoken. She was young and under any other circumstances Alaric would have called her pretty. Her breasts were pushed up in an obvious way to gain the attention of her male customers. Again Alaric's mind was too far preoccupied to notice.

"A mug of ale please," was all he said.

Chapter 7: Doctor's Orders

The physician arrived at the inn an hour after they arrived. Accompanying him was the local magistrate and a tall slender man. Both men looked at Alaric with distain, but his attention remained on the physician as he moved closer to his friend.

"The city guard has told us some disturbing news," the magistrate spoke with an officious tone. "It seems there is some indiscretion on whether you know this elf. What we have been told is very disturbing and if true you will face the hangman's noose."

Only the last comment was able to break Alaric's concentration. He looked away from the physician and faced the other two men. The concern that had been on his face ever since the physician had first taken a look at Palentonal and shook his head was now gone. What replaced it was a mask of anger.

"How dare you come here and accuse me of injuring my friend?"

"Well for starters, let's have a look at these papers you told the watch had been stolen." The magistrate had a wry smile on his face.

It took Alaric a minute to locate the paper. He hadn't thought to take it after Palentonal had shown the gate guards. He was sure that made him look even guiltier and the last thing he needed was to be held up by an overzealous magistrate.

The magistrate read the letter of passage before handing it to the tall, slender man. Once the man had read it he handed it back to the magistrate. The magistrate folded the paper a couple of times before stuffing it into his back pocket. Alaric scolded himself for not reading it himself. He was sure there was information on it he needed. There was no way the magistrate was going to give it back for him to read and he'd be a fool to ask.

"So tell me why the two of you were on the road this afternoon?" The magistrate sat at a small round table as he spoke. His friend followed suit and sat on the other side.

Alaric thought about telling them the true story, but he didn't think that either of them would understand. The only thing he could do was to continue with his original lie. "My friend and I are travelling the Seven Kingdoms. We were waylaid by bandits not far from the city. My friend, as you can see, was badly wounded. Most of our possessions…"

"Yes we've heard this version already and we don't believe it. Now you either tell us the truth or we will drag you away and you can spend the night in the cells." The magistrate's tone was harsh. There was no doubt he was telling the truth. The look in his eyes made Alaric uncomfortable.

"That is the only story I have." Alaric held his ground. He couldn't tell them the truth and he couldn't think of a better lie. The only thing that saved him was movement from the physician.

The physician stood and shook his head before addressing the three of them. "I've never seen anything like this before." There was a great amount of concern in his voice.

"What's wrong with him?" Alaric could only just bring himself to ask. His voice breaking as he spoke.

"Your friend has been poisoned." The physician turned to speak directly at Alaric. "As I said I have never seen anything like it before. The wound has festered more than I would have expected considering the time frame. He is running a high fever, higher than what should be possible. Now I admit I have never treated an elf before. We don't get too many of their kind in Bellarome, but I don't think that his illness is natural."

"So what can you do to help him?" Alaric was starting to get desperate.

"I'm afraid there is nothing that I can do. If I had a fresh sample of the poison I might be able to create an antidote," the physician looked enquiringly at Alaric, but when there was no response he continued. "I will be very surprised if he makes it through the night."

Alaric couldn't take his eyes off his friend. He kept going through his head what he could have done differently. He didn't know what he was going to do without Palentonal's aide. With the others gone he was relying on the elf to help him with his quest. He didn't think he could go on by himself.

"In light of this news we shall leave you tonight. Be warned there will be soldiers posted outside the inn. If you try to flee then you'll be arrested. We shall continue our conversation in the morning." Alaric only vaguely heard the magistrate's voice.

He didn't look up as the three left the room. His friend lay dying and there was nothing he could do about it. He wished Eldred was with him. He knew the wizard would be able to save Palentonal. Alaric scolded himself, if he had been a faster learner he was sure he would know what to do. As it was, magic was going to be no use to him.

Exhaustion got the better of Alaric as he sat vigil by Palentonal's bed. Alaric had not planned on sleeping. He wanted to stay awake in case Palentonal regained consciousness, but his body needed sleep and it was more powerful than his mind.

It was late in the night when Alaric stirred. He woke with a jolt when he remembered where he was. The room was dark and all he could hear was Palentonal's laboured breathing. There was a rasp that Alaric knew was not a good sign. He stumbled around until he found a small lantern on the table. After fiddling for a moment he managed to light it and as the sudden light lit the room there came a stir from the bed.

"Palentonal," Alaric's voice barely broke a whisper as he moved towards the bed.

"Alaric, are you there?" Palentonal tried to sit up, but he didn't have any strength.

"Rest, my friend, don't try and sit," Alaric spoke softly.

"I know I don't have long to live." He coughed.

"Don't be silly," Alaric nearly choked on his words. "A little rest and you'll be up and about."

"You don't have to lie. I know my time is short." Palentonal's voice was weak. "You have to be strong Alaric. You can still defeat Nyrra." Palentonal stopped what he was saying to cough again. "Move on Alaric. You don't have time to grieve. Move on or you will risk everything."

"What is written on those travel papers?" Alaric swallowed hard before he spoke. "Palentonal...?" Alaric spoke louder when there was no answer. "...Palentonal!" He cried out towards the roof, but he knew it was too late.

Palentonal's body now lay completely still. His chest had finally stopped rising and falling and Alaric dropped his head onto his folded arms which rested next to the elf. He couldn't hold back the tears any longer. The exhaustion he felt only added to his despair.

After he regained his composure Alaric wrapped Palentonal's body in his bedding. It was the best he could do. When he was sure he had done all he could he left for his own room. He was surprised at how much he had missed a soft bed. It seemed like a lifetime ago when he had last slept inside and as soon as he lay down he fell asleep.

He was rudely awoken in the morning by his door being bashed open. He sat up quickly as a number of soldiers rushed into the room. The first soldier quickly made his way to Alaric's sword, which was resting against a chair. They then blocked any exit and chance for Alaric to escape.

"It seems that your *friend* has passed," the magistrate's voice was less than sympathetic. "I think you should now come with me." It wasn't an invitation.

Alaric slowly rose and dressed himself. He seemed less than worried about the magistrate and his entourage. The new day had brought a new trial. He had taken Palentonal's final words to heart and he needed to be strong if he was going to survive. The magistrate was clearly planning on blaming Alaric for his death and it would not be easy to explain.

"I would appreciate it if you would dress the body in the appropriate death wraps. I will give him a proper elven send off when we leave the city," Alaric's words were cold as ice. The magistrate even took a step back in surprise.

"I don't think you'll have to worry about that in a hurry," the magistrate spoke when he regained his composure.

Alaric was quiet as he was escorted from the room. There was a prison wagon waiting for him outside. He had no idea how he was going to get out of his current situation.

There was a window in the back of the portable prison, but Alaric wasn't interested in the view. He sat in the back trying to come up with a solution to his problem. The wagon rattled through the streets for over half an hour before it came to a stop. Alaric still had no idea what he was going to say.

He thought about using magic to free himself, but the more he thought about it the more he knew it was a bad idea. He knew that he was strong enough to break the lock on his prison, but that would simply give away his location. By himself he was too vulnerable to risk being found by Nyrra's agents.

It wasn't long before the prison carriage rattled to a halt. No idea had come to him on how he could escape. He hadn't been able to think about much since his friend had died. He wished his other companions were with him. He was sure they would know what to do.

"Come on then. We haven't got all day," a gruff voice spoke from outside as someone banged twice on the side of the carriage.

Slowly Alaric made his way out the back. A pair of rough hands gripped his shoulders and pulled him the rest of the way out. His dawdling had obviously upset someone.

"Don't drag your feet. We have a lot to get done this morning and we don't want you slowing us down," yelled the magistrate.

"Please. I haven't done anything wrong and I really need to be on my way." Alaric thought forbearance might serve him better.

"There is no point speaking to me. It is well out of my hands. Lord Richmond had taken an interest in you. It seems the elf you killed is known to him." Hearing the accusation made Alaric lose his composure and he made a lunge for the magistrate. Alaric came within inches of wrapping his hands around the man's throat before he was cracked on the back of the head with a cudgel. Alaric sunk to the ground, barely able to stay conscious. "Now I trust that you won't try that again." There was something smug in the magistrate's voice.

Before Alaric could regain his composure the same pair of rough hands gripped his shoulders and lifted him to his feet. He kept his head bent as the ringing in his ears seemed to quieten when he did. The last thing he wanted to do was to earn another blow. He didn't think things could get any worse. The only way he was going to get out of his current predicament was to tell the truth and hope that Lord Richmond believed him.

At first, when Alaric could finally bring himself to raise his head again, he thought he was being marched into a rather large courtyard. When he stopped he had a chance to survey his surroundings. He was at the northern end of what looked to be some kind of arena. A ten foot wall surrounded him with a large gate at the southern end and a smaller one at the northern end. Bending around from the western extreme to the eastern extreme from north to south were rows and rows of empty bench seating. On the northern end, dead in the middle, sat four high-backed thrones covered by a large canvas awning and surrounded by a large platform. Two men sat on the middle thrones.

"My Lord," the magistrate spoke clearly from Alaric's side. "This is the man you requested. We are yet to know his name. He has been quite adamant about not revealing that to us." The magistrate twisted the truth slightly. As much as Alaric had avoided telling them his name he had never been directly asked.

The magistrate spoke the burly man, who had twice manhandled Alaric and clobbered him once again before shackling him to the ground. He had not even noticed the chains and shackles that were mounted to the ground beneath his feet. Any thought of escape, which was all but impossible anyway, was completely gone. He would have to rely on the mercy of Lord Richmond if he didn't want to spend the rest of his life in a prison cell.

"I see," Lord Richmond mused from his throne. "And why is it that you feel the need to hide your name? In my experience many thieves and cutthroats try to hide their identity. Which one are you I wonder?" Richmond had a soft tone which seemed quite out of place.

From the distance Alaric could see that Richmond had short brown hair. Although he couldn't be sure, but he thought he was also a man of middle years. There was hint of lines on his face and even in his lose fitting robes Alaric could tell his body held muscle. There was something kindly in his face that Alaric thought he might be able to use to his advantage.

"I am neither my Lord. I am just an innocent traveller who has fallen on bad times. As I am sure you know already that my travelling companion died late last night."

"Do you take me for a fool?" Richmond's voice boomed throughout the arena. "I have been fair in giving you a chance to explain yourself, but instead you decide to lie to me. If you wish to spend the rest of your life in my prisons I suggest you continue your lies."

The words ripped at Alaric. His shoulders visibly dropped as he realised what he had done. His lies might have cost him his freedom. There was no doubt that his only chance of release was to tell the truth.

"My name is Alaric and my companion's name was Palentonal," Alaric took a deep breath as he tried to think of what to say next. "We were on a quest to find some friends of ours who have been kidnapped. They were taken by the same people," Alaric used the word people very loosely, "who murdered Palentonal. Now I must hunt them by myself and my time is short. To make matters worse I have no idea where they are, only their destination and I need to find them before they reach it." He didn't think it was worth giving away the nature of their captors.

"I believe that you're now telling the truth." Alaric could see Richmond was holding a sheet of paper. "But I believe that there is more to your story than you are telling me."

There was a moment when the entire arena went quiet. Alaric didn't believe Richmond had asked him a question and as much as he was sure that it didn't help his cause he wasn't going to offer any more information. He didn't know where he would find Nyrra's agents, but he was sure if he made his true presence known they would find him sooner or later. His life was already in grave danger and he didn't want to make the situation even worse.

"I don't think that you are making your life any easier by remaining quiet," it was clear Richmond was trying to think as he spoke. It was as if he was trying to recall something he had heard in the past.

"You're right, my Lord. There is more to the story, but it's not one I can freely speak about. The enemy has eyes and ears everywhere." It was as much truth as he was willing reveal.

Even from the floor of the arena Alaric could see the look of realisation cross Richmond's face. Whatever Alaric had said seemed to do the job. Despite that he received a whack on the back of his head and he sunk to his knees.

"As you see my loyal subjects take quite an offence to what you are saying." There was a large smirk on Lord Richmond's face.

"Be that as it may," Alaric spoke as he rubbed the back of his head. He decided it would be safer to stay on his knees instead of rising to talk. "I don't know who these men are and the information I have cannot fall into the wrong hands."

Richmond thought for a long moment and stroked the short, brown goatee that grew from his chin. He looked very pensive. "Very well. If you are who you say you are then everything will be alright for you. However, if you are lying you will hang from my gallows before nightfall."

Even though he spoke with a level tone there was something very menacing in his words. There was also something knowing in his tone, as if he knew something he didn't want anyone else to know. There was a sudden click and Alaric was pushed forward and he slid face first into the ground.

Before he could resist, shackles were placed on his wrists and ankles. A thick chain joined the four shackles together, making movement extremely hard. There was no chance for Alaric to make a run for freedom, if there had been somewhere for him to run to.

The magistrate and his burly friend led Alaric through the gate at the northern end of the arena. It led to a dimly lit corridor. On either side of were many small holding cells, all of which were empty. There was a smell of stale blood in the air, which almost made Alaric vomit.

Once they were at the end of the corridor they passed through an iron barred door. The magistrate opened it with a set of keys that hung on a large ring. Alaric wondered if one of the keys would open the locks on his shackles. Even if he was able to steal the keys it would take him too long to find the right one.

They entered another small corridor and at the end there was a small archway that led out into the open. To the left hand side, before the archway, was a flight of stairs. As he climbed the stairs he tried to think of some lie to tell Lord Richmond that would help him to escape, but for some reason the nobleman seemed to know when he was lying. He just hoped Richmond would believe the truth even though the truth was more unbelievable than any lie he could think up.

The top of the stairs came up at the back of the platform behind the thrones. Lord Richmond was standing behind his throne and two men stood on either side with half a dozen guards to protect them. Alaric found it difficult to climb the stairs in his shackles and was glad when they reached the top.

Lord Richmond was much older than Alaric had thought when he was looking up from the bottom of the arena. The subtle signs of age where more prominent on his face and there were strips of grey in both his hair and his goatee. There was a power in his age, not a frailty. There could be no doubt the sword that hung by his side was not just for decoration.

"Well what is it that you have to tell me?" Richmond asked.

"I told you. What I have to say is for your ears only," Alaric remained calm as he spoke. There was something about Richmond's appearance that settled his nerves. He had a friendly, compassionate look about him.

"Very well," Richmond nodded at the men on the landing.

Everyone started to leave except for the man standing on his left. The magistrate seemed the most annoyed at being dismissed. He was about to protest, but the look on Richmond's face made him change his mind. He knew better than to upset the Lord. He had fought hard to reach his position as the local magistrate and he didn't want to do anything to jeopardise it.

"I said everyone." Alaric spoke when everyone else had left the platform. He tried to remain composed, but there was something very disturbing about the way the other man was staring at him.

"This is Tancred. He's my advisor and I trust him with my life. He will stay and you will talk or we call the others back and take a trip to the gallows." There was no waver in Richmond's voice.

"If that is what you want," Alaric spoke slowly. He hoped he could trust the two men with the truth.

There was nothing else he could do. Alaric was completely out of options. He had to tell the truth about how Palentonal and he happened to be travelling through Bellarome. He still had to be careful not to tell the entire truth. Some things needed to be kept secret at all cost. He didn't know how much of his journey was documented throughout the Seven Kingdoms, but he knew he couldn't reveal all the facts.

"Are you familiar with *the Prophecy of the Stone*?" Alaric asked. He thought it best if he tried to find the boundaries of the Lord's knowledge.

Lord Richmond was about to speak when Tancred cut in. "We know as much as any in the times we live in. The Evil One is on the move and has broken through his prison to the north. We have heard the many rumours and theories on how he is to be defeated. We keep our own council on what we believe. We are also servants of the crown and do as our King instructs." He spoke as though he was repeating a practised speech. "What does this have to do with your current situation?"

"Well, if you know of the prophecies then you will know that there is a man who is named as the Chosen One. That man is me!" Alaric paused and watched the reaction on the other men's faces. He could tell instantly that they were sceptical, yet their expressions showed that they didn't completely discount what he had told him.

Alaric slowly started to tell his tale, careful not to make any reference to the Ruby Stone. He thought it best to omit its existence since he no longer had it as proof. "And then we were waylaid on our way to the battlefield," he spoke the truth, but an underlying truth. "Two of my friends were captured and taken to Jarrat. Palentonal was gravely injured. I took it upon myself to go for help whilst the rest of my companions continued on to the battlefield."

"If you are the Chosen One, then why did you not continue on to face the Evil One? I don't believe you are telling the truth," Tancred was not convinced. There was doubt in his mind and he had not yet condemned Alaric to the gallows.

Tancred looked around the same age as his master, although the lines of age weren't as apparent on his face. He also had short brown hair, although it was lighter than Richmond's and had no grey through it. It looked as though he was freshly shaved and Alaric assumed that was a daily ritual for him. Although he was referred to as an advisor it looked as though he was built for battle. Although his physique wasn't as muscular as his Lord he looked as though he could handle himself in single combat. Alaric had to admit there was something very strange about the pair.

"That is a long story," said Richmond "and I'm not really sure if it'll answer your questions." In truth Alaric didn't know where Nyrra was. In the final chamber of the Cauldron Mountain he had fought only an illusion, a powerful illusion, but an illusion nevertheless. He hoped that Nyrra wasn't in Jarrat. He had struggled against the illusion and he didn't believe that he could defeat the real thing, especially since he no longer possessed the Ruby Stone. Things were not playing out to plan and now he was just following his nose. "I chose to follow the trail of my captured friends in hope of discovering the truth."

"I think that he's telling the truth?" Lord Richmond spoke.

"You are always too trusting," Tancred didn't sound convinced.

"Nevertheless it makes sense, although I don't believe you have told me the full truth. There are too many holes in your story. I do believe you are who you say you are." Lord Richmond had a fatherly tone to his voice. "I thought as much when the magistrate brought me your right-of-passage letter. It was not something that could easily be forged and I doubt anyone would let it fall into the wrong hands." When he finished speaking he produced the papers from his pocket. "I believe that we can trust you," he nodded towards Tancred.

The advisor produced a set of keys from inside his coat pocket. The set was only slightly fewer than that of the magistrate. He cautiously unlocked the shackles, not that Alaric had any thoughts of sudden movements. He rubbed his wrists when he was set free. There was no pain, but the feeling of the shackles remained for a moment.

"We have much to discuss, but we shall not do it here," Lord Richmond's voice remained friendly. "You shall be my guest at my home."

"I thank you, but I am in a great hurry and I really must be on my way." Alaric was starting to become excited.

"These are troubled times and travelling through Darshival is not easy. I take it that you have read through the papers that your friend was carrying. You were lucky and these right-of-passage papers will only get you so far. You were fortunate to gain entry to Bellarome, but I doubt they will gain you access to Kiarome," Richmond explained.

"What are you talking about?" Alaric was starting to become annoyed.

"As I said we can't speak here. Now please come with us. I don't want to have to call the magistrate back. I'm sure he would be more than pleased to drag you kicking and screaming," Lord Richmond's tone was cold. There could be no doubt that he would go through with his threat if Alaric didn't acquiesce. "I don't think he likes you very much."

Alaric dropped his head. He thought about trying to fight his way free. Since he was out of his chains he was confident he could unarm the other two and escape, but here was something in the back of his mind telling him he should do as he was told. Even though Richmond had been nothing but officious with him he had a feeling that the man was a friend and he should listen to what he had to say.

It was not his mind that made the final decision. As he stood there contemplating his next move his stomach started to rumble. It had been a long time since Alaric had eaten a decent meal and he knew he would not get far without help and Lord Richmond seemed to be offering. His food supply was soon to run out and he had no money to buy any more. Despite the fact he wanted to stay on the path of his friends he knew that for the moment he had to remain in Bellarome.

"Very well, I accept your hospitality with great pleasure and gratitude." Once Alaric had agreed to stay it was like a great weight had been lifted off his shoulders. He didn't know why, but he knew that he had made the right decision. Alaric felt as though Lord Richmond was important to his mission.

"Now there is only one more thing." Something in Richmond's tone made Alaric think he was not going to enjoy it. "We must chain you again and have you transported to my home as a criminal."

Alaric took a sudden step back from the shackles which lay at his feet. Something strange was happening. First they take away his freedom and then they give it back only to take it away again.

"Please, you have to trust me. I will explain everything once we get to my home."

A sinking feeling came over Alaric as the shackles were returned. Whatever happened he was at the mercy of Lord Richmond. He only hoped that initial feeling about him was accurate.

Chapter 8: Lord Richmond

His home was more than a house. It was a small palace in the centre of the city. A small wall, more for decoration than defence, circled the gardens surrounding the palace. The gardens were one of the most spectacular features of the palace. Lush, well cared for lawns were broken by a multitude of flowers and trees. A number of small streams meandered their way through the gardens to end in small fish ponds.

The palace itself was nothing out of the ordinary. It was made of polished stone, but that was the only extravagant thing about it. There were no fancy designs to the façade and only one small tower rose from the centre.

Alaric kept his head down as he was led towards the palace. Richmond had instructed him not to look around and again the Lord didn't give him any reason for the strange request. Alaric had to take the advice on its merits and trust that Richmond would explain everything once they arrived.

"Thank you for your wonderful service magistrate." Richmond said when they reached the main doors to the palace. It was nothing more than to placate him and keep up the façade of Alaric being a desperate criminal.

"Shouldn't I take him to the dungeon for you?" the magistrate said with his chest puffed up with pride.

"No, thank you. I think I will be able to manage from here. There was a touch of impatience in Richmond's voice. The magistrate didn't seem to notice.

"At least let me leave some of my soldiers for your protection, until your own guards arrive." He was now starting to get on Richmond's nerves. His pompous attitude was starting to show. Lord Richmond took offence to the assumption that the soldiers belonged to the magistrate. All the city's soldiers, and the magistrate himself for that matter, were on Richmond's payroll. He swallowed his anger before he spoke again.

"That will be fine. I'm sure that you have more pressing matters," the dismissal was subtle, but it didn't miss the magistrate's ears. If he was at all offended he didn't show it.

"Very well, my Lord. We shall leave you here." The magistrate tried to make it sound as though it was his decision to leave and he motioned for the soldiers to move.

Lord Richmond stood at the door until the magistrate and his soldiers walked out of view. Lord Richmond, Alaric and Tancred remained with the two guards standing on either side of the door. Richmond wanted to release Alaric from his bonds, but he knew he would have to wait until they were safely inside. If anyone figured out who Alaric really was then they were all in danger.

"Step lively lieutenant!" Tancred boomed, louder than was really necessary.

The guard on the left side of the door suddenly snapped into action. Both of them had been following the conversation so closely, and what had transpired afterwards, that they had forgotten they had a job to do.

The main entrance to the palace was a huge wooden double door. The doors were only used on ceremonial occasions when large numbers needed to be admitted at once. It had been such a long time since the doors had been opened, but the lieutenant moved to open a small, regular sized door cut into the left one.

Alaric gave Lord Richmond a fierce glare before he was ushered through the door. The situation was becoming stranger and stranger. Just when he thought he was doomed Richmond would do something very unexpected.

"Would you mind telling me what this is all about?" Alaric's voice was dripping with annoyance.

"Not now," Tancred whispered from behind Richmond as a serving girl appeared from behind a corner.

The three of them continued through the palace. Alaric was in the lead and was being directed from pokes from Richmond behind him. Every now and then, when Alaric thought they were completely alone, a serving girl or a page boy would come out of nowhere. The journey was becoming very unnerving.

It wasn't until they reached a large stone door before Richmond began to relax. Around his neck was a large golden key, which slipped into the lock perfectly. There was an audible click when he turned it and the door slowly ground open ajar. Richmond quickly, but with quite an effort, pushed the door open and pushed Alaric through. Once Tancred had walked through the doorway Richmond took a quick look down the corridor before disappearing inside, closing the door behind them. The same click could be heard as Richmond secured the door.

Tancred lit the two torches which hung on sconces on either side of the door. They all stood on a small landing at the bottom of a large stone stairway. Alaric was about to speak, but Richmond shook his head. It was clear they were still not safe to talk. Without saying a word Richmond motioned for Alaric to climb the stairs.

Alaric looked at the stairs and then down at the shackles which remained securely locked around his wrists and ankles. As much as he could make it up the stairs in his current restraints he would prefer not to.

Richmond noticed the look on Alaric's face and motioned for Tancred to release him.

The shackles made a loud clink as they dropped to the stone floor and Alaric rubbed his wrists as soon as they were released. He kicked the shackles in disgust before making a start up the dust covered steps. It was obvious no one had used them in a long time.

It wasn't until they were at the top of the stairs that Richmond finally spoke. At the far end of the small landing was another large stone door. "I am sorry for all this intrigue Alaric, but I can assure you it's necessary." As he spoke he moved to open the door. He used the same golden key to unlock it.

"What's this all about?" Alaric's voice was tense. It was clear he was going to get his answers once he walked through the door, but he didn't know if they were the answers he was looking for.

"All in good time," Tancred spoke as his Lord strained to open the solid stone door.

"Well, don't just stand there. Do you know how long it has been since this door has been opened?" Richmond spoke through clenched teeth as he struggled.

Even with all three of them the door was difficult to open. They gave up when it was open far enough for them to squeeze through.

On the other side was a small room. Long ago it had been a prison. A rather nasty nobleman had it built especially to imprison a Lord, who had previously controlled Bellarome. Over the years it had been used to imprison only the vilest of criminals. It was Richmond's grandfather who had stopped using the tower as a prison and had converted it into a study. When his grandfather had become too old to climb the stairs the room had been locked and hadn't been opened since. There were a number of chairs around a small table and a large number of scrolls and books lined the walls. Cobwebs covered the walls and the books and everything was covered in a thick layer of dust.

"This is not the most comfortable of places, but you can be sure that it is safe from prying ears," Richmond explained once they were safely inside.

"I still don't understand what's happening. At one time you seem to believe me and then just as soon you seem like you don't. Would you please tell me what is happening?" Alaric had stayed near the door, just in case they decided to lock him in.

"Of course. Please have a seat and I will try and explain," Richmond offered.

Tancred had quickly made himself useful by dusting the chairs and table and once he was done he waited for the other two to be seated before he joined them. Tancred watched Alaric as closely as Alaric was watching them. Richmond was the only one who seemed able to relax and he was quick to notice their discomfort.

"I can assure you that we are all friends in this room," he spoke as much to Tancred as he did to Alaric. "I will try and explain it all to you. If I skip over something please forgive me. This story is extremely complicated."

A growl from Alaric's stomach was the only reply. Alaric looked around the room, but there was no sign that there was any food. When he remembered the room hadn't been used in years he silently cursed himself. His head was still sore from the two blows and he wasn't thinking straight. He wished he could have eaten and rested before hearing any information.

"I'm sorry Alaric, but you will have to wait. It is important that you know the situation. This is the right-of-passage paper that Palentonal gave to the magistrate. As you can see it was easy for the man to get the situation mixed up." Lord Richmond passed Alaric the paper that he so desperately wanted to see.

He snatched the paper out of the Lord's hand before flipping it over a couple of times. He couldn't believe what was written on it. There was one solitary word written 'help'. Alaric tried to understand its meaning, besides the obvious.

"Don't try and understand. That is the reason for the word. It will only make sense to someone who is expecting it. It also causes the reader to contact the correct people. It ensures that I am contacted when you arrive. It also means that no one else knows that it's you." There was a slight look of understanding on Alaric's face, but he was still not convinced.

"Why did I have to go through the interrogation?" Alaric sounded confused.

"If Palentonal wasn't close to death he could have explained the situation. Since he was in such bad condition it was important for us to make sure that it was you. I'm sure you can imagine what would happen if it was not you sitting here now?" Richmond explained as best he could.

"Well that crosses one thing off my list." Alaric slid the paper back across the table. "The next problem is, what are we doing here?" The question was directed at the tower room.

"As you know these are troubled times, and that is an understatement. Unfortunately Darshival has been swarmed by agents of evil. They are subtly taking over the land." Richmond stared out the window at the overcast sky. There was the feeling of rain in air and it was only a matter of time before the clouds would break. "I know that he has spies in my palace and throughout my staff. The only problem is that I don't know who they are. Besides Tancred, there are only a handful of people I can trust. I believe that it will only be a matter of days before the Evil One launches an attack on the palace."

"Does he have an army nearby?"

"No. There isn't an army at least a day's ride in any direction," Tancred explained.

Relief filled Alaric's chest. He was worried that he would have to make his way past an enemy army. What replaced it wasn't hope, but confusion. Things had not made sense to him for a long time and the conversation was only making things worse, not better.

"I know that it sounds odd, but if you let me explain you will understand. The Evil One doesn't need to invade to take control of the city. He has grown smart over the years and has changed his tactics. He's not into open warfare any more. His tactics are a lot more subtle. He is using subterfuge to take control of major cities around the Seven Kingdoms. A coup from the inside is a lot easier than a full blown attack." The words coming from Lord Richmond drained hope from Alaric's heart.

"Then everything has been a lie?" It seemed to be a common occurrence.

"It seems so. We concentrated so much on prophecies and what happened in the past that we ignored all the signs. Looking back now it's been happening for years. The Evil One has planted so many spies that it's impossible to tell who is loyal any more. Not only that, but they are gaining support amongst the council. Their tactics are so subtle that no one notices and that it's impossible to know who the spies are and who the gullible followers are. They gain support from the commoners and the soldiers. I believe their front men are just puppets, but again it's impossible to tell." The news just got better and better.

"So I will have to stay in this room whilst I'm here?" Alaric said as he looked around the room.

"No, that has all been taken care of. The man who was arrested this morning, as far as anyone knows, is cooling his heels in my dungeon. As far as anyone else is concerned you are my cousin from the country. My uncle has sent you here to learn the life of the city. Your name will be Dyrk. I suggest you get used to that name. I would advise, at least as long as you are in Darshival, you go by it. The name Alaric is slowly becoming known throughout the Seven Kingdoms and I'm sure the Evil One's agents will be looking out for you. The only other name you'll need to know is my Uncle and his name is Obert. You'll be given a comfortable room where you will be able to stay without being disturbed. Everyone will be instructed that you are here for quiet study and contemplation."

Alaric had to think about what he'd been told. There was a lot of information to consider. "That's all well and good, but I don't think that I'll be staying here long."

"I know your friends have been kidnapped, but rushing after them is not going to do you any good. Your friends will be safe until you reach them. They have been taken for a reason and that's what you now need to consider." There was something strange about the way Richmond spoke. It was as if he knew more about Alaric's situation than what he'd been told.

"I appreciate what you're saying, but I must rescue my friends." He pictured Alena and Eldred being tortured and his blood started to boil.

"Calm down Dyrk." Richmond could see Alaric was starting to become upset, he also wanted to him to get used to being called Dyrk. "There is more that you need to know, but I think for now you should get something to eat. The sun is on its downward arc and the kitchen will be preparing for the evening meal. We've had Palentonal's body and all your possessions brought to the palace."

"And I think it would be good for you to bathe and change those clothes. No one will believe you are cousin to our lord dressed and smelling like that," Tancred added.

Alaric had become used to his situation and simple things, like clean clothes and bathing had become uncommon to him. He quickly sniffed his clothes and pulled his head away in disgust. He had become so used to being dirty that he hadn't even noticed the stench he had been omitting. Reluctantly Alaric had to agree to their conditions. Something deep inside him told him he should stay and listen to what Richmond had to say.

"There'll be new clothes waiting for you in your room. You'll need to look the part of a spoilt nobleman if you're going to play the part," Tancred continued after Alaric slowly nodded his agreement.

"Very good. I think that we should go now. It will only be a matter of time before someone realises I've disappeared," Richmond ended the conversation.

The three of them rose and Richmond led them out of the tower. At the bottom of the stairs he listened intently at the stone door to hear if anyone was on the other side. The effort was fruitless as the thick stone blocked all but the noisiest of sounds. When he was satisfied it was safe, that is to say he waited a good minute, he took out his key and unlocked the door. Again it took all three of them to push the door open enough for them all to squeeze out. Tancred stuck his head around the corner first, to make sure there was no one in the corridor and when the coast was clear they quickly rushed out and pushed the door shut.

"If anyone speaks to you keep your answers short and try not to talk about anything you don't know. Remember that you're here for quiet contemplation," Richmond reminded them as they started for Alaric's room.

Lord Richmond walked with purpose down the corridor. The three of them would have received some strange looks if the servants didn't recognise the look on Richmond's face. They knew if they caught their lord's attention then they would be in trouble. After one quick look they all walked past with their heads lowered and their eyes firmly fixed on the ground. It took all of Tancred's self-control not to start laughing. Alaric didn't see the joke, but he did make sure he didn't make eye contact with anyone.

The three of them definitely looked the part as they walked along the corridor. Lord Richmond was the scolding uncle who was displeased with the job of looking after his brother's wayward son. Tancred looked like the passive teacher who kept the peace and taught both uncle and nephew. Alaric, albeit unintentionally, played the part of the obedient nephew. Everything about his posture as he walked along the corridor, a step behind the other men, was that of an obedient man who had been scolded one too many times.

The room that had been prepared for Alaric was more than he could ever have imagined. It was the largest bedroom he had ever seen. On the far wall was a large four post bed made from rich mahogany with an intricately laced canopy. On either side of the bed were large windows which overlooked the Southern Gardens. Many large, colourful paintings lined the walls and in-between them were lit torches in their sconces, all ornate in design. As well as the torches there was also a magnificent glass chandelier hanging from the ceiling. The candles had been recently replaced, although they weren't lit. The floor had a soft, woven carpet with a number of even softer rugs. Towards the back of the room there was another smaller room. This was his private bathroom. Although he could not stay long in Bellarome it seemed as though he was going to enjoy himself. A little luxury before he hit the road again was just what he needed.

"A bath has been drawn for you. Leave your dirty clothes out here. Someone will be in to get them. I think that it would be best if we burn them," Alaric looked at his tattered rags when Tancred finished speaking. They were once a very fine set of clothes, but they were not even worth cleaning. "A meal shall be brought in for you as well as your possessions. We shall return after nightfall to continue our discussion."

They left Alaric alone with his wonder. His amazement only lasted a few seconds before the reality of his situation returned. He walked to the window to see if there was any chance of escaping. They were on the second and top level of the palace with only a short drop to the ground below. Alaric thought he could easily escape and continue on his way, but he knew that it would not be a reality until he had his sword, *The Prophecy of the Stone* and the two elven horses. Without those two items and his means of transportation there was no way he could finish his quest.

The thought of escape made him suddenly tired. He could smell the sweet dampness of the bath in the next room. It had been scented with rose petals and all of a sudden he could feel the build up of sweat and grime on his body. Without thinking Alaric stripped off his clothes as he made his way towards the bath.

Once his body touched the warm water his troubles slowly drifted away. There was something very calming about the water and he felt as though he could spend the rest of his life lying in the tub. He closed his eyes and let his head sink under the water. He couldn't remember the last time that he had been able to bathe. It was like he didn't have a care in the world. If only that was the truth.

Whilst he bathed a myriad of servants came and went. The young woman who had to take away Alaric's old clothes didn't seem pleased. She picked them up between her thumb and forefinger and carefully placed the offensive clothes into a cloth sack making sure not to touch anything more than she had too. Other servants brought his possessions, new clothes and a steaming plate of hot food.

It was the smell of food that roused him from his bath. His stomach growled loudly from below the water. Slowly as he lifted himself out he nearly slipped over in shock when he saw another young woman standing before him holding a large bath towel. The embarrassment was evident on Alaric's face and caused the serving girl to also become flustered. She quickly handed Alaric the towel and then retreated out of the room.

Silently Alaric scolded himself. He was supposed to be playing the part of a spoilt nobleman's son. He imagined that it must be commonplace for nobles to be treated in such a manner. He hated to think of what the girl would say to the other servants. As much as it took a while for Alaric to come to terms with the ruse he had to admit to himself he would rather not have anyone know where he was. If the enemy knew where he was and how vulnerable he was then his life would be in even more danger.

Once he had dressed he sat at one of the tables to eat his meal. He ate heartily and when he finished he felt as though he could eat another serving and still have room for more. He thought about ringing the bell pull which hung beside his bed, but he decided that he would rather avoid speaking to any of the servants.

His head became heavy once he had cleared his plate. He had been so used to travelling hard and sleeping less and less. Now that he had nowhere to go the thought of sleep was overpowering. He knew that he should take the opportunity to study the prophecy, but the thought only made his head heavier and his eyelids began to droop. It wasn't going to be long before he would fall asleep, whether he wanted it or not. He figured if he was going to sleep he may as well do it in the comfort of a bed.

He fell asleep almost as soon as his head hit the pillows. He had thought the guest rooms in Lel Dinion had been nice, but they were nothing compared to the bed he now slept on. He thought he could get used to the life as a noble. That was the last thought that entered his mind before he fell asleep.

***

"What do you think?" Richmond asked as he sipped on a cup of tea.

"Sorry, what did you say?" Tancred had been deep in thought. He hadn't even touched the cup that sat on the table in front of him.

"What do you think about Alaric?" Richmond was about to continue, but was silenced by the look on Tancred's face.

"I don't think that we should be discussing this here," Tancred kept his voice low. "You know that there is always someone listening in at the door."

Richmond started to laugh. Intrigue was a daily ritual in Bellarome. Someone was always looking for a way to take control of the city. Richmond had wrested control of the city from the last Lord over twenty years ago. His family had ruled Bellarome for many generations before Lord Luther betrayed Richmond's father and stole control. Richmond had only been a boy of ten at the time. When his father was hung in the main square, he, his mother and brother were exiled to the farm where his brother resided. Richmond left home and returned to Bellarome where he secretly became a page boy under another name. When he was old enough he gathered enough information and enough support to have Lord Luther removed. He didn't have Luther hanged, but instead had him imprisoned in the palace dungeons where he would remain for the rest of his life, unless one of his family returned to power.

"There is nothing to worry about. Don't take this the wrong way, but you are not my only friend within the palace. I still have some trusted servants that are loyal to my family. No one will disturb us for at least an hour. Everything we say will remain between the two of us." Richmond didn't bother to keep his voice low.

"Even so, now that he's here, I don't feel comfortable speaking outside of the tower. We know there are enemies everywhere and there's no point in taking unnecessary risks." Tancred didn't believe what Richmond had told him. He knew, better than most, the cost of court intrigues and anyone could be bought at the right price. The life of a servant wasn't glorious and the thought of bags of gold could easily sway even the most trusted.

"You still haven't answered my question," Richmond's voice was firm.

"I don't know. He could be the Chosen One. There is a power about him. It is hard to explain, but there is something about him that I can't put a name to. He could be the Chosen One, but he just as easy might not be," Tancred kept his voice as low as he could.

"I see. I had hoped you would have been able to feel something. We are taking a great risk and we need to know we are making the right decision. Are you sure there is nothing you can do to confirm that he is who he says he is?" Richmond's voice had returned to normal as Tancred had started to speak.

"I'm afraid not. Whoever he is he is very powerful. The only way for us to know for sure is to watch him very carefully." Tancred could not bring himself to speak at a normal level.

"You know I don't like to leave things to chance. We can't continue with our plans until we know for sure who we are dealing with. If we make our move and we are wrong then we'll be in a lot of trouble," Richmond warned.

"I know the risks, but we also need to be on the move soon. We cannot remain here for much longer. Time is as critical now as it ever was." Tancred shared Richmond's concerns.

"Did you have someone check through his possessions?" Richmond asked, changing the subject only slightly.

"Of course I have," Tancred raised his voice for the first time, offended at the implication of the question. "There was nothing of any great importance. Although there was a rather strange artefact that could shed some light on his identity, it's a great tome named *the Prophecy of the Stone.*"

"So the stone wasn't there?" Richmond could hardly contain himself as he asked the question.

"No, but then we weren't really expecting it to be there. If he still had the stone then I believe that things would already be over." Tancred continued in a quiet voice.

"That's what frustrates me the most. There is so much conjecture on what's going to transpire. If we knew then it would make life so much easier." Richmond's shoulders had slumped and he took a long draught on his tea almost draining the cup completely.

"Now if everything was neatly laid out for us then where would the fun be in life?" Tancred again returned his voice to a normal level.

"I guess you're right. Now do you think he has slept for long enough?" Richmond asked.

"I don't think that it really matters. The sun set a long time ago and we have too much work to accomplish today. If he hasn't slept enough then he'll have to catch up another time. I think we'll get a better response if he's still sleeping. If his brain isn't functioning in a fully awake state then he might let something slip that he normally wouldn't," again Tancred spoke in a whisper.

"I knew there was a reason why I like you so much. You have an even more devious mind than I." Richmond laughed when he finished speaking.

"Now I don't know whether to be offended or not." Tancred faked the sound of offence in his voice.

"All jokes aside I think it is time."

Chapter 9: Wasting Time

Alaric had been rudely woken when he was having the best sleep of his life. He hadn't realised he'd slept for so long until he looked out the window and saw the moon high in the sky. The two men who woke him didn't give him a chance to regain his composure. They quickly made him dress and then pushed him out the door.

The corridors of the palace were empty. Some of them were still lit, but others were completely dark. It was eerie and it made Alaric very nervous. He wasn't sure if he trusted the two men and at any moment he expected a group of assassins to jump out of the shadows and kill him.

Even though it was obvious the majority of the palace was asleep or busy doing other things Richmond still remained cautious. He stopped and listened intently at the stone door before producing the key from around his neck to unlock it. It took all three of them to open it and it wasn't until the door had been safely locked behind them that Richmond started to relax.

"I am sorry for all this intrigue, but as I explained before things aren't right in Darshival at the moment." Richmond apologised once they reached the top of the stairs. Alaric caught the Lord passing his advisor a strange look.

"What is it you want?" Alaric asked, still feeling the effects of being woken.

"There will be enough time for that, but first we have some questions for you and I'd advise you to answer them honestly," there was nothing friendly in Tancred's voice, yet the threat didn't seem as menacing as it should.

Alaric thought that he should react, but he was still trying to wake up. It was taking him a rather long time to shake the cobwebs of sleep. The room seemed hazy, more so than that it should. The firelight from the torches seemed to blur at the edges and he shook his head slowly as he returned his attention to the others. They were both watching him closely.

"We are curious to know more about what's been happening," Tancred started. "There's a lot going on in the Seven Kingdoms at present and we need all the information we can get."

Alaric knew there was something underlying in Tancred's words, but he couldn't put his finger on it. Something very strange was happening. "Well what do you want to know?" he said.

"Do you know what is happening with the army to the North?" Tancred blurted.

"I can't really comment much on the war. We left half our party there and continued on towards the City of Night." Alaric wasn't sure why he was divulging so much information. "The army was growing. They were waiting for the first of King Lisle's army to arrive from Hondin Lel. Nyrra's army hadn't arrived when we left so I can't tell you anymore."

Lord Richmond looked at Tancred as Alaric finished speaking. Something passed between the two that Alaric couldn't understand. There was something very wrong with the situation. He was still battling with the incessant sleep in his mind and he knew that once he had completely woken he would work it out.

"So what happened once you left the war-camp?" Tancred asked, figuring it was better for him to continue forward in Alaric's timeline. There would be less chance for Alaric to realise what they were doing if the questioning followed a logical progression.

Slowly Alaric started to recall his story. He started with entering the Kingdom of Nostiria and continued with their meeting with the Nomad tribe. Tancred and Richmond listened in awe as Alaric told them of the harsh land and the beautiful oasis. The more he spoke the more they believed he was indeed the Chosen One. Alaric spoke with such enthusiasm right up until the point where he reached the City of Night. Finally the veil of sleep lifted from his mind and Alaric realised he was saying things that he really shouldn't.

"Then what happened?" Richmond asked, his voice thick with anticipation, when Alaric stopped speaking.

"What's this all about?" Alaric barked, strength returning to his voice.

Richmond shot Tancred a questioning look. "I am sorry Alaric, I mean Dyrk. What you must understand is that we had to be sure that you were who you said you were." Alaric stood quickly, sensing something was wrong. As he did he pushed the chair back, knocking it over.

"I think it's time that you tell me what this is all about." Alaric looked around the room to see if there was anything he could use to defend himself. There were a few items, but nothing of any use.

"Please, sit down Alaric, we mean you no harm," Richmond's voice was calm, with a touch of regret. Alaric returned to his chair, which he picked up off the ground. "We didn't mean to upset you, but it was the only way we could be sure that you were telling us the truth."

"What are you talking about?" Alaric was still poised to defend himself.

"We drugged your food to make you more pliable. You must understand our point-of-view. Our city is full of the Evil One's agents and more are coming in every day. For every agent that our guards turn away there are a dozen sneaking in. If a man turned up with a dying elf at your gates what would you expect?" Tancred's words made some sense.

"But you said that the right-of-passage paper was all the proof that you needed?" Alaric was trying to come to terms with the situation, so he skipped over the fact that he'd been drugged.

"It tipped us to your arrival, but under the circumstances we had to sure," Richmond explained. "There is much that needs to be discussed."

Alaric wanted nothing more than to find out the reason why the two men were so interested in him, but his head started to swim. The room began to spin and he felt as though he was going to bring up his entire meal. The drug's effect had worn off on his head, but it was now taking effect on his body. He suddenly he felt deathly cold as a sweat broke out. He wasn't sure if he was going to be able to remain conscious.

"What... Why... do you... Who...?" Alaric's voice was weak and he struggled hard for breath.

"Dyrk, are you alright?" Richmond's voice was thick with concern.

Alaric's head dropped to the table. His breathing remained heavy and his eyelids drooped, but he remained conscious even though his entire body went completely limp. His arms hung down by his sides and it was only by pure luck that he remained on his chair.

"What's going on?" Richmond asked Tancred.

Tancred tried his best to defend his actions. "I don't know. I've used this herb many times and it's never done anything like this before. If anything I gave him a weaker dose than normal."

"Well look at him. He can't move. Do you call that normal?" Richmond tried his best to keep his voice level.

"Something must have gone wrong... but I don't know what it is." Tancred rubbed his forehead as he started to panic.

"Well what are we going to do?" Richmond also started panic.

Alaric sat in his seat, unable to move. He could hear everything and the panic in their voices did nothing to calm him. Feeling close to death was nothing new to him, but that thought was no comfort. He just hoped that the two men would come up with an answer soon. He felt so awful he almost wished he would die. Although he couldn't move anything he could feel great pain rushing through his body. The muscles in his arms and legs were starting to cramp and there was no way for him to relieve it. He wanted to scream out, but his lips wouldn't move.

"We are going to remain calm for starters. We must get him back to his room without anyone seeing us. If someone sees us carrying him back then the rumours will be impossible to stop," Tancred said as he looked as Alaric.

"I think that you are forgetting one thing Tancred. It takes three of us to open the door. Without Dyrk to help us I don't think we'll be able to get out."

Hearing this brought a wave of fear into Alaric's heart. He was sure if he didn't receive treatment soon he would die. He was beginning to think he should have taken the opportunity to leave the palace when he had his chance. The only thing that could save him was that his mind was still awake. His first challenge was to communicate with the other two.

The pain rippled through his body. He tried to slow his breathing, but he had no control over his lungs. The pain threatened to rip his mind apart and drive him crazy. Taking a mental breath Alaric prepared himself. Reaching through the pain he tried to feel the energy in the room. Two beacons stood out, but he knew that he couldn't draw power from them. For a moment he thought they deserved what he would do to them, but he knew that he would seal his own fate if he did.

The room was strangely stagnate. The energy was as stale as the dust on the floor. Alaric had never experienced the feeling before, but he was sure that it would work all the same. As another intense wave of pain rushed through his body he started to draw in the energy around him. The sudden rush blocked the pain and Alaric sucked up a deep breath as his body returned to normal.

"No, Alaric!" Tancred cried out at the top of his voice.

As he spoke another jolt of pain struck Alaric and he completely lost his concentration and the energy instantly left his body. This time Alaric couldn't breathe as the intense pain returned and it took almost half a minute before the air returned to his lungs. Although Alaric had been trained to filter away unnecessary distraction, channelling energy with excruciating pain made it impossible.

"What do you think you are doing?" Although Tancred asked the question he knew he wasn't going to get a response. "The city is crawling with the Evil One's agents. If you continued to do what I think you were doing then you would have sent out a beacon that even the lowliest of magicians could have seen."

"What are you talking about?" Lord Richmond seemed confused at Tancred's sudden outburst.

"We must find a way out of here and soon. I don't think Dyrk is going to last much longer." Tancred deliberately ignored the question.

Alaric silently cursed himself as the pain continued to rip through his body. He had been trained to mask the tell-tale signs made when someone draws in energy. The pain had made him lazy, looking for a quick escape. He knew if he was able to shut out the agony he could channel the energy without anyone knowing.

"We could try climbing down from the window," Richmond suggested, although he knew it wasn't an option.

The pain attacked Alaric's consciousness trying to take away his senses. It pulled at the very fibres of his being. It would not be long before it completely consumed him. He had to act quickly if he was going to survive. Whatever poison was coursing through his body it was working quickly.

With one final effort Alaric cast the masking spell. Since he was only going to use a small amount of energy to create the spells he needed he didn't have to draw any energy to cast the masking spell. Once completed Alaric started to draw in more energy. This time Tancred didn't seem to notice. He just continued his futile conversation with Richmond.

"We have to try the door. There is a chance that the two of us can open it," Tancred was almost pleading with Richmond.

"I see that we have no other choice, but I doubt that this is going to be any use," Richmond conceded it was their only chance.

As the two men moved closer to the door there came an audible click from the lock. Both men took a step back and gave each other a questioning look. They then looked towards Alaric who remained, motionless, slumped over the table. Alaric lay with his eyes wide and sweat pouring from his body, the only sign he was still alive.

Shortly after the door was unlocked it slowly started to grind open. Tancred and Richmond drew their swords and prepared themselves for whoever was on the other side. Richmond was confused as he thought he was the only one who had keys to the tower.

When the door finally stopped they waited. When no one entered the two of them looked at each other again. Slowly there came a knowing expression on Tancred's face. That only increased Richmond's confusion. He didn't like being left out in the dark in any situation.

"What are you grinning about?" there was a distinct tone of annoyance in his Richmond's voice.

"It seems that Dyrk is who he says he is," Tancred pointed at the door as he spoke.

"Sometimes I don't think I will ever understand you," Richmond shook his head. "Sometimes I wish you would just speak plainly. Your riddles can hurt my head sometimes."

"Don't you see?" The question was rhetorical. "It was Dyrk who opened the door."

"But how? He didn't move and you can feel when people are using magic?" Richmond didn't like the knowing smile on his advisor's face.

It was something about his advisor and best friend that he never understood. Although Tancred didn't seem to be able to create any spells he had an uncanny knack of being able to sense magic. It didn't make any sense, but it was fact nevertheless.

"It seems that he is stronger that I gave him credit for. He masked the energy used to create the spell." There was a touch of awe in his voice. "Quickly now. We must get him to the physician."

The two men carefully carried Alaric's body down the stairs. Time was of the essence and Richmond had to risk the fact that no one was on the other side of the door.

The corridor was completely empty besides the three of them. Although they knew their time was short in getting Alaric help they also needed to protect the secret of the tower. There was only a moment of indecision before they both put all their strength behind pushing the huge stone door shut again. Their muscles ached as the stone door slowly stared to slide back into place. Richmond thought his muscles were going to snap with the strain. Quickly he produced the key from around his neck and locked the door before he collapsed, letting his back slide down the door until his was seated on the ground.

"Go Tancred. Get help!" Richmond puffed from the ground.

Tancred himself was also trying to catch his breath. His head was resting against his arm, which was leaning against the door. He was about to protest, but remembered his place. It wouldn't look good if the advisor was sitting by the Lord's nephew whilst the Lord ran looking for assistance.

Once Tancred had scampered to the end of the corridor Richmond slowly lifted himself to his feet. According to Tancred there could be no doubt that the man lying on death's door before him was the Chosen One, the saviour of the world. Since they had been so untrustworthy they had more than likely done the Evil One's work for him. Whatever had gone wrong with the herb was working fast. Richmond still didn't understand what had gone wrong. He had never heard of anyone having an adverse reaction, except for its purpose. The thought almost made Richmond physically sick, but nothing would matter if he didn't get Alaric help.

"Come of Dyrk. Let's get you back to your room and try not to drink so much next time," Richmond spoke as he heard footsteps at the end of the corridor.

Two boys in their teenage years were busy with their own conversation and didn't notice Richmond until he spoke. When they realised who it was they stopped. Taking one look at each other the boys quickly turned and started for the other end of the hallway. At that point it was obvious to Richmond they were up to no good and not sent there by Tancred to help him.

"Come here boys!" Richmond tried his best to sound commanding and hide the fatigue in his voice, he did a good job.

The boys stopped again as soon as they heard his command. They thought for a moment about pretending they didn't hear him and making a dash for it, but if they were caught then they didn't want to think about the consequences. Slowly they turned and made their way back towards their Lord. They looked guilty, but Richmond was too concerned with the safety of his supposed nephew to worry about what two boys were doing lurking in the corridors in the middle of the night.

"Don't dawdle. Can't you see that my nephew needs assistance? You two take him back to his room. You do know where it is?" Richmond put on his best voice to speak to two obviously guilty boys who both nodded their agreement. "And I think you should make your way to the Mistress' room once you are done. I'm sure she would love to know why you are roaming the corridors at this time of night!" He added knowing the boys would have been expecting it. He didn't want to throw any more suspicion on the situation.

The two boys struggled to carry Alaric along the corridor. They looked relatively strong for their ages, but Alaric was a dead weight. Richmond wanted to give them some assistance, but again it would look too suspicious for the Lord of the house to be carrying a man through the corridors, even if it was his nephew.

Once the three of them had disappeared around the corner Richmond quickly took off in the direction of Tancred. He hoped he would find him before he let the entire house know what happened. He knew his advisor would be subtle, but information like sick nobility would soon be all over the household. Servants were the worst when it came to gossip, some say even worse than the nobility themselves.

He found Tancred with two strong looking men. Richmond didn't recognise them, but he was sure they would have done a better job than the two teenage boys. He thought about sending the men on ahead to give them assistance, but he thought the least amount of people who saw Dyrk in his current state the better.

"It is alright now Tancred," Richmond stopped them before they could walk past him. "It seems my nephew has regained his consciousness." Tancred gave him a questioning look. It seems his advisor had made up his own story. Richmond only hoped that his version of events wasn't too different from Tancred's. "It seems that he has had a little too much to drink tonight. That's the reason he collapsed. He is on his way back to his room now. I think that we should have the physician have a look at him anyway, just to be on the safe side."

"Well, you heard your Lord. Back to your duties!" Tancred didn't like scolding the two men for trying to help, but it was expected of him to act unreasonably towards servants. The two men would leave grumbling about being disturbed so late at night, but come morning it would be the last thing they remembered.

"Is the physician on his way?" Richmond asked once the two of them were out of earshot.

"Yes, but if Dyrk is up and walking then there might not be any reason for him to see the physician," Tancred sounded a little relieved. "The least amount of people that know about this the better."

"I totally agree with you. The only problem is that Dyrk isn't up and about," Richmond quickly recounted his meeting with the two boys. "You see it was the only way I could explain our being in the corridor. If I let the two boys go then the story would be all over the household by morning. At least now they will be too busy trying to explain themselves to the Household Mistress to worry about gossip." Richmond felt a little sorry for the boys and the soreness of their backsides once the Mistress was finished with them.

"Sometimes I think you're more devious than I," Tancred had to laugh as they started towards Dyrk's room.

Although they wanted to run to see how Dyrk was fairing they didn't want to look conspicuous. Richmond swore at the damned nature of his Kingdom. It was not just Bellarome that was filled with intrigue. All the major cities had regular espionage for control. Even the King had to be careful in his palace in Kiarome. Although no one would openly challenge the throne it didn't mean there weren't families waiting in the background for a chance to challenge for succession. Sometimes he wished he could have the royal guard come through and clean out his house of all the spies and traitors, but then he also wasn't sure the Kingdom could run without her little intrigues.

They arrived at Dyrk's room just in time to see the two boys scamper away. They took one look at Richmond and doubled their speed. The last thing they wanted was to be named for another job. The Lord's nephew must have really had a lot to drink because he didn't stir once when they were dragging him back to the room. They were just thankful that Lord Richmond didn't see the way they were handling him.

Richmond, although he didn't want to, entered the room first. Inside the boys had placed Dyrk indiscriminately on the bed. They didn't even bother to put him under the covers. Both men quickly moved to his side and tried to make him as comfortable as possible. Since he couldn't move it was hard to tell if he was conscious or not. Occasionally his eyes opened, but again it was too hard to know if it was a voluntary movement or not.

Shortly after they finished making Alaric comfortable the physician arrived. He looked less than happy at being woken. He had only been told that the Lord's nephew was sick. On his way to the bedroom he had heard the rumour that he had been drinking too much and that really irritated him. If the man wanted to over indulge then he could pay the price for it and there wasn't much he could do anyway.

"Let's make this quick. Some of us have sleep to get back to." In his irritation the physician forgot that he was talking to the Lord of the land.

"Is there somewhere you would rather be?" Lord Richmond had picked up of the physician's tone and was not going to let him have the upper hand.

"Of course not, my Lord. Sorry, I'm still waking up," the doctor tried his best at deference. "What seems to be the problem," he moved closer to the bed, wanting Richmond to make the accusation on Dyrk being too drunk.

The situation was going to be even harder to explain, if they were going to tell the truth, yet keep the lie true. The only answer was to create another lie. Richmond wondered at when the lying would stop.

"Some of the kitchen staff have had some problems with Dyrk in the past and it seems as though they have put something in his meal," Richmond spoke slowly as he made up the lie.

"That's funny. I haven't heard…" the physician let what he was about to say trail of into the silence of the room. "Do you happen to know what it was they gave him?"

"I believe it was wheatworte," Tancred spoke before Richmond had a chance. "We found some leaves in the bin when we investigated the rumours." The lie rolled off his tongue more naturally than it did for Richmond.

The physician took one look at Dyrk and then turned to leave. "If you are going to lie to me at least make it believable."

"What are you talking about?" Tancred protested as the physician made his way to the door.

"Wheatworte doesn't have that effect on anyone. It is obvious to me that he has had too much to drink and just needs to sleep it off." The physician didn't care if he was speaking to Lord Richmond or not, he didn't like being woken for something as frivolous as alcohol poisoning.

Just before the doctor reached the door Tancred moved to block his path. To make his intentions known he had his sword drawn. He was not about to let him leave.

"What's this all about?" the physician looked at Tancred and then at Richmond.

The physician was known to both Richmond and Tancred, but neither knew him well enough to trust him with the truth. Information was power in Bellarome and if the physician wasn't completely loyal then he would be very popular in other circles. The constant web of lies had to continue.

"It seems that someone has a grudge against my brother's son. If this is not wheatworte then what is it?" Richmond tried to sound reasonable, even though he knew very well what he had been drugged with.

The physician's shoulders dropped as he realised he had no choice. He knew there was something awry. If he could find out what it was he might be able to use it in the future. He knew people who would pay good money for information. He didn't have any real allegiances to any factions. He was more interested in his own wellbeing.

"Well I suppose I could have another look at him," he sounded as though he had a choice in the matter. "I'm sure I will be able to get to the bottom of this."

The physician slowly walked back over to the bed whilst Tancred returned his sword to its sheath. Dyrk looked to be in a great deal of pain even though he lay motionless. The doctor had a serious look on his face as he examined him. He poked and prodded and took Dyrk's temperature. When he was finished, with what seemed to be completely useless procedures, he turned to the others.

"There are a number of herbs that can do this to a man, most of them are lethal," the last was unnecessary to say, but he wanted to make the other two squirm. "It is impossible to tell without a sample. All we can do now is wait. If he is strong he may survive. If he is not then he is definitely dead."

Both Tancred and Richmond looked towards the table where they assumed Dyrk would have eaten his meal. They both knew that his food would have been cleared away a long time ago. His servants had been told to be extra attentive to his nephew's needs. All that was left on the table was a half drunk glass of water. Richmond instantly dismissed it, thinking there must have been another herb added to his meal. Tancred was also about to dismiss the glass when he thought he saw something strange. As he came closer to the table he could clearly see something floating in the water. He picked up the glass and gave it a closer inspection. He saw some yellow powder floating in the water. When he shook the glass the yellow spot slowly disappeared.

"Well since there is nothing I can do I think I shall return to my sleep," the physician sounded nonchalant as he walked towards the door again.

Tancred waited until the yellow powder was visible again. "What do you think about this?" The physician's hand was already on the doorknob.

The physician's shoulders dropped when he heard Tancred speak. He was so close to being out the door and on the way back to his room. He didn't know what was happening, but he knew he didn't want to get involved. Whatever information he could obtain by staying was not worth the risk of having a knife plunged into his back. Slowly he turned and walked back to Tancred. His shoulders and his heart sunk even lower when he saw the yellow flakes in the water. He knew whoever it was that wanted Dyrk dead they had powerful and dangerous connections. If word got out it was he who cured him then his life would be over.

"I take it from the look on your face you know what it is?" Tancred had been watching him carefully.

"Ah… No I don't think I do," the physician backed away from Tancred as he stammered his reply.

Unbeknownst to the physician Richmond had moved in behind him, blocking any chance of escape. The physician kept back stepping until he bumped into him. He jumped in surprise. When he saw the look on his Lord's face he took a quick step forward. Richmond watched him carefully. He could see the fear in the man's eyes. Whatever was in the glass had the physician scared.

"I think you better be honest." The threat was clear in the coldness of Richmond's words.

"Honestly, I don't know." Fear was evident in his voice. He figured he had a better chance of surviving if he lied to these two men then face what was outside.

"I don't think you understood what I was saying," Richmond drew his sword. "Now I know that you know what this drug is and I think it's time you started talking."

"I wouldn't worry about who did this. If you don't cure Dyrk then you will not live to find out." Tancred's threat was not exactly true, but it had the desired effect.

"Okay, okay. The drug is called pepperstone and it's one of the most deadly drugs I know of. It is also one of the rarest. I have never seen it before, except in books. Whoever it was that poisoned your nephew is a powerful man." The physician shook as he spoke.

Richmond looked at Tancred. Both men were thinking the same thing. Someone must know Dyrk's true identity. No one would go to such lengths to kill Richmond's nephew. Such a drug might be used to kill Richmond himself, but never someone so insignificant. The repercussions of what that meant weren't worth thinking about. What they had to concentrate on was making sure Dyrk didn't die.

"At this point in time we don't care who poisoned him or how he managed to slip such a rare poison into his drink. What we do need to know is how to get him better." The physician thought he might take advantage of Richmond's concern and try to lie again. The thought was written all over his face and Richmond was quick to put a stop it. "And I wouldn't advise you try and lie again. This is too important for you to try and weasel your way out."

"I'm offended," the physician started in a mock-hurt tone. "The fact that you don't trust that I'm going to do the right thing by…"

"Enough dribble physician. By the looks of Dyrk he doesn't have much time. Now here's the way it's going to be. If Dyrk dies then you die."

Hearing the words the physician went deathly pale. He had been stalling for time, trying to find a way out of helping the Lord's nephew. He thought with enough time he might be able to talk his way out of the room. Now there was no doubt that he had stay and cure Dyrk of his illness.

"Of course, but I can't do it here. I need to read through my books. I've never encountered this drug before and it is only by pure chance that I have read about it." The physician was desperate to find an answer. "If there is a cure I am sure that it will be in one of my books."

Tancred had moved to the bellpull besides the large four poster bed and tugged. He knew as soon as the physician was out of their sight there was no chance of ever seeing him again. The four, short, sharp rings would alert the master of the servants that all his available servants were required. As there was at least two hours before sunrise some of the servants would be busy, the rest would still be in bed.

"What are you doing?" The physician seemed genuinely confused.

"Do you honestly think that we would let you out of our sight for a second?" The question was rhetorical.

"What are you talking about?" The thought of escape hadn't crossed his mind. Since Tancred brought it up he thought it might have been his one last chance. "I wouldn't even think about leaving. I am loyal to the crown and have been all my life. Without those books and my herbs there is nothing I can do." He was desperate for two reasons. One he still had a chance for escape and two he didn't want to die.

"You don't have anything to worry about. There will be a number of servants here very shortly. They will be able to bring anything you need here." Tancred had a large grin on his face.

"But I don't know the name of the book I need. I will only know it when I look at it." For once the physician spoke the truth. He knew he owned the book with the answer to his problem, but he didn't know which one it was.

"That's alright. There are a lot of servants in the palace. Once we have woken them all up I am sure it will not take long to bring here whatever it is that you need," the smile remained on Tancred's face as all the hope of escape left the doctor.

Richmond pulled Tancred to the side of the room where they could speak privately.

"What are you doing? This is going to alert my entire household to Dyrk's condition. We wanted to keep this secret." Richmond whispered.

"It's all for naught if he dies. Someone has already made an attempt on his life. I doubt secrecy is an option anymore."

Suddenly there was a soft knock on the door ending their conversation. Even if Richmond didn't agree with Tancred there was little choice. The servant was hoping whoever was on the inside wouldn't answer. It was common for nobles to need something in the middle of the night only to fall asleep before the servant arrived. A loud knock on the door might wake them.

"Don't drag your feet?" Richmond boomed from inside. He was not going to give the servants any chance to escape.

Slowly the door opened and two bleary eyed boys entered. They looked around the room trying to work out what was happening. They seemed surprised to see the three men. They could feel the tension radiating around the room.

"Now firstly you must go to the master of the servants and tell him to wake everyone. Then all of you must go to the physician's room and bring back all the books and scrolls you can find." Tancred ordered on Richmond's behalf, as was proper for the situation. "The physician will tell you where to start looking."

Chapter 10: A House at Work

It started slowly at first, like the first drops of rain before a storm. As soon as the two young servants had woken and fully understood the situation they left at a run. Tancred thought about berating them and giving them a lesson on etiquette, which would have been the appropriate thing for him to do, but time was precious and for the sake of a silly protocol he knew it was best to let them go.

It was almost dawn when the first of the books started to arrive and the physician was quick to move into action. As he flicked through each book and scroll he rubbed his head once before tossing them aside. Every time he added to the pile of discarded books two piles of fresh ones had already appeared. Richmond wondered how many medical books the physician had when finally the last of the servants arrived with another arm full.

"That is the last of them my Lord," the young man bowed as he spoke. "Is there anything else you wish for us to do?" The man was visibly shaking at having to speak to Lord Richmond. "Or should we go back to our regular duties?"

The master of the servants had not been happy at being woken in the middle of the night, but he would not openly abuse Lord Richmond, at least not without proof that it was a frivolous order. With all his servants at Richmond's beck and call he had no one to complete his daily tasks. There would be many noble men and women who would go without their breakfast as there was no one to serve them and it would be the master of the servants who would have to explain why.

"Nobody leave until I say so. You can all wait out in the corridor," Richmond spoke with command, even though he was too tired to really put up the charade.

The boys and young men all trudged out of the room thus removing all the spying eyes and ears. He knew well that a lowly paid servant could easily be bought for information. It was much better for them all to wait outside and only surmise what was going on inside.

The physician was sweating as he poured through the books and scrolls. He was clearly upset at the pressure that had been put on him. Every so often he jumped up to check on Dyrk, who remained in his semi-comatose state. It was hard to tell if he was still alive. His breathing was still shallow and laboured. The only saving grace was that he had not worsened. The physician thought each time he checked it would be his last. The fact that he was still alive renewed the physician's vigour. He would find the answer if for no other reason than to save his own life.

The books were still piled up on both sides of the table when the physician let out a cry of relief. The sudden noise startled Tancred and

Richmond who had been constantly pacing as the books kept coming in. When the last of the books had been dropped off they finally sat down. Since then they had been watching the physician intently, but finally it was all they could do to keep themselves from falling asleep. The physician would leave what he was doing and make a run for his own freedom if they did. The sudden noise brought them to their senses.

"What is it?" Tancred barked.

"I've found the book I've been searching for. At least I think this is right book." The physician sounded less confident as he finished. He rubbed his eyes and looked at the book again. "No, I am sure this is the right one and I think that it shouldn't be long until we have an answer," he actually sounded excited for the first time.

Richmond and Tancred returned to their seats and looked at each other. Something passed between them without having to speak. Neither of them wanted to get too excited, but finally something was happening. It had taken so long they were surprised that Dyrk was still alive.

At first the physician skipped through the pages as quickly as he could. The book seemed to be larger than he remembered. When he was about half way through he started to slow. He hoped he wasn't wasting his time. If this wasn't the book he needed then he wasn't sure if there was time for him to flick through another. Just when he was about to give up hope he came upon the page that he was looking for. In bold letters, at the top of the page was written: Pepperstone. Underneath was written: *Applications, Causes and Cures.* The physician let out a sigh of relief making sure no one heard him before he returned to the page in question. He wanted to make sure he had all the information before he alerted the other two. There might still be a chance for him to escape if he was able to think quickly. The last thing he wanted to do was to get in the middle of the conflict. Men like him never survived such things.

As he read down the page he began to relax and when he reached the bottom he started to laugh. He knew there was something very strange about the situation and now it all started to make sense. The noise brought the attention of the other two. He knew the answer and he didn't care what the other two thought and he might just get out alive.

"What are you laughing at?" Tancred asked. The sound of the physician laughing irritated Tancred, but it also brought hope.

"If what you said earlier was true it seems that your two separate druggers have been working against each other." There was a large smile on the physician's face.

"What are you talking about?" Richmond asked. "Hurry up man because you are stretching my patience." It had been a long night and Richmond was very irritable.

"If you just relax and wait a moment I will tell you what is happening." The physician took a deep breath and paused to build some unnecessary tension. "I knew that I had heard the combination of wheatworte and pepperstone before, but I just couldn't place it."

"I mentioned that you're trying my patience. If you don't get to the point I will kill you and to hell with my brother's son!" Richmond was ready to take his threat seriously.

"I'm sorry." Although the physician thought he was in complete control of the situation he didn't want to push his luck. "There is only one cure for pepperstone and it must be taken within hours of ingestion. There is no exact time frame as the study in pepperstone is still fairly unknown. All that we do know is that if the patient hasn't been administered with the cure quickly then it's certain he will die." The sound of swords being drawn was the last straw. The physician knew if he didn't give them the good news soon he would receive at least one through his chest. "The cure is wheatworte. This means whoever it was that served him the wheatworte obviously didn't know he was being poisoned with pepperstone. It seems your nephew has more than one friend. I would be very careful if I were you." The physician looked at Richmond as he stood. "Now if you don't mind, since there is nothing more I can do here I think I would like to go back to sleep. I would appreciate it if you had all these books returned to my office."

Before the physician could make his way to the door Richmond stopped him. "So what do we do now?"

"The fever and the paralysis is all part of the recovery. Pepperstone poisoning is one of the most painful ways to die and the recovery is no better, if anything its worse. Give him a day or two. Try and pour some water down his throat so he doesn't die of dehydration and wait. Once the fever has broken he should gain some movement and then it shouldn't be long before he regains consciousness." The physician returned to his normal boring tone, as if he was telling the most common of knowledge to the dimmest of people.

Although Richmond didn't appreciate being spoken too in such a manner he was too tired to care. He was just happy Dyrk would soon make his recovery and truth be told he was sick of the sight of the physician and wanted nothing more than to have him out of his sight.

Both Richmond and Tancred were quick to sit down. It had been a long night and they were both exhausted. They were thankful Dyrk was going to be alright, but knew there were many more problems to worry about.

"How long do you think it will be before this news is all over the palace?" Richmond asked Tancred when he was sure the physician had left.

"I think the question you should be asking is how long will it take for the gossip to reach the city? As long as it remains in the palace we can contain it, but once it reaches the city there's nothing that we can do." Richmond didn't seem to understand where Tancred was going. "Once the news reaches the local taverns then the merchants will hear there has been an assassination attempt on your brother's son. Then it will be a race to see who can make it to your brother first. Once the merchants see that Dyrk is alive and well and still on your brother's estate it won't be long before they return to the city. I don't think it will take long to figure out who Dyrk really is once that happens."

A look of both knowing and horror crossed Richmond's face. "That's not the only problem. Once the assassin hears Dyrk is still alive I do not think that it will be long before they try again."

"That's a very good point. At this stage besides you and I the only other person who knows that Dyrk is going to live is the physician."

"Then we need to work out a way to keep him silent. Gold is always a good way to get people to come around to your way of thinking."

"Don't you worry about the physician, I will make sure he doesn't spread any unnecessary rumours," Richmond wasn't sure what Tancred meant. His words were ominous, but he was too tired to question it.

"Very good. Now all we have to do is work out how we are going to stop the rumours from reaching the city," as Richmond finished speaking he yawned.

"I don't think that there is anything that we can do about that now. By the looks of you I think you need a good sleep." Tancred followed suit by also yawning when he finished speaking.

"It looks like I'm not the only one who could use some sleep. I think that we can both use some rest. I'm sure we will have some time to sleep before anything major happens. I will have some guards posted at the door. All we need is someone to look after Dyrk." The thought of sleep was starting to overpower him.

"Leave that to me. I have just the person." Tancred had a wry grin on his face that made Richmond worry.

"I don't know if I trust that look. The last time I saw that look I think I ended up naked wandering the street of Kiarome. Now tell me what it is you have in store this time."

"I'm offended," Tancred put on his best mock-hurt voice. "I can assure you there is nothing underhanded going on here. All I mean is that I know a very reliable nursemaid who is more than qualified to tend to your nephew's care."

Richmond didn't want to know why Tancred knew a nursemaid. There was only one reason and that didn't bear thinking about. He knew if he was going to ask the question then his advisor would explain it to him in detail. It was better if he just trusted him and ignored any implications.

"Very good then. I will arrange the guards. I think someone from my personal retinue would be better suited for the job. It might seem out of the ordinary, but I don't think we should take any chances with his security. You can take care of his wellbeing." Richmond, with the aid of pushing himself up, rose from the table. "I think we should meet again soon. I am sure in our current state we are missing some obvious answers."

"And some obvious problems," Tancred added in an ominous tone as he also rose from the table.

Tancred waited by Dyrk's bed as Richmond organised the two guards and their replacements. There was no chance they would leave him alone. Once Richmond had finished his duty he left for his own chambers. His need for sleep was overwhelming and the palace was alive with its daily businesses. Not one of the multitudes of his staff noticed he was dead on his feet. They pushed papers into his hands and asked for his signature. They didn't even notice when he simply signed without even looking at the documents, just to be rid of them. Finally when he was rid of them and made it to his own apartments he made straight for the bed. As he drifted off to sleep he couldn't help but think that there was something important that he was missing. There was something seriously wrong, but he couldn't figure out what it was. The thought was just out of his reach and there was nothing he could do to recall it as he fell fast asleep.

***

Things had not gone to plan. When word reached him the enemy had survived his assassination attempt he wasn't pleased. The message boy was so young and innocent and he didn't even look at the letter before he delivered it.

Na'garoz smiled as he remembered the look of pure horror on the boys face. There was nothing sweeter in the world than that first look on someone's face when they realised they were going to die. The only thing that came close was the look on their faces when they were suffering the painful death he had laid out for them.

The boy really didn't deserve the death he had been given, but it made Na'garoz feel better. The fireball had consumed him quickly, but not quick enough to save him from a painful death. He normally liked to work a lot slower, but he couldn't risk the young boy's screams reaching someone's ears. That sort of thing was frowned upon in this world. He couldn't understand it; the pure, innocent joy of watching someone die in pain was one of the greatest things to experience. It had been a long time since he had been able to kill someone. It was dangerous, but he couldn't control himself. The news was just too disturbing and he needed a pick-me-up.

Everything had been going so well. He had murdered and usurped the magistrates position months ago. It had been easier than he had thought. The old magistrate had been a cruel and sadistic man. No one noticed the change. Na'garoz had been able to go about his business without suspicion and when he had been overly vicious no one noticed or thought anything about it. He had to use all his will power not to take it to the next level. He wanted nothing more than to administer the deaths he had commissioned, but that would be too suspicious. He had to pleasure himself by watching his cruel and unusual punishments instead. Life had been good. He was almost getting used to it, but now that was all going to change.

He knew he had made his run for glory too soon, but it had seemed like such a simple idea. When he had noticed Alaric had not been taken straight to prison it had been obvious Richmond must have realised who he was. The sudden arrival of the Lord's nephew and the disappearance of his prisoner seemed all too coincidental. No one thought anything of the magistrate wandering through the kitchen. They were all too scared of him to comment. He enjoyed that. He loved filling the hearts of these creatures with fear. That was the beautiful thing about being the magistrate. He didn't have to change his personality to get the desired result. The magistrate had truly been a malevolent being, yet he had begged for his life like a small child. When he looked death in the eye he had broken like all the others. Na'garoz had looked death in the eye on more than one occasion himself. Each time he laughed at the top of his voice and embraced the warmth.

Now all that he worked for was gone and it wouldn't be long before they realised who poisoned the Cursed One. Once someone told them who had been lurking around the kitchens there would be no way he could avoid the inevitable. No one saw him sprinkle the pepperstone in his water and if he had died there would have been no way for them to find the cause of his death. Na'garoz would have been able to sneak away from the city without anyone being the wiser. That's what he hated about the foolish creatures. Most of the time they were no smarter than the orglin, the dim-witted creatures that his master liked so much, but they could be somewhat intelligent when they wanted to be.

He didn't know how the wheatworte had made its way into the food. There was no way anyone could know what he was planning. The creature he had bought the pepperstone from had managed to have himself a fatal accident before he could speak to anyone. Na'garoz knew the best way to remain anonymous was to kill anyone who might know who he was. The creatures loved to gossip and it would only be a matter of time before he told his acquaintances he had sold pepperstone to the magistrate.

He had made the right decision, not to mention how much he enjoyed the particularly evil way the trader died. There was no chance anyone could have known he was planning on poisoning the man they were calling the Lord's nephew. That still didn't explain how the wheatworte had managed to make its way into his food. His head was starting to hurt as the thoughts raced through it. He liked things when they were nice and easy. He didn't like having to think too hard. He couldn't think of anyone else who knew about the pepperstone, unless someone had been spying on him when he was making the purchase.

There were too many inconstancies in his plan. It had been so perfect, so easy, he should be exalted now, sitting at his masters right hand. But he had to look forward now and not worry about the past. Na'garoz screamed in frustration. He would have to leave the city, at least until he found a new guise. No one would be as convenient as the magistrate, but that was in the past.

As he thought the form of the magistrate slowly started to fade. In its place was a figure robed in black. Na'garoz was glad to be back in his original form. It had been a long time since he had worn his old body and it felt good. He knew he couldn't wear it around town, but he was not unhappy to be himself again for a while. As soon as the sun went down he would make his way out of the city. No one would notice him if he acted like a beggar making his way to a better place.

Security would be tighter than ever around the Cursed One now. There was no hope he would be able to get close enough to make another attempt. At least he knew where the Cursed One was. That was more than any of his brethren knew. All he had to do was to work out where the Cursed One would go next. He could try and reassimilate himself amongst the Lord's staff, but he really didn't have the time. It wouldn't be long before the Cursed One would be on the move again. Now all Na'garoz had to do was to work out where he would be travelling next. If he could get a big enough head start then he could set another trap. This time he would set a trap that would not fail.

The next logical step would be for the Cursed One to travel to Kiarome. It was the largest city in the area and for some reason the man creatures like living close to each other. There were many bandits along the road, however, and he thought that might be too risky. He didn't know how many man creatures would be travelling with him and he didn't like the chances of convincing a group of bandits to fight heavily armed guards. Bandits were generally cowardly untrustworthy creatures. He could force his will upon them, but there was a good chance that they would turn him over to the guards as soon as they had the chance.

Three small towns were built along the highway for travellers to rest in comfort on their journey between Kiarome and Bellarome. He would have enough time to assimilate himself into one of the communities. Each town was sparsely populated so it wouldn't be hard for him to kill one of the creatures and take their place.

Drool started to drip down Na'garoz's distorted face with excitement. All of a sudden things were looking up. He had never liked intrigue in the past. He had always liked to race in and destroy. Thinking had always made his head hurt, but now he was starting to enjoy it. It was a new world. He was adapting to his new way of life. There was nothing more rewarding than watching the subtle chaos that he had caused. To watch from the shadows while the wretched creatures suffered the confusion and pain that he caused brought a strange joy to his life.

Yes, that is what he was going to do. He would meet the Cursed One again and next time he would be glorious. Next time he would feel the pure elation as the Cursed One's blood flowed over his body. The thought made him quiver as the drool continued to slather from his mouth. That was one of Na'garoz's major faults. He could only ever see the positives in his plans and never for a second thought he could fail.

It would be at least another day before he could transform himself again. The art of transformation took a great deal of energy to create, but once he had changed then it only took a minute amount of energy to continue the ruse. Now the spell was broken he was at his most vulnerable. He doubted whether he would have enough energy to light a small fire.

He pulled his hood tight around his face as he stood so no one could see inside. There would be no way he could explain his grotesque features to someone if they saw him. He would have to leave the city that night and find somewhere safe to hide until he was strong enough to carry out his plans. The thought of having to sneak out of the city did not please him. He should be riding out as a God not sneaking out like a scolded dog. He slowly opened the door and nervously looked out into the night. When he was sure there was no one around he crept out into the street and started to slink away.

Chapter 11: A Slow Recovery

Richmond woke in the morning feeling refreshed. It had been two long days since the Chosen One had joined them. The sun shone through Richmond's bedroom window and as much as he wanted to return to sleep he knew he had more pressing matters to attend to. With any luck Alaric, the man who they now called Dyrk, would be awake, but he knew deep down this wouldn't be the case. He had given the guards strict instructions to be woken if there was any change. He didn't realise that Tancred had also instructed the guards not to wake him under any circumstances.

The thought of bathing crossed Lord Richmond's mind. He had been so tired he couldn't do anything except sleep after he had finished his daily duties. He sniffed under his armpit and screwed up his face in disgust. Even though his body odour was enough to repulse himself he didn't bathe, instead he quickly dressed and dabbed some fragrant flower essence oil on strategic parts on his body. Taking a deep breath he was happy that he had sufficiently covered his own stench. There was nothing that was going to delay him checking on Dyrk's health and he knew if he took the time to bathe then it wouldn't be long before servants, noblemen and his officials would be knocking down his door. At least he could try and make a secret dash for Dyrk's room.

The palace corridors were strangely empty. It was the first thing Richmond noticed as he made his way to Dyrk's room. He thought he would be dodging people every step of the way, but it was as if everyone was making a point to avoid him. It did nothing to calm his nerves as he quickened his step. He had a very bad feeling that something had gone very wrong.

When he reached Dyrk's room he was relieved to see the two guards still standing outside. They stood a little straighter when they saw him approach.

"Any news?" Richmond kept the concern out of his voice as he spoke.

"Nothing sir! Tancred is inside, but as far as I know there has been no change to your nephew's condition." The soldier looked straight ahead and Richmond thought he looked nervous. There seemed to be something that everyone was hiding from him.

"Very good." Richmond waited for one of the soldiers to open the door for him. He didn't really need or want to wait, but he thought he better hold on ceremony. When neither of the soldiers moved Richmond coughed softly.

"Sorry, my Lord," one of the soldiers said as he quickly jumped into action.

Inside the room he could see Tancred standing over Dyrk's bed. Next to him was a beautiful young woman in a small white dress and cap, the standard garb of the palace nursemaids. She stood rather close to Tancred, but when Richmond entered she moved away quickly. Richmond could not suppress the smile that crossed his face.

"Excuse me my dear. I would like to have a private word with Tancred." There was no real reason why he needed to dismiss the young woman, but he thought she might appreciate an easy way out.

"Thank you my Lord," there was a clear waver in her voice. She was obviously very nervous being in his company Lord Richmond hated the effect he had on people. If only they realised he was a man like anyone else.

Tancred's eyes didn't leave the young woman until she left the room, then he smiled. Richmond was concerned with what his advisor had been doing in his absence. He now knew why Tancred was so keen for Richmond to retire. He had to let out a laugh when he thought about it.

"What are you laughing about?" Tancred asked as Richmond approached the bed.

"What exactly were you doing last night?" Richmond did his best to keep the smile from his face.

"I can assure you we have been keeping a close eye on Dyrk. I managed to sneak away for a quick nap, but Frida remained here all night. She made sure he remained hydrated and kept his fever down. Nothing untoward happened here I can assure you."

Richmond burst out laughing as his friend tried too hard to defend himself. It was obvious something was happening between the two of them. "Relax Tancred. What you get up to in your own time is none of my business," he said once he had finished laughing. "But, we have more important matters to discuss."

"Yes indeed we do," the embarrassment quickly left Tancred's face. "There has been very little change. I do believe he is getting better, but it's taking longer than what we thought."

"What about our other little problem?" Richmond was quick to change to subject.

"I'm afraid things aren't any better on that front. The physician disappeared last night before I had a chance to get to him. It seems that our friend was shrewder than we thought. It seems he has skipped town. I noticed there were a few essential items missing when I searched his apartment. He left in a hurry though and there were quite a few items left behind. I have a very bad feeling he knew more about this situation then he let on last night."

"Do you think that there is any chance of finding him and bringing him in for questioning? I mean if we find out who it was that tried to assassinate Dyrk we would gain the upper hand. At the moment we are running around in the dark and that is one thing that makes me very nervous."

"Given enough time I have no doubt we will be able to find him. The only problem is we don't have enough time. I think it would be a fruitless exercise to try. People will start asking questions if we send out a manhunt for the physician who apparently saved your nephews life. Things are bad enough as it is without adding wood to the fire. All we can do is hope Dyrk recovers before another attempt is made on his life or someone else realises our ruse." Tancred sighed.

"What can we do now?" Richmond shot a quick look towards Dyrk's still lifeless body before taking a seat at the table. He let his head drop into his hands.

"All we can do is hope that Dyrk recovers soon and we can continue with our plan. In the mean time I have already started a rumour there was a small case of food poisoning and Dyrk was one of the victims." Richmond shook his head as he figured where Tancred was going. "I did have to poison a few dinners to make the story more convincing. It wasn't easy to find a non-lethal poison that has the same effects, but I think the story should hold up for long enough to see us leave the city."

"So we wait?" Richmond asked the question, even though he knew the answer.

"Yes, we wait."

And wait they did. They spent the rest of the day sitting and watching Dyrk. Occasionally a servant would enter with requests from his council to attend meetings and each time they were sent away with very little information, only that Lord Richmond was not to be disturbed for the rest of the day. Tancred and Richmond had both decided if Richmond was to attend meetings then he would be bombarded with questions about the man everyone believed was Dyrk. Eventually there would be inconsistencies in his stories that would get the palace thinking on the true cause of his illness.

Besides the servants the nursemaid, Frida, was the only other person allowed to enter the room. Richmond couldn't be totally sure, but he thought that each time she entered she was disappointed to see him. Tancred was a little too obvious in the way he treated her. He tried too much to treat her with indifference that it was obvious there was something going on between them.

"You know you really don't need to act like that when Frida enters the room. If there's something happening between the two of you then I am happy for you." Richmond couldn't help himself after Frida left the room leaving them to eat dinner.

"I don't know what you're talking about." Tancred made sure he didn't take his eyes off his meal as he spoke.

"Hah!" Richmond stifled a laugh and nearly spat half his dinner out.

"What?" Tancred sounded hurt.

"I know there is something happening between the two of you, but if you want to keep it to yourself then that's your business," Richmond said after he cleared his mouth.

"You know what things are like in the palace. Someone like me doesn't associate with nursemaids, at least not for anything serious. We have been seeing each other for almost a year now, but it's essential to keep everything quiet." Tancred watched Richmond closely as he spoke. "Life would be very uncomfortable for her if it got out that we were seeing each other."

"As I said, you don't have to explain to me. Sometimes I wish I could shack up with a nursemaid, but unfortunately it will never happen," there was no humour in his tone.

It was more than three years since Richmond's wife had died. She had been pregnant when she contracted a strange disease. Both mother and the unborn baby died only weeks from the delivery date. Lord Richmond had been devastated and promised himself he would never fall in love again. It was one of the main reasons why Tancred had kept his relationship a secret, but he would never tell Richmond.

There was no change in Dyrk's condition as the night wore on. Eventually Tancred had insisted that Richmond leave and get some rest. He had to promise he would wake him as soon as there was any change. Each day that passed was another set back to their plan.

As soon as Richmond had left the room Frida returned. Tancred quickly brought her into his arms and held her close. The one good thing about Dyrk being ill was that he had more time to spend with the woman he loved. It broke his heart he couldn't tell her he was leaving and would probably never see her again. It wasn't that he didn't trust her, but once the secret was told it was no longer a secret. There was no way Lord Richmond could sneak out of the city if everyone knew what he was doing. She seemed so content in his arms and he wanted so much to take her with them. He was sure that a nursemaid would be handy on their journey, but he couldn't expose her to the risks they were about take.

It wasn't until first light that Dyrk's fever broke. He still remained unconscious, but the colour had returned to his skin and there was no more sweat. Tancred was true to his word and had one of the guards send for Richmond. Frida had spent the night, but left as soon as the morning sun shone through the window. She quickly checked Dyrk before leaving.

"Frida assures me he will regain consciousness today," Tancred explained as Richmond rushed in.

"Does she know exactly what happened to him?" Richmond gave Tancred a stern look.

"As much as I thought it would be better for her to know since she is expected to care for him I knew it was safer for her to remain ignorant. According to his symptoms she believes he will be up and about at the very latest by lunchtime tomorrow," Tancred continued.

"And when will he be ready to travel?" Richmond asked.

"I didn't think it was prudent to ask that question. As far as Frida knows as soon as Dyrk is better he will resume his life in the palace."

"You could always say that once he is better he will be returning to his father's estate," there was a moderate tone to Richmond's voice.

"I could have said a lot of things, but I thought it best to keep her in the dark as much as possible." Tancred sounded hurt at what Richmond was insinuating.

"I suppose you're right. I'm sorry, but the situation is starting to get to me. I don't like it when things are out of my control."

"I noticed." Tancred had to have his little dig.

Once they were done with their conversation they returned their attention to the man who was still lying motionless. Things had taken a nasty turn. It was only by sheer luck the man who was called the Chosen One, the man who was supposed to save the Seven Kingdoms from utter annihilation, didn't die from the poison he had been given.

"Have you heard any rumours about whether Dyrk's true identity has been discovered?" The thought had been plaguing Richmond all morning.

"It seems our ruse is still strong. The food poisoning story is holding. I don't think anyone suspects it was an assassination attempt. I think that everyone still believes he is in fact your nephew." Tancred seemed confident with what he was saying.

"So that means that whoever it was who masterminded the attack was either after your nephew or working alone. Either way I think it works in our favour. If we only have to look out for one man then we have a greater chance of protecting Dyrk." Richmond sounded a little happier.

"Be it one or be it a dozen I think the only way to truly protect him is to discover who it was that made the attempt on his life. That will be the only way we will know if they know Dyrk's true identity." Tancred wasn't as positive as Richmond.

"If Dyrk's identity has been discovered then maybe our entire plan has already failed." It was the first time Richmond fully accepted the fact someone might know who Dyrk really was. It had been plaguing his mind for the past two days.

"I agree with you that our plans will take a backward step if our ruse is discovered, but I don't think we are all together lost. I think we will have enough time to tweak them for us to continue. There is too much at stake for us to give in at the first sign of trouble." Tancred stood firm, the pillar of strength of the pair.

"I guess the first thing we need to do is discover the identity of the assassin." Richmond stroked his beard as he spoke.

"Of course you're right. I would have started straight away, but I thought it better to keep an eye on Dyrk. Since we can't let it be known that we are looking for an assassin there wasn't much I could do."

"I'm sorry, I didn't mean to imply you weren't doing your job. I know this is a very delicate situation. Sometimes I wish I wasn't involved in all of this intrigue." Richmond's voice trailed off as he spoke and he rubbed the side of his head. "The last few days have been very stressful on the both of us. The lack of good sleep hasn't helped. Now that Dyrk is on the mend we need to move quickly to discover the assassin. If we leave here without that knowledge there is no telling when they might strike again."

"Of course you're right," Tancred was still somewhat hurt, although he knew that Richmond had not meant anything bad. He also knew what had to be done, he could tell by the look on Richmond's face.

"I think it would be best if I stay here and look after my nephew and you ask around to see if you can gather any information. I think it will be less suspicious that way." Tancred slowly shook his head when he was sure that Richmond wasn't watching. Most of the time Richmond and Tancred were on an even playing field, at least when they were alone, but every now and then Richmond would slip into what Tancred called 'His Lordship mode'.

"I will get on it right away," he didn't really mind Richmond's lapses into 'His Lordship mode'. Most of the time he just shook his head and moved on, it was easier than trying to explain the situation.

Tancred knew it would be up to him to uncover the assassin. If Richmond was to ask around it would raise too many questions. He knew Richmond was again going to state the obvious, but it was better if he just let him go.

"I think you should go down to the kitchens and see what you can find. I'm sure someone will know if there was something amiss," Richmond kept his view on Dyrk so he didn't see the look on Tancred's face.

"Good idea," was all Tancred said as he stood from the table. "I will check in later and let you know if I uncover anything."

Tancred was glad to leave the room. As much as he wanted to know when Dyrk regained consciousness there was not much he could do. Time was precious and he could no longer waste it waiting for Dyrk to wake up. He would have to be careful with the questions he asked down in the kitchen. It had been a great risk for him to maintain the food poisoning ruse. If he wasn't careful he could ruin everything.

The second benefit with him doing the snooping is that he knew most of the women who worked in the kitchen. They would be more relaxed around him. There was a better chance he would be able to get the information he needed.

"Good morning ladies," he said as he walked into the kitchen. "How are we all this morning?" Tancred spoke in his friendliest voice, masking all the tension that filled his body.

There were quite a few giggles and a couple of replies. Tancred was a favourite amongst the kitchen women. He had a certain suaveness to his personality that women couldn't resist. There was also a kind of innocence about his appearance that made him very popular with the ladies.

"Hmm, something smells good," he kept up his usual banter when he entered the kitchens. He thought it would be a better idea if he kept to his regular routine. It would be too suspicious if he strayed.

"Now Tancred you know we can't give you anything to eat. What would Lord Richmond say if he heard about it?" A plump woman in a white dress spoke. She had flour smeared across her face. Tancred always thought she looked a lot like the puddings she was so famous for.

"But I am so hungry," he rubbed his stomach in mock hunger.

"Now you get out of here Tancred," a skinny, rat faced women came storming up from the back of the kitchen. In her right hand she held a rolling pin which she waved it at him. "If Hulda comes back and finds you here we'll all be in trouble. We have been given strict instructions not to let you in here." That wasn't exactly true, but the kitchen women would get in trouble from the Mistress of the Kitchens, Hulda, if she caught them.

"She's a pussy cat. She wouldn't do anything to me," it was false bravado on Tancred's part. In truth he was petrified of her.

Hulda was a strong, heavyset woman. When she was younger she had been quite attractive. She had been the Mistress of the Kitchen for almost twenty years. When Tancred had been a boy he remembered sneaking into the kitchen and trying to steal food. She had only been a scullery maid then, but she had given him such a spanking each time she caught him. He tasted the round end of her wooden spoon on more than one occasion. The punishment had never been done with malicious intent, but Tancred had left the kitchen with tears in his eyes. Now, although she could no longer issue him a beating, Tancred was still afraid of her.

His words brought a round of laughter from the kitchen women who knew full well he was still afraid of Hulda. Tancred's cheeks slowly started to turn crimson. It wasn't often he blushed, but he did now that he had been caught. He liked the women in the kitchen. They were the only group of people in the palace that didn't treat him like a nobleman. They teased him as much as they teased any small child who tugged at their aprons.

"I'm wondering if anyone knows about the food poisoning I've been hearing about." He knew that the mention of food poisoning was going to get him some evil looks, but there was no way to dance around it.

"I don't know what you are talking about," Thilde, the rat-faced woman, spoke with venom in her voice. She took offence the accusation of food poisoning.

Tancred took a step backwards as he recognised the look in her eyes. She might be old, but there was no doubt she would box him around his ears with her rolling pin. Thilde scared him only slightly less than Hulda. Thilde had also been the Mistress of the Kitchens before Hulda took over and had also punished a young Tancred when he was somewhere he shouldn't be. Not only that, but she still felt as though she still had to protect her girls. Any insult to the kitchen was a personal insult on her.

"I mean no disrespect." Tancred raised his hands in defence. "It's just that Lord Richmond's nephew was one of the people who were poisoned. Now I'm not saying for an instant someone deliberately poisoned the food, but you know how paranoid Lord Richmond can be. He always thinks there is a master plan to assassinate him and now he thinks someone is trying to kill his nephew." The ease in which Tancred could lie was quite disturbing. He knew the women would believe every word he told them. He listened to conversations when people didn't think he was listening. In doing so he was able to gather a wealth of information about the way people felt towards Lord Richmond. "He has asked me to come down here and ask if you ladies have seen anything, or anyone acting suspiciously two days ago."

"I don't know what you are insinuating, but I can assure you that nothing untoward happens down here. Hulda runs a very tight ship. Now I think that you should leave before Hulda catches you here." Thilde's eyes looked from left to right as if she was hiding something.

Tancred looked at her while he thought. There was something out of place. Thilde's harsh words sent all the women back to work. The fact Tancred hadn't moved only fuelled the fire brewing in her stomach.

"If you just stand there gawking I will hit you over the head." She waved the rolling pin above her head to indicate she wasn't joking.

"Yes, of course." Tancred was very pensive. There was a riddle here and he was going to work it out. "I'm sorry if I offended you." The apology didn't sound real, but Thilde accepted it.

Tancred watched the other women closely as he walked out of the kitchen. They seemed to be working just a little too hard, making a point not to make eye contact with him. He was sure someone knew something. He had to work out the kitchen before he could move on with his investigation. He stopped just outside. There was no door leading into the kitchen, just an archway, so he was able to lean against the wall and try to listen in.

"I don't want to hear another word about this," Thilde's voice dominated the room. "If I hear anything else then you can be sure Hulda will hear that you haven't been working."

Tancred knew the threat of Hulda would be enough to silence the women. He could stay where he was for the rest of the afternoon and still not get any information. Just as he pushed himself off the wall and started back towards Dyrk's room he heard someone approach.

"Tancred, thank the Gods that you haven't left yet," the woman who looked like a pudding spoke softly.

It was obvious she was afraid. She was shaking slightly as she waited for Tancred to reply. There was something about her disposition that really worried him.

"What is it Didrika?" Tancred kept his voice low.

"Something you said to Thilde. You wanted to know if anything strange had happened." Didrika looked over her shoulder nervously. "I don't think I should talk to you here," she looked over her shoulder again. "I have some time off after the lunchtime meal has been prepared. Is there somewhere I can meet you?"

"Meet me in my office. You know where that is don't you?" Tancred could hardly contain himself, but he could see the fear on Didrika's face and knew he shouldn't push too hard.

"Didrika!" Thilde's voice rang out from inside the kitchen. "What's taking you so long?"

Didrika simply nodded her head before she rushed back into the kitchen. Tancred also rushed away in case Thilde decided to check what Didrika had been doing. Didrika seemed afraid of Thilde. Tancred had never liked her and the situation only increased his distaste for the ex-Mistress of the Kitchens.

After checking in on Dyrk and Richmond he returned to his office. Tancred thought Dyrk was looking better, but Richmond did not share his enthusiasm. Tancred thought it would be better for him not to share the non-information he had received. It was mid-morning when he arrived at his office and although he was early he didn't want to miss Didrika. He had a feeling her information would be very useful in figuring out the identity of the assassin.

Shortly before noon there was a soft knock on the door. Tancred quickly jumped to his feet and opened it. Standing on the other side was the woman he had been waiting for, Didrika. She quickly entered the room and then looked behind her to see if anyone was there. Tancred also couldn't help but check the hallway before shutting the door. There was no one.

"What is it you need to tell me?" Tancred tried his best to contain his enthusiasm. He still didn't want Didrika to know what was happening. He hoped she was too concerned with her own safety to worry about what he was doing.

"I really shouldn't be speaking to you," Didrika slowly sat down. "If Thilde knew I was here I would be in for such a beating."

"You can relax Didrika. Whatever you say to me is completely confidential. You know I always wondered why you haven't been given the position of Mistress of the Kitchens. You are much better with the girls than Hulda."

"Thank you, but I don't think I would be any good at the job." Tancred's words were meant to calm Didrika and they seemed to work.

"Now what is it that you want to tell me?" Tancred didn't have time to continue the small talk.

"At the time I didn't think anything of it, but when you mentioned the food poisoning it all started to fall into place."

"What did my dear?" Tancred could hardly contain himself.

"For the last week or so the magistrate has taken a fancy to Ottila. Every now and then I saw him in the kitchen talking to her. Rumour has it they have been having an affair for the last month. She seemed to be completely smitten with him. I don't know if the affair was true, but I find it hard to believe." Didrika seemed very nervous.

"Why don't you believe it?" Tancred knew he had to push a little to get the answers that he needed. If he pushed too much then she might run away. It was obviously something was upsetting her.

"I know that she was in love with Fremont, a young man with the city guard. They seemed so perfect together. Then all of a sudden Ottila became so… cold. She stopped laughing, except when the magistrate was around. Something changed in her, but I don't know what it was. It was as if the magistrate had put a spell on her. But that is not the only strange thing," she paused again.

Tancred was starting to get frustrated with the lack of information coming from the plump woman. She was too nervous for it to be idle gossip. She had more information and he had to pry it from her. "What else is there Didrika? This could be very important. If someone is trying to kill Lord Richmond's nephew then I need to know."

"It was well known throughout the kitchens that Thilde was in love with the Magistrate. Although the two of them never had an official relationship it was widely spoken about. At least they were at one point in time," Didrika stopped speaking again when it was clear that there was something else she wanted to say.

"You can trust me Didrika. Tell me what you know and I will make sure you're safe." Tancred spoke as softly as he could.

Hearing Tancred's words brought tears streaming down her face. She lowered her head and started to sob. She was shaking almost to the point of falling out of her chair. As much as Tancred was concerned for her wellbeing he was starting to become annoyed. The information was on the tip of her tongue.

When her sobbing died down she looked up at Tancred. Her eyes were red, but the tears had stopped flowing. "Two days ago Ottila went missing. No one has heard from her. I have a bad feeling she was involved in the attempted murder. It's just not like her though. We were good friends and I know that she couldn't have done this on her own. Someone must have forced her to do it."

That was it. That was what she had come to tell him. She thought that it was her good friend who had poisoned the food. Tancred knew she couldn't have done it on her own. The complexity of the crime was more than a simple kitchen girl could devise. The question was where to look next. The magistrate would be the next logical step.

"Thank you Didrika. You can be sure that I won't tell anyone what you have told me. Tell Hulda you are sick and take the rest of the day off. I don't think you should be working at the moment. If you have any problems tell her to speak to me." Tancred ended the conversation.

Once Didrika had left the room Tancred pulled on the bell-pull hanging to the left of his desk. Within a minute there was a gentle rap on the door. Tancred stayed seated as he called for the pageboy to enter.

"I need to speak to the magistrate straight away. It is of the utmost importance and I do not wish to be kept waiting." Tancred's voice was commanding.

"Yes sir," the boy bowed quickly and then scurried from the room.

Tancred didn't know what he was going to say to the magistrate. He didn't know if he should come right out and accuse him or try and trick him into giving up information. He knew the magistrate would be a tough adversary. He was a cruel man, but he was also very clever. Tancred didn't believe it was going to be easy to get information.

It was late in the day when the pageboy returned. He knocked very tentatively on the door before he was admitted. The look on his face showed Tancred that the news was not good.

"Well, boy, don't just stand there. Where is the magistrate?" Tancred was less than impressed at having to wait so long.

"The thing is," the boy twisted as he spoke, obviously very nervous. "I looked everywhere, honest I did, but the magistrate was nowhere to be found. I spoke to the city watch and the palace guards, but no one knew where he was," the pageboy spoke quickly. "I looked everywhere, but I couldn't find him. It was as if he has disappeared off the face of the Seven Kingdoms. I asked everyone I could and no one knew where he was."

"Okay, I get the picture. You may leave now." Tancred dismissed him with a wave of his hand.

Things were getting more disturbing than he had originally thought. It was clear the magistrate and the kitchen girl had a big part to play in the attempted assassination. The main question now was whether or not they knew Dyrk's true identity. He needed to speak to Richmond.

Richmond put his index figure up to his lips when Tancred entered the room indicating him to be quiet. "What is it?" Tancred spoke softly.

"Dyrk was awake for a short while and just got back to sleep. He's still very weak so I don't want to disturb him." There was a smile on Richmond's face.

"That's good news. I wish I'd been as successful." Tancred didn't find joy in Dyrk's recovery.

"What have you found?" Richmond let the smile fade from his face.

"Just more mysteries I'm afraid." Tancred went on to explain what Didrika had told him.

"That is quite disturbing. I must admit I have never liked the magistrate's tactics, but he was always very efficient in his job. There has been something unusual about him recently. His methods have been a little suspicious and one might have called him outright malicious. I think you might have stumbled across something here. The only question now is where is the magistrate and his mistress?" Richmond mused.

"The only connection we have now is Thilde and she will not be an easy one to break." Tancred added.

"Are we sure that Thilde and the magistrate were romantically attached? I don't want you upsetting the women in my kitchen."

"I think we are beyond saving someone's feelings. There is more at stake than the stability of your household." Tancred didn't like what Richmond was implying.

"Of course, but we still have to step lightly. If anyone finds out what we're doing then all is lost. I want to make sure there is as little turmoil when I leave as possible. Remember we want the city to survive or else what are we doing this for?"

Tancred knew Richmond had a valid point, but his views were very narrow. There was more than his city at stake. They were trying to save the world. If their city had to be sacrificed in the process then that was a small price to pay. He knew he couldn't voice his opinion. Richmond could be extremely patriotic at times and Tancred didn't need another argument.

"I'll be very careful with what I say to her," was all Tancred could bring himself to say.

"Hah!" Richmond laughed out loudly, before he put his hand over his mouth, forgetting that Dyrk was still asleep. "Don't think I don't know the relationship that you have with the girls in the kitchen. I would be very surprised if Thilde will tell you anything."

"Be that as it may she is the only one with information that might be able to help us solve this mystery. I don't think it would be a wise idea for you to start questioning the staff. That, I'm afraid, is my job. Whether she will like it or not I can be very persuasive when I have to be. Unless you have a better idea I don't think that we have much choice. Dyrk should be up and about in the next couple of days and then we have to be on the move. This doesn't give us any time for subtleties." Tancred pressed his opinion.

"Very well. I can't say that I like it, but I don't see we have another option. I'll send out word to the city watch that I wish to speak to the magistrate on a private matter. I'm sure that will avoid any unnecessary rumours. I'm sure between the two of us we will be able to get to the bottom of this."

"On that note then I think I will find Thilde and try and get some answers out of her. I trust that you will be able to cope with out me." Tancred knew he was pushing his luck, but he hoped Richmond would see the humour in his jibe.

"Get out of here." Richmond dismissed both Tancred and his comment.

Tancred was only too happy to acquiesce. He didn't want to be around Richmond in his current mood. The situation was tough on both of them, but it seemed Richmond wasn't handling it as well. He wasn't looking forward to confronting Thilde. He would have to tread very carefully if he was going to get the information he needed. He was sure she would be able to shed some light on the situation.

He found her in the kitchen, busily working away on the evening meal. He thought about waiting until she had finished, but decided he would have more impact if he interrupted her from her work.

"Thilde!" Tancred called out from the archway.

"Be gone child. I have no time for your silliness," Thilde didn't have to look up to know who was speaking to her.

"I need to speak to you now. This can't wait!" Tancred used his most commanding voice, although he knew it would have little effect.

Thilde's body physically slumped. It was a reaction Tancred was not expecting. He thought he was going to have to carry her out of the room kicking and screaming. She looked up at him, her eyes were red as if she was about to start crying. There was something very different about her demeanour.

"Okay. I will speak to you," she stopped what she was doing and followed Tancred out into the hallway. "What is it that is so important that you disturb me from my work?"

"I am looking for the magistrate and it has come to my attention the two of you are close?"

"Lothar and I were close, as close as you could be without getting married. It was impossible for us to marry, but we did love each other. Then all of a sudden he changed. He became cold and calculating. He wanted to know things about the kitchen. At first I thought he was just interested in my work, but then he starting asking about the other women. It seems he was looking to replace me. He didn't even try to hide the fact. It was obvious he had seduced Ottila. Now the two of them have run off to be together." Thilde then broke down and cried.

Things were not going at all like Tancred had planned. He had thought Thilde would have been in on the poisoning, but it seemed she was as much a victim as anyone. There had to be someone behind the attack. He couldn't understand why the magistrate would suddenly decide to kill someone, other than the wanted criminals.

"It's alright Thilde. I'm sure there is a logical explanation to what happened." It was all he could say. He didn't know how to make her feel better. "You better get back to work."

Thilde sniffed once and wiped the tears from her eyes. She looked up at Tancred. It was the first time he had ever seen her vulnerable. "Please don't tell anyone about this," was all she said before she went back to the kitchens.

There was nothing else he could do. If she was lying to him then she was very convincing. He didn't think it was worth pushing her on the off chance she wasn't. All he could do was to go back to Dyrk's room and relieve Richmond. Their only chance of uncovering what happened was to find either the magistrate or Ottila.

Chapter 12: More Bad News

The night came and went with no news on Lothar or Ottila. Richmond left Tancred with the job of watching over Dyrk, but neither men were happy with their current situation. There was nothing they could do about it, all they could do was wait for answers.

Dyrk had woken briefly during the night, but he was still too weak to talk. Frida had remained with Tancred after Richmond left and tended to Dyrk's needs. She was very careful not to do anything to over-exert him. Frida was pleased with his condition and said he was responding well to her treatment. She suggested he would have the energy to leave his bed in a day or two. The good news did nothing to ease Tancred's nerves. Without truly knowing his ailment there was no way she could accurately diagnose his recovery. He thought about explaining the situation, but knew he couldn't. Even though he trusted her implicitly he could not reveal the truth. It was more so for her own safety. Once they had left the city he was sure she would be questioned and her ignorance would be her only defence.

Richmond returned to the room at first light. The two of them shared a silent breakfast as the vigil continued. The room was thick with tension. Neither of them wanted to break the silence before the other. It wasn't until there was a knock on the door around mid-morning that one of them spoke.

"Enter!" Richmond boomed out from his seat. His voice croaked slightly.

The door opened and a page boy entered. He was the head page and nearly old enough for a different job within the household. It was obvious whatever the message was it was too important for anyone else to deliver. They both knew there was very little chance the news was going to be good.

"Excuse me, my Lord," the page seemed somewhat nervous. That wasn't a good sign.

"What is it boy, we don't have all day?" Richmond became very irritated.

"Yes, my Lord. We have found the magistrate." The pageboy looked even more nervous now.

"Well that is good. I don't know why you look so concerned." Richmond sounded relieved.

"Sorry my lord, you don't understand. We searched everywhere in the city we thought he could be. We checked his house and all the local taverns we thought he might custom. When we couldn't find him there we started checking the seedier parts of the city." The page was now starting to babble. There was obviously something that he didn't want to say.

"That is all very interesting, but is there any chance that you are going to get to the point soon?" Tancred spoke as it was obvious that Richmond was starting to lose his temper.

"We searched everywhere and there was no sign of him. Then we got the idea to check under the city. We went through the sewers and that's where we found him." The page continued.

"So he was hiding in the sewers?" Tancred spoke directly to Richmond.

"No sir, you don't understand. He wasn't hiding in the sewers. He wasn't doing anything in the sewers. He was dead."

"Damn it!" Richmond cursed. Before he spoke again he looked up. It was clear there was still something that the pageboy wanted to say. "What is it boy?"

"This is what we can't understand. The body has been in the sewer for a least a week. It was obvious even to me the body had been there longer than the time Lothar had been missing." Now it was obvious why the page had not wanted to speak.

"Are you sure?" Tancred was trying to process what he had just heard.

"Absolutely, not that I have seen a dead body before, but the city physician arrived and confirmed it, he is sure the body has been in the sewer for over a week." The page grew in confidence, but was still quite nervous.

"What about the other person who was missing? That girl from the kitchen?" Tancred tried to be as blasé as possible. He didn't want the pageboy to get the idea that the two events were related.

"No Sir. To be honest I don't think anyone has been searching for her. We've been focused on finding the magistrate. I figured that Ottila has run off with some young man. She has a reputation for falling in love too easily. I didn't think it was worth wasting our time." The pageboy has a sly smile on his face.

The words enraged both Tancred and Richmond. The pageboy just stood there smugly as Tancred raised an eyebrow towards the Lord who simply nodded in return. He was just as angry as Tancred with the disrespect the pageboy had shown them, but he knew it was better that Tancred dress him down. If Richmond lost his temper then it would soon be all over the palace and that would start the rumours flowing.

"I see." Tancred started off slowly. "Who is the head of the Palace staff?" Even though the question was rhetorical Tancred still waited for an answer.

"Lord Richmond." There was a confused look on the page's face.

"I see." Tancred looked down before hardening his gaze on the page. "Then why is it that you decided to ignore a simple request. We want to find Ottila because she is a member of Lord Richmond's staff and she is missing. Now I suggest that you disappear and continue doing your job before you find yourself cooling your heels in the dungeons." Tancred's voice was harsh, but he refrained from yelling. A moment later the page was still standing before them, stunned at the harsh words. It was enough to break Tancred's calm. "Get out of here boy and find that kitchen girl. If you don't find her you can be sure that you will be horsewhipped in the palace courtyard at sundown."

Whether it was the threat of being horsewhipped or the tone in Tancred's voice, it forced the page into action. He almost jumped in his hurry to leave the room. Tancred couldn't help but laugh when the door shut behind him. The pageboy had enraged him, but the look on the boy's face after he had been scolded was enough to lighten his spirits. When the reality of their situation returned to him his face hardened again.

"This is disturbing news," was all Tancred could say.

"It is indeed. All it has done is open up more questions. If the man in the sewer was Lothar then who was the man masquerading as the magistrate...? and why didn't anyone realise who he was?" Richmond began to get anxious. "If people realise what is happening then there'll be no way for us to contain the rumours and then there's no telling what will happen."

"We need to leave the city and we need to do it soon." Tancred spoke softly, as if to himself.

"That's all well and good, but we cannot leave him here." Richmond nodded towards Dyrk.

"What's going on?" The voice coming from the bed was cracked and broken.

The two men spun around from their seats and looked at the bed. They had been so involved in their own problems they hadn't noticed Dyrk had woken and was sitting, rather tentatively, on the edge of his bed. He still didn't look like his normal self, but then they didn't really know what he normally looked like. He looked fragile and unsteady as if he would collapse at any moment.

"Dyrk, you're alright." There was a clear relief in Richmond's voice.

"Who is Dyrk, what are you talking about?"

Richmond looked at Tancred before he spoke again. "You are Dyrk. Don't you remember the story? You're my nephew, sent here to learn the way of the city."

"Oh," Dyrk lowered his head and thought for a moment before returning the men's gaze. "And who are you?"

"I am Lord Richmond, your uncle. Don't you remember?" Richmond seemed confused.

Tancred signalled for Richmond to follow him to the other side of the room before Dyrk had a chance to speak. He knew if Dyrk was to reveal his true identity there would be nothing they could do. He also had a theory on why Dyrk was acting so strangely.

"I don't think he remembers who he is," Tancred kept his voice low.

"I have figured that out for myself," Richmond said as he struggled to keep calm.

"That's not what I mean. I think that he has amnesia. I don't think he can remember much at all. Follow my lead." Tancred didn't wait for Richmond to respond before heading back towards the bed.

"What year is it?" Tancred blurted out the question at a bewildered Dyrk.

"What are you talking about? Of course I know what year it is," but just as Dyrk was about to call out the answer he paused. He looked around the room for something that would give him a hint, but he couldn't think.

"Who is the King of Darshival?" Richmond asked when it was clear that Dyrk did not know the answer.

Dyrk didn't even try to respond. The look on his face was enough to confirm Tancred's suspicions. Richmond thought the situation had just become worse, but Tancred could see the bright side. If Dyrk didn't know his true identity then there was no way he could reveal it to anyone.

"That's alright Dyrk. I am sure that your memory will come back to you eventually," Tancred spoke softly. "You should eat something. You haven't eaten in a long time."

Dyrk noticed a bellpull hanging beside his bed. The instinct to pull on it was almost impossible to deny. At the mention of food his stomach started to rumble. He hadn't realised how hungry he was and now he was starving. He resisted the urge as he felt as though it was not proper for him to do so. Instead he waited for Tancred to walk over and pull on it for him.

"Bring some food for the Lord's nephew," Tancred barked when the door was opened.

Dyrk didn't know why he didn't summon the pageboy himself. If he was indeed of noble blood and the nephew of the city's very Lord then he should have been able to summon someone to his room. There was something not quite right about the situation, but why would the two men before him lie? His head was clouded over with doubt. Until his memory returned he didn't think he had a choice but to believe them. They seemed to be looking after him so he didn't think he was in any danger. Sitting on his bed he made a private vow. If the men before him were not true then he would kill them both.

"Please, lie back down Dyrk. You need to save your energy." Tancred said.

He did feel tired, but it was as if it was from sleeping too much, not sleeping too little. His muscles felt weary from lack of use, not overuse. He tried to ignore the request for him to rest and tried to stand, but his strength hadn't returned enough for him to carry his own weight. Instead he did as he was told and lay back down. He didn't feel very comfortable, but he didn't have any other choice.

"What do we do now?" Richmond kept his voice low.

"Once he is strong enough we must leave. In fact I don't think we are going to be able to wait for him to regain his strength. I think we should leave at first light tomorrow. Everything is moving too fast against us. We need to change the tide if we are going to be victorious. I will make sure that everything is ready." Tancred had to assume Richmond was going to agree with him. Sometimes Richmond's nobility stood in his way. As much as they spoke as equals it was still ultimately Richmond's decision.

"I don't agree with you, but I also don't think we have another option. Get everything ready and we'll leave at first light." Richmond sighed.

With Tancred out of the room Dyrk thought he would try and get some answers out of his so called uncle. He had followed their body language as he couldn't hear their words. It seemed to him that Tancred was the dominant of the two. Lord Richmond was in the position of power, but it was Tancred who called the shots. If he was going to get any answers it would be best to get them from Richmond.

"What's happening?" It seemed the best place to start.

Lord Richmond took a deep breath. He thought about telling Dyrk the truth, but decided against it. The lie the two had created would have to do. "It seems as though you have been poisoned." Richmond almost bit his tongue as the words came out of his mouth. "There have been quite a few cases of food poisoning recently. At first we thought that someone was trying to attack you, but the cases have been too random." Richmond hoped that his explanation wasn't too rushed. "It has come at such a bad time. We were planning on taking you to Kiarome to see King Unwin. We were supposed to leave when you became sick. Now we're running terribly late. I don't think we can leave the King waiting much longer. In these troubled times we need the favour of King Unwin. There is no telling where the Evil One's army will strike." Richmond could have throttled himself. At the sound of the enemy Dyrk sat bolt upright in his bed. It was obvious something had registered inside his head.

Before Dyrk had a chance to question Richmond there was a knock on the door. Richmond let out a sigh of relief. He quickly called out for whoever it was to enter and he was grateful to see a serving girl with a large tray of food. He hoped the food would take Dyrk's mind off their conversation.

The food worked a treat. As soon as the aroma reached Dyrk's nostrils all thoughts of conversation left his mind. Richmond was able to sneak out of the room whilst Dyrk ate. He could tell Dyrk didn't completely believe their lie, but the main thing was not to give him any more excuses not to trust them. He should have been ready for the questions, but Dyrk had taken him by surprise. He had to clear his head if he was going to convince Dyrk of the lie. The stress and lack of sleep was really starting to get to him.

The soldiers were still posted outside the door. The threat to Dyrk was still real and they thought it best that they kept the guards. Regardless of how suspicious it looked they still had to make sure Dyrk was safe. Before he left, Richmond made sure the guards knew no one was to enter or leave the room unless it was himself or Tancred.

Richmond walked the halls as if he was in a trance. He had spent most of his life in the palace. He had travelled for a short while, but most of his time was spent either in the palace or around the city. Bellarome was his life and soon enough he was going to leave it all behind. His palace staff tried to get his attention around every corner. It was well known he was not to be disturbed whilst he was with his nephew, but since he was wandering the corridors and he was fair game. Richmond hardly even saw them. At best he dismissed them with a nod or a grunt; at worst he didn't acknowledge them at all. He was grateful Tancred was organising their escape. He didn't think he had the heart to leave the palace, but it was the only way they were able to leave without the entire city knowing. If they had organised to leave the city then there would be an entire fanfare. There would be no way for him to sneak out. It was going to be difficult enough as it was, especially if Dyrk wasn't able to walk on his own.

When he had done a circuit of the palace Richmond returned to Dyrk's room. Inside he found a scene he had not expected. He wasn't sure if it was a good or a bad sign. Dyrk was dressed and out of bed. He still had the same confused look on his face, but he was also looked determined. Richmond was going to have a hard time convincing Dyrk to stay in his room. He didn't want to risk the chance of the assassin having another chance of killing him, especially since they were so close to leaving.

"You are up, that's great" Richmond tried to sound as excited as possible. "It seems all you needed was a little food to get your energy back."

Dyrk had a strange look on his face, as if he was looking for something. He would quickly look around the room before returning to his previous stare. He didn't seem to acknowledge Richmond at all. Richmond wished Tancred was there with him. He was sure his advisor would know what to say. All he could do now was hope that he didn't ruin everything.

"What are you looking for Dyrk? Maybe I can help you find something?" Richmond spoke with a calming tone.

For the first time since Richmond had entered the room Dyrk looked at him. Richmond could see there was a question on his face, but instead he answered Richmond's. "I don't know. I feel as though I am missing something, something important. It's hard to explain, but I don't feel whole at the moment. Not to mention these clothes don't feel right." Dyrk made a show at looking at the clothes he was wearing. He had found them in the wardrobe and assumed they were his. The navy blue silk shirt fitted him perfectly, but the yellow stars on its trim seemed out of place. The blue tights felt uncomfortable and the suede shoes didn't quite fit properly. There had been a matching cap hanging on a hook, but he thought it was unnecessary to wear. The navy blue outfit had been one of a dozen different outfits that were hanging in the wardrobe. He didn't know why he needed so many clothes, he was sure he never had so many.

"A large storm hit just before you arrived at the city and most of your clothes were destroyed. We had to have a lot of clothes made up for you." Richmond hoped that his lie didn't sound too fake. "If they are not too your liking I can have the seamstress come by in the morning."

"No, thank you. I'm sure I will get used to these," Dyrk didn't sound so confident. "So you say my name is Dyrk? Why doesn't that sound familiar to me?"

Richmond looked away as Dyrk looked towards him. He knew if he looked into Dyrk's eyes his face would give away the truth. Without his full memory he didn't think the man standing before him would understand what they were doing.

"I'm sure it will come back to you in time. I think for now you should rest though. We will be leaving for the capital in the morning and you will need all you strength." It was the best Richmond could do.

"I think if I could walk around the palace that might help to jog my memory." Dyrk's tone was confrontational. It was as if he was trying to make Richmond slip up.

"As I said I think it best if you rest. I will have a physician come in and have a look at you. He might be able to shed some light on how long it will be before your memory returns." Richmond quickly left the room without giving Dyrk any real answers.

He sent for the physician who returned shortly after. Richmond anxiously waited outside the room until he arrived. Richmond could hear Dyrk pacing around inside and only hoped he didn't try to leave. It was bad enough he was sitting outside the room with the soldiers.

The new physician had Dyrk sit down whilst he examined him. Richmond sat on the other side of the room, his anxiety growing. The physician asked some standard questions that Dyrk could not answer. The physician stroked his short beard as he thought about what could be the cause of his amnesia. When he was done he walked over to where Richmond was seated. Dyrk had to move to listen to his diagnosis.

"Well there doesn't seem to be any real reason for the amnesia. From what I can tell he hasn't had any trauma to his head and no case of food poisoning could cause amnesia. All I can put it down to is some form of psychosis," The physician didn't sound overly confident.

"So what does that mean?" Richmond asked.

"I have seen this before. When something terrible happens in a person's life the brain can block out the horror. It's a defence mechanism. In extreme cases, like this one, the patient can block out more than just the traumatic experience. They can block out entire stages of their lives. It seems as though Dyrk has repressed all his memories. It's something that I have never seen before." The physician looked just as confused as Dyrk.

"Is there anything we can do?" Richmond said.

"In my experience, no!" he spoke softly, as if trying to keep the news from Dyrk.

"So there is no hope of my memory returning?" Dyrk sounded forlorn.

"I didn't say that." The physician wasn't giving away much information. Richmond found it to be a trait of the physician's within the city.

"Well?" Richmond could play the same game. The tone in his voice was all the question needed.

"There is nothing you can do to get your memory back, but that is not to say your memory won't return on its own. There is very little known about the diseases of the brain. All I can suggest is that you take it easy and try not to get too stressed. You have to get over whatever it is that caused your amnesia." The physician spoke as if he was educating a child. This was something else that Richmond noted was common amongst the medical profession. "There is no telling what could trigger a memory."

"Thank you for your assistance." Richmond tried to keep his voice as grateful as he could, which wasn't easy.

The physician simply grunted his acknowledgement. When it was clear there were no more questions he stood and left. Richmond hated to think how they would treat the rest of the people in the city if this was the way they treated a Lord. The news was neither good nor bad, but at least they knew what they were up against.

"This isn't right," Dyrk said. "There is nothing familiar here. That just doesn't make any sense."

"Everything will be alright. It will all start making sense soon enough. Until your memory comes back you will just have to trust me. Both Tancred and I only have your best interests at heart."

Dyrk returned to sit on his bed. He looked somewhat downtrodden. The fire that had been in his eyes earlier had completely extinguished. He let his head rest in his hands. Richmond felt somewhat sorry for him, but not enough to tell him the truth.

"I suppose you're right. There isn't much I can do until my memory comes back. I will trust you for now, but be assured that if you are lying to me then I will have your head on a plate." There was something cold in Dyrk's voice that made Richmond shiver.

Once Dyrk had returned to bed Richmond was satisfied that he could leave him alone. He was glad to leave the room and needed to speak to Tancred about their new revelation. He needed his advisor more than ever.

It was late when Tancred opened the door to Richmond's office. He knew it was not going to be easy organising their journey, but he had hoped to speak to Tancred earlier. There wouldn't be a lot of time to discuss their next move and they both needed rest. Richmond started to tell Tancred the diagnosis, but to his surprise Tancred cut him short.

"That's all well and good. I think we should stick with the original plan. We don't tell him anything he doesn't need to know. At least until he starts remembering things. If he hasn't recovered by the time we reach Kiarome we will tell him everything once we are in the safety of the palace."

"Is Unwin's palace going to be that much safer than mine? Whoever it was who is masquerading as Lothar is still out there. If he can infiltrate my palace there is no telling how far he can go. I don't know if this is the right way to do things. I think the sooner we tell him the truth the better. The longer we go on like this the more chance we have of being discovered." Richmond didn't entirely agree with his advisor's assessment.

"I don't think we are going to come up with any new answers tonight. Things haven't been going to plan. Tomorrow morning we will travel to Kiarome. Hopefully from there things will start going in our favour." It was obvious to Richmond that Tancred wanted to leave.

"Is there somewhere you would rather be?" The question had accusing undertones.

"Of course not, but I don't see what banging our heads against a wall is going to achieve. I think that it would be better if we both got a good night's sleep. We will be travelling hard and there is no telling what we will have to endure." There was something else, but Richmond couldn't put his finger on it.

"I suppose you're right. I still think that we should be honest with Dyrk. He needs to know his true identity and he needs to know we are here to help him."

"Very well. We shall sleep on it and see what the morning brings. I will meet you here an hour before first light." Tancred stood as he spoke.

Richmond thought about speaking, but he knew that would be no use. Instead he flicked his hand at Tancred indicating he was able to leave. Sometimes they both fell back onto formalities. It was easier then getting into an argument. There was something strange about Tancred and Richmond really wanted to know what it was. He knew Tancred well enough to know if he didn't want to speak then he wouldn't. There was nothing left for him to do besides eat the evening meal and then go to bed. He wished he had more time. He wished he was able to prep his staff about his departure. He hoped they would be able to run the city without him. He knew they could. He just hoped there was still a city for him to come back to, although he had no doubt that someone would supplant him in his absence.

***

As Tancred left his Lord's office he hoped he had not been too rude. His mind was elsewhere and he didn't have time for something he could not change. Having another pointless conversation was not going to change the facts that Dyrk had lost his memory, his assassin was still on the loose and their entire plan was up in the air. It was his last night in Bellarome for a long time and possibly forever. He didn't know what was in store for him in the future. He did know, however, the adventure he was about to embark on was dangerous and could possibly take his life. Everything else was ready for their departure and there was only one more thing that was left for him to do. He would spend one more night with the women he loved. It broke his heart that he could not tell her where he was going or why. All she will know is that one day he was there and the next he was gone. That was all anyone would know, at least until they reached the palace. From there it would be more difficult to hide their identity. Unwin was expecting them, but it would still be hard to hide.

He knocked softly on the door when he reached Frida's room. His heart was racing as he waited for her response. After a moment he heard her soft voice call out for him to enter. A tear appeared in his eye for a moment as the thought of leaving her overwhelmed him. He brushed it aside before he entered the room. He couldn't show any sign of sadness. If she asked the question he didn't think he could lie. She was his one weakness. That was the reason he couldn't tell her he was leaving. If she asked him to stay he didn't think he could say no.

Her scent hit his nose as he opened the door. He took a deep breath as he walked into the room. It was dark with the only light and a cool breeze coming from the open window. A lump stuck in his throat as he thought this would be the last time he would feel Frida's touch.

"What's the matter my love?" her voice was soft and sweet.

"Nothing my dear," Tancred walked into the room, not realising how long he had been standing in the doorway. "It's just been a long day." He wished so hard that he could tell her he was leaving. He knew she would be heartbroken when she heard the news he had left. There was nothing for it. What he was doing was more important than his own feelings. He took one last thought of what was lying ahead and then lost himself in Frida's embrace.

Chapter 13: Leaving at Long Last

Dyrk's was not as mobile as the others would have liked it, not only that but he didn't understand their need for stealth. Nothing made sense to him anymore. There didn't seem to be any logical reason why the Lord of Bellarome would be sneaking through his own palace.

"If you're the Lord and we're on a regular journey to the capital then why do we have to sneak out of the palace?" Dyrk whined as they crammed into the secret exit behind his wardrobe.

"Things are more complicated than they seem," was all Tancred said.

The tone in Dyrk's voice made Tancred believe he knew more than he was letting on. It was possible he was starting to remember. If he realised who he was before they left the city then their plan might come unstuck.

The passageway they were in had not been unused for many years. To add to the discomfort of the narrow walls and low ceiling it was covered in dust and cobwebs. They all had to walk hunched over to avoid banging their heads on the ceiling. Tancred took the lead with Dyrk and Richmond following behind. They all coughed and spluttered and Richmond tried his best to support Dyrk as they walked.

Luckily the passageway was only short and they came out at a small landing at the top of a flight of stone stairs. The only light came from a torch which Tancred held. It had a small flame which didn't give off much light and it was impossible to see more than half a dozen steps below them.

"How are you feeling?" Tancred asked Dyrk as he looked out over the edge of the stairs.

"I'm a little shaky on my feet. I don't think I have all my strength back," as if to emphasise his statement he reached out and steadied himself on Richmond's shoulder. Richmond quickly moved to take the extra weight.

"We'll wait here until you're ready." Richmond suggested.

"No, we need to keep moving." Tancred didn't completely believe Dyrk was as sick as he said. There was something in his tone. "We don't have time. The sun will be rising anytime now. We need to be out of the city before it's completely awake."

Without waiting for a reply Tancred started down the stairs. Holding the torch gave Tancred the power. If the other two wanted to see where they were going they would have to follow. Richmond did his best to help Dyrk. They were able to walk two abreast with Richmond just able to support him. Tancred heard them struggling behind him and sneered to himself. There was something not right about Dyrk and until he could figure out what it was he knew it was best to keep his mouth shut. If he had a chance to speak to Richmond privately he would share his concerns.

At the bottom of the stairs there was another small passage leading to a small door. The door was about half the size of normal door with a small lock and a handle in the middle. Tancred produced a golden key and unlocked it with a soft click.

"Well, here goes nothing," Tancred spoke, as if to himself. "Actually here goes everything," he corrected himself as he pushed the door open.

They came out of the passage just outside the palace walls. The grey of dawn shrouded the small public garden. The door was hidden behind a number of small bushes and it took a little effort to push through. Again Richmond had to help Dyrk. Tancred extinguished the torch before he went searching through the nearby bushes. He came back shortly holding a bundle wrapped in a goat pelt.

Placing the bundle on the ground he untied the two strings revealing three black cloaks. Tancred quickly picked one up and motioned for the other two to do the same.

"These should hide us whilst we move around the city." Tancred wrapped the cloak around him and pulled the hood over his head.

The three men skulked through the shadows of the still sleeping city. Only the very early risers and the night watch were on the streets. Even so they still couldn't risk being seen. Even the lowliest of people would recognise Lord Richmond. His disappearance would not be apparent to the palace for another couple of days and the information would not reach the city for another two or three days. Once it was common knowledge then their plan would really kick into gear.

They reached the stables where Tancred had booked a team of two horses and a carriage. Two extra horses were also there with saddle bags loaded onto their backs. The perfectly white stallions did not look happy with the extra weight and Dyrk thought the animals looked familiar. He wondered if the horses were his.

Tancred finished the deal whilst the other two waited outside. The fast purchase of their transportation had bumped up the price. Tancred thought about berating the stable owner, but it would do no good. Unless he dropped Lord Richmond's name there was no way he would get a discount. It was not that they were short on money for their trip, it was just the principle. He grumbled as much as was warranted before handing over the gold.

Richmond opened the door to the carriage and helped Dyrk inside. Tancred took the driver's seat and when he was sure the other two were seated he started the horses. He drove with his hood drawn close over his face so no one would be able to recognise him and Richmond kept the curtains drawn. To anyone on the street the carriage could have been any number of nobles or rich merchants.

Everything was going well until they reached the Southern Gate. The guards stopped them just before they were about to pass. Tancred had been expecting it. He peered through his hood and instantly recognised the guard. Tancred drew his hood closer; he knew the guard would recognise him if he saw his face.

"What's your business outside of the city? These are troubled times and the outside world is not a safe place," the guard spoke officiously.

Tancred kept his head low as he reached inside his cloak. After making an effort of searching he pulled out a crumpled piece of paper. Without looking at the guard he handed it to him. The guard looked at the crumpled piece of paper with disgust. Once he had opened the note and read it his attitude quickly changed.

"Go straight through sir," the guard even saluted.

Tancred simply nodded and reached out for his note. The guard, who had forgotten himself since reading it, quickly returned it, apologising and then jumped out of the way as Tancred flicked the reins.

Tancred let out a sigh of relief, the note had been genuine and with Richmond's signature and the royal seal they could have got away with anything. If the guard had checked the carriage, which would have been proper procedure, then their ruse would have been discovered. Their plan had been to shock the guard with awe and hope he forgot his job, it worked and they were on their way to Kiarome.

The highway between Bellarome and Kiarome was a good four day ride. There were a number of farm houses dotted along the highway and three small villages allowed comfort for travellers. The first village was called King's Rest, the second, which was the largest and could almost be called a town, was Stellerville. The third and final village before the capital city of Kiarome was Lord's Wait. In-between Stellerville and Lord's Wait there was a small forest that was notorious for bandits. Lord Richmond had done his best to clean it up, but it was too far from his domain. He had petitioned King Unwin to send his soldiers, but he had denied the request. It would be the hardest part of their journey. Tancred would have to be extremely vigilant if they were going to come out unscathed. He thought about the upcoming peril as he gently steered the horses along the highway.

"Why is it we are travelling under disguise, Uncle?" Alaric asked. It was the first time Dyrk had called him uncle. Richmond was quite pleased with the turn of events.

"Things are very difficult to explain. Since I don't have any children you are the next in line for my title. It has come to our attention that some of my rivals are prepared to try and assassinate you. This is why we must travel to the capital. King Unwin has promised he will protect you. I thought I would be able to, but I was wrong. Now we must sneak out of the city so no one will know where we have gone." Lord Richmond had practiced that speech many times. He knew Dyrk would ask the question. He was pleased with the way it went. He sighed with relief when he saw a look of understanding in Dyrk's eyes.

"That makes sense," he thought for a moment. "Life as a nobleman is hard."

"You don't know the half of it," Richmond replied.

Dyrk returned his gaze to the small crack in the curtain. He could only just seem the landscape around them. Richmond was glad there were no more questions. He didn't agree with lying to Dyrk, he thought he should know the truth.

The journey to King's Rest went without incident and they arrived in the village by mid-afternoon. There was plenty of daylight left, but not enough to get them to Stellerville. Richmond double checked the curtains before they reached the village and although it was far away from the city the locals would still recognise him.

Tancred made arrangements for them to stay at one of the local inns. He had planned for them all to stay in the one room figuring it would be safer that way. Dyrk, on the other hand, had other ideas. As nobility he believed he should have a room to himself. Even after Tancred explained they were in hiding until they reached Kiarome he didn't care. It seemed the man was starting to believe what they were telling him. Tancred wasn't sure if it was a good idea or not. He could very easily get into bad habits acting the way he was. Richmond calmed Tancred and was happy to acquiesce to Dyrk's demands. It was better than trying to fight.

***

Dyrk sat in his room after he had eaten his evening meal. A serving woman had brought him a plate of steaming hot food and mug of foaming ale. Tancred had given him specific instructions not to leave. Dyrk had agreed, anything to get the other two off his back. Ever since they left the city Dyrk had been dying to be by himself.

He knew that Dyrk wasn't his real name. He knew he wasn't Richmond's nephew. The amnesia had not been fake and at the start he couldn't remember anything, but as the day wore on things had started coming back. At first he thought of telling the others, but then he realised he was not who they said he was and knew he could not trust them. He was going to play along until he could figure out what they wanted with him. They claimed to be after his best interests, but there was an agenda they were keeping to themselves. Until then he would remain the spoilt son of a nobleman.

It did have its bright side however; he had seen a rather large tome in his possessions when they were being loaded onto the back of the carriage. It had only been a glimpse, but he knew it was somehow important. That was the main reason why he wanted a room to himself. He wanted to be able to read the book without the other two becoming suspicious. He was sure there were going to be answers for him in it.

He was glad that Richmond had not decided to wear the trip away with conversation. The memories weren't great and didn't really give him any answers. They were more feelings than anything else. He couldn't remember anything specific, but he did have a feeling that he was in the middle of doing something important before he lost his memory.

He didn't feel as though he was native to the land he was travelling through. If he wasn't born there he wondered why he was there at all. The feeling he had was that he was born a long way away. He couldn't think of any reason why he would travel half way across the Seven Kingdoms. He didn't think he was a merchant of any great importance, he didn't think he was travelling on business and he was sure that he wasn't on vacation.

Sitting on the small timber chair Dyrk breathed a deep sigh of frustration. The more he thought about what he was missing the further away it became. The feelings only came to him when he didn't try and focus on them. That was the most frustrating part. To take his mind off his problems he started reading the tome. On the spine of the large volume were the words '*The Prophecy of the Stone*'. Dyrk wondered if they had any significance to what he was doing. He had a sudden feeling it was pivotal to recovering his memory.

There was no book mark, not that he remembered any of the book if there was, so he decided to start from the start. It was not long before he was engrossed with what he was reading. It was late in the night, or early in the morning, when he finally put it down and went to sleep. Nothing in the book made sense to him, but that didn't make him feel any worse. There was something between the lines in the words, but he couldn't put a finger on it.

***

Tancred had Richmond and Dyrk up and out of bed at first light. Neither of them seemed excited to be on the move again. Tancred couldn't figure out why. He knew Richmond had gone to bed early.

"What's wrong?" Tancred asked as they made their way to the stables. They wore the same black robes with the hoods drawn close.

"I don't know. I just have a bad feeling this is not the right day to be travelling," Richmond sounded resigned.

"And do you feel the same?" Tancred asked Dyrk as a matter of interest.

Dyrk yawned openly before answer. "No. I just don't like being woken so early." The spoilt noble's son act was starting to wear thin. Tancred didn't believe it for a second, but again it was typical behaviour so he couldn't make the accusation.

"Very good. I think that we should be off," Tancred took the final vote, although he doubted they would have stayed regardless of who wanted to.

Again the travelling was mundane. The weather was pleasant, but not out of the ordinary. There was the usual amount of traffic, but no one seemed to take any notice of them. Tancred was still very wary regarding Richmond's bad feeling. With what had happened recently he couldn't take any risks.

The two others spent another day in silence. Dyrk made sure that his attention was outside the window, not giving Richmond any chance to make conversation.

Shortly after midday Tancred stopped the wagon. He jumped down from the driver's seat and opened the carriage door.

"We have crossed our check point. You can remove the cloaks and pull back the curtains. Now we must remember we still have to remain incognito. There will be people that will still recognise Richmond and some that will know the…" Tancred left what he was about to say short.

Dyrk raised an eyebrow at the comment, but quickly lowered it as Tancred looked at him. For the first time Richmond noticed something pass between the two of them. He had been so concerned with his own lie he had not noticed the tension between Dyrk and Tancred. He thought about speaking, but then thought better of it. Neither of them had mentioned anything and it was not his place to put ideas in their heads. The tension would have to continue until their entire situation could be resolved.

"We should continue. Keep an eye out for anything unusual," was all that Tancred said before returning to the driver's seat.

They were travelling again before Dyrk had a chance to question what Tancred was about to say. Tancred was very close to giving away the truth and that was one thing he didn't want to do. He didn't enjoy lying, but he truly believed it was the best way. There was no telling what Dyrk's reaction would be. He would have to know before they reached the capital, but until then Tancred would let him believe that he was Richmond's nephew.

"What's the story with you and Tancred?" Dyrk asked after they had been travelling for an hour.

"What do you mean?" Richmond was surprised to hear Dyrk speak.

"He's your advisor, but it seems that half the time he tells you what to do. I would think that it should be the other way around. He should advise, not command." Dyrk watched Richmond closely.

"I suppose that's true. I don't believe this should be the case. Tancred has been my advisor for a long time and he was my very best friend when I was growing up. He's a very smart man. I don't believe I should control him just because my father was who he was. Tancred will do what I ask when I ask him to do it and that is enough for me."

Dyrk thought about pressing him for answers, but decided against it. He had learnt what he needed to know from Richmond's brief answers. In the courts it was Richmond who led, but in privacy it was Tancred who called the shots. He was sure that piece of information would come in useful.

It was coming on dusk when they arrived in Stellerville. The village was at least twice as large as King's Rest. The carriage moved slowly through the streets as most of the village residents made their way home for the night. The narrow streets were busy making Tancred nervous. The enemy's spies were everywhere. As much as they had left in secrecy he had no preconceptions that the enemy didn't know what they were doing. To be over confident or complacent would be the death of them.

There were a number of inns in Stellerville, unlike the other two villages which only had the one. Some of the inns were nicer than the others, but only one had the reputation of being the best. That was the Royal Sleep. It was a tough decision to choose which inn to stay at. The Royal Sleep would be the most conspicuous of all the inns, but then for someone who travelled in such a carriage to stay at a lesser inn might also be suspicious. In the end Tancred figured if they were going to be noticed they may as well at least be comfortable.

There were no complaints from the other two when he reined the horses in at the Royal Sleep's stables. Richmond was pleased to be out of the carriage. It was more comfortable than riding up front, but he still didn't enjoy it. He much preferred to be on horseback. He thought about riding one of Dyrk's white horses, but that would also be too suspicious. It was possible to masquerade as a guard, but he didn't think Tancred would agree.

"I think a drink is in order," Richmond sounded jovial.

"Do you think that's wise?" Tancred did not sound impressed.

"We have to play the part. Who would stay at the Royal Sleep and not drink in its tavern?" Richmond slapped Tancred on the shoulder.

Tancred had nothing to say. He still didn't agree with Richmond, but he knew better than to argue with him in public. It was one thing for him to take command in private, but in front of Dyrk it wouldn't be a good idea. He had to play along as Richmond's advisor for the moment. When the time was right he would take command. Both men knew it was meant to be, but Tancred was sure that Richmond wouldn't take the transition well.

The inn was much cosier than the last. Dyrk had insisted again that he had a room by himself. Tancred protested the expense, but since he didn't want to create a scene there was nothing that he could do. He watched Dyrk closely as he walked away towards his room. The man strutted more than walked. It didn't look right.

"There is something very odd happening here," Tancred commented when the porters had left with their bags.

"I don't know what you're talking about. I think he's acting exactly as a noble's son should. At least one who thinks he is better than everyone else."

"That's just my point. He's not the son of a nobleman. He shouldn't know what a nobleman's son should be acting like." Tancred finally spoke his mind.

"Well, we don't really know what he was like before he arrived in our city. Maybe this is just who he really is." Richmond's retort was thin.

"Maybe you're right, but I think we should be very careful around him. I think he's playing a very underhanded game."

Tancred had come around to Richmond's way of thinking and followed him into the tavern. The long day on the road had made him parched and he was looking forward to the Royal Sleep's famous home brewed ale.

"Two ales please," Tancred ordered.

"Not from around here?" the serving women asked the obvious question as she poured.

"No, we are from Bellarome. We are doing our annual pilgrimage to the capital. Maybe this year King Unwin will grant us an audience." Tancred spoke the lie as if it was the truth.

"I hear rumours that he had closed his court," the woman said. "I hate to be the bearer of bad news, but I think you are wasting your time."

"What are you doing here?" A man bumped into Tancred at the bar, slurring his words.

"Now Delbert what have I told you about annoying my guests?" The serving women spoke in a motherly harsh voice.

"I'm sorry Bethinda. You know my feelings on foreigners!" Delbert left the bar after giving Tancred an evil look.

"What was that all about?" Tancred looked over his shoulder and watched Delbert take a seat at a table on the other side of the bar. A smell of unwashed body odour followed in his wake.

"Nothing much. He lost his wife and child not two days ago. He claims an outsider came and took them away. He has been here the last two nights drinking to excess. Whenever an outsider comes in he tries to start a fight." Bethinda handed Tancred his ales.

As much as he wanted to find out more Richmond was waiting for him. He simply thanked Bethinda and walked to the table where Richmond was seated. They both took a long drink before they spoke to each other.

"What took you so long?" Richmond asked.

"It seems that man has a problem with outsiders," Tancred nodded to Delbert before explaining the story.

The man looked broken. His shoulder length black hair was dishevelled. Stains covered his clothes, there was dirt on his face and his brown eyes were bloodshot. Tancred wasn't sure if it was from crying or excessive drinking. Either way he felt sorry for him.

"That does seem odd. Do you think it's a coincidence?" Richmond already knew the answer.

"I don't think that anything is a coincidence. The fate of the Seven Kingdoms lies on our companion's shoulders. I don't think if anything happens to us whilst we're in his company that's a coincidence. I think there's a reason why this man's family went missing and why he has stumbled into our lives." Tancred kept his voice low.

It was still early and there weren't many in the bar. Besides Delbert and Bethinda there were only another half a dozen men. Their voices carried, forcing them to speak quietly.

"What do you think the link is?" Richmond asked.

"I don't know, but I wouldn't be surprised if this has something to do with the assassin."

"But how would the assassin know that we were travelling here?" Richmond asked.

"Remember it's the prophecy that pulls us in the direction we need to go. I am sure that the same prophecy is drawing evil to follow us. There can be no doubt even in secrecy we are not safe." Tancred's words were ominous, but they also made sense.

"Still, I don't think we need to concern ourselves about it now. We will be gone in the morning, well before anyone can figure out who we are. All we have to do is relax and enjoy ourselves." Richmond was trying to convince himself as much as he was trying to convince Tancred.

There was no reply from Tancred. He only took another drink of his ale before looking towards the bar. The bar woman returned his gaze when his eyes moved onto her. She didn't look at all happy with him staring. All he could do was finish his ale and approach her, as if he was waiting for her to serve him.

"What can you tell me about Delbert?" Tancred asked as he dropped a silver coin on the bar.

"He was once a loving, caring man. He never touched a drink. He was a model citizen before his wife and son left him. He believes they were kidnapped, but everyone thinks she just left him." Bethinda made sure no one else in the tavern could hear her.

"I don't understand. If he was a loving, caring person as you said, why would his family leave him?"

"He might have been loving, but that's not all that a marriage is about. Apparently, and I can only go on the rumours that I have heard, he was a boring man. He had no inspiration and talking to him was like having conversing with a stone wall. Now I am not saying that is a good excuse to leave your husband, but again the rumours say she ran away with another man. A merchant who was passing by swept her off her feet and took her away with him. I don't know which story is true." Bethinda didn't seem at all troubled in telling Tancred the man's life story.

"I see. Wouldn't you think the man would try and find his family? Why is he just sitting in the bar getting drunk?"

"You know I asked myself that very same question. When it is said and done where would you start looking? If the story was true that she ran away with a rich merchant then where would you look? No one in town knows who this man is and no one knows if he was heading north or south. If they ran away together then they would be sure not to leave a trail for Delbert to follow. Now if they were kidnapped there is no telling where the kidnappers would have taken them. All he can do is wait for their ransom. Finally if they have been murdered then there is no telling where the bodies could be. Now I ask you, what would you do in his stead?" Bethinda had obviously thought about it.

"I get your point, thank you." Tancred took the fresh ales and returned to the table.

He quickly and quietly explained to Richmond what he had learnt about Delbert. Richmond listened intently, making his own judgement as he did.

"Do you think this might be related to Dyrk's assassination attempt?"

"I don't think it could be anything less. It's too convenient all this happened the same time that Dyrk was poisoned," Tancred answered.

"If the assassin was able to murder Lothar and take his place as the magistrate without anyone knowing then it is quite possible that he would be able to murder this poor man and his family and then take his place within the town. It would make sense he would take the place of someone who is not well known about the town. From what I can gather he kept to himself and didn't socialise much. No one would notice if there was a change in his personality." Richmond's words made sense.

"We need to be very careful. If the assassin is here then he will know we have arrived. I don't think we can be as cavalier as you first thought." Tancred warned. "We must find Dyrk and make sure that he's safe."

"What will we say to him?" Richmond asked. "If we don't tell him the truth then it's going to be very hard explaining why he is not safe in his own room."

"You're right. I think that it will be better if we invite him to join us for dinner. During the night one of us will have to stand guard outside his room. There is no other way to make sure he is safe." Tancred was not going to yield.

Richmond stood to leave, but Tancred motioned for him to stay seated. Richmond shot him a questioning look, but did as he was instructed.

"We shouldn't rush off. It is still early and it might look suspicious if we disappear now. As long as we keep an eye on Delbert we should be alright. We'll get Dyrk when we are ready to eat."

Delbert had been watching the two men out of the corner of his eyes. He was suspicious of all outsiders. Tancred and Richmond were no exception to the rule. Tancred had not realised that he had been staring. If he did he would have been prepared for Delbert's attack.

The drunken man stumbled his way over to their table. Once he was close enough he slammed the palm of his hands down and almost overbalanced. He was able to recover himself just at the last moment.

"What do the two of you think that you are doing here?" There was a glazed look in his eyes and his speech was broken.

Richmond raised his hand as Tancred was about to respond. He knew the look in his old friend's eyes. He was not going to be subtle in his response. Richmond knew tact was better than outward aggression. There was nothing reasonable in Delbert's attack and he would find nothing reasonable in their response.

"We are just passing through. We don't want any trouble." Richmond kept looking at Tancred as he spoke. He thought it would be less threatening if he didn't look Delbert in the eyes.

"Well I think you should keep passing through. The last time there was a stranger in town my wife and child were stolen. Now who is it to say you didn't have something to do with it?" The man wasn't making any sense. He was ranting, but knew to keep his voice low. If he started yelling then Bethinda would call in the village watch to have him removed.

"I am sorry for your loss, but we didn't have anything to do with it. We are just here for the night and will be on our way at first light." Tancred coughed as he thought Richmond was giving away too much information.

"Leaving so soon? That means you have something to hide. What is it you could possibly be hiding?" Delbert started to sway as he spoke. Tancred believed the only reason he was still standing was his hands on the table.

Richmond gave Tancred a questioning look. That only made Delbert angrier.

"What was that look for? You two are definitely hiding something. If you know where my wife and child are you better tell me. I'm warning you. I may look drunk, but I could still skewer you alive," the threat didn't even sound real.

"I think it's time you leave. We don't want any trouble and really don't want to be threatened. You should return to your table and think about what you are doing." Tancred's voice was firm. As he spoke Richmond tried to get Bethinda's attention.

The serving woman had seemingly disappeared. Richmond felt very uncomfortable and if they were not very careful then their secrecy would be ruined. It wouldn't take long before the entire village knew that Delbert had started a fight with some foreigners.

"Please, let me buy you a drink." Tancred was trying to calm him down.

"Don't think that you can buy me off with a drink. I know you know where my family is and you are going to tell me." Delbert fumbled under his shirt for a moment before pulling out a rusty knife waving it in front of them. It did nothing to worry them expect for the attention they were getting. A few more people had entered the tavern and they were all watching the performance.

"I don't think you want to start waving knives around." Tancred's voice was cold. His eyes didn't leave the knife that was slowly passing back and forth between them.

"What did I tell you Delbert," the voice came from across the other side of the room.

Both men breathed a sigh of relief when they saw Bethinda approaching. She moved quickly and didn't look very happy. She grabbed Delbert by the arm and pulled him away from the table. As she did she looked over her shoulder and made an apologetic face. She sat Delbert back in his chair and had a quite word with him. He didn't look happy, but whatever she said to him made him stay.

"Have a drink on the house. I am so sorry that he attacked you. He is truly harmless enough. I'll make sure he doesn't bother you again tonight." Bethinda left to get the ales.

"There's definitely something not right here." Tancred spoke. "This Bethinda woman doesn't seem right either."

"I know what you mean, but I think that we might be just a little paranoid. Do you think that we would be thinking this way if we weren't doing what we are doing?" Richmond spoke softly.

"True, but that doesn't change the fact that this is a very strange situation. I am a little bit dubious now on whether we should bring Dyrk into the tavern. If the assassin is in this room then we would be showing them we have Dyrk with us," Tancred added.

"I don't know. I don't think there's a wrong or right way. I'm sure whatever we do choose we should have chosen the other.

Bethinda returned to the table with the ales. "Meals will be served in an hour. Are you staying for dinner?" She was now being extra friendly. She smiled warmly as she spoke.

Tancred looked at Richmond before he spoke. "We will be and our other companion will be joining us."

"Very good."

Chapter 14: Forgotten Memories

Alaric sat in his room. He had realised his name was Alaric and not Dyrk. Sitting by himself reading *The Prophecy of the Stone* seemed to have helped his memory. Again through the day flashes came back to him, nothing solid, but it made him feel better. Since he had started flicking through the giant tome he had at least remembered his name.

Again the words in the book made no sense to him. Nevertheless he knew the tome was the key to him remembering. The book was the key to everything he was searching for. It was just impossible for him to understand what it was trying to tell him.

As he read he remembered he had been travelling. He had travelled a long distance. He had come from a small town named Arsiliac. He didn't know which Kingdom it was part of, but he knew it was a long way from where he was. He was happy he was starting to remember, but it also made him worried. He knew his life was in danger and until he could remember why he would not be able to keep himself safe. All he could do was rely on the fact the two men he was travelling with didn't want him dead; if they did then they would have already killed him already. He couldn't work out any other worse case scenarios.

Something else had happened to him earlier in the day. The feeling came on slowly, as if someone was tapping him on the shoulder. He started to feel what he could only describe as a presence. He could feel it all around him. Some places it felt stronger and other places he could hardly feel it, but no matter where they went it was always there. He thought about asking Richmond if he knew what it was, but he didn't want to risk them finding out that his memory was starting to return. Instead he kept quiet and mused what it might mean.

He had not been reading for long when there was a soft knock on the door. The sound made Alaric jump. He didn't realise how involved he was in the tome. He wanted to be left alone, but when the knock came again he knew that he had to answer it.

Standing on the other side was Richmond and Tancred. They both looked as though they wanted to speak, but was waiting for the other. After they stood there for almost a minute in silence finally Alaric spoke.

"Can I help you gentlemen with something?"

"Lord Richmond and I thought that it would be nice if you'd join us for dinner." Tancred kept his face straight, but Alaric knew there was something else.

"If we are going to do this then you have to be honest with me," Alaric kept his voice level.

Richmond looked pleadingly at Tancred. Tancred looked at Alaric and then back to Richmond. Eventually he gave his master a slight nod of his head.

"We believe that the assassin is here in Stellerville. We think it's safer if you stay with us." Richmond's voice was filled with concern. He wanted to reiterate to Alaric that it was his best interests they were thinking about.

"Then wouldn't it be better if I stay in the room? Out of sight out of mind?" Alaric really didn't want to leave the room, but then he thought he might be able to gain some more information from the other two if he did. "Then again, I suppose it couldn't hurt to eat something."

Alaric walked out without waiting for the other two. Both men quickly followed after, both perplexed with his sudden change of mind. They didn't believe he was doing it out of any favour to them, but they also couldn't work out why. They were just going to have to keep an eye on him.

The inn's tavern was almost full when they returned forcing them to use the dinner room. Inside there were a number of tables and chairs scattered around and at the end there were two large rectangular tables joined together. The tables were dressed with silky white linen. On top there was a large roasted boar sitting on a silver platter with a variety of vegetables, fruits, breads and cheeses.

"I doubt there is much chance of another attempt to poison your food. They would have to kill all the people in here for that to happen." Tancred sounded somewhat joyful, but Alaric didn't see the humour in his words. "Go on Dyrk, don't be afraid to eat."

Alaric slowly walked towards the table. As much as he didn't believe the food was poisoned he couldn't bring himself to even pick up a plate let alone eat. He stood and stared at the wild boar. It looked appetising, although he didn't know what animal it was.

"What is this?" he asked as he slowly picked up a plate.

"Don't you know?" Richmond looked at him strangely.

Tancred interrupted before Dyrk had a chance to answer. "Of course he doesn't remember. He has amnesia," he spoke to Richmond first before returning to Alaric. "This is wild boar. It's native to this region of Darshival. It's quite a delicacy. As far as I know they're not found anywhere else in the Seven Kingdoms." Tancred almost bit his tongue when he finished speaking.

Alaric felt as though that made perfect sense. It was not as if he had eaten boar before and just couldn't remember. He felt as though he had never eaten it in his life. He smiled to himself, but then quickly returned his previous gaze. He didn't want the others to get suspicious.

He quickly picked up the carving knife and started cutting himself some meat.

At the table Alaric felt much less conspicuous, but he still couldn't help thinking everyone in the room was looking at him. He wondered if one or more of them were trying to kill him. The most disturbing part was he had no idea why. He was fairly confident it wasn't because people believed he was Richmond's nephew.

They ate their meal in silence. Tancred silently scolded himself for giving away too much information and Richmond was still upset he was not able to tell Alaric the truth. He knew it would only be a matter of time before he realised who he was. If the stories were true about his abilities and strengths he didn't want to be on his wrong side.

Once they had finished eating they returned to the tavern. As there were no seats left they had to stand at the bar. Alaric looked at Bethinda. He thought there was something strange about her, something exotic. He couldn't take his eyes off her until she came to serve them. When she looked at him he had to look away. There was something accusing in her eyes.

"Three ales please?" Tancred ordered watching her very closely as she poured them. If she was going to try and poison them then he wanted to know before it was too late.

"What did I tell you people about drinking in my tavern?" Delbert stormed through the crowd to the bar.

He was clearly a lot more intoxicated than earlier. Even with the extra alcohol he seemed more focused. His movements were a lot more controlled. Tancred was worried he was not all that he seemed.

"I asked you a question. I don't want to have to make you leave, but you're not giving me any choice." Delbert kept his gaze on Alaric. He was staring, as if he was trying place where he knew him from.

"We don't want any trouble, sir." To everyone's surprise it was Alaric who spoke. "I am sorry for your loss, but there is nothing that we can do about it." His last comment was even more perplexing. They were sure there was no way Alaric should know about Delbert's family.

No one knew what to say, especially Delbert. Alaric's presence was strangely compelling. Delbert was less confident in his tirade. He had been ready to fight, but now he didn't know whether he should just leave them alone or join them for a drink. Instead he just stood there and stared.

"Now Delbert. This is the last time you will annoy these people tonight. If you can't behave then you will have to leave and you won't be able to come back. You know that if Obert finds out you've been disturbing customers then it will be my job as well."

"Yes, ma'am. I think it's time for me to go home. I think I'm going to have a long day tomorrow." Delbert's attitude had completely changed. He seemed less focused and more distant.

The three men watched him leave the tavern before returning to their drinks. At the same time Alaric's presence also seemed to change. Tancred was the only one who noticed it. Richmond was just glad not to be involved in a tavern brawl.

After they had drained their ales Alaric spoke. "I think I might retire for the night. We have another long day on the road tomorrow."

Richmond and Tancred agreed, but decided to stay for one last ale. Alaric had an uncontrollable urge to leave and return to his room. He didn't understand why, but there was something drawing him there. Once he was inside the feeling went away. He didn't know what it was he was supposed to do, so he sat down to read *The Prophecy of the Stone*.

He found the great tome on his bedside table. It was open about half way through. Alaric could neither remember leaving the book there nor having it open. Although it seemed odd Alaric quickly brushed it aside. Since he couldn't remember what page he had just read he decided to start from the one that was opened in front of him.

The day will come when the one
Will lose all that he has and remember none
He will try and try
And eventually it will come
Two will try and deceive
Though their hearts may be true
The facts will remain the same
Regardless of what they try and do
If the mind fails and so does the truth
Then all will be lost and none will be saved
The chosen one and saviour
All hope he will lose
But that is not all said and done
If the two remain true
Then hopes still run abound
Don't push too hard
But don't wait too long

It was almost as if the last lines were speaking directly to him. He was finally starting to understand the words that were previously so hard to read. The passage made perfect sense to him and it unlocked a part of his brain that had previously been shut. A large smile crossed his face. His memory had not completely returned, but he knew enough not to be vulnerable. His life had taken a new twist and he felt as though he was getting back on track.

His urge to read had completely disappeared. It was still relatively early, but he felt as though he had achieved everything he was going to. He thought it would be better to take his own advice and get an early night sleep.

The night passed without incident and Alaric woke with a fresh outlook on his life. He almost forgot to wipe the smile from his face when the other two men came to get him. He had deliberately not packed his bags and even though he knew he was not Dyrk he still had to play the part. If he deviated from his previous attitude then they would know he was starting to remember. Until he could work out their motives he needed to play his part.

Once Tancred had collected Alaric's possessions they made their way to the stables. Tancred had taken on the role of making sure Alaric was ready. Richmond would have done it himself, but they both thought Alaric would find it strange if a Lord was acting as a pageboy.

As they started out from the inn stables someone called out to them. Tancred looked around to see who it was. When he realised who it was he thought about putting the reigns to the horses, but instead he brought them a gentle stop. As Delbert approached, Tancred wondered why he had stopped. The man had been nothing but trouble and he doubted the situation was going to change.

"Please wait!" Delbert cried out from behind them.

"We're leaving, alright. Leave us alone." Tancred snapped when Delbert stopped outside the carriage.

He looked surprisingly well for someone who had been drinking almost non-stop for the past three days. He had bathed, changed his clothes and brushed his hair. His eyes were still bloodshot, but only time could change that.

"No, please listen to what I have to say. I apologise for last night. When I've had a few drinks my mouth runs away with itself. I have nothing against you or your friends. This is what brings me to what I have to ask you?"

"Well spit it out man, we don't have all day." Tancred was fast becoming angry.

"I only ask that you let me travel with you?"

"You have got to be joking. There is no hope in the heavens that you can come with us." Not only was Tancred still angry with what Delbert had done the night before there was still the chance that he was the assassin.

"I understand that you are upset…"

Tancred didn't let him finish his story. "You understand nothing. Now get out of my way before I teach you a lesson in manners," Tancred started yelling.

"What's all this hubbub?" Alaric asked as he stepped out of the carriage.

"Nothing Dyrk. Get back in the carriage. I will sort this out." Tancred had to clench his teeth not to yell at him.

"You're the man from the bar last night, aren't you?" Alaric completely ignored Tancred.

"My name is Delbert."

"My name is Dyrk. I know your story and it's a sad one. What is it that you want from us?" Tancred was fuming, but could not bring himself to interrupt.

"My family was taken from me. I believe if I travel with you I will be able to find them. I can't explain why, but I need to travel with you and your friends." Delbert didn't seem too confident with what he was saying.

"I understand." Alaric made a scene of thinking before speaking. "Do you have a horse?"

"Yes I do." There was a look of hope in Delbert's face.

"Good, then get your horse and your things and meet us along the highway. We are travelling to Kiarome and you are more than welcome to join us." Alaric sounded more confident than usual.

"Now wait a moment Dyrk. There are things you don't understand." Tancred did his best to keep his anger under control.

Alaric turned to Tancred and gave him a look that nearly made him jump from the carriage. The look only lasted for a second, but it was enough to take effect.

"Delbert will come with us," the statement needed no reply, but Tancred felt that he had to speak.

"Very well, let it be on your head."

"You will meet us on the highway. We will not wait for you, but you are welcome to travel with us," Alaric's words were cold.

"Thank you, I will be with you shortly," Delbert spoke quickly, bowed once, before rushing away to get his horse.

"Ride up with me." Tancred said once Delbert had left. He had recovered from his initial shock and wanted to speak with the man he thought was still Dyrk.

"I don't think so. I am the son of a noble and will not ride up front." Alaric slipped back into the role of Richmond's nephew so seamlessly that Tancred wasn't sure his memory served him correctly.

Once he was back in the carriage Alaric thought the drama was over. He didn't want to have to explain himself to Tancred. What he didn't know was that Richmond had been watching. Although his so called uncle was less assertive than Tancred he was no less part of the entire scheme.

"What was all that about?" Richmond asked the question before elaborating. Unfortunately Alaric was up for the challenge.

"What are you talking about?" Alaric kept his gaze out the window.

"What you said to Tancred wasn't very diplomatic. As a nobleman you must take note of what your advisor tells you." Richmond had his doubts that Alaric still believed he was Dyrk, but he had to keep up the pretence.

"I apologise. I was just touched by that poor man's story. I didn't think about the repercussions." Alaric tried to put on his best Dyrk voice, but his heart wasn't in it.

"Well next time see that you listen to what Tancred tells you. He is a wise man and deserves your respect. Not to mention the man who tried to assassinate you is still on the loose. There is no telling who he could be." Richmond didn't seem to notice the slip as he continued his lecture.

Alaric thought for a moment before he replied. "How could he be the assassin? That man has lived here his entire life."

Richmond almost swore as he realised what he had said. If he wasn't careful he was going to give away too much. He wished he was driving the wagon and Tancred was in the carriage. It was Tancred's idea to keep secrets from Alaric. He looked out the window for a moment before he realised what he had to say, although he didn't sound very convincing.

"Of course I don't think Delbert was the man who tried to kill you, but I also don't think whoever it was worked alone. There is no telling how many people were involved in the assassination attempt and there is no telling how many people still want to see you dead. What you must understand is that this is a very dangerous time for you and you must trust our judgement." Richmond hoped that Alaric didn't see through his lies.

Alaric thought about pushing him for more information in an attempt to uncover the truth, but he thought better of it. In his own attempt he might give away his own secrets and he wasn't ready to reveal them.

Both men sat in silence, the tension thick in the back of the carriage. They both wondered if the other was suspecting their lies. In truth both men were suspicious of the other, but only Alaric knew for a fact Richmond was lying.

Neither man spoke until the sounds of horse's hooves could be heard beside the carriage. Delbert slowed his horse to a walk and he leaned into the window until he was almost face to face with Alaric.

"Thank you so much. I owe you a debt." Delbert was puffing as he had obviously been riding hard. His horse was also covered in a fine sweat.

Tancred reigned in the horses as they approached the edge of the forest. He dismounted and approached the back of the carriage. On passing he shot Richmond a quick look.

"What's happening?" Alaric asked Richmond as Tancred rummaged around at the back.

"We're at the edge of the forest. There are bandits everywhere. It is very dangerous to travel without an armed escort," Richmond explained.

"Then why don't we get an armed escort. I am sure you have enough money and no one needs to know who we are." The words made sense, but Richmond knew Tancred would never allow it and either way it was too late.

"That may be right, but we still can't risk being discovered. Tancred is getting our swords. We are all capable of defending ourselves, even you." Richmond kept his voice low as he noticed Delbert was near the window.

Before Alaric had a chance to speak Tancred opened the carriage door. First he handed Richmond his weapon, a large double handed sword, then he gave Alaric a much slender sword. Alaric pulled the blade a couple of inches from its scabbard so he could see the steel. There was something very familiar about it. The hilt felt natural in his hand. He had never once thought he might be a great warrior, but since he had a sword he thought it might be true. He wanted to draw it, but there was no room in the carriage.

"Now we must all be vigilant. The ride through the forest is a good three hours. We must be aware the bandits will see the carriage as an easy target. We cannot let them get the jump on us." It felt as thought it was a speech from a general to his legions.

"I will not let you down," Delbert said.

Tancred was about to say something to him, but the look on Richmond's face told him not to. Alaric was glad there was no argument. He knew the other two thought Delbert was part of the assassination plot against him, but he felt the man was important to him.

Once Tancred was back in the driver's seat they continued along the highway. The trees soon loomed up on either side almost completely blocking out the sun. The gloom added to the suspense of an impending attack. Alaric peered through the window into the forest. The shadows were thick under the trees making it difficult to see. Occasionally something moved in the corner of his vision, but when he tried to focus on it there was nothing there. Alaric had a bad feeling that there was someone or something watching them.

It did not take long before they were stopped by two men on horseback. Tancred remained calm and made sure the men couldn't see his sword. He wanted to see what they wanted first before he threatened them. He hoped they were just fellow travellers, but by the looks of them he knew they were not.

"I am afraid that I am going to have to lighten your load." The man spoke with an arrogant tone.

"And I am afraid that we can't do that. I don't think the two of you can take on the four of us," Tancred kept his voice level.

Delbert sat nervously in his saddle. The only weapon he had was a small cudgel which he kept in front of his saddle pommel. He tried to look the part of a bodyguard, but he failed miserably. There was no way he would scare anyone.

"I think you should have paid more money for your security guard. It looks as though a strong breeze could blow him off his horse. You may be able wield the sword, but I am certain your friends in the carriage wouldn't know the pointy end from the blunt one."

"I would think again if I were you. I could take the both of you without the help of anyone else." Tancred believed in what he was saying, but really didn't want to test the theory. He showed his sword, but did not take it out of its sheath.

Tancred's confidence had the men shaken. "Be that as it may, but the problem you have is the half a dozen archers in the trees. You would be dead before you drew your sword." The arrogance had left the man's voice.

Tancred started by laughing, but his eyes remained fixed on the man's. "If there were men in the trees we wouldn't be having this conversation. No, I think you two are on your way back or to somewhere and have come across us by accident." Tancred stroked his chin. "Now that you know that I know that you're alone you are hoping you're going to get out of this situation alive." Tancred paused for a response.

"Go on." The man was now clearly uncomfortable.

"This is your lucky day. I am in no mood to be killing anyone. However I cannot let you go free either. I am sure that if I let you go then you will run back to your friends and then come after us. Now as much as I believe we could beat your entire gang we simply don't have the time. Therefore my guard here will tie you to a nearby tree. I'm sure that your friends will come for you before the wild animals do. Now if you would kindly relinquish your weapons we will be on our way." Tancred kept the smile from his face as he spoke. His words wouldn't have the same effect if his face wasn't hard.

The two bandits looked at each other before unstrapping their swords and letting them fall to the ground. They looked at Tancred who returned their glare. He waited a moment before shaking his head. The bandits sighed and unstrapped their daggers which were concealed under their pants. Tancred thought for a moment and when he was satisfied that they had no more weapons he stepped down from the driver's seat.

The two men were safely tied to a tree in a matter of minutes and Alaric watched out the window as the carriage trundled passed them. They glared threateningly at Alaric. He could tell that they were afraid; even though they looked menacing he knew it was only a façade. He didn't know their fate, but he knew it was not going to be good. Deep down he knew they were not evil; they did what they did to survive. It was not the life they had dreamt about when they were children. The life had been thrust upon them and it was for that reason that he called out for Tancred to stop.

"What is it Dyrk?" Tancred's voice was thick with annoyance as he stopped the horses. He was beginning to lose his patience with Dyrk's attitude and it showed in his own.

"Let the men go." Alaric's voice dripped with command. It was enough for Tancred to take a moment before he spoke.

"Have you lost your mind? These are dangerous people. If we let them go then they will come back with the rest of their gang," Tancred warned.

"If they come back then we will deal with them. At this moment in time we will show compassion." Alaric would not be deterred.

"This is not up for discussion." Tancred flicked the reins and started the horses on their way again.

"Delbert," Alaric poked his head out and spoke to the man who was riding next to them. "If you wish to continue with us you will do as I command."

Delbert was surprised at the command which remained in Alaric's voice. He was no longer the spoilt son of a nobleman. He was the General of an army. There was nothing in his voice that left contradiction. Delbert simply dismounted and did as he was told.

"Drive on," even though the carriage was still moving Alaric felt as though he need to say it.

Richmond's mouth was open as he was staring at Alaric. Even as the Lord of his land he had never commanded with such a presence. He had no doubt that the man sitting next to him did not believe that he was the son of a noble. He knew he would have to be extra careful with what he said.

"What?" Alaric asked in his most deferential voice. He was now playing the part again.

"Exactly what I should be asking you. That was something different," Richmond didn't know what to say.

"I didn't do anything." Alaric's feigned look of confusion did the job.

The look of confusion was enough to silence Richmond's next question. The physician had told him that he could have sudden flashes of memory recovery. Normally the memory would stay, but in rare occasions the flashes would only last for a moment. Richmond had to wonder if this was the case. He had his doubts, but he still could not voice them.

Alaric smiled as he looked out of the window. The doubt was the only thing that kept his secret. Something had opened inside him. He didn't know exactly what it was and he didn't know if he could control it. A power had come over him and he knew what he wanted and there was nothing that could stop him. The thought was somewhat scary.

They had not been travelling for more than half an hour before they were stopped by more bandits. This time Tancred was not as confident as he was with the first two. There were three bandits standing on the road in front of them. He could see at least another two in the trees, one to either side of them.

"Drop the reins and step away from the carriage." The man, standing in the middle, spoke with a deep voice.

Tancred thought about trying to charge, but he knew that there was every chance he would soon be hit by an arrow. The odds of escaping were slim to none. It was Alaric who caused him to make his decision.

"Do as they say!" Alaric commanded "These are the men we have been looking for," he whispered to Richmond.

Tancred wasn't sure exactly what he meant, but he had to take his advice.

"Tell the other two to get out of the carriage and tell your guard to dismount."

Alaric led the way as he exited the carriage. He carried his sword in his left hand. He still felt connected to the blade, the same way he felt connected to the large tome. He felt safe with it in his hand. He knew that bandits were going to instruct him to drop it. He had yet to decide what he was going to do. If they saw the value in his sword there was no doubt they would steal it and he couldn't let that happen.

Once Richmond was out of the carriage and Delbert was off his horse the lead bandit spoke again. "Drop your weapon, nobleman, you're no match for us. All we want is your money, but if we have to take your life then so be it."

Alaric thought about leaving his sword behind, but the threat to his life was enough to change his mind. He didn't know exactly how he was going to defeat the bandits, but he knew that he could not surrender.

"I will not surrender to you. If you wish to fight then you will die." Alaric's voice wasn't as confident as it had previously been.

All the bandits in view started laughing. The lead bandit motioned for someone to join them from the woods once he had finished laughing. A man, holding a bow and arrow aimed directly at Alaric, walked out of the forest. His eyes didn't leave his prey. Alaric had no doubts if he made a wrong move there would soon be an arrow protruding from his chest. The sudden threat did nothing to perturb him.

"And this threat is supposed to worry me?" Alaric asked with a mocking tone.

"Just a warning. There are a dozen more archers hidden in the forest. I would advise very strongly that you drop your weapon and surrender."

Delbert looked up at the archer. Instantly his composure changed. His face went bright red and he took a step forward. Alaric noticed the change and held out his hand to impede his advance.

"What are you doing?" Alaric kept his voice low.

"That man, the one holding the bow and arrow," Delbert spoke through clenched teeth.

"What about him?" Alaric asked.

Delbert pointed at the archer and spoke so everyone could hear. "He's the man who came to town and stole my family."

"I didn't steal your family, they left with me willingly."

Delbert took the bait. He tried to free himself from Alaric, but it was no good. Alaric increased his grip so the man couldn't move. Delbert was surprised at how strong the nobleman's son was.

"This is getting us nowhere." Alaric spoke to Delbert.

"I whole heartedly agree. I believe it's time for action. Either you surrender or die." The lead bandit spoke.

"I don't think so, but I believe there may be another solution. Take us to your campsite. I wish to speak to your leader." Alaric's words brought another round of laughter from the bandits.

"And what makes you think that we will do what you say?"

"Because if you don't you will all die here today." Alaric's words were cold as ice.

"Enough." Tancred barked from the front of the carriage. "You must let us go. Our mission is of the utmost urgency. You can have our money, but please let us keep the carriage."

"You are in no position to ask for anything. We will take what we want and you will be thankful if we leave you with your lives." The lead bandit turned his attention to Tancred.

"This is your last chance. What will your decision be?" Alaric felt a sudden surge of energy as he prepared for the impending attack. It was clear the bandits were not going to surrender. He didn't know what he was going to do, but he had a feeling he was doing the right thing.

"Fire!" The lead bandit raised his hand and then quickly lowered his arm.

In unison a dozen twangs could be heard as the archers released their arrows. Alaric raised his arms out in front of him with his palms facing forward. Just before the arrows struck their targets they froze in mid-air. They stayed there for a second before they dropped to the ground. No one could believe what they saw.

"Fire again!" The head bandit was the first to recover, but there was no response to his command. "Fire, or I will be the one who takes your head off."

The second command, with the added threat, had a greater effect. The archers all fired again, this time in a staggered attack. Each time an arrow came within a foot of its target it would freeze for a second before dropping to the ground. Everyone watched on in horror as the arrows couldn't reach their targets.

"Now I think you will take me to your leader now." Alaric spoke when the arrows stopped.

The lead bandit dropped his head. There was nothing left for him to do. He could try charging the group, but there was a greater risk all of his men would be slain. If he could stop arrows in their paths there was no telling what else he could do. With a sigh of regret he motioned for everyone to follow him.

Chapter 15: A New Friend

The forest floor was too rough to travel on so, they left the carriage on the side of the highway. Neither Richmond nor Tancred wanted to the leave it, but Alaric had insisted they visit the bandit's campsite. There was no denying Alaric was in control of the situation as they unhitched the horses and unloaded their packs.

They took the five horses with them as it was easier to hide the carriage without them attached. Alaric assured the others the carriage would be safe where they left it. Tancred shook his head as he walked away. He had believed he had been in charge, but it was clear that he was not. He didn't know when he had lost command. Alaric had wrested it away when he wasn't paying attention.

There was no doubt that Alaric had regained his memory. Richmond couldn't be sure when it happened, but he was sure it had been for a while. He wanted nothing more than to talk to him, but he couldn't whilst the bandits were around. That conversation was going to have to wait.

They reached the campsite without being harmed. The bandits didn't look happy and the bandit leading them didn't know how he was going to explain things to their leader. There were sixteen bandits in total and they were defeated by two nobles, a wagon driver and a poor excuse for a guard.

The bandit thought there was something strange about the younger of the nobles. He had a presence that commanded attention, more so than any other minor noble he had stolen from before. Normally nobles were just thankful to be alive, but this man stood up for himself and not only that but he defeated them. He would not have believed his men if he hadn't seen if with his own eyes. He only hoped the other men would tell their leader the same story as some would be inclined to lie to further their own agenda.

The campsite was an hour's walk from the highway. It was deep in the forest hidden behind thick growth. One could easily pass by without even knowing it was there. The tension grew within the group of bandits when they came close. It was obvious that no one wanted to admit what had happened. They would be the laughing stock of the forest. They were part of the largest gang and had great respect amongst the other bandits.

Alaric walked side by side with the lead bandit as they entered the campsite. He wanted to make sure from the start that everyone knew he came as an equal and not as a captive. It was not going to bode well for the head of their party.

The leader of the bandits was a large man by the name of Guido. He had short black hair and a bushy brown beard. If it wasn't for his immense stature he would look comical. His strength was second to none within the bandits and his height only beaten by one. He stood up when he saw the group return and frowned when he saw Alaric walking side by side with his commander.

"What is this all about Horst? Why are these men with you? I gave you strict instructions not to take any prisoners. If they were giving you trouble then you should have slain them and hidden the bodies. Now what am I going to do?" Guido didn't sound happy.

"I know what you said, but this is not my fault

"I asked Horst to bring us to you. It seems there is a problem that we need to solve," Alaric started.

"And who do you think you are to address me in such a manner?"

"I am Dyrk, but that's not the point. This is Delbert. He believes that one of your gang has kidnapped his wife and child," Alaric explained.

"I don't believe that is true. We are not in the business of kidnapping. It always ends up messy when you start playing around with people's lives."

"That man stole my wife and son away." Delbert pointed at the man who he believed kidnapped his family.

Guido looked at the man in question. "I didn't steal anyone. I think you have me mistaken for someone else," the man tried to defend himself.

"Delbert, is that you?" The voice came from one of the small tents that scattered the campsite.

The tent flap opened and out came a woman of middle age. She had blonde hair and a body of someone who had given birth. She had a broad smile on her face. "What are you doing here?"

The confusion was not just saved for Delbert. The men standing around all looked at each other, hoping that someone had answers. Delbert could only stand and stare. He couldn't believe he had actually found his wife alive. The confusing part was that she was obviously not a prisoner and she didn't seem to have run away.

"Rolanda, what are you doing here?" Delbert finally asked.

"I don't understand. Didn't you get the letter I wrote for you?" Rolanda now seemed just as confused as everyone else.

"What letter?" Delbert had lost all his fury.

"I wrote you a letter explaining where I went. This is Roland, my brother. I grew up with these bandits. Roland came to town to tell me our father was dying. I had to leave in a hurry to see him one last time. I wrote a letter telling you where I had gone so you wouldn't worry," Rolanda explained.

"So you didn't leave me?" Delbert could hardly bring himself to ask.

"Of course not!" Rolanda rushed towards him and threw herself into his arms. Tears started rushing down Delbert's face.

Delbert had never known about Rolanda's history. Whenever he had asked she had always told him that it was too painful. Her life was with him and whatever had happened in the past was in the past. As much as Delbert didn't like the response he never pushed her further.

As they embraced Delbert's son raced from the tent and joined them. Delbert couldn't believe his luck. He had truly believed that he would never see his family again.

"What do we do now?" Richmond whispered to Tancred who was standing next to him.

"I don't know. This is completely unexpected," was the reply. "I think you should ask your nephew."

Richmond gave Tancred a hard look. "I think we both know he is no longer my nephew." Richmond looked around quickly to see if anyone had heard him. He breathed a sigh of relief when he realised no one had.

"Well this explains a lot, but it still doesn't forgive you barging into my land without my permission," Guido spoke with conviction.

"I do apologise for intruding, but there is more than one reason for my visit," Alaric spoke mysteriously.

"Do tell. I would love to hear the story of how you convinced sixteen of my best men to invite you along for a holiday." Guido crossed his arms around his chest.

"Of course, but I think this conversation is better done in private," Alaric suggested. Everyone just started at him. "Is there somewhere we can talk?" Alaric added when there was no response.

Guido thought for a moment. He looked around his campsite. All of his men were still looking at him. He had to make a tough stand or he risked losing their respect. On the other hand something was telling him to listen to what the strange man had to say. He had a very commanding appearance and there was not a scrap of fear about him. Guido had a feeling he was going to regret getting out of his tent that morning.

"Very well, we can speak in my tent." Guido made a sign for Alaric to follow him.

Guido's tent was almost in the centre of the campsite. It was larger than any of the other tents. Inside there was a large throne like chair on a raised dais. There was another room at the back of the tent via an entrance behind the mock throne. Guido quickly moved to sit in the throne leaving Alaric standing before him.

"Well what is it that you want from me?" The question was loaded. Guido was dying to give the order to have him and his friends put to death.

"I am here to recruit for my army." Alaric got straight to the point. He continued speaking before Guido had a chance to interrupt. "My name is not Dyrk and I am not the son of a noble. As you may know the Evil One has broken out of his prison to the north and is now roaming somewhere in the Seven Kingdoms. He agents and his army are also here. The Alliance marches to fight, but it needs more men before the final battle. It will be travelling through here in a few weeks and I need you to gather all the bandits together and join it."

"Okay then, if your name is not Dyrk what is it and why should I help you? You come in here and demand that I join some pointless crusade. There is always some threat to the Kingdom, but it is never a threat to me and mine. I don't care who rules, we will always survive in the forest." Guido gave the response that Alaric was expecting.

"It doesn't matter who I am. All you have to know if that you must play your part. It is no coincidence that brought me to your campsite. What you must understand is that Nyrra is like no tyrant you have ever seen before. He doesn't just want to take your land he wants to take your lives. He feeds on death and misery. He won't let you live out your life in the forest, he will hunt you down and he will kill you. This fight involves everyone. No one can hide from it." Alaric felt a tingle through his body. It was similar to when he stopped the arrows, but it was more subtle than before.

"I don't think I will be able to assist you. I am sure you believe you are doing the right thing, but we are a small gang of bandits who do what we do to survive. We do not get involved in the politics of the outside world."

Alaric wasn't sure what he needed to do. He didn't know why, but he knew that he needed to help someone by the name of Bern. He didn't know who Bern was, but he knew he was trying to help him. Bern, he thought, was also trying to save the world from utter destruction and that was enough to make him try. With his memory still scratchy he wasn't sure exactly what he should say to try and convince Guido.

"So I don't think we are going to be able to help you," Guido had been talking whilst Alaric was deep in thought. "I will grant you all our hospitalities whilst you stay, but I would advise you to leave before sundown."

Alaric left the tent. He didn't think it was going to be that hard to get Guido to do what he wanted. As he left the tent the reality of what he was trying to do sunk in.

"What's wrong?" Delbert asked as Alaric walked away from the tent.

Alaric looked up into the smiling face of Delbert. He thought about telling him the entire story, but decided not the burden the man with his problems. "Nothing. How is your reunion?"

"Wonderful, you have no idea how grateful I am. Now please tell me what happened with you and the gang's leader. I may be able to help you." Delbert seemed so concerned that Alaric felt compelled to tell him.

"Now you must not tell anyone what I tell you." Alaric started before beginning his tale.

Delbert listened to Alaric's story with bated breath. When he finished there was a large smile on his face. "Then it is quite fortunate that you told me your problems."

"Well, what is it that you have to say?" Alaric was somewhat annoyed with Delbert's attitude.

"You see, my wife's father was the leader of this gang and as are the way of things in the world the first born child inherits his position. As you can guess, Rolanda is the first born and therefore has claim to the position of leader. Guido just assumed the position whilst her father has been too sick to lead. Now that my wife is in charge, or soon will be, I can help with your dilemma." Delbert seemed quite pleased with himself.

"That is good news. If you can take care of this situation then I can continue on my way. Now please do not tell my companions of this tale. I think that it's best that they do not find out," Alaric explained.

The two men said a quick goodbye before Alaric left to find his two companions. He found them standing nervously around a group of bandits. Alaric didn't know what had happened, but the bandits didn't look happy. He thought about leaving them and continuing on by himself, but the thought only stayed in his head for a moment. He was still curious about their motives and he didn't think they deserved the death the bandits would give them.

They were all escorted back to their carriage by a couple of bandits, who seemed displeased with their latest job. They grumbled quietly to themselves the entire journey. Alaric thanked them when they reached the carriage and all they did was grunt at him before disappearing back to the forest.

"You're lucky we didn't end up dead." Tancred scolded Alaric as he harnessed the horses.

"Be that as it may, but we are alive and we have done a great deed for one of your citizens. Now I do believe I shall retire to the carriage."

"He knows he's not Dyrk." Richmond kept his voice low as he helped Tancred.

"I figured as much. Yet he still pretends to be, which makes me wonder what his game is?" Tancred pondered. "Until we know what he's up to I think we should play along."

Richmond shook his head. "I don't think there is anything to be gained by this trickery. If he knows that he's not Dyrk then I think we should explain to him what we are doing."

"Let us wait until we reach the capital. We cannot risk him leaving us until we speak with Unwin. It is of the upmost importance."

Richmond was still not happy. He was sure all the secrecy was not going to end well, yet he had to take his advisor's words on board. He would at least wait until they were out of the forest. There were still many bandits in the forest and they would have to be careful. They couldn't rely on Alaric to save them next time.

The remainder of the journey passed without incident. The forest was strangely quiet, as if it was waiting for them to leave before it came to life again. There was something very peculiar that even made Alaric uncomfortable.

Everyone relaxed slightly once they had reached the outskirts, but they didn't truly feel at ease until they reached the village of Lord's Wait. Tancred was quick to lead them to the one and only inn. Not only was it the only inn, it was also the only stables, the only tavern and the only smithy. The owner was a short, fat and bald man by the name of Emil d'Reiche. Emil seemed excited at the new arrivals when he met them at the front desk.

"Welcome to the Lord's Wanderer, I trust that you made it through the forest unharmed?" There was a large smile that looked out of place on his face.

"We did indeed," Richmond said, not giving anything away. "We require two rooms for the night, one for my advisor and myself and one for my nephew."

"You are very lucky to pass through without a group of guards. Now, say, don't I know you from somewhere? I am sure I recognise your face." Emil peered at Richmond.

"I'm afraid not. I am but a minor noble from the north-west provinces. This is the first time I have made the pilgrimage to the capital. I have been told I have a very familiar face." Richmond fumbled through his lies.

"That must be it. Now I trust your horses have been taken care of?" Emil continued in his friendly manner.

"Yes, thank you. You run a very fine business here. I will be sure to mention it to King Unwin when I see him." Richmond smiled as he spoke.

"Thank you my Lord. King Unwin has stayed here before, but I'm sure a good word from you will go a long way." Emil's comment, scything as it may be, lost itself on Richmond who was more concerned on getting to his room.

"We wish to be away early in the morning. I would appreciate if you bring the evening meal to our rooms. Be sure I will pay well for your assistance." Richmond continued his pre-planned oration.

"Of course my Lord and let me know if there is anything else we can do to make your stay more pleasant. Here at the Lord's Wanderer we pride ourselves on offering the very best of services in the land." Emil bowed his head slightly as Richmond turned to walk away.

When the three had left the inn's entrance the smile from Emil's face turned to a sneer. Emil new exactly who had been standing before him and he didn't appreciate the lie. He called out to his porter who came promptly.

"See our new guests receive their luggage," was all he said.

There was much to be done. He had been waiting for such guests to arrive and he was not going to let them down. The smile returned to his face as he thought of the future.

***

Alaric had been quite happy to resume his reading. Things had felt familiar to him during the day, but nothing that jogged his memory. He hoped the book would help. At first he thought there was something coming back to him, but the more he read the more futile it became. When there came a knock on the door Alaric's rage was close to breaking point.

Opening the door his anger left his body in such a rush it made his head spin. He took four steps backwards allowing the man on the other side of the door to enter the room. Alaric knew instantly who it was.

"Your meal is ready?" Emil spoke with a kindly voice.

"Thank you, but I'm not hungry." Alaric's voice was shaky, he continued backing away until he was sitting on his bed.

"But it has been bought and paid for," Emil said as he walked further into the room. "Now I'm sure your uncle will be displeased if you don't eat something. It is a long ride to the capital tomorrow, so you'll need your strength.

"Leave it there and I will eat it shortly." Alaric tried to contain himself.

"Good then, I will come back shortly with your dessert." Emil left the room.

As soon as the door was shut Alaric let out the breath that he had been holding since Emil had entered the room. Now he had a chance to prepare himself. His sword was hanging on a hook behind the door. He quickly snatched it and instantly felt better with it in his hand. Next thing he had to do was find the room the other two were in.

He looked at the food sitting harmlessly on his table. The roasted meat and vegetables did smell appetising. The aroma almost forced him to sit and eat, but his mind overpowered him. The last assassination attempt had been poison in his food and he had no doubt his food had been poisoned again.

Outside the room the hallway was vacant. He looked nervously up and down before he left. He had no idea which room the other two were in, but if his suspicions were correct they would not be close. There was no point knocking on the doors close to his.

Alaric took one step forward when he heard footsteps coming from behind him. He looked over his shoulder, but the sound was coming from around the corner. Without waiting to see who it was he took off down the corridor.

He rounded a corner and passed a number of doors before he was compelled to stop. Something was telling him not to go past the door to his left. He thought about putting his ear to it and listening to who was inside, but the sound of footsteps could be heard again. Instead of waiting he turned the handle and pushed it open. He didn't wait to see who was inside before closing the door behind him. To his relief he had found the room that contained Richmond and Tancred.

"What in the Gods' names are you doing Dyrk?" Tancred was taken aback.

They had finished their dinner and were drinking ale. They both looked surprised to see Alaric come barging into their room. The look on his face only added to their confusion. Alaric rested against the door and listened to sound of passing footsteps outside and only relaxed when he was sure they were gone.

"What are you doing here?" Tancred asked again.

Alaric moved away from the door and sat on one of the beds. There was a fine covering of sweat across his forehead. It was clear something had shaken him. Neither Richmond nor Tancred could think what could have done it.

"Bad news," Alaric puffed a couple of times before he continued. "The assassin is here."

The words were enough to silence any reply they were thinking. Since Delbert was not the assassin, as they thought he was, they had relaxed a little. They had not seen anyone who they suspected of being the assassin. They had kept to the room and kept to themselves and they assumed Alaric had done the same. That narrowed down the suspects considerably.

"Who is it?" Tancred asked eventually.

"Emil, the owner of this establishment," Alaric watched their reaction closely.

"That's impossible. Emil has been the owner of this inn for many years. I have met him a number of times when I was travelling through to Kiarome." Richmond didn't sound convinced.

"You were the one who suggested that Delbert was the assassin and he was accounted for at the time, so why should it come as such a surprise that Emil is the assassin?" Alaric watched them carefully. There was a chance he was going to be able to gather some information.

"You are right Alaric," Tancred spoke deliberately. "We have not been entirely honest with you." Richmond scowled at Tancred, but he was happy he was finally being honest. "You see when you lost your memory we thought it best we stayed with the original plan that you travelled under the guise of Richmond's nephew. If you knew the truth we were afraid it might put you in danger. Now that you seem to have your memory back there is no point in continuing our ruse. However, it's still important that we treat you as Dyrk." Tancred did his best to keep his explanation short. He continued to tell Alaric everything that had happened since he had arrived in Bellarome.

"Thank you for your honesty. I think that you should have told me earlier, but better late than never." Alaric had the upper hand. The other two thought his memory had completely returned. He felt no need to tell them anything different. There was nothing they could tell him to help him remember who he really was. "Now I can tell you that Emil is the one who is trying to kill me. At least he now looks like the man who you once knew as Emil. I don't know exactly what he is, but he is definitely some kind of shape-shifter."

"I thought that was just a tale to tell naughty children. I didn't think anyone or anything could actually shape-shift. I thought that it was just a myth," Richmond said.

"The path to the Evil One does have its benefits. It's clear this is one of his agents. I don't know who he is, but he is not the owner of this inn anymore." Alaric had a fair idea who it was he was pitted against and it scared him to his bones.

"What should we do?" Richmond sounded worried.

"I need to think. I don't really know what to do," Alaric mused as he lay back on the bed.

Tancred and Richmond both armed themselves. It was the only thing they could do. If the man, or creature, they faced could shape-shift then there was no telling what else it could do. They didn't know whether their swords would be any use against a magical being, but it made them feel better. They returned to their table and sat in silence as Alaric thought.

He knew that it was one of Nyrra's Dark Knights that he faced, but he didn't know which one it was. There was something in the back of his mind telling him that he had faced a Dark Knight before and if that was the case he must have succeeded. The thought did nothing to ease the fear in his heart. Without more of his memory returning he didn't think that he would be able to face one of Nyrra's Dark Knights. He also didn't believe his two companions would be any use.

"I think we should pack up and keep travelling toward Kiarome." Alaric suggested after five minutes of quiet contemplation.

"It's very dangerous to travel the highway at night," Tancred replied.

"I think it's more dangerous staying here. It will not take long for Emil to realise I know who he is. He brought my dinner, and when he's seen that I haven't eaten it he will know. There is no telling what he will do. With his failure at Bellarome I don't think he's going to leave anything to chance," Alaric added.

"The problem is we need to get the horses and carriage from the stables. If Emil is smart he will instruct his stable boys not to help us, or at least to inform him if we were leaving," Richmond added to the confusion.

"So we are damned if we do and damned if we don't," Alaric pondered aloud.

"Then we must stay and fight," Tancred didn't sound too optimistic.

Alaric didn't like their chances, but he also didn't want to show the other two he doubted they would survive. At least they thought they had a chance. That was better than if they knew they were going to die.

"Then we find him and kill him," Alaric stood up from the bed as he spoke.

"What if you are wrong? We can't just go randomly killing people," Richmond protested the idea.

"Don't worry. There is no doubt this is the man who has been trying to kill me. The true Emil is already dead

"Even so, we have to be careful. Just because we know he is not the real Emil doesn't mean we can just walk up to him and run him through. I'm sure King Unwin will not be pleased to hear we killed one of his subjects." Tancred came to Richmond's defence.

"I don't see we have any choice. If we stay the night and not do anything about Emil then there is a good chance we will all be dead. What is it that you propose?" Alaric didn't sound convinced.

"I think we should all go to your room and wait for him. If he is after you then I am sure that he will come for you. When he does we will be able to capture and question him," Richmond suggested.

It was the best idea that they were going to get. Unless Alaric wanted to share the true identity of his assassin he was not going to be able to convince the other two they must kill him. It would be almost impossible to capture the man who looked like Emil. At least if he died whilst they were trying then they could not scold him.

Once they were back in Alaric's room it was obvious that something was wrong. Alaric's clothes had been thrown across the room. His bed was dishevelled and one of the chairs had been upturned. Someone had been looking for something.

"What were they looking for?" Richmond seemed perplexed.

"I think I know," another shot of fear rushed through Alaric's body.

As he spoke he walked towards the place where he had left *The Prophecy of the Stone*. As he suspected it was missing. That was all that had been taken. The trashing of the room was obviously a distraction from their real goal. Alaric saw through the ruse immediately. Whoever it was who broke into his room knew about the tome. He hoped it was a random hit, but he knew deep down that it was Emil. On the bright side he doubted the Dark Knight was coming back to kill him.

"What was it?" Tancred asked when Alaric had spoken.

"It was a book." Alaric replied.

Both men let out a sigh of relief. Alaric instantly realised they didn't understand the importance of it. He thought about explaining, but he didn't think they would understand. All they needed to know was that he had to get it back. He didn't truly understand its significance, but he knew that he could not let one of Nyrra's agents possess it.

"Then we have nothing to worry about," Tancred said.

"That is not exactly true." Alaric looked at both of them before he continued. "One good thing is that I don't believe we are going to be attacked tonight. The bad thing is we have the get that book back.

"Would you like to tell us why?" Tancred asked, with one eyebrow raised.

"No, but you have to trust me that it is of the utmost importance we recover the book." There was no doubt in Alaric's voice this was the right thing to do.

"Okay then. We find the book and hopefully we might get some answers to these riddles." Alaric wasn't sure if Tancred was speaking to him or Richmond.

Chapter 16: Chasing a Thief

As Alaric had expected Emil had already left the inn. He didn't completely understand why. He thought the Dark Knight's mission was to kill him, but he had decided against that to steal the prophecy. He felt a little jealous the book was more important than his life, but he was relieved to still be alive nonetheless. There was no other option but to chase down the man who was trying to kill him. He didn't know why, but he knew they needed to retrieve the prophecy from the Dark Knight.

Richmond and Tancred were relieved that the assassin had left. They both wanted to take advantage of their safety. If the threat of attack was gone then they should be able to rest for the next day's journey. Alaric insisted they leave immediately.

"We need to leave now. We can't waste any time," Alaric urged as he through his clothes back in his packs.

"I don't think that is a wise plan," Tancred interjected. "It is a dangerous road to Kiarome during the night and we don't even know if that is where he is heading."

As much as Tancred's words made sense Alaric knew exactly where the Dark Knight was headed. There was a sensation in the back of his mind leading him towards the South. He knew that it was the prophecy calling to him. It was further away than what he would have expected, but he was sure that if they left immediately then they could catch the Dark Knight before he reached Kiarome.

"We don't have any time to waste. Let's go!" Alaric didn't wait for a response as he made his way from the room.

None of the staff knew where Emil had gone. He was nowhere to be found. As much as Alaric assured them he had left they wanted to make sure. When they were positive he was no longer at the inn they made their way to the stable.

Outside the sun had already set and a crescent moon dimly lit the sky. A number of torches burned inside the stables giving enough light to see where they were walking. It didn't take long to find the stable boy who was on duty. By the looks of him he was just about to finish for the night.

"Hey boy!" Alaric called out to the stableboy as he was about to walk away.

"What do you want? My shift is over and I want to go home." His words sounded too rude to be an accident.

"I want you to treat your betters with a little respect." It was Tancred who took it upon himself to scold the boy. "Now come here and look sharp."

The boy did as he was told. He walked to where the others were standing, his head down and his hands in his pockets. It was clear he had been punished before for his attitude.

"Hands out of your pockets and look up, boy!" Tancred barked and the stableboy quickly did as he was told. Alaric was impressed with Tancred's control. He waited for the stableboy to look him in the eye before he spoke again. "We are looking for your boss. Do you know where Emil went?"

The boy looked around nervously, as if he was looking to see if anyone was watching. He lowered his head again when he answered. "No I haven't."

"Don't lie to me boy," Tancred's voice became harder. "Tell me the truth and there won't be any more trouble."

The stableboy's shoulders dropped even further. He didn't know which threat to take seriously. If he told he would be in trouble and if he didn't he would be in trouble. In the end he decided the imminent threat was the worst. "He said he was leaving for the capital. He said he had important business there. He told me that if anyone asked to tell them that he had gone into the forest." The boy's voice was raised and he looked Tancred in the eyes as he spoke.

"Is this the truth?" Tancred believed him, but he still had to ask. It would have been too suspicious if he didn't.

"Yes, sir, honest sir," the boy sounded worried.

"What do we do now?" Tancred asked Richmond.

"We go after him," Alaric was not going to be dissuaded so easily.

"At this time of night?" Tancred turned to Alaric. He had to make him understand that it wasn't worth the risk. "He has a good half hour head start. There is only a small moon out tonight so the travelling will be slow. Even if we could catch him before he reaches the capital, what are we going to do? There are plenty of nooks and crannies for him to hide in. There is just as much chance of us riding right past him." Tancred was trying to be as logical as possible. Alaric was ready to rush off after Emil, but they still didn't know what they were up against. If the man could shape-shift then there was no telling what else he could do. "I think we should stay here tonight and make a fresh start in the morning."

Alaric drew his sword and placed its blade across the stableboy's neck. "Is there anything else that you should tell us?" his voice was stern.

The stableboy was visibly shaking. Whatever it was that Emil had told him made him scared. "You should not fear us boy. Emil will not be returning. You can tell us whatever he told you to do." Tancred's kept his voice soft.

"He told me he would have me horsewhipped if I told anyone, sire. He told me he would have my entire family horsewhipped. I dare not go against the master of the inn. He is the most powerful man in the village." The boy's voice was broken as he spoke. The fear was evident in his lack of composure.

"You have nothing to fear. We will make sure that you are safe." Tancred was desperately trying to reassure the boy.

"I am sorry sire," the boy would not relent.

"Let's put it this way. If you tell us what Emil has instructed you to do then there is a chance that he will punish you for it. On the other hand if you do not tell us what Emil has instructed you to do then I will definitely punish you." Alaric skimmed his blade along the boy's neck causing a small nick to draw blood. The boy squeaked, out of surprise more than any pain. "Do we understand each other?" Alaric knew the soft approach wasn't going to work. The boy obviously needed to fear something more than an innkeeper.

Richmond didn't agree with what Alaric was doing, but he couldn't bring himself to speak. They needed the information and it seemed to be the only way they were going to get it.

"Yes sire, I will tell you," the boy was terrified, even though Alaric had lowered his sword. "The boss said to me that no one was to leave tonight. He told me that if anyone asked to leave then I was to deny them entrance to the stables. Then he told me when they had left to let their horses go and burn their wagon. I didn't want to sire, but he gave me no choice. There has been something strange about the boss over the last couple of days. He ain't been his usual self."

Alaric looked at the other two. There was concern on his face. After hearing the boy's words he knew that they were right. There was no way they would be able to catch Emil during the night. If the man was who he suspected him to be then they would be in great peril. There would be no doubt there would be a trap somewhere down the highway.

"You should go home now boy. Have a good night sleep and don't come to work tomorrow. In a day's time this will all have settled down and it will be safe for you to return." Alaric didn't know where the words came from, but he knew that it was what the stableboy needed to hear.

Richmond and Tancred stood and waited for the boy's racing footsteps to disappear into the night. When they were sure he had left they turned to Alaric and waited to hear what he had to say.

"We shall return to our rooms and stay the night. Firstly you shall come to my room and we shall discuss out next move." Alaric didn't wait for a reply. He simply turned around and walked back into the inn.

Tancred looked at Richmond who in turn shrugged his shoulders. Whatever the reason for Alaric changing his mind really didn't matter. They had achieved what they wanted to and that was all that mattered.

Alaric felt a little better once he was back inside. There was something disturbing about the night air, but there was no doubt in his mind he had made the right decision. Even though Emil had a good head start Alaric knew where he was going. All he had to do was to work out how to catch him. He knew exactly where *the Prophecy of the Stone* was and he felt as though if he closed his eyes he would be able to point to its exact location. Even if the Dark Knight was able to change his appearance again he would still be able to locate the book.

"What was that all about?" Richmond asked when they reached Alaric's room. He had controlled his temper whilst he was in front of the stableboy, but since they were alone he could not contain himself. "You say we have to chase Emil down and then you suddenly back flip. That boy is going to be telling his story all over the village. Whatever chance we had in secrecy is now gone."

"You have to think before you speak. Remember that this is our land. We know what people think and how they act. You have to let us take the lead," Tancred added his own lecture.

"Are you quite finished?" Alaric had his back to them as they scolded him. He turned to face them when it was his turn to speak. The look on his face immediately silenced the other two. They simply nodded their agreement before taking a seat at the table. "Very good then. I know a little more about this situation then you do. Although my memory has not completely returned I do have an idea about what we're up against." Alaric took a deep breath as he decided on what to say next. He knew Richmond and Tancred were keeping secrets from him. If they were going to be able to retrieve the prophecy then they would need to work together. "I believe the man we now know as Emil is one of Nyrra's Dark Knights." He paused as he waited to the information to sink in. "Things have just become a whole lot worse."

"What are we going to do? If he had left to go to the city then maybe you are safe. It has to be a promising sign that he no longer wants to kill you." Richmond had calmed down and was now trying to think logically.

"I don't think that this is a good thing. Obviously Emil believes the prophecy is more important than my life."

"What is the significance of *the Prophecy of the Stone?*" Tancred sounded worried and Alaric didn't sound pleased at his question. Tancred remembered seeing the book when he was going through Alaric's possessions at Bellarome.

"*The Prophecy of the Stone* is the one true prophecy," Alaric replied softly.

"Then things are more perilous then we first believed." Tancred looked at Richmond. Richmond nodded before Tancred returned his nod. "There are things you need to know."

"How do you know about the prophecy?"

"We are part of an ancient Order of Knights." Tancred started slowly. "We are part of the Knights of the Prophecy. We are bound to the success of that ancient text. The original prophecy was stolen from our main chapel in Castalia over a thousand years ago. There are many copies, but no one knows if they are accurate. There are many subtle differences in each. It is as if the person who rewrote them added his own agenda."

"So what does all this mean?" Alaric sounded confused.

"If you are right then *the Prophecy of the Stone* might actually be a true copy of the original." Tancred silently cursed himself for not taking more notice of the tome when he saw it in Bellarome. He had been too focused on Alaric to take any interest in the book. "That is the only reason why a Dark Knight would steal it."

"We are here to help." Richmond said as he felt Tancred was getting off topic. "We serve the prophecy and we go where ever it leads us. We had to be sure you were who you said you were. With the Evil One loose he has a lot of spies in the Seven Kingdoms. He infects the prophecy with his evil and without the original copy we cannot be certain."

Alaric thought about telling them that he believed *the Prophecy of the Stone* was the original and even with that they could not be certain of its meaning, but decided that he couldn't completely trust them. There had been too many lies and they would have to prove themselves for him to trust them completely.

"When you lost your memory we thought it was better to play along with our original ruse. We didn't know how you would react so we thought the lie would be just as good as the truth."

"Okay, say I believe what you're telling me. If this is all written out in the prophecy then what do we do now?" Alaric asked.

"As I assume you have read the prophecy you will know it's not that easy to read. Many of our order have spent their entire lives trying to decipher some prophecy or another. No one has been able to completely translate the words. Some people have been able to understand certain passages however. All we know is that we are to take you to Kiarome to see King Unwin. It seems we now have another job to complete. We must also recover the prophecy from this Emil character. Our major problem is we won't know what he looks like. He could be one of any of the thousands of citizens who call Kiarome home."

"That is not exactly true." Alaric had a smile on his face.

"What do you mean?" Richmond asked when it was clear he wasn't going to elaborate on his own.

"It takes a few days to recover from changing. Since he has changed twice already recently I would assume it will take even longer for him to recover. I don't think he will stop on the way to Kiarome. He will have to use the same guise when he reaches his destination. That gives us a great advantage." Alaric seemed somewhat pleased with himself.

"Then why has he gone to Kiarome. Wouldn't it make more sense for him to hide in the country somewhere? At least until he was able to change his appearance. This doesn't make any sense," Tancred returned.

Alaric knew the answer before the question was asked. He also knew he had given away too much information. Until he was able to remember more he would keep what he knew to himself, unless it was imperative they all knew.

"The answer to that question is I'm sure we'll find out in due course. Let it be known that none of this has happened by pure chance. I think we will get the answers we seek once we have arrived in the city." Alaric was finished speaking. He had all the answers he wanted and had given all that he was going to give.

Alaric's words brought the conversation to an end. They were not going to solve any of the many questions that had been left unanswered. All they could do now was wait for morning and make a fresh start.

In the morning they were on the road at first light. The stableboy had not done what his master had ordered and they found their animals unharmed and their carriage untouched. The morning stableboy fetched their things and readied their horses without question. Alaric had been worried there may have been trouble leaving, but they were back on the road quicker than anticipated.

Instead of riding in the back of the carriage Alaric had ordered that stable boy to have Adelanta saddled. Now they all knew who he was he didn't see the point of keeping up the charade. Tancred had claimed it was important for everyone to still think that he was Richmond's nephew. Alaric agreed to go by the name Dyrk, but would not ride in the back of the carriage.

Adelanta felt much happier with Alaric on his back. He had never liked being used as a pack animal. There was a new spring to his step as he carried Alaric along the small dirt track of the village. Tormenta, on the other hand, seemed even more put out having to carry the load. He snorted at his fellow stallion before finally accepting his role.

It was much easier for the carriage to travel on the smooth highway once they were out of Lord's Wait. It would take them most of the day to get to Kiarome, but if they pushed the horses hard, which they were planning to do, they would reach the capital by mid-afternoon.

The day was overcast and the clouds threatened to break. The weather seemed to reflect their moods. As their emotions stayed in check so did the weather. There was no unusual traffic on the highway. They passed merchants every now and again and they passed by without saying a word. No one seemed to give them a second glance. Despite his fancy clothes Alaric looked the part of the armed guard, more so than Delbert had.

Alaric was tempted at stages to stick his heels into Adelanta and make a dash for Kiarome. He could feel the prophecy tugging at him. It was more general than it had been the night before, but there was no doubt Emil had reached the city.

By mid-afternoon they crested a small hill. On the other side they could see Kiarome, the capital of Darshival. The sight of the city took Alaric's breath away. He had seen many cities, he knew, but he had never seen anything like Kiarome. It was the second largest city in the Seven Kingdoms.

Like most cities the huge outer walls encased it leaving only scattered farmhouses on the outside. The royal palace was on the Eastern side of the city, its three white towers rose up above the city walls and looked out over the city like a loving father.

Like all other cities security at the main gates had been increased. It was more difficult to control the flow of traffic of a city the size of Kiarome. The guards did their best, but they made very few friends. At least this time Alaric had a legitimate excuse for entering the city and Richmond would have the appropriate documentation.

"What is your business in the city?" The head guard spoke in an officious tone.

There were at least twenty guards on duty. The main gate was twenty paces wide and a daunting task for the guards. They couldn't stop everyone who was coming and going. All they could do was stop the ones who either looked suspicious or they didn't recognise. It was only out of pure chance they were stopped at all, let alone by the head guard himself.

"We are here to see the King," Tancred kept his voice low as he didn't want the people passing by to hear.

"Papers," was all the guard said in reply.

Tancred rifled through his coat until he found the parchment he was looking for. Alaric hoped there would be no problem gaining entrance. He felt a tugging at the back of his mind. He knew the prophecy was close. It could only be a couple of paces away. He looked around at the people coming and going. He felt as though one of them might hold the key to finding Emil.

"These all seem to be in order. Though I will give you word of advice," the guard peered around slyly to see if anyone was watching them. When he was sure that no one could hear he spoke again. "There is something strange with King Unwin. He is not the same man that he was a year ago. He has a new advisor and I believe that is part of the problem. Now move it along."

Tancred wanted to ask for more information, but it was clear that the guard was not going to help. He flicked the reins and started the horses into the city. Alaric sat for a moment before he followed behind. The feeling he needed to stay was almost overwhelming. There was something drawing him to the gate. The traffic was starting to build and there was no way for him to return. Once they were through the gate the feeling disappeared. He didn't know if this was a good thing or a bad thing.

Tancred continued with the traffic for a couple of hundred paces before it started to thin out. Slowly he moved the carriage across the road until he was able to turn off into a side street. Every now and then Alaric would get an urge to turn off into other side streets. Even Adelanta would get restless when they passed by those streets. Until he knew what the feelings meant he would continue to ride next to the carriage.

Once they were out of view from the main streets Tancred reined the carriage to a halt. He motioned for Alaric to join him in the carriage.

"I know the guard who stopped us in front of the main gate. He would not have done it unless he had a good reason. I believe he was trying to tell me something. The obvious answer was what he told me, but I know there is something more underlying in his words," Tancred mused. "I think we should find an inn and stay there while we ask around. We need more information before we go into the palace. Something is not right and I don't feel like walking into a trap."

"I think that Tancred is correct. There is more to this than meets the eye. I don't think a little more information could hurt. No one knows we are in the city, so it shouldn't be too hard to gather information. I think we should change our appearance though. Three rich men asking questions about the King might start people talking. Three poor men talking to people at a tavern are much less suspicious," Alaric added.

"Okay, we will do it your way, but let it be known that I believe we can gather more information inside the palace, not outside in the city." Richmond had to concede to the idea, but he would not concede the point.

It didn't take them long to find an inn that would be suitable to their needs. Since they would be socializing away from the inn they didn't have to keep up the pretences. The first port of call was to find some clothes suitable for their purpose. It was Tancred's job to do that as he was the only one who wasn't dressed like a noble.

Richmond sat by the window in their small room whilst they waited for Tancred to return. He was more than a little concerned with their plan. He knew the city could be dangerous and the parts where they were looking for the information were the worst. He was sure things couldn't have gotten so bad in the palace that they would not be safe.

Alaric sat on the other side of the room. He could not shake the feeling he should be out looking for Emil. The man was somewhere in the city and he possessed the prophecy. The worst part was he didn't know what Emil planned on using it for. There was something very disturbing about the fact he would prefer to steal the prophecy and not kill him. It didn't make any sense.

The tension was thick in the room when Tancred returned. It had taken him a long time to find the market where he could buy second hand apparel. They wouldn't have had the same effect if they wore new clothes, regardless of how poor they looked.

With their new clothes they looked the part and the fact that they had been on the road all day and had not washed also helped. No one would mistake them for being nobles.

The sun had well and truly set when they left the inn. There was no moon in the sky which made streets very dark. The only light came from the windows of the houses where people were home. The poor district didn't have any lanterns, except on the main streets. It was a very dangerous part of the city and the night watch avoided it unless they were called into action and only then for emergencies. Richmond was again ruing their decision not to go straight to the palace.

The night was still young and they received no problems as they made their way to the nearest tavern. They were only just more comfortable inside the tavern than out on the streets. Inside there was a strange smell of stale alcohol, sweat and pipe tobacco. There was a cloud of smoke in the air and it hung, creating a constant haze. Alaric coughed once upon entering and his eyes started to water.

Tancred walked to the bar whilst the other two looked for somewhere they could sit. They figured they would be less obtrusive if they eavesdropped instead of directly asking questions. Tancred, on the other hand, thought he would ask the bartender if they knew anything.

"Three ales please," Tancred spoke a little too politely to be one of the locals. He spoke without thinking.

"Yes, sir. Though may I ask what brings you here tonight?" The serving woman asked in a suspicious manner.

Tancred had to think quickly. He had already let himself down, but he had a chance to recover. "Been kicked out of the Drunkin'

Horseman, thought I better be polite for once," he hoped his lie would hold. He knew the tavern existed, but he had never been inside.

The serving woman nodded her head. It was obvious it was not the first time she had received patrons from other taverns. He was also sure she had sent patrons the other way. He almost chuckled out loud at the thought of bums wandering the streets from tavern to tavern.

"Hey, I've been hearing some disturbing rumours coming from the palace. Do you know anything about it?" Tancred kept his best slovenly voice as he spoke.

"Ha, no more than usual. You know ever since King Unwin, the Gods preserve his good name, got himself that new advisor there have been nothing but strange tales coming from the palace. I heard he was putting a bounty on anyone travelling in the country side after dark. Don't know what that is going to prove, but that's what I heard. Now here are your ales. That will be six copper coins," she held out her hand with an accusatory look on her face.

"That's a bit steep ain't it?" Tancred made a show a trying to find the coins.

"Ya, but the taxes keep goin' up so I gots to put me prices up," the serving woman didn't question his comment.

"Here we go," he spilled the coins onto the bar before quickly grabbing the mugs. He noticed there were some thirsty looking patrons eyeing off his ales.

He carefully picked his way through the tavern until he reached the others against the far wall. They had managed to find a table to sit at, although they almost got into a brawl for it. Tancred placed the mugs on the table before sitting himself.

"It seems that Unwin has himself a new advisor," Tancred kept his voice low as he spoke to the others. "This could be the reason why the guards warned me at the gate. This doesn't bode well for our cause."

"Be that as it may, Unwin is my cousin and I am sure that this advisor will have no huge power over him. Once I am in the palace I know that I will be able to talk him around. Remember that he is also a member..." Tancred silenced Richmond before he could finish what he was saying.

"I think caution is the method to be used here. We don't know anything about this new advisor of his. If we're not careful we could easily end up in the royal dungeons. I know you are cousins, but you are not that closely related. When was the last time Unwin sent you a missive updating you on the state of the Kingdom? The only time you have heard from him is when his collectors are chasing taxes, which as you know have gone up considerably in the last year."

Richmond almost snarled at Tancred's comments. He didn't look at all impressed, but he knew Tancred was right. There was nothing that he could say in his own defence. When it was said and done he was trying to convince himself of Unwin's intentions more than the others. The rumours had to be right. Somehow the new advisor was calling the shots.

"You are right, but that doesn't change the fact that we need to get into the palace to see him. What are we going to do?" Richmond asked, his voice downtrodden.

"We need to gather more information. I think I should visit a few taverns to see what I can get," Tancred offered.

"We should all go together," Richmond said. "We should not split up."

"This outer city can be very dangerous. I don't think we all need to put our lives in danger." Tancred was holding strong.

The two of them passed arguments back and forth over the table. Alaric simply sat back and drank his ale. Both of them made good points, but neither persuaded the other. Eventually Alaric knew he was going to have to settle it, but he wanted to finish his ale first.

"I'll get another round whilst you two are working out our brilliant plan," both men just waved Alaric aside.

"What can I get ya darlin'?" the serving woman asked as Alaric reached the bar.

"Another three ales please," Alaric replied.

"Not from around here are you?" The woman recognised the foreign accent immediately. "Sounds like a Remidian accent to me, the Duchy of Zenza if I am not mistaken?"

Alaric thought about trying to lie, but there was no way she was going to believe he was from Darshival. "That is very good," Alaric put on as much surprise in his voice as he could.

"What brings you to Kiarome?" She asked when she returned with their ales. "It's a long way from home."

"I'm visiting family," Alaric looked at the other two men on the table. "I lost my family and all my possessions in a house fire. I spent all my money to come here and start a new life." Alaric's lie was very convincing.

"And how's it all working out for ya?" She seemed interested in Alaric's story, although there was something in her eyes that worried him.

"To be honest, not real well. You see I used to work in the palace for the Duke of Zenza, now I am trying to get a job in the palace. The only problem is I can't get in to apply." Alaric tried to look forlorn.

"I think that you're goin' to be waiting for a long time. You see, I don't normally like to listen to gossip, but if people are goin' talk then I'm goin' to listen." She had a cheeky smile on her face. "It seems there's a new advisor in the palace. His name is Gearalt and he's a nasty piece of work. From what I hear he is the one who makes all the decisions now."

"That's very interesting. I thought King Unwin was a strong leader. I didn't think he would let someone usurp his power." Alaric had no idea what sort of person King Unwin was, but it was a safe bet if he was King then he was a powerful type of person.

"That he was, but now he defers all his decisions to Gearalt." Alaric could have sworn she winked at him as she spoke. "I don't really have any more information unfortunately. I know a lot of staff drink at a tavern near the palace gates. I think it is called the Drinker's Arms, but I could be wrong." She smiled warmly at him.

"Thank you very much. I will head there and see what I can find." Alaric picked up the three mugs and turned to return to the table.

"Oh I wouldn't bother about going there tonight. It's strictly palace staff only tonight. They get cheap drinks or something like that. Tomorrow night it's open to the public again." Alaric looked over his shoulder as she spoke to him.

"Thank you," was all he said as he returned to the table. The warm smile he gave her was all the gratitude she needed.

"What was that all about?" Tancred asked when he returned. The two men had continued to argue whilst he was gone. Even so Tancred had still kept an eye on him at the bar.

"Just gathering some information, it seems we need to go to the Drinker's Arms tomorrow night. It's where the palace staff go to drink. We should be able to get the information we need." Alaric seemed pleased with himself.

"Let's go then. There is no point waiting until tomorrow." Tancred stood as he spoke.

"Relax," Alaric explained the situation and Tancred returned to his seat. "We have time. We can't go anywhere until we recover the prophecy. There is more information that we need to gather."

*****

Na'garoz, or Emil as he was now known, sat in his room at the Patriot. Once he had taken the like of one of the pitiful creatures he found if he concentrated enough he could assume their memories. He knew the innkeeper Emil had stayed at the Patriot before and he knew the inn was one of the better inns in the outer city. If he was going to keep up the pretence he would have to follow routine. He learnt from his mistake with the magistrate. No one had noticed until it was too late, but they still noticed and that wasn't good.

He knew the little worm at the stable would have told them what they wanted to know. He would have preferred to have more time, but he didn't think they would believe his ruse either way. They knew who he was and that wasn't a good thing. He should have killed the Cursed One, but the prophecy was there to be taken. With the book in his possession he had just climbed the ranks of his brethren. The only problem was he didn't know what to do with it. He had never been good with the words of the worms. They always twisted around in his head until he couldn't look at them anymore. There was only one he could trust enough to show the prize. They had been close once upon a time. They hadn't spoken in over a hundred years, at least, but he was the only one he could trust. He was the only one he knew who could read the words. He would have much preferred to keep the book to himself, but it would do no good.

Now he had to work out how to get into the palace. The word on the streets of Kiarome was that the palace was shut off to the public. His brother had shut the King off from the world and had done well, the thought almost made him sick. The Great Lord would be proud with what he had achieved. Fenaroz would be ahead of him in the Great Lord's favour and that was unacceptable. With a translation of the worm's prophecy it would bring him back into his master's favour. The only problem was that he needed Fenaroz. It was not that he didn't trust his old companion, but he knew that given the same opportunity he would steal the knowledge.

The only advantage he had was the prophecy. When Fenaroz heard he had it then he would have to admit him to the palace. The next problem was how he was going to get word to him. For starters he didn't know what pseudonym Fenaroz was using. Secondly, Emil had known quite a few people in the capital, but none had any sway within the palace.

Na'garoz had heard a rumour there was a tavern near the palace gates that serviced mainly people from the palace. He thought if there was any chance getting word to his brethren then that would be his best chance. He had tried the tavern earlier in the evening, but he was not allowed in. Apparently they were only letting palace workers in that night. He thought about breaking into the palace, but if he got caught then there was no telling how long it would take for him to break free. He would have to use subterfuge again. He had grown used to it, but it was starting to wane on him. He ached for attack, for total chaos. He wished he was on the battlefield leading a legion of menace.

Drool started to appear in the corner of his lips at the thought of battle. He wiped himself and regained his composure. Even though he was in the privacy of his own room there was a chance someone could walk in. The last thing he wanted was to be caught acting like a madman. It would be hard for him to explain, even though he was starting to think like one of them. The ability was starting to come in useful, but it was also a hindrance to his final plan.

There was a knock on the door, he had been expecting a visitor, but he did not think she would arrive so early. "Enter," he called out.

A young woman entered the room. She was dirty and her blonde hair was tattered. He assumed that she was quite attractive despite the dirt stains across her cheeks, although he was still getting used to his new body's desires. It was one thing that he definitely enjoyed about being in the worms' bodies. Lust was one of the benefits that he was starting to become used to. A grin, which almost looked like a snarl, appeared on his face as he thought of all the wicked things he was going to do with the young lady before him.

"Are ya ready, sire," the girl asked with a broken accent.

"Certainly," he almost hissed the words at her in anticipation.

Chapter 17: A Race to the Palace

The day passed without much incident. All three men woke up with a ringing heads and pains in the stomach. They had stayed on at the tavern for the rest of the evening, trying to gather information from the local drunks. All they ended up achieving was having very annoying conversations that led absolutely nowhere.

They stumbled back to the inn about an hour before sunrise, all the worse for wear. Their spirits were surprisingly high as they walked through the streets in the grey light of predawn. They were all happy to be back at the inn and given a chance to sleep. It would be another long night ahead of them and they would need to be well rested to achieve their goal. The information would not be given easily and they needed all their guiles.

It was midday before they surfaced from their rooms. It was only pure hunger that motivated them. None of them wanted to brace the light of day or be seen in public, but at least their behaviour would suit the parts they were trying to play.

An hour before dusk they made their way to the Drinker's Arms. The night was upon them by the time they made it to the door. The lights were on inside and by the sound of it the tavern was in full flight. The effects of the alcohol from the night before had worn off, but the memory was still thick in their minds. They knew they couldn't go into the tavern and not drink, but they would definitely make sure that they didn't drink to excess.

The Drinker's Arms was a much nicer inn. There was a scent of perfume in the air that masked any bad odours. The floor had been swept and one of the serving girls would do the rounds before it became too filthy. There was only a hint of pipe tobacco in the air as there was a courtyard out the back for smokers.

Even the clientele looked a lot cleaner. The palace staff, even after a long day at work, were dressed nicely for a night out. All three felt much more comfortable in their current setting. Although Alaric did not think he came from a noble background he did believe that at least once in his life he had enjoyed the finer things. They had all dressed appropriately for their night out. They wore the clothes suitable of middleclass workers and they blended in nicely.

The Drinker's Arms was a large inn with three rooms inside for drinkers, a courtyard and a room set aside for meals. Even though it was relatively early in the evening the drinking rooms were almost full. There was nowhere for the three of them to sit so they made their way to the bar.

The serving woman was too busy to speak to them as they ordered their drinks. Tancred tried to make conversation, but she simply ignored him. After she had served their drinks and collected the coin she was off to serve someone else.

"I don't think that we are going to get much information from her," Tancred commented before he took a draught on his ale. "Although I must admit the ale is a lot better here," he said as he took another sip.

"I don't think we should just go around asking questions," said Alaric. "If what we have already heard is true I am sure people here would rather slit our throats than risk their jobs." Alaric's observation was a little off, but the point was still there.

"Then how are we going to find out what's happening?" sighed Richmond.

"There is an old saying, there is more than one way to skin a cat. If we split up and listen to the conversations happening around the inn then I think we should be able to gather the information we need. I know people get a lot more talkative when you buy them a few ales too, so that might not be a bad idea either."

"Just not too many drinks, if we don't get into the palace soon then our money supply is going to start running short. We didn't allow for a long stay in the city. Just remember that before you start giving away all our gold," Tancred warned.

To his surprise Alaric nodded his agreement. He had expected an argument. There had always been an argument when Tancred suggested something that contradicted Alaric's plan.

"Good, then let's see what we can find out. We should meet back here after a couple of hours to see what we have discovered." Alaric placed his empty mug on the bar. He looked around the tavern before heading off into one of the other rooms.

Tancred looked at Richmond and slowly shook his head. He didn't need to speak for his Lord to understand what he meant. At least their relationship was still intact. Tancred would be in a lot of trouble if Richmond decided to take command like Alaric had. Slowly the two of them spilt up and made their way around the bar. Tancred decided to see what was happening in the meal room, mainly because he was hungry, whilst Richmond found himself a nice solitary spot behind a large group of gossiping women.

The night passed and they returned to the front bar to discuss what they had found. Alaric was the last to arrive and he found Tancred and Richmond deep in conversation. He thought about eavesdropping, but Richmond looked up when he approached.

"Thank the Gods you are here," there was a look of concern of Richmond's face.

"I don't think you will say the same thing when you hear what I have to tell you," Alaric's voice was also grave.

"Well I think that you should go first then," Tancred suggested.

"I don't think we should do it here. When I was out the back I saw Emil. He's here in the Drinker's Arms. I think it would be better if he didn't know we are here as well." Alaric looked around the bar nervously.

"Let's get out of here and try and find somewhere a little more private." Tancred finished his ale and started for the exit, making a point to keep an eye out for Emil.

As much as Alaric wanted to stay and follow Emil to try and regain the prophecy he knew they needed to discuss what they had heard. There was more at stake and rushing into action wasn't their best course. He would need to be more secretive to achieve his goal.

"We should stay close to the tavern. If Emil leaves then I want to follow him," Alaric whispered as they walked out.

Opposite the tavern, about fifty paces down the road, there was a narrow alley way. Once they had checked that it was empty they made themselves comfortable. There was only one door leading in and out of the tavern so it was easy for them to keep watch.

"Now I don't believe that you should go after the prophecy by yourself. We do not know what we're up against with Emil, so we need to be careful. There is no point in recovering the text if you are going to die in the process. We will all wait for Emil and see where he goes. From there we will decide on the best course of action for recovering the prophecy." Tancred did his best keep his voice low. There were still people in the streets and he didn't want to be discovered.

"Has anyone found a way to get into the palace?" asked Richmond.

"I think I might have something useful," Tancred looked out into the street before he continued. "It seems that they are hiring in the palace at the moment. More than one of the servants has disappeared recently and they need replacing. Most of the positions are for young boys and girls, but I believe there are also some openings for senior positions. I think if Richmond writes us a good report I don't think it would be too hard to gain entrance to apply for the jobs."

"That seems like a good idea," Richmond agreed. "Do you have anything Alaric?"

"I heard a group of young men talking about a secret way in and out of the palace. They use it when they want to sneak women in and out. I didn't get its exact location, but I believe it's somewhere near where the palace wall meets the city wall. If we can find it we can get in undetected. Once we are inside we should be able to find our way unhindered. I believe it is only getting in and out of the palace that is difficult. Once you are inside everyone assumes that you are supposed to be there so no one questions you," Alaric explained.

"They are both very good ideas. I don't know which one is the better," Richmond mused.

"I don't think it really matters at this point. Our first priority must be regaining the prophecy. There is no point gaining access to the palace until we have recovered it." Alaric almost raised his voice as he spoke.

"I have to agree," Tancred added. "At least until Alaric regains his memory we should do everything we can to recover the book."

"Don't you mean Dyrk?" Richmond added after recognising Alaric's true name.

"I think our ruse has run its course. King Unwin will know he's not Dyrk and I don't think anyone else is going to know the name Alaric. If no one knows who you are out here in the city then I don't think they are going to recognise him."

They sat in silence as they watched the door of the tavern. The further the night continued the more the temperature started to drop. It started becoming quite uncomfortable as they watched people come and go from the tavern with no sign of the man they were looking for. All three of them were starting to shiver.

"This is starting to get ridiculous," Richmond's shivered.

"We have to wait," Alaric's voice did the same as he replied.

"Catching our death in the streets is not going to prove anything. Richmond is right. We need to make our way back to the inn. We can do no more tonight." Tancred agreed with Richmond, but Alaric had already ignored him.

Whilst Tancred was speaking there was movement out the front of the tavern. Adrenaline started to rush through Alaric's body as he watched Emil speak to a small group. It seemed as though the Dark Knight in disguise had made some friends. Alaric wondered if they would see the light of day.

"I think that it would be better if I continue on alone. There will be less chance that he will see me by myself."

"You can't go wondering around by yourself. Emil aside, this is still a very dangerous place. There is no telling what could happen to you," Tancred said as he peered out to get a look at Emil.

"Don't worry I know how to protect myself," Alaric opened his cloak to reveal his sword. "As you know this is no ordinary man we are following. There are things about Emil that you don't know and you don't want to know. Trust me when I say that it will be safer if I travel alone." There was something in Alaric's voice that made the other two listen.

"I don't think there will be any advantage to you travelling alone. At least let us follow behind to make sure there is no one following you," Tancred suggested.

"I appreciate the offer, but if you want to do something productive try and find the hole in the wall. We may still need to use it to gain entrance into the palace," Alaric suggested.

"Very well, but be sure that you are careful. The city is full of shady characters." Tancred had to agree as Emil was starting to walk away from the tavern.

"I will see you back at the inn in the morning." Alaric crept out into the street, making sure he kept to the shadows.

Emil had left the others at the tavern and was making his way down the street alone. Alaric had to be careful not to reveal himself to the people Emil had been talking to.

Emil didn't seem to notice that he was being followed. The man seemed to be rather pleased with himself and Alaric wondered what he was up to. If he was trying to get himself into the palace then Alaric didn't want to know what the ramifications could be.

Soon they were in a part of the city where there was no one on the street. The buildings loomed up around them, mainly warehouses that were shut for the night. Alaric was beginning to become suspicious. Although he did not know the city he could still feel the presence of the prophecy and it was not in the direction they were travelling. The feeling was coming from somewhere behind him. As much as he thought he was heading for a trap he had to see where Emil was leading him.

They rounded a corner down a narrow alley and Emil walked straight into a dead end. A large stone wall stood at the end of the small avenue and there was a lantern at the end of the street, which was more like a large courtyard. Once Emil reached the end of the courtyard he turned around. Alaric crept back into the shadows. The man didn't seem to know that Alaric was there.

Alaric almost jumped when he heard the sound of many footsteps coming from the street behind him. He pressed himself up against the nearest wall and found a small nook. He hoped the shadows were enough to hide him.

Rounding the corner was a man dressed in finery, followed by a dozen soldiers dressed in the clothes of the Royal Guard. They all carried torches which lit up the entire courtyard. Alaric knew instantly there was something wrong with the leader. He couldn't tell what it was until he stood side by side with Emil. His first thought was to run for his life, even though he had to pass the soldiers, but he remained where he was. If he was going to gather vital information he needed to remain strong.

"So you have finally made your way to my city." The man spoke with an undeniable tone. There was a confidence and cruelty that didn't match his appearance.

"What about them." Emil moved his head towards the direction on the soldiers.

"Them? Don't worry about them. There are completely under my control." A snarl appeared on the man's face.

Emil didn't look sure. There was no confidence in his stance. He looked around the alley nervously. His gaze lingered on the small gap in the wall where Alaric was hiding. For a moment Alaric thought he had been discovered, but then Emil continued looking around. "Are you sure this is safe?"

"You came to me, now I think you should start talking or crawl back to where you came from," nothing changed in the man's demeanour, but his tone gave away his mood.

"I have something that you might be interested in Gearalt," again Emil looked around nervously. He was beginning to doubt that Fenaroz, Gearalt, he had to remember his new name, was the right one to get to help him.

"Hurry up and stop wasting my time," Gearalt spoke harshly. Again Emil looked at the guards standing at the entrance to the alley. "You can speak freely in front of them. They won't speak to anyone unless I instruct them.'

Emil didn't want to think what that meant. If Gearalt could control the minds of twelve people at once then he had indeed grown more powerful. He was seriously considering not telling him about the prophecy. There was every chance Gearalt would try and steal it from him

"I have the Cursed One's text. I have *The Prophecy of the Stone*!" Emil couldn't control the smile on his face as Gearalt had a look of disbelief on his.

It only lasted for a moment before a look of knowing appeared as Emil's hopes dropped. The snarl returned to Gearalt's face.

"So you want something from me, or else you would not be telling me this little titbit. What could it be?" Gearalt pondered his own question.

"I need you to translate to the text for me," Emil felt uncomfortable admitting he couldn't read the scrawl.

Gearalt started to laugh. The sound sent chills down Alaric's spine. There was something very creepy about the new arrival. If he was powerful enough to make one of Nyrra's Dark Knights scared then there was more to him than meets the eye. Alaric knew that the man was familiar, but he did not know why.

"And why would I want to help you? I am going alright by myself. I think I will kill you now and just take the prophecy."

"You don't think I am that stupid do you? There are quite a few mystical traps around its location. You wouldn't get within five steps of the prophecy before you were obliterated." Hearing the words made Alaric's heart drop. There was very little chance of him recovering it. Even if he could remember he didn't think he would be capable of getting passed Emil's wards. "You see, you need me as much as I need you."

Gearalt turned his back on Emil and looked towards his soldiers. He had to decide whether he thought Emil was bluffing or not. What would he do in the same situation? He knew the answer to his own question immediately. There was no way he would trust one of his brothers and he would place as many wards around the book as he could without giving away his location. That was the only saving grace. The wards could not have been too powerful or he would have felt Emil casting them. Even so he didn't think it was worth the risk. He would be able to play Emil along, get what he wanted from him and then leave him for dead.

"Very well, brother, I will help you translate the prophecy. I will come with you to where you're staying." Alaric's heart skipped a beat when he heard the first words come out of Gearalt's mouth. Now he knew why he recognised the man. It was not his features, it was his commanding presence. There was no doubt that he was facing two Dark Knights. Alaric shrunk back against the wall as close as he could, if he got caught there was no way he would survive.

"I don't think so." Emil twitched slightly as he spoke. All of a sudden there was an unusual amount of fear in the air. He brushed it off quickly before continuing. "I will bring it to the palace. You can put me up in a room there."

"I think that you might be overestimating your own powers. I have set up nicely in the palace. I don't need you there messing things up for me."

"Well that is not an option. You see the Cursed One is in the city. It will only be a matter of time before he finds where I am staying. If I am in the palace then you will be able to stop him from gaining access."

"What do you mean the Cursed One is in the city? That is impossible. There is no way he could know that I'm here. The only way is if…"

"It makes no difference the reason why he is here the point is that he is and I am not safe in the city. If you are not going to help me then I will move on and leave the Cursed One here for you to deal with." The threat hit the mark.

"It makes a great difference why he's here. It has taken a long time for me to convince Unwin to my way of thinking. The old man's mind was surprisingly strong willed. I have convinced him not to send any more troops to help the enemy, but I think it will be a different story if I have to get him to attack them. I don't think he would send his army against his old allies. I am close, but it will still take a while to convince him. If the Cursed One gains an audience with Unwin then there is no telling what could happen."

"Then you should be doubly careful on how you treat me. It would be quite easy for me to find him and tell him what you are doing. I am sure he would go easy on me with such information. I might even be able to barter myself out of this mess." Emil felt that he was gaining the upper hand.

"Very well, but remember what happened here tonight. I will have my revenge." Gearalt turned his back and started walking back to where his soldiers were waiting. Once he reached them he turned around to address Emil, who was still standing at the end of the alley. "Go and get what you need. I will let it be known at the gate that you will be arriving. I will have a room ready for you in the palace." Gearalt spun around, swirling his cape in the process. He pushed his way though his gang of soldiers and made his way out of the alley.

Once the soldiers had gone Emil slumped to his knees. He was surprised that the meeting ended so well. He thought for sure his old brother would have tried to kill him. If he was in Feranoz's position he certainly would, but in the end there would be nothing gained. He doubted the Great Lord would take too kindly if they started killing each other. There were better ways to gain his favour.

As soon as he had composed himself he returned to his feet and walked out of the alley. It was Alaric's turn to breathe a sigh of relief. He thought about returning to the inn without the information that he came for, but that would be just as disastrous. He had to follow Emil to the prophecy before he went to the palace.

When he was sure the courtyard was empty he slowly stepped out of his hiding place. Carefully he moved about in the small, dark alleys of Kiarome. Once he was out of the light and back in the shadows he felt a lot safer. His heart sank though, when he realised that the alleyway in front of him was completely empty. He could only hope that Emil had returned the way he had come.

Alaric had been concentrating so much on the two Knights he had forgotten the path back to his inn. There was no chance for him to find Emil. All he could do was to return to the others and tell them what he had found. Their next step was for them to infiltrate the palace.

He made his way in the direction he thought the palace was. The only problem was that the streets and alleys didn't always run straight. The streets were dark and empty and Alaric continued until he came to a fork. A lantern hung from a pole in the centre casting and eerie light. Curiosity got the better of him and he wondered who had placed a lantern in the back streets of the city.

"Look what we have here fellas." A man stepped out of the darkness from one of the branches of the fork. He was brandishing a cudgel and slapped it against the palm of his left hand. "Looks like you walked down the wrong alley, my friend." There was nothing friendly about him. As he spoke three more men walked into the light, each holding their own weapons. "Now if you would be so kind as to give me all of your gold then we can be on our way."

"I'm afraid I don't have any gold. I don't have any coins to give you."

"Then I am afraid this is your unlucky day. You see that if you don't have any money to give us then we have to take our payment out of your hide. There is good money for body parts in this city. By the looks of you we will make some good money." The others laughed.

Alaric kept his eyes fixed on the leader as the other men moved around to encircle him. He hoped he would be able to get out without having to fight. He really didn't have time to waste on petty criminals.

"I do not wish to fight you," Alaric started, his eyes remaining dead straight. He could see the others moving out of the corner of his eyes. He took a step backwards to make sure they didn't move out of his view. "We can all go our separate ways and no one needs to get hurt."

His words brought more laughter from the gang. It was only the leader that didn't find Alaric's words funny. He recognised the look on Alaric's face. There was no fear in his eyes, he was prepared for whatever they were going to do to him.

"Well I am afraid that my crew needs to eat. It has been a slow evening and I do not think they wish to go hungry. A hungry cat will fight longer and harder than a sated one."

Alaric kept his head high. His heart rate was calm and his breathing level.

"I don't believe there is anything else to talk about. You are either going to let me walk away or you will all be visiting the dark land of death. I hope you have paid your way because your debts are all due," Alaric sneered.

"Ha, if I didn't have to kill you I think I might have liked you. Anyway I suppose we should get this show on the road, so to speak." The leader of the gang signalled for the other three to attack.

Alaric quickly took a stance that felt comfortable for battle. He could feel a twinge in the back of his mind, as if he was remembering something. He reached for his sword, but at the last moment decided against it. The men before him only carried cudgels and he felt that his sword would be too much of an advantage and he would risk killing them all. As much as they were looking to kill him he didn't feel the same way. If he could defeat them without taking a life he could rest easy.

The three men slowly started to walk towards him. Alaric put himself in a position so he could see all of them.

When the attack came it came at once. The three men charged at Alaric with their cudgels swinging. The attack was less than organised and Alaric simply sidestepped at the last moment and sent the three men crashing into each other. It was a perfect moment for Alaric to attack, but he felt he should wait for them to recover.

He stood with the three men in front of him. It would be more difficult for them to attack at once. It was the result Alaric was looking for. The man on Alaric's left was the first to attack with the other two not far behind.

Again at the last moment Alaric waited to attack. The bandit swung his cudgel towards his head and Alaric easily grasped the man's wrist with his left hand, stopping the blow. With a quick movement Alaric swept the other mans feet out from under him, knocking him to the ground.

Another attacker had already started his advance before Alaric was finished with the first and he only just managed to deflect the blow with his right arm taking a glancing blow to his shoulder.

Alaric danced backwards as the two men swung their cudgels. He knew if one of their blows was to strike then it would crack his head open. The ferocity of their attack was also their downfall. Every time they swung their weapons they were aiming to kill, but it also put them off balance. Alaric had noticed the similar movements in their attacks and instead of dancing backwards Alaric pushed forward to the left after the bandit had swung his cudgel. He was able to knock the man of balance enough to push him into his partner's attack. The cudgel sunk deep in his head, killing him almost instantly. The bandit's body dropped to the ground, twitching for a number of seconds before it lay still.

The shock of the attack was enough to make the man drop his cudgel, but the first bandit had returned. Facing only one of them gave Alaric the complete advantage. Again he waited until he saw the rhythm of the man's attack. At first he dodged left to right and underneath the man's blows. When the time was right he struck out with his fists and caught the man in the neck. The bandit instantly dropped to his knees, coughing and gasping for breath.

"Do you wish to continue?" Alaric asked the leader as he kicked the fallen man in the side of his head. It was enough to knock the man unconscious, but not enough to kill.

The leader didn't and as soon as his one remaining thief was with him the two of them disappeared into the night. They didn't even wait to help their one fallen friend who was still alive.

Alaric looked at the two fallen men. There was no pride in what he had done. He had no choice, but he would have preferred if none of them had died. His mission was to save these people. He was supposed to be their saviour, not their executioner. He knew deep down they were good people, just trying to survive. People could stoop to any level if it meant their own survival.

He didn't linger long in the street. Even though the bandits had run off scared there was no reason why they wouldn't come back with more men. He was sure he could take on whatever they threw at him, but he did not want to take any more lives that night.

It was the adrenaline that had been coursing through his veins that had kept the fatigue away. Now that he was safe again the strain took its toll. Alaric had to sit and rest whilst he caught his breath. He had to keep going though. His life would be in greater danger if he stayed on the street for the rest of the night.

When he started again the buildings loomed up in front of him and all around. The sky was covered in clouds and there was no way for him to tell which direction he should be travelling. He kept moving although he didn't know if he was going in the right direction. There was something disconcerting about being lost in the city.

It took Alaric over an hour to find his way out of the maze of streets that were the inner city. He was attacked once more by a small gang of thieves. This time he managed to defeat them without killing anyone. His exhaustion almost caused him to lose consciousness when the adrenaline subsided.

It was close to dawn and Alaric was close to exhaustion when he finally returned to the inn. He found the other two inside, asleep in their beds. He thought about waking them and giving them the bad news, but he figured it could wait until he had slept. There was nothing they were able to do for the moment, so there was no point in waking them.

Alaric lay down in his bed, although he was still wired from the night's events and despite his fatigue he could not sleep. He could still feel the gentle tug of the prophecy somewhere within the city. He still couldn't pinpoint its exact location and that frustrated him. Soon, if he was not already there, Emil would be in the palace and under the protection of not only Unwin and his entire guard, but also his fellow Dark Knight. Gaining entrance to the palace would be hard enough, but convincing King Unwin that his advisor and new friend were part of Nyrra's army would be almost impossible.

Eventually Alaric was able to fall asleep. His dreams were filled with nightmares. They reflected the feelings he felt before he fell asleep. It was not completely hopeless, but recovering the prophecy was going to take more strength than he currently possessed. Unless he was able to completely regain his memories by breakfast he didn't know what he was going to do. There was a horror in that thought that followed him throughout his dreams.

Chapter 18: The Palace

In the morning Alaric felt as though he had not slept at all. The others had already started to stir, but they had decided to let him sleep a little longer. He felt as though he could sleep all day, but knew he had a big day ahead of him. Time was his worst enemy and he sighed as he slowly lifted himself out of bed.

"Did you find where Emil was going?" Tancred asked when he realised that Alaric was awake.

"Not as such, but I have some more disturbing news." Alaric yawned before he continued. "It seems that Emil has a friend inside the palace." Alaric paused. He thought about telling them the true identity of Unwin's new advisor, but he wasn't sure if they would be able to control themselves if they knew who they were facing. Alaric had come to the realisation that he needed Richmond and Tancred's help if he was going to succeed.

"This is not good news at all," Tancred looked at Richmond. "How is it that someone pretending to be an inn keeper from King's Rest came to know a King's advisor? Something is not right here. Do you think that this is a coincidence?"

"No I do not. It makes sense that if one shape-shifter was to infiltrate your court then another would infiltrate the King's. The only question now is what they are up to?" Both Richmond and Tancred looked at Alaric when he finished speaking.

"It seems that the one posing as Unwin's advisor is trying to undermine his army. I overheard him talking about not letting any of Unwin's soldiers join the Alliance. Then they were talking about getting Unwin's soldiers to join the Evil One's forces instead and destroying the Alliance." Alaric watched the other two closely as he spoke.

"That's impossible. Unwin would never lead his soldiers against the Alliance." Richmond looked accusingly at Alaric.

"Remember that Unwin is in the thrall of this Gearalt character. It will not be the King in his right mind making the decision. We do not know the extent of his power. We have no idea what he is capable of."

"So what do we do know?" Richmond asked.

Alaric wasn't sure exactly what the best plan of attack was. The previous night he was sure that they needed to gain entrance into the palace, but in the light of day he wasn't sure it was the wisest plan. Once they were in the palace there was no telling what trouble they could get into. He knew there was an army nearby, but he did not know how far away it was. It could be another month before the Alliance reached Kiarome. He wasn't even sure if the army was going to come so far south. His next problem was bringing a hostile army, as the citizens would see it, into the city. It would be just as bad if he brought the Alliance against Kiarome. He quickly let that idea leave his mind. The army had its own course to run and its own part to play. Alaric couldn't change the course of history without bringing disaster to the world.

"We must find a way into the palace. Our mission has changed now. We must not only recover the prophecy, but we must also release Unwin from his enthrallment." Alaric had no idea how they were going to accomplish it. He doubted his ability against one Dark Knight, but against two he knew he had no chance.

"So do we think that this Gearalt has been working for the Dark Knight parading around as Emil?" asked Tancred.

"I don't know."

"It's more than likely this Gearalt is a Dark Knight himself." Richmond's comment was so casual no one was sure he exactly knew what he was saying. It wasn't until he noticed the other two staring at him that he realised what it was. "Well? It would make sense. Unwin is a strong willed man. I doubt anyone less would be able to control him."

As the thoughts raced through Alaric's mind he remembered something. He knew he had a feeling that he had fought one of the Dark Knights sometime in the past. Not only did he fight the Knight, but he also destroyed him. There was something comforting in that thought. If he had succeeded in the past then maybe he would succeed in the future. The only difference was that he knew what he was doing in the past, now he was fighting blind. On the bright side he had already won a number of battles that he was sure he should have lost.

"I don't think there's any chance we are going to be able to walk through the front gates. I'm sure by now Gearalt, whoever he may be, will have stopped all from gaining entrance to the palace. He won't risk us slipping by unnoticed. The only chance we have is by finding that hole that you spoke about last night." Alaric wanted to change the subject. Although they didn't seem overly worried about another Dark Knight he didn't want to give them a chance to realise the futility of their mission.

"Very well then. I think that we should get something to eat before we continue. Hopefully an idea might come to us that we have not already thought about. I don't think this current plan of ours is any good. I have a bad feeling we are going to end up the King's dungeon." Tancred's words were ominous. Alaric only agreed because his stomach started growling. There was no point running an assault on an empty stomach.

They found a moderately priced tavern that served breakfast. The city was alive with action by the time they left the inn. The sun was shining and there was no breeze blowing through the streets. It was going to be a hot day. The morning was already starting to become uncomfortable.

"I don't think this plan is going to work either." Richmond voiced his concern again as they neared the end of their breakfast.

"That is because there is no real plan." Tancred added. "I think we should reassess our situation. We can't just rush into the palace."

Alaric swallowed a mouthful of smoked ham. He had been enjoying his meal and the silence that had gone with it. He had been trying to think of what they were going to do once they were inside the palace grounds, but nothing came to him. Unless they knew exactly what they were facing there was nothing for them to plan. He knew the others would not like it when he told them, but there was no other option. The longer the two knights were in the palace the harder it would be for Alaric to wrest control from them.

"There is nothing we can do. We have to get inside the palace to gauge the situation. Once we are inside we will have a quick look around, see what the situation is and then return to our room. From there we will be able to make a plan," Alaric didn't sound at all confident.

"And what if we don't make it out of the palace?" Tancred asked.

"Then we will have to cross that bridge when we get to it. Time is against us my friends and that means that sometimes we will have to act without forethought. It is the only way for us to succeed."

Once they had finished their breakfast they started towards the palace. They all wore the dark robes with the hoods pulled over their faces. Although the weather was already becoming hot it hid the clothes they were wearing underneath and that was more important than their comfort. To blend in once they were inside the palace they wore finery, suitable of the nobility underneath. They left their swords behind as it would look out of place if nobles wore weapons of war around a palace. It was a risk, but since they were just doing a reconnaissance mission it was one they were willing to take.

Richmond knew a noble family who they could pretend to be as they couldn't risk using their own identities. The Lord of Sillarome had a son and an advisor who were around the same age as his two companions. Richmond himself was a few years younger than his fellow noble, but he didn't think anyone would notice. Sillarome was a city to the south of Kiarome. It was a minor state of the Kingdom, not nearly as important as Bellarome. The Lord was powerful enough to be admitted into the palace, but not powerful enough to really be noticed. It would not be unusual for him to be there and the King would not even know. Richmond just hoped that the Lord was not already in the palace.

Alaric didn't get any great information about the location of the hole, so the first port of call was the make their way to the wall. They walked, almost completely unnoticed through the streets of Kiarome. To the people of the city they were just another group of paupers. To the other paupers they were competition. They brushed through the crowd without being recognised.

At the palace wall the crowd started to thin out. There were guards posted on the wall keeping a close eye on the people below them. Not only were they watching outside the wall they were also watching the inside. The further the three of them continued the more conspicuous they became. Not only because there were three beggars walking near the palace, but also because they were walking together. Most of the beggars of the city were solitary creatures. They could become violent when they thought another beggar was trying to take over their territory.

"I think we should leave the wall," Tancred kept his head low so no one could see him speak. "We're drawing too much attention from the city guards."

They followed Tancred's lead and moved down a number of large and small streets until they found themselves alone in an alley. They all removed their hoods when they realised they were alone. Sweat covered their faces. The heat of the day was starting to take effect.

"What do we do now?" Richmond asked. "It's too dangerous for us to try and find the entrance into the palace. The city guards have the walls completely covered."

"It seems Gearalt is expecting us. I was hoping he would put all his attention towards the main gate. He's much smarter than I gave him credit for." Alaric pondered their new situation. "I still think we have a chance to enter the palace. It wouldn't be a secret entrance if it's clear for everyone to see. Even with the guards on the wall there has to be a way to get in unseen."

"Did they say if the hole was in the wall itself?" Tancred was thinking.

"No, but where else would it be?" Alaric looked surprised.

"I think I know?" Richmond spoke with a half grin on his face. "It is possible that there is an entrance under the palace walls. The sewage from the palace needs to come out somewhere."

"Wouldn't the sewage run outside the city and not into the city?" Alaric asked.

"It all depends on the sewer system. It's quite possible that the sewers run from the palace, under the city and then out," Richmond explained.

"Do you know how to find the sewers, let alone which one leads into the city?"

"No," Richmond had to admit. "But I am sure we will be able to find someone who does."

"The next problem is if we take to the sewers then by the time we reach the other side we will stink like human waste. No one will believe that we are nobility smelling like that

"He's right Richmond. Our plan relies on us being ghosts once we enter the palace grounds. If we smell like the sewers then there is no chance of that happening. We have to find an entrance above ground." Tancred had to agree with Alaric.

"Then we have no chance. We are too conspicuous on the outside if we stay above ground and we are too conspicuous on the inside if we travel below the ground. I think we need a new plan altogether."

They stood in silence for a moment before Alaric spoke. "We continue on the original course."

"But…" Tancred and Richmond both spoke at once and were both silenced at the same time.

"You have to trust me on this one. I will explain later." Alaric didn't explain his plan. It was another time where he just had a feeling he was doing the right thing. "We will follow these streets until we hit the city wall. From there we will make our way back to the palace wall. Hopefully it will not take long for us to find our entrance. The temperature is starting to get hot and I for one want to get out of these robes." There was a new confidence in his voice that made the others suspicious.

There was no doubting him. So far everything he said had come to fruition. Since neither of them had any better ideas they had to go along with Alaric.

Alaric started off in the direction of the city wall while Richmond and Tancred remained behind.

"That didn't sound like Alaric?" Richmond commented. "What do you think is happening here?"

"I think he is starting to remember who he was, or at least who he needs to be. I don't think this confidence can be a bad thing."

"Are you two coming?" Alaric called back down the street.

The two men returned their hoods over their heads and followed after him. Even though the streets were empty they needed to keep up their ruse. There was no telling which corner would take them directly into a crowd.

Alaric paused once he reached the city wall looming over them. It was supposed to comfort those in the city, but it made Alaric feel very small. He felt a tingle in the back of his neck and his head felt extremely hot. His eyelids drooped until they were almost closed. If anyone had of been able to see inside his hood they would have thought he was about to lose consciousness.

"Where to now?" Tancred asked.

Alaric ignored him. In fact Alaric didn't even hear the words. His entire body was tingling. He could feel a stream of power ebbing and flowing all around him. He felt as though he could touch it, but it was just out of his reach. Whenever he reached out the power pushed away from him, it was the most frustrating thing in the world

Suddenly a rush filled his body. The other two watched with concern as they saw him convulse for a second. The movement was so sudden and so quick that when it had finished neither of them was sure it had actually happened. Just as soon as it had begun it ended and Alaric returned to normal. He looked at the others to see if they had noticed anything, but it was impossible to tell with their hoods drawn. He felt somewhat self-conscious, but he had no idea what had happened.

"Let's go," was all he could say to break the uncomfortable silence.

If Alaric was not going to speak about what had happened the other two were not going to ask. They weren't completely sure what they had seen and they both felt different.

As they walked they noticed people were bumping into them. Most city folk ignored the poor and putrid in the city or pushed the poor out of their way and kept on walking. These people where giving them some strange looks before they continued on their way. If it wasn't for their disguise Tancred would have given them a piece of his mind. Instead it was easier for them to avoid the people as they walked towards them.

Once they reached the corner where the two walls joined they paused again. There was a guard standing directly above them on the palace wall. The guard didn't seem to take any notice of the three men standing below him. Instead he seemed more concerned with what was happening further out of the city.

"We have to be careful now." Tancred kept his voice low. "If we get caught by one of the sentries then this masquerade will quickly be over."

"I don't understand why that guard doesn't look at us." Richmond also kept his voice low.

"I guess it is true what they say. The city's serfs are the invisible people of the Kingdom." Alaric didn't sound so convinced with his own revelation. "Whatever the reason is I don't think standing here is going to help."

Alaric's words made sense. The longer they stayed in one place the more conspicuous they would become. Slowly they started to move along the palace wall. Every step they took they thought they were going to be discovered. Every time they passed a sentry they would press themselves against the wall and prey they remained hidden.

After half an hour of creeping along the wall they came to a part that was completely overgrown by bushes. There was no easy way for them to pass through.

"It looks like we are going to have to walk around," Tancred spoke softly.

"Wait!" Alaric stopped the other two. "I think this is what we have been looking for."

Alaric took a closer look at where the bushes met the wall. He was able to see scratches against the wall and it was clear it was from the branches being moved back and forth. Alaric slowly pulled the branches back and saw there was a space for someone to enter. Without speaking to the others Alaric disappeared into the bush. Tancred and Richmond waited outside keeping as close to the wall as possible

Alaric slowly returned from the bush and stuck his head out so he could speak to the others.

"Hurry up you two!" Was all Alaric said before he disappeared back into the bushes.

Richmond took one look at Tancred, who in turn shook his head, before following Alaric. Tancred sighed in resignation before he followed the others. Once they were inside they were surprised to see it was so roomy. The bushes were only six feet thick before it turned into a bushy cave.

In the middle of the wall there was a hole that could easily accommodate a man. Alaric was standing by the hole waiting for the other two to join him. He had a smile on his face that didn't disappear with the other two's glares.

"I have been on the other side and there doesn't seem to be anyone around," Alaric spoke with renewed hope. "I think we should leave our robes here and assume our new personas." To accentuate his point he started to take his robe off.

Richmond waited for Tancred's lead before stripping off his outer shell. The bush cave was sheltered from the heat making it much cooler. They were all much more comfortable without the black robes, but they would also be more conspicuous.

"So what do we do once we are on the other side?" Richmond asked just before Alaric was about to head into the hole.

"We have to try and make our way into the palace. From there we should be able to start gathering the information we need." Alaric didn't wait for a response before walking into the hole.

A small tunnel led through the palace wall to a similar bush cave on the other side. Alaric again waited for the other two to join him. There was something exhilarating about what was on the other side of the bushes, the anticipation of what was waiting for them. Alaric's heart was beating faster than normal. Sweat was visibly pouring down his face even though it was much cooler in the caves and the tunnel.

"Are you alright?" Richmond asked when they were all together.

"Yes, I am fine. Why do you ask?" Alaric didn't notice anything different.

Richmond and Tancred looked at each other. It was obvious that something was happening to Alaric, but they didn't know whether it was good or bad. Neither man knew how to reply to Alaric's question. If he didn't feel uncomfortable then there was obviously nothing wrong with him.

Alaric shook his head in confusion when no one answered him. Sweat flicked around the cave, but Alaric didn't seem to notice. He made his way to the palace wall, where he poked his head out first to make sure the coast was clear. When he was sure there was no one there he left the safety of the bush.

The other side of the wall was completely different to the city side. The dirty, dusty streets had changed into a beautiful garden. There were a few people sitting and walking in the gardens, but no one seemed to take any notice of Alaric. When he was sure that no one was looking he signalled for the other two to join him.

Again, no one seemed to take any notice of them as they walked around the garden. It seemed quite odd that no one looked up when they walked by. It was as if everyone was making a point not to look at them. This made Alaric feel even more self conscious.

"I have a bad feeling about this," Alaric spoke softly when they stopped to look around.

"Nothing about this situation is good," Tancred also kept his voice low.

"I agree, there is definitely something amiss. I think you should go back to the inn. If we don't return by nightfall then you will have to work out a way to rescue us," there was nothing comforting in Alaric's words.

"What are you talking about?" Tancred sounded confused and was starting to raise his voice.

"There is no time to explain. There is an army on its way South. The commander of the army is a friend of mine." Alaric didn't know how he knew what he was saying, but he knew it was true. "I know it's a last resort, but if we can't help Unwin then a full frontal attack might be the only chance."

Tancred was going to protest, but Richmond silenced him. "Do what he says Tancred. I am sure we'll be alright, but if we get caught we need someone on the outside." Richmond's words made.

"Very well, but if you are not back by dusk I will start to make preparations." Tancred took one last look around the palace garden before returning to the group of bushes.

They waited for Tancred to disappear before starting to move again. Alaric had a burning sensation that someone was watching him. The feeling was very disturbing. He couldn't help but look around to see if anyone had noticed them. There was no one in the garden that even looked interested in them.

"I think we should make our way to the palace," Alaric suggested.

"I thought we were just going to have a look around. I didn't think that we were going to enter the palace today?" Richmond looked concerned as he spoke.

"Things have changed. We need to get into the palace, now!" Alaric's words were strained.

"I don't know if that's a good idea," Richmond called after Alaric.

Alaric didn't stop as he made his was towards the main entrance and Richmond hurried to catch him. Alaric didn't look right to Richmond, he was still sweaty and out of character

Before Alaric reached the main avenue leading to the palace he saw a sight that made him freeze where he stood. Walking down the palace steps was Gearalt leading a group of soldiers.

"What is it?" Richmond asked.

The sudden sound of Richmond's voice urged him into action. Alaric quickly pulled Richmond behind a nearby bush. Alaric's breathing was laboured and his face had turned pale. Richmond was worried that he was about to lose consciousness.

"What's wrong?" Richmond almost breathed the words as he tried to keep his voice low.

"That is Gearalt." Alaric pointed through the bush even though there was no chance Richmond could see. "He is one of Nyrra's Dark Knights." Alaric's voice shook with fear. As much as he wanted to keep the revelation a secret the words came unbidden.

The sound of Alaric's voice was enough to get Richmond's heart racing, even before what he said had registered. He looked around the garden seeing if there was any chance they could make it back to the hole in the wall without being seen. No matter which way he looked they had travelled too far into the garden. The only way they were going to escape was if Gearalt and his soldiers walked by.

The sounds of many footsteps could be heard approaching and Richmond thought about making a run for freedom, but it was clear Alaric wouldn't make it. Before Richmond could decide what to do Gearalt and his soldiers were upon them. Gearalt was standing before them, with his soldiers in an arc behind him. The soldiers had strange blank expressions on their faces

"Okay, I think the jig is up. You can drop the act and show yourselves." There was a cruel sneer on his face.

Alaric looked at the group in front of him. He didn't know what to say. Richmond didn't want to speak. He knew he was not strong enough to face a Dark Knight. He had heard stories of the Dark Knights when he was a child. Even if a tenth of the stories were true then he was right to feel terrified.

When there was no answer Gearalt spoke again. "If you want to play it like this I think I am a little stronger than you."

After a moment Alaric felt a slight tug, as if someone was gently pulling the small hairs on the back of his neck. Within moments the gentle tugging changed suddenly. The sensation was not painful, but it was uncomfortable enough to make him start twitching and rubbing his neck. Richmond looked at him, but he was too scared to speak. There was something seriously wrong.

Before Richmond was able to react Alaric suddenly collapsed to the ground. One moment he was fine, albeit with a little discomfort, and the next he felt as though someone had squeezed all the air from his lungs. Not only that but he felt as though someone hit him on the back of his head with a cudgel. There was nothing he could do but roll around on the ground in pain, gasping for breath.

"I take it that was the first time someone has broken one of your spells?" Gearalt was now looking directly at Alaric. There was a slight look of surprise on some of the soldiers' faces, although their features looked out of place. "Now it is going to be a while before you recover, but that is no concern of mine. There is truly nothing that you can do to stop me. I do have a few questions for you, however, so this is going to interesting."

"Carry him to the throne room. Take the other one to the dungeons." Gearalt turned to walk away, but stopped. "No. Take him to the throne room. I think it would be good for him to witness this."

The soldiers quickly snapped to their orders. With Alaric immobilised they had to pick him up. His body was bent over, all twisted in strange ways. The only part of he could move was his eyes. He looked around wildly, trying to see what was happening. No matter how hard he tried he couldn't see what the soldiers were doing to Richmond.

Any thoughts of making a run for freedom left Richmond as the soldiers started him towards the palace. The soldiers carrying Alaric remained in the lead, slightly behind Gearalt. Whenever Richmond lagged in pace he was pushed along. There was nothing in their treatment that gave Richmond any hope of escape. He still thought, if they got to speak with Unwin, there was a chance he could talk him around.

Alaric tried to relax as he was carried towards the palace, but with his body completely seized up and there was nothing he could do. All he could do was watch the palace rise up in front of him and hope he would soon regain his mobility. He doubted very much it would come back in time to escape. To make matters worse there was a ringing in ears, like he had just heard an explosion. His head was also aching. It was hard for him to focus on a single thought.

At first the people in the garden looked at the cause of the commotion. When they realised who was there they looked the other way. From then on everyone made a point not to look at them. They all knew better than to get involved when the new advisor was around. It would not be the first time that someone had stared at Gearalt and then disappeared shortly after. It was well known Gearalt was a dangerous man even if they didn't know his true identity. No matter what they thought the man had the blessing of King Unwin and that was all he needed. No one knew why.

The guards standing at the large golden double doors to the palace snapped to attention when they saw Gearalt approaching. They quickly opened the doors so he didn't have to break stride. The guards looked nervous as the man walked passed. They looked straight ahead when they saw Alaric being carried inside. Again they didn't want to gain any attention from the King's advisor.

Once they were inside the palace they made their way directly to the throne room. The room was at the back end of the palace from the main doors. Inside there were a number of people trying to talk to Unwin. Unwin sat on the throne looking out disinterestedly into the room. He didn't even seem to be listening to the people around him.

The King did not look well. That was the first reaction Richmond had when he entered the room. The King he had known in the past was a strong, powerful man, not only in body, but his mind and personality as well. Now he was hunched over in his throne. His rich brown hair had turned grey. His once well trimmed goatee was now stingy and overgrown. There was nothing domineering about his appearance. He looked like an old and dishevelled serf.

Richmond recognised the man standing by the King's right shoulder. Emil did not look as though he was enjoying himself. He looked even less impressed when he saw Gearalt enter the room, but there was a spark in his eyes when he saw what the soldiers were carrying in. He had felt the same thing as Gearalt when Alaric had cast his spell and he wondered how he managed to capture the Cursed One. He was right with his original forecast of Fenaroz's abilities. His brother was growing in power whilst he was staying stagnate. He desperately needed to use the prophecy to gain in power, but Fenaroz would also learn from the book.

"Your majesty," when Gearalt spoke the entire room went silent. The sarcasm was thick in his voice when he called Unwin 'your majesty'.

The soldiers dumped Alaric on the floor in front of the throne and pushed Richmond to the side. Alaric was starting to get some movement back and his ears where no longer ringing. His headache had disappeared, but in its place there was a strange throbbing. Alaric knew that it was not a good sign.

"These two bandits were caught breaking into the palace grounds. There is no telling what they would have done had they not been captured." There was a certain amount of satisfaction in Gearalt's voice. "I suggest that they be put to death!" The words echoed through Alaric's mind. He didn't think Gearalt would try such a bold move. If he didn't regain his movement completely then there was a very good chance he would end up on the block.

King Unwin stood from the throne. Even in his dullard state he still knew that something was wrong. He walked down the two steps from his dais to get a closer look at his prisoners. He didn't recognise Alaric, who had nearly stretched himself out on the floor. When he reached Richmond something sparked inside him. It was clear on his face, but only for a moment.

"I know this man," Unwin's words were a hoarse mumble.

"Of course you know this man. It is the evil Lord Richmond from Bellarome. It has been long known that he has been plotting to overthrow your crown. Now that we have finally caught him we can give him the death that he deserves," Gearalt spoke with utter confidence.

King Unwin looked confused. He had to believe the words that Gearalt was saying to him, but he also knew the same words were a lie. He didn't know what to do and it was evident on his face. Alaric saw a glimmer of hope in the old man's confusion. He had almost completely stretched himself out, but he was still unable to move freely.

"I don't know," was all Unwin could mumble.

Gearalt knew he could not sentence anyone to death without Unwin's permission. Of course he could, but he knew it would be the end of his ruse. The people would never stand for it if he disobeyed King Unwin's command and he needed Unwin to control the army when the time came.

"Your majesty, there is nothing you can say to save these two. They are traitors to the Kingdom. They worked together to subjugate your command. Their treason deserves death and nothing less." Gearalt couldn't control the anger in his voice.

"Is this true?" A slight amount of drool appeared on the side of his mouth. It was clear that every word was strained.

"No, your majesty," Richmond dropped to one knee as he spoke. "It is all a lie."

Before Richmond could continue Gearalt turned and struck him across the side of his face. The blow knocked him to the ground. Unwin looked as though he wanted to protest, but the words wouldn't come out of his mouth.

"Send them to the dungeons. We will do this again when the King has his senses." Gearalt almost screamed at the soldiers.

The soldiers did as they were told. Like Unwin they didn't look as though they agreed with what they were doing, but they did it anyway. With the aid of one of the soldiers Alaric came to his feet. Before Unwin could protest the two were escorted from the throne room.

The dungeons were deep below the palace. They were cold and damp and carved out of the rocky foundations. A few torches hung in wall sconces giving off a dull light. There was a smell of pure filth, a mixture of rotting food, sweat and human excrement. Alaric dry retched a couple of times before he became accustomed to the smell.

By the time they reached their cell Alaric was walking on his own. The soldiers placed the two men together as it was the only cell they had left. Since Gearalt had assumed the role of Unwin's advisor there had been a lot of people sent to the dungeons. There had been even more people sent to their deaths.

"Alaric! Are you alright?" Richmond asked once the guards had left.

Alaric looked around the cell. A small amount of light came through the small opening in the wooden door that kept them imprisoned. The dark stone glistened in the dull light. He felt much better. He had full movement back, although the throbbing sensation was still in his head.

"Yes, I am fine Richmond." There was something different about Alaric.

"I don't understand. If both Emil and Gearalt are Dark Knights then why aren't we already dead?" Richmond's voice was shaking.

"I don't know, but I am sure there's a reason. I have no doubt that Gearalt is controlling Unwin with a powerful spell. Those he cannot control he has imprisoned or murdered."

"Things are worse than what I thought."

Alaric moved to sit on the solitary bed in the prison cell. There was very little room for the two of them. Only having one bed was going to make their living arrangements even more uncomfortable. He looked around one more time before speaking to Richmond.

"There is another problem." Alaric paused, but this time Richmond did not speak. "I cannot reach the power," he didn't expect Richmond to understand, but he just wanted to say the words out loud.

"What does that mean?" Richmond also sat on the bed. The floor didn't feel too clean and if one of them was going to have to sleep on it Richmond was not going to give in without a fight.

Again Alaric had to decide whether he was going to tell Richmond the truth or not. The shock to the system he had received when Gearalt had broken his spell had jolted his memory. He had not even realised he had cast a spell until after it had been broken. Not all of his memories had returned to him, but there was enough for him to fill in the blanks from the last few months. All it managed to do though was to remind him how hopeless their situation was.

"It means there is no way for us to escape. We must wait for the others to arrive," Alaric didn't seem too worried, which lifted Richmond's spirits for a moment.

Alaric needed time to think. Something had sparked inside him and he needed to collect his thoughts. He was sure what he knew was not part of his previous memories. He also knew it had to be Emil who was shielding him. Gearalt was not powerful enough to control Unwin and half his household as well as stop Alaric from using magic. At least Alaric knew if he was that powerful there was nothing that he could do anyway. His main problem was working on a way out of the prison cell. Without any magic it was going to be a near impossible task. His only hope was for Tancred to find the army. If he was correct the army should be somewhere between Bellarome and Kiarome. If he was wrong then he didn't think he would be living long enough to find out.

***

Night had fallen and Tancred had started to feel concerned when the sun started to set. It had completed its journey for the day and he was very worried. He was also unsure of his next move.

He had agreed when Alaric told him to find the Alliance Army, but that was before he believed they were going to get caught. There was still a chance they would return. Alaric had said by nightfall, but Tancred knew even the best laid plans sometimes failed. If he left too soon he might miss them completely and then everything would be out of balance. He would fail the prophecy and that meant the destruction of the Seven Kingdoms.

With each passing hour Tancred's hopes diminished until he finally resigned himself to the fact they were not coming back. The thought of what would happen to them if they had been caught almost made him physically sick. There was no telling what Gearalt would do. He couldn't leave the city if he knew his Lord had been captured. He didn't know how long Richmond would survive in the palace dungeon as he had grown up in the lap of luxury.

The decision he had to make was whether he was going to listen to Alaric and find the army or if he was going to trust his heart and try and rescue them himself. He fell asleep with the plans racing through his head. It was pure exhaustion that got to him in the end.

In the morning he woke with a plan in his head. He knew he couldn't go against Alaric's wishes. If he was going to storm the palace then he would need an army at his back. Even with the secret hole in the palace wall he would not be able to sneak into the dungeons. If subterfuge was going to work then he would need someone on the inside. With the palace locked down there was no chance of him speaking to anyone inside, let alone convincing them to help.

The only option he had was to find the army. He hoped Alaric knew what he was talking about. If the army was not on its way south then there was no telling where it might be. He did not have time to go chancing around the Kingdom to look. If Gearalt was a friend of Emil's then he was sure it would not be long before they would convince Unwin to execute them.

He made his way to the stable where their horses were kept. If he was going to make the time that he needed then he would have to take one of the elven stallions. Neither looked pleased to see him. For no real reason he chose Tormenta. He did not seem happy at being saddled and when he realised Alaric wasn't coming he started to buck.

"Please horse. I need to save the other two." Tancred called out in frustration. To his surprise the horse settled down. Tormenta's eyes were not as wild and his breathing returned to normal. "Thank you!"

He would have to ride hard if he was going to reach the army in time. He was sure the white stallion was up to the challenge. There was something about the horse that was different to all other horses Tancred had ridden.

It was a slow ride through the crowded streets of Kiarome. Tancred couldn't help but feel a thousand pair of eyes watching him. He looked around nervously, but he couldn't find anyone watching him. Sweat dripped down his body. It was from the stress of his situation more so than the temperature. Once he was close to the northern gate he kicked Tormenta into a gallop. He didn't want to risk being held up at the gate. All he hoped was that the stallion could outrun any archer's arrows that would be fired at him from the wall. If not it would be the shortest rescue attempt in the history of the Seven Kingdoms.

Chapter 19: The Alliance

The army had been on the move for over a week marching harder than they had for a long time. Bern had assumed command of the army, through necessity more than desire. Although Jarwe had show signs of his old self he always slipped back into his malaise. As frustrating as it was all Bern had to do was point the army in the right direction; at least the direction he felt was right. When it came time to make any serious decisions he hoped Jarwe would return to his command.

At first Bern didn't like being in charge of the army. After five days when Jarwe had still not reclaimed his right of leadership the command group officially made him the commanding General. Even though Bern had protested his new, official, position the others would not take no for an answer. In the end he resigned himself to the fact that if everyone was going to look to him for direction he may as well accept it. It was either that or have everything go into complete chaos. He was still working on the feeling he had in the back of his mind. He knew it was telling him to go south, but he had no idea where in the south they were heading. Worse than that he had no idea what he was leading them towards.

He kept to himself as much as possible. Whatever, or whoever, it was inside his head making all the decisions had gone quiet once they had broken camp. Enough information had been left inside Bern's head for him to convince everyone to travel south, but not enough to explain anything. Bern decided if he was by himself there would be no one to ask him questions. He rode at the head of the army leading them wherever his feeling led him.

Now he had reached his first challenge. It had been easy at the start; all he had to do was ride at the head of the army. General Sorrell would name the start and finish times. He knew when the army had to march and when it had to rest. He happily stepped into the role of Bern's lieutenant, but now that they had reached the first major city Bern would have to speak to someone. Although they were in Darshival and Sorrell was General of the King's Army it would be expected of Bern to speak to the local dignitary.

Bern reined his horse at the crest of a small hill and looked down on the city of Bellarome with both hope and doubt in his heart. Their supplies were almost completely exhausted. They only had a day or two of food and water remaining and replenishing supplies in the city was the only chance they had of survival.

Not only did he have the problem of having to barter for supplies he also had the problem of having to control the men in his army. Six thousand men could cause havoc even in the largest of cities. Bern had no idea what they would get up to in a city the size of Bellarome, or if there was even room for them. He only hoped that Sorrell's standing with the King still meant something. He had heard rumours from his scouts that there had been trouble with him. They were only rumours, but he had to take them on board.

Bern's horse stood nervously on the hill. It was as if she knew her master's feelings and reflected them in her own. She stepped lightly as she waited for the order to move. Bern stroked her neck to try and settle her.

A strange feeling of longing for his family came over him. Ever since his personality had started to change so did his feelings towards his wife and children. He still loved them very much and would do anything to protect them, but he didn't long for them as much as he used to. The feeling felt somewhat foreign to him.

Shaking his head he turned his horse around and rode back towards the army. The thoughts of his family disturbed him and he wanted to keep himself busy. He also didn't want to think about the impending meetings. If the Lord of Bellarome didn't cooperate he didn't know what he was going to do. He didn't want to lead his army into a battle against one of his allies, but if they refused his request there was a chance that the Lord was his enemy. That was the problem; he didn't know who he could trust.

"What's the matter?" Duke Hadar asked when Bern returned.

As the leader of the Hondin Lel army he was automatically brought into the command group. There was something about the large man that brought Bern comfort, more so than the two dwarves he had travelled with for so long. He liked the dwarves, but they were nothing like Hadar.

"There's a city ahead. I fear that all is not right. I do not wish to lead this army into war with ourselves."

"I am sure Sorrell will be able to ease your burden. He is with the troops at the moment, but when he returns he should be able to shed some light on the situation." As usual Hadar's words brought him comfort.

"It's close to the midday meal," Bern got off the subject, for his own sanity more than anything else. "It will give us a chance to think."

The army was still out of view of the city. That was one of the other reasons why Bern wanted them to stop. He didn't want to alert the city that they were there, at least not before he had a chance to speak to Sorrell. He needed all the information he could on the local nobleman before he asked for assistance.

Bern had sent a number of his ever growing retinue to find the General. The two dwarves and the remainder of the command group joined him for lunch. Bern didn't want to discuss his plan until he had spoken to Sorrell. In fact he didn't even have a plan. He didn't know what he was going to do. He really hoped his alter-ego would appear. He was starting to remember small events that happened when he was in his comatose state. He liked the way it felt to be in control and he liked being confident in his own decisions.

General Sorrell arrived just before they had all finished eating. He looked tired. He had been working hard to keep the morale of the troops high. Since Prince Hawthorne had taken almost half the army back to Remidia the soldiers had been wondering what they were doing. Their fighting was supposed to be in the empty Kingdom of Avalon and since the battle had been a ruse they were becoming disillusioned. Most of the soldiers believed they should be returning home. Sorrell was doing his best to keep morale high.

"You need to rest more," Captain Aimon offered when Sorrell joined them. "You will have yourself in an early grave."

"That is the life of a General. The work never ends." Sorrell picked at what remained of their lunch. He didn't look too enthused, but he ate anyway.

"I need information about the nobles and the city," Bern asked, getting straight to the point.

"The city is Bellarome and the nobleman is Lord Richmond. He's not married and he has no children. He is very passionate about his lands and his people. He supports the cause. I am sure there will be no problems gaining supplies from him," Sorrell explained before taking another mouthful.

"That is good news. I wasn't sure whether we were going to have any trouble," Bern sounded slightly more relaxed.

"Well don't get your hopes up just yet." The more Sorrell ate the more he wanted to eat, which made the conversation frustratingly slow. "The city of Bellarome is a dangerous place, especially in the palace." He stopped again to take another mouthful. "Intrigue is rife. In fact it is one of the favourite pastimes of nobles throughout Darshival. Nobleman can change in power without a single battle being fought."

"Then what is our best plan of action?"

"We must speak with Lord Richmond. I am sure he will give us everything that we need." Sorrell scraped the last of the food off his plate.

"Good. We will ride to the city immediately." Bern turned to speak to Aimon. "Captain, have the army wait here. I don't want anyone to know we are at the head of a large army. It might make people nervous if they think they are under threat."

"I don't think that is a great idea," Sorrell added.

"Why not? I don't what Lord Richmond to think that we are here to invade," Bern protested.

"That could be true, but you must understand the politics of the land." Bern had to admit he knew nothing about it. He would need all the advice he could get if he was going to survive at the head of the army. "If you are going to ask for help from Lord Richmond for the army it would be best if we show him that we actually have an army. Also, if the discussions don't go to plan then we can use the size of the army as intimidation."

"That makes sense. Aimon, tell the men to make camp within sight of the towers. We will make our presence known." Aimon was already on his way before Bern was able to finish his orders. Although it could have been seen as disrespect Bern was quite happy for Aimon to second guess his instructions. It made his life a lot easier and he was still not comfortable with being the leader.

General Sorrell, Duke Hadar, Dorn, Hulkan, Lord Pernian and Bern started slowly towards the city leaving Captain Aimon in charge of the army. Bern rode at the front of the group with the others behind. No matter how slowly he rode the others would not ride with him.

Shortly after they left, a number of standard bearers ran up to walk beside their appropriate nobleman or leader. It was Aimon's idea to have the announcement of their approach. Bern was still yet to receive a standard, although it was not through lack of trying. Each day someone presented him with a new standard for his approval and each time he rejected them. The other leaders said it was important for the head of an army to fly his colours, but Bern always stated he was not head of the army. He had always said he would draw the line at the numerous pages and servants who always flustered around him. They had been the remnants of those who had travelled with the Remidian army. Prince Hawthorne had left in such a hurry it had been impossible for him to take everyone and a lot of the lesser servants and pageboys had been left behind. They had all taken the opportunity to increase their status with a new position on Bern's staff.

Bern looked around the country side nervously before looking at the turrets on the city walls. He knew there would be archers poised along them, waiting for the word to shoot. Being at the front of the line did nothing to calm his concerns. For all the city watch knew an invading army was approaching.

The traffic on the road, as they approached the city looked at them strangely. Some of them were afraid whilst others looked on with morbid curiosity. No one knew what to make of the strange group. Sorell rode up with Bern before they reached the gate.

"Let me do the talking once we reach the gates. I am sure the guards are going to be somewhat confused," Sorrell said as they neared the main gates.

Bern didn't speak. He didn't want his voice to betray how relieved he was. He had come a long way since the first day the entity had taken control of his body and mind, but he was still not confident on his own. With each day the entity didn't return Bern would sink back into his old self. He hoped it would return when it came time to speak to the Lord of Bellarome as he could not rely totally on Sorrell.

There was a line of people trying to gain entrance into the city. Some were admitted and some were turned away. Those who were turned away did not look happy as they passed by them. Sorrell moved the group away from the line and headed straight towards the gate. He managed to take the lead by himself allowing Bern to drop back with the others.

Before they reached the gates they were stopped by a group of unhappy looking soldiers brandishing their spikes. Bern had a bad feeling things were not going to end well.

"Stop where you are. There are many people trying to gain entrance into the city. You have to wait your turn and hope that you're admitted. Go back to the end of the line." Sorrell only reined his horse to a halt when it was clear that the guard was not going to move.

"I am General Sorrell of the King's Royal Army. I have business within the city and it cannot wait," Sorrell's voice boomed over the din of the crowd causing everyone to stop and see what was happening.

"There is no record of any special visits today. In these days everyone must be pre-announced to gain entrance." The soldier stood his ground and looked around to his fellow soldiers to make sure they still had his back.

"Stand aside soldier. You do not wish to stand between me and the city," Sorrell's boomed again.

"Even if you are the King's General, there is still nothing I can do. The orders have come from Lord Richmond himself and his power precedes yours. There is nothing that I can do without his specific written consent.

General Sorrell's face had gone red from rage. His hand trembled on the hilt of his sword. There was nothing that upset him more than having to kill his own countrymen, but gaining entrance was more important. He hoped it would not come to it, but it was something he was prepared to do.

Just before Sorrell was about to dismount Bern rode up beside him. It was clear by the look on Sorrell's face that he was about to start trouble. The last thing Bern wanted was to start a confrontation with the city's guards.

"We have urgent business with the Lord of the city. We have news from the battle in Avalon and news of pending battles to come."

The confidence in Bern's voice showed the entity had returned, and just in time.

Sorrell didn't know if it was the command in Bern's voice or the words he spoke, but it was obvious the guards were listening. Sorrell could have cursed the men who had previously ignored his commands. Instead he sat in his saddle and glared at them.

"These are truly troubled times and I can understand why you don't allow anyone into the city without papers. What you must understand is that we do not have time to wait. We need entrance into the palace and we need it now."

The guard looked at Bern, trying to judge the character of such a man. "Do you speak for the entire army?"

"I am the General of the Alliance. I have the power to command the army."

"Instruct your army not to move any closer and I will see that you are admitted, as far as getting into the palace that will be entirely up to you." The guard watched for any reaction.

"The army has already been instructed the hold its ground and wait for our return. Be sure that if anything untoward happens to us they have been instructed the level to city at all costs." Any thoughts of detaining them further had completely gone from the guard's mind. The iciness in Bern's voice proved it was no idle threat.

"Hurry along," the soldier stood aside and waited for the group to continue. "Before I change my mind."

Bern almost fell from the saddle has they started towards the city gate. He felt a rush of blood to his head and his eyes fluttered. It only lasted for a moment, but it was enough to make him feel self-conscious. He let Sorrell take the lead and waited for the others to join him. None of them seemed to have noticed his little spell, or at least no one was willing to comment on it. At least their first test had been a success. Bern couldn't remember what had happened, but he was glad that they were still alive.

Sorrell led the way into the city. He had been to Bellarome a number of times in his life. Many on the call of duty, but he had also had a short affair with one of the city's residents. He knew his way around almost as well as he knew Kiarome.

They were not stopped again as they approached the gate, even though there were a number of different soldiers stopping people. As they rode through they received many dirty looks from other people trying to gain entrance.

"What's the matter? Hadar asked when they were all together.

"We have to be careful now. There is something not right within the city. I know a lot of cities have become paranoid with the Evil One on the loose, but there is something different here. I don't know what it is, so stay alert. Lord Richmond is a fair man, but if this is his doing then there is no telling what sort of reception we will get once we are in the palace." Sorrell looked around nervously.

"What do you suggest we do?" Hadar asked.

"Just take notice of what's happening around us. Let me know if you think something is out of place. All being well we would should be back with the army by nightfall." Sorrell made sure that no one else wanted to ask any questions before he left.

Since Sorrell had mentioned it the others had started to notice something strange. People looked at them and then turned away before they got caught staring. They walked around as if they were scared of something.

Bern tried to remember what had happened outside the city walls. He knew he had said something to make the soldiers let them in. He knew the entity had taken over and he just wished he could remember. Although he was starting to get used to the entity he wished that he control it. It could come in handy under certain situations.

The group must have looked a sight riding through the streets of Bellarome. A group like theirs travelling with purpose towards the palace was not something that was seen every day. There would be a lot of excited stories and speculation and it would not be long before their visit would be known throughout the entire city.

Once again they were detained when they reached the entrance to the palace grounds. Sorrell looked around with concern at the many guards on duty.

"Sorry, there is no one allowed into the palace today." One of the guards spoke to Sorrell.

"What is going on? Why are there so many soldiers here?"

"That is private information. I am not at liberty to divulge anything at this time," the guard looked staunch as he spoke.

Sorrell dismounted and motioned for the others to do the same.

"I am General..."

"I don't care what your rank or your name is. There is a situation within the palace and I am not permitted to let anyone inside."

Sorrell looked towards Bern for assistance. Bern shrugged his shoulders. It was obvious the entity wasn't going to help, but Sorrell needed it. He motioned for Bern to join in the discussion.

"This is..."

"Again there is nothing I can do. Unless you are King Unwin himself I cannot allow you in the palace." The soldier was starting to become agitated. He looked around nervously as if someone was watching him.

"At least tell me why we're not allowed in?"

"What's going on over here lieutenant?" A voice boomed from somewhere closer to the palace gate.

"Nothing Captain, just telling these gentlemen that it is time to move along." The lieutenant's eyes didn't leave Sorrell's

There was a moment of silence as the captain of the guard came over to see what was happening. He took one look at Sorrell and the expression on his face changed. Before he said anything he turned to the lieutenant.

"Good work soldier. Now I think it is time you took a break." The captain slapped the lieutenant on the shoulder, sending him on his way.

"General Sorrell," he turned to face the General and saluted in the process. "It is good to see you again sir."

Sorrell took a closer look at the captain. There was something very familiar about the man's face. He had trained and commanded so many men in his career that it was not inconceivable that the captain knew him. Suddenly a smile crossed his face as he recognised the man.

"Well I never," Sorrell quickly returned the man's salute. "If it isn't my old friend Karel, or should I say Captain Karel?"

The two men shook hands ferociously before taking a step back to look at each other. They had been cadets in the Darshival Regular Army and had been best friends during training. Once they graduated they were sent to different stations. They had not seen each other since. Sorrell hoped their old relationship would gain them entrance to the palace.

"What brings you here and with such illustrious company?" Karel looked at Sorrell's companions for the first time.

"We need to see Lord Richmond. It's a long story and time is short." Sorrell didn't mean to be obtuse, but he didn't want to give too much away whilst they were out in public.

"Of course. Time is always in short supply these days. Come with me. I know somewhere we can talk," Karel replied.

"I would love to catch up with you Captain, but we're in a hurry." Sorrell tried to be as polite as possible.

"I can appreciate that, but I have some information that you need to hear first," Captain Karel kept his voice low.

His words and his tone piqued Sorrell's curiosity. There was something telling him that he should listen to what Karel had to say. Regardless they would not get access to the palace without Karel's permission.

"Lead the way," Sorrell offered.

Captain Karel led the group towards the guard house. Inside a number of guards, including the lieutenant who first spoke to them, who were having a break. Karel quickly ordered them to leave. The soldiers did as they were told, albeit moaning and grumbling.

"Things have changed in the city over the last few days it's hard to know where to start." Karel paused as he thought. "I suppose the most pertinent problem is the location of Lord Richmond."

"What are you talking about?" Sorrell sounded both confused and frustrated.

"Lord Richmond has been missing since this morning. He has been avoiding his duties over the last few days, but when he wasn't seen at all we thought we better look for him. It was midday before anyone noticed that he wasn't here. It wasn't long before it was realised that he wasn't anywhere in the palace, or at least he was nowhere anyone could find him."

"I am sure that isn't out of the ordinary. I know sometimes I like to disappear for a while. When you are in a position where people look for you all the time sometimes it's nice to disappear."

"Be that as it may his advisor, Tancred, is also missing. If Richmond was on a simple sabbatical then Tancred would remain to continue his work," Karel continued to explain. He had more to say, but Sorrell interrupted him again.

"I admit that does sound strange, but again I do not think that there is any need to jump to any dire conclusions. I am sure that there is a simple explanation." Karel wished that Sorrell would let him finish his story.

"That's not all. A few days ago Lord Richmond's nephew arrived in the city. Apparently he was here to learn from his uncle on how to be a leader. Now I am not saying this is a fabrication of the truth, but I have seen the Lord's nephew a few years ago and he didn't look anything like the man in the palace. The man in the palace looked to be a good four inches taller and his hair looked lighter."

"What does this have to do with anything? Did I mention that I was in a hurry?" Sorrell was starting to become annoyed.

"If you would let me finish, General, it will all start making sense. Or at least it will not make any sense at all." Karel's words were somewhat mysterious. "This so called nephew has also disappeared. All three of them disappeared at the same time. I believe they are not telling us what really happened. Now this isn't even the full story. They found the city magistrate dead the other day. I have seen the body and if he had been dead for only a day then I am the son of an orglin. The body looked as though it had been there for over a week. If this is the case then how is it that the magistrate was seen up and about until only a day ago? Something is not right and I think you need to be very careful once you're inside." Karel warned the group. He continued on to explain about the other deaths and the poison attempt on Richmond's supposed nephew. Karel knew more than most within the palace. He made sure he knew more than others.

"This is indeed disturbing." Sorrell looked at the others as he spoke. He had his suspicions of the identity of Richmond's nephew, but he wanted to speak to Bern first before he voiced them. "Thank you captain, this information will be more than valuable. Tell me, who is it in control of the city if Lord Richmond is no longer here?"

"That's going to be your problem. There are a lot of minor officials trying to wrest control. None of them would openly try to supplant Richmond without knowing his exact whereabouts. I fear with the current political climate if he doesn't return in the next week or two it will be a different story." Karel was a little more pleased now that he had been able to explain the situation in its entirety.

"I see. Who is it that we should speak to once we are inside?"

"The man who by rights should be in control is the Chancellor of the Exchequer. He is an elderly man, but what he lacks in physical strength he makes up for in character. He will do alright whilst there is some level of control, but I fear he will not last long if Richmond doesn't return. His name is Medwin Bargeld. I am sure he will help you with whatever you need. The only problem is whether he has enough control over the other officials to help you." Karel seemed somewhat pleased with himself. "Now I think we have taken up enough of each others' time. I hate to think what my soldiers will be doing without me."

"Thank you for all your help Captain. I will make sure that Lord Richmond hears of your service," the compliment was more than Karel deserved, but it showed on his face that he appreciated it. "Now if you would give us a few moments to speak before we leave that would be greatly appreciated."

"Off course General. Take all the time you need." Captain Karel stood, saluted and then left the room.

Sorrell turned to the others. "This is very disturbing news." He watched for the others' reactions. "I think the most concerning piece of information is this supposed nephew of Richmond's. Does anyone want to hazard a guess at his identity?"

"It's Alaric!" Bern spoke before anyone had a chance to.

"How do you know that?" asked Hulkan.

Bern simply raised one eyebrow in return and they all knew the answer. There was no doubting that Bern's instincts were always correct. They had all thought the mystery man was Alaric, but they did not want to assume.

"If it is Alaric, then what happened to the others?" Dorn was the first to recover from the initial shock.

Everyone looked at Bern, even though he didn't specifically ask anyone the question.

"How am I supposed to know the answer that question?" Bern became quite defensive.

"We are getting off the track here," Sorrell took control. "We need to get into see Chancellor Medwin. If it is Alaric who is with the Lord then he might be in great danger. Either way he is no more than a day away. The sooner we can get back on the road the sooner we will know what is happening."

There could be no arguing with that logic. The day was already starting to fade away. There was no chance that they would be moving the army that day, but if they weren't quick then it would be at least another day before they were moving again. Their only hope for a quick turnaround was if the Chancellor agreed to their demands. Sorrell knew with Lord Richmond missing any chance of help was going to be very difficult to gain. Sorrell knew how cutthroat political life could be in Darshival. No one would want to make a move to help or hinder without a guarantee that it would bring them favour in the court.

Chapter 20: Ask For Help

They found the chancellor in Lord Richmond's chambers. He looked out of place sitting at the large desk. He looked old and fragile with a soft crop of white hair on his head. The weight of the world had rested on his shoulders more than once. After the page announced them, they entered the room. The chancellor looked up, but there was no expression on his face.

"What can I do for you gentlemen?" his voice sounded friendly even though his expression didn't change.

"We need assistance," said Sorrell.

"I don't think there is anything I can do. Lord Richmond is missing and he hasn't left anyone in charge. I am doing my best to keep the city running, but I think that is as far as my power extends. What is it that you need?" Medwin sounded dejected.

"We need supplies. Food, water, bedding and anything else you can spare. We could also use reinforcements," Sorrell sounded hopeful.

"Do you have a list of exactly what you need?"

Pernian produced a list of requirements. He passed them across the table to Medwin. It was a number of pages long and Medwin picked up a small pair of spectacles and put them on. He looked at the first few items before flicking through the rest of the pages. As he read some of the items on the first page he started shaking his head slowly. The further he read the more he shook his head. When he was finished he took the glasses off and looked across the table.

"This is a long list. Even with the permission of Lord Richmond I don't think I could allow this. Giving away this many goods would cause a depression that I don't think the city could survive, lucky for me I do not need to make that decision." Medwin sounded relieved as the words came out of his mouth.

"I understand this is hard, but we require more supplies. This is a letter sealed by King Unwin, as well as Faxon and Oriana," Pernian said as he passed the letter across the table.

To our loyal subjects,

Please supply those who carry this letter all the assistance that you would to me and my family. These are grave days and we must do all that we can to defeat the evil that plagues the Seven Kingdoms. All those who hinder these men will be considered traitors of the state and will therefore be charged with treason.

Those who entreat with these men will be rewarded when the battle is won.

King Faxon   *Queen Oriana*   King Unwin

Medwin read the letter carefully before placing it on the table. The first two signatures were foreign to him, but there was no denying the last. He had seen Unwin's signature many times on the various documents coming in and out of the treasury. He also recognised the royal seal, which had already been broken, in wax on the outside of the letter. Now he had a real dilemma, he knew a royal order could supersede one from his Lord, but since his Lord was not there he doubted he had the authority to delivery their request.

He lowered his head into his hands. He wished he had more time to make his decision, but he knew the men seated before him would need an answer. He needed a way to keep his honour without creating the treason that the letter so clearly stated.

"I wish I could help you, but you see that I cannot exceed my authority. With Lord Richmond's absence I can make mandatory decisions for him, but for something this large we really must wait for him to return." Medwin wasn't deliberately being difficult, he just really wanted to keep his job and his life. There was no doubt in his mind that he would end up dead if he agreed to their claim and refusing wasn't going to much better.

"I am sure that you are not being deliberately troublesome, but we are in a great hurry and need your assistance now. I am sure Lord Richmond would honour our King's request." General Sorrell spoke knowing full well the position Medwin was in.

"The best I can do is organise a conference with the heads of the household. Between all of us I am sure that we can make a decision. As you can appreciate I cannot speak for Lord Richmond unless he specifically commands it. If I was to agree to give you everything on this list I would be condemning my people to death." Medwin was trying his best not to be bullied.

Sorrell knew the full list could not be supplied by the one city. He knew how important it was to keep the army going, but he could not sacrifice such a beautiful city as Bellarome. If they received half of what they asked for he was sure it would be enough to get them to their next location. He only wished he knew how far away their next location was. Relying on Bern's intuition wasn't a great way of leading an army.

"Very well, have the palace council summoned immediately. In the meantime have a room ready for us and have some food sent in," Sorrell ordered.

"I certainly have a room you can make yourself comfortable in. I do not think that I will be able to assemble to appropriate people today. I think it would take at least a week to get everyone together."

The old man had just overstepped his boundaries. Sorrell took a menacing step towards him and slammed his fist on the table. The force caused everything to bounce and Medwin to jump in his seat.

"You will do as I command. Time is of the essence and I do not have any to waste sitting around the palace. My soldiers are close to starvation. If you leave me no choice then I will have to enforce my King's edict and take the city by force. Anyone who resists will be arrested and tried for treason. Now I believe that you have a job to do."

No one had ever seen a seemingly feeble old man move so fast. He had not liked the threat, but he also knew he had no choice. Even if he doubted the letters authenticity he could not go against such a powerful edict. Again his only saving grace was his own lack of authority.

"Once you have assembled all the available members we will discuss the best way for you to help with our current situation. Those who cannot make it will abstain their votes. Now go." Medwin was almost out the door by the time Sorrell had finished his speech.

They were not alone long before a pageboy came to take them to their room. The palace was full of guest rooms for visiting dignitaries and one was more than sufficient to accommodate their needs.

"I don't think that I could lead the army against the city. We cannot fight against the people who we are trying to protect," Bern said once they were alone.

"Do you think it will really come to this?" Lord Pernian asked from the other side of the room as he was staring out of the window.

"I don't know. I believe that they will do the right thing. Bellarome, more so than any other city in Darshival, is rife with political unrest. If someone thinks they can wrest control from Lord Richmond by blocking our request then they will. I do not think anyone will truly disobey an order from the King. The only way they could resist is if they try to claim his signature is fake," Sorrell explained.

"Either way we better get this situation sorted soon. If this mystery man masquerading as Richmond's nephew is indeed Alaric then we need to find him. With Alaric had the head of the army it will put to bed any doubts on its legitimacy," Duke Hadar spoke.

"I don't think that we are going to have any chance in catching Alaric. There are only three of them and there is an entire army of us. All we can do is hope that they left under their own volition. If they were kidnapped then there is no telling how long it would take for us to catch them," Pernian mused.

"I don't think that Alaric has been kidnapped." Bern's words were as mysterious as ever.

"How do you know that?" Hulkan asked.

"The same way that I know everything else. I am sure that if Alaric had been kidnapped then I would know about it. I can't explain why and I don't know if I ever will," Bern explained as best he could.

"Then what is he doing?" Dorn asked.

"If only I knew. All I can tell you is that he is doing what he thinks is right." Bern stood up and walked to the window. His life had taken a huge turn. Life on the farm had been so simple. He got up in the morning and went to bed at night knowing exactly what he had done and what he was doing. Now he had no control over his life. With each new day came new challenges. Sometimes he wished that he was back on the farm, with his wife and children. With the thought of his family a tear appeared in his eye. He quickly wiped it away and returned to the others.

"We just need to concentrate on getting the supplies for the army. We cannot afford to go to war with our own side," he said to get his family out of his mind.

A knock on the door was a welcome distraction to everyone. No one wanted to think about what would happen if the council did not accept their proposal. A small group of servants came in with their food.

The meal brought another distraction. Whilst everyone was eating no one spoke. They all used the food to quietly contemplate their own lives. When they had all finished there was nothing they could do to avoid conversation.

"I suppose we should plan for the worst." It was General Sorrell who spoke the words that no one wanted to hear.

"That's true." Hadar agreed.

"If we move quickly enough I am sure we can move the army into the city without them knowing. If we keep our heads in this meeting and not lose control then it will work. If we move at night with no lights then we can control the gate before they know what we are doing. There is no way they will be able to resist." There was a strangeness to Bern that suggested the entity had returned, but it was not as strong as before. Bern's consciousness remained, but he knew the entity was speaking through him.

"I think that is the only way. We can ill afford to create a siege situation. We do not have the time or the infrastructure for that," Sorrell agreed with Bern's tactics and began to ask the others.

Before they had time to discuss their plans further there was another knock on the door. The door was pushed open before anyone had a chance to react. A nervous looking pageboy was standing on the other side. He looked as though he had a message, but he didn't want to speak.

"Come in boy!" Sorrell snapped at him, annoyed at being disrupted. "Tell us why you are here."

The pageboy stepped nervously into the room. His hands were behind his back and he played with them as he walked. There was no confidence about is demeanour and that made everyone nervous. Finally, after waiting almost a minute, the boy finally spoke. "The council is ready to see you sir!"

"Very good," Sorrell kept the commanding tone in his voice. "Give us a moment and then show us where they are."

The pageboy bowed awkwardly in a show of respect. In the end he just looked clumsy. He quickly moved out of the room and shut the door.

"Let me do the talking when we reach the council. They know who I am and will respect my judgement. They can be very particular about rank. They will not recognise any foreigners as their equals or betters," Sorrell looked at everyone, but his eyes stayed on Bern longer than the others. "We need to step very carefully if we are going to avoid a war."

Everyone nodded their heads, except for Bern.

The pageboy jumped when the door opened and the men started walking out of the room. They didn't know whether he was just a nervous character or whether he knew there was going to be bad news. Either way his attitude didn't fill anyone with confidence. The walk to the meeting was tense enough as it was. The pageboy was only making things worse.

They were all relieved when they reached the door to the meeting room. The pageboy had one last job to do and then he could return to his normal day-to-day tasks. He knocked once on the door and then entered. He quickly shut the door behind him, leaving the group waiting. When he returned he did not look happy at having to speak again.

"You may go in," he said, his voice shaking.

Sorrell took the lead. He didn't dismiss the pageboy so the young man had to wait as they all entered the room. As soon as the door closed the pageboy went racing down the corridor. He was so relieved to be gone he didn't notice the man who had been watching from a nearby doorway.

The council chamber was the largest room in the palace. It was almost twice as large as the throne room and nearly half again of the main dining hall.

The chambers themselves were shaped like a half colosseum. Rows of chairs stepped down to the main floor where a small group of men sat around a long rectangular, oak table. Behind them there was an even longer rectangular, much more impressive table made of marble. Finally behind the marble table was a large podium which held a jewelled throne. There was a thin layer of dust over it, indicating it was only used by King Unwin himself when he presided over their meetings. It had been well over a year since the King had visited Bellarome.

"Come and join us," Chancellor Medwin called from the table. Even though the man was aging his voice carried clearly around the room.

The smaller table only had seating for ten people. Medwin sat at the head with three people to his left and four to his right. As there was only room for Sorrell and Bern so the others were forced to sit in the gallery. No one had a problem with being left out. They had no idea what they would say if they were involved. Sorrell could see what they were doing as soon as he stepped into the room. They had created a situation where they had the strength of numbers.

"Take a seat. Unfortunately there is not enough room for all of you." A thin, middle-aged man who was sitting next Medwin spoke. He had an arrogant look on his face and his words were dripping with ignorance. Bern took an instant dislike to him.

Sorrell sat at the foot of the table, so he was directly facing Medwin. Bern sat to his right, next to a young, fat man. The man seemed nervous to be sitting next to Bern. There was a thin layer of sweat on his brow. Bern didn't know if he knew something that was not good or whether he was just in awe of their company.

"I have briefly explained the situation to the council," Medwin spoke. "Now it is your turn to plead your case."

"Thank you Chancellor," Sorrell started to speak, but was interrupted before he could continue.

"This is highly irregular. I was under the impression that a Remidian was at the head of this so called Alliance Army. Why is it that you speak on his behalf, Sorrell?" The skinny man spoke again. It was clear he was against the idea of giving them support.

Sorrell looked around the table before he spoke again. For the first time he could tell which way most of the councillors where going to vote. It was clear that the man to the left of Medwin was going to be as difficult as possible.

"It is true that General Bern is in command of the army, but as his advisor I reserve the right to speak to this council." Sorrell had already thought that someone would mention the fact that he was not in charge of the army. It was not going to bode well for them that a Remidian was in charge and even more so if they knew Bern's background. He hoped any rumours had yet to reach the city. "I am General of the King's Royal

Army and come to you on his behalf. If you deny me then you are denying the King himself."

"We have heard about the letter and we have our doubts of its authenticity. It is widely known that the King is not in his right mind." The words coming from the councillor's mouth infuriated Sorrell. The councillor was so smug with his comment that he didn't notice the look on Sorrell's face.

"What is your name councillor?" Sorrell spoke between clenched teeth.

"My name is Councillor Redwor Stadtuhr. I am in charge of monitoring the city watch. Why do you ask?"

"I just want to make sure the magistrate announces your name correctly before the executioner takes your head off," Sorrell's voice boomed throughout the chambers.

His words echoed for a moment and then there was silence. Redwor looked around the table for support, but there was none coming. Those who had supported Redwor and opposed the help to the army were suddenly unsure of themselves. None of them had believed the threat of being charged with treason had been real.

"Now would anyone else like to speak ill of our King?" Sorrell looked hard at everyone around the table. No one made contact with his eyes as he looked at them. "I didn't think so. There can be no denying the authenticity of our letter. It is a command sent to you directly from your King. Now, I ask all of you, who will stand in?" Sorrell was now trying to be as diplomatic as possible.

No one spoke for a moment and Councillor Redwor regained his courage. "That is all well and good to speak of patriotism, but that is not the only question on the table. Of course no one will defy an order from the King, but we cannot authorise what you ask. Only Lord Richmond has the power to enforce what you are asking. In his absence we only have the power to run the city and that is all."

"We ask only what you can spare," all eyes turned to Bern. "It is a time of war and the threat is to everyone. Richmond has left you all in charge of the city in his stead. If this was not the case then he could have instructed you of his wishes. I therefore implore you to do the right thing. Without these supplies good men will die before they have a chance to fight for your freedom. This army is the last chance that we all have for survival. If the Evil One wins then you will all be his slaves or worse."

"Your words are all well and good, but a decision like this needs to be made by a majority vote of the entire council, not just the eight of us. The city will be in disarray if we approve the movement of our supplies. Unfortunately we are not going to be able to help you with your request." Redwor wasn't about to back down.

There was silence for almost a minute as everyone took in what had just been said. Bern looked at Sorrell who in turn shrugged his shoulders. Originally he did not want Bern to speak, but since he didn't want to talk himself he was happy to let him go. Bern had gained some ground with the other councillors, but he doubted it was enough to take them to a vote.

"Unfortunately we do not have time for the other councillor's to arrive. We need to gather together the supplies now and have them loaded by morning. The army must be on the march again at first light. We have camped a short way outside of the city. It should not take long for you to fill our wagons," Bern continued.

"That still doesn't change the fact that we cannot authorise…" Redwor was about to repeat himself, but was cut off by Medwin.

"That is not entirely true. It is possible for the sitting members of the council to take a vote in extreme circumstances without the remaining members being present. I would suggest that these circumstances are quite extreme." Medwin commanded the attention of the other members.

"I do not know of this law, Chancellor. I think that you will have to show proof," a middle-aged councillor spoke from down the table.

His words were followed by a few mumbled agreements as well as nodding of heads. Redwor smiled at the response. The councillors who agreed with his decision were still holding strong. He would make sure that there was no way the army was going to receive their supplies. In doing so he would gain enough support with the other councillors to usurp control from Medwin. That was the start of his plan, then, if Richmond did not return soon he would be able gain control of entire city. Lord Redwor had a good ring to it.

Chancellor Medwin was up to the challenge. He knew they would not take his word on the law. He produced a large tome that he had secreted under the table. The leather bound book had large silver lettering on the front. The words read *Laws & Regulations in Time of Crisis*. There was an awed hush over the table as Medwin flicked through the pages. There was little doubt that the Chancellor of the Exchequer knew what he had been talking about and it was not long before he found the passage he was looking for.

He passed the book to his left. Once one of the councillors had read the passage they passed it on to the next. Once everyone had finished reading the book of laws they returned it to Medwin. The look on the other councillors' faces brought a smile to the old man's face. He had won a small victory. He knew Richmond would have agreed to help the Alliance if he was still around. Lord Richmond supported King Unwin to a fault and would not have disobeyed his edict.

"As you all can see that there is a way we can make the decision now. I urge you all to vote towards helping the Alliance. We cannot survive if we do not support the impending war."

"Now here is where we have another difference in opinions. There is no hard evidence to say that there is actually going to be a war. Everyone was so sure that the war would take place on the fields of Avalon, but obviously that did not happen. There has been no sign of an invading army in these parts. I have not heard news of an invading army in any Kingdom. If you can quite categorically prove that there is a threat to our lands then I will be more than happy to support the war, but if you cannot than I do not think that we should vote to decimate our own supplies," Redwor spoke again.

"Don't keep your head in the ground. There is a threat to all Kingdoms. It is true that we have been duped into thinking the battle will take place in Avalon, but mark my words that there is no doubt the Evil One in now somewhere within the Seven Kingdoms. His army is also here somewhere. The fact that we do not know where it is makes things even more perilous. We move to find his army and destroy it. If you do not help us then you risk the lives of all who you hold dear. This threat affects everyone and everyone must do their bit to help." Bern's words were inspiring and Redwor could see his support was slipping.

If Redwor was not able to convince the council to vote against the support then his plans for supremacy would be over. He was running out of ideas. The strange man who was in charge of the army had a compelling argument. Even Redwor was beginning to believe him. His only chance was to try and discredit the General.

"Who are you to tell us Darshivallians what to do? You are from Remidia and you speak for that Kingdom not ours. How can you sit there and tell us what to do?"

Sorrell's face had gone red due to the councillor's words while Bern's composure had remained the same. He knew there was no strength to Redwor and the other councillors felt the same. All that needed to be said had been said. There was nothing more he could do to convince them. Bern placed a reassuring hand on the General's shoulder. That was all that it took to refrain Sorrell from speaking.

"Time is getting away from us. I think that it is time to vote."

Redwor looked around the table for support. None of the other councillors, even the ones who backed his plan, would speak on his behalf. Redwor knew he had lost. There was nothing more that he could do. His last attack had failed miserably. In the end it did more harm to his cause than good.

"Those who oppose to support the Alliance, raise your arms now." Medwin looked around the table.

Redwor quickly raised his arm and then looked around the table. At first no one made a move to vote. Slowly two more arms were raised in the air. When it was clear that no one else was going to vote Medwin spoke again.

"There are three voting against the move to support the Alliance. Now for those who support the move, vote now."

Medwin was the first to raise his arm. There was one more who raised his arm immediately. Redwor felt a glimmer of hope. There was still a chance the other three remaining voters could abstain. If that was the case then he would win.

Slowly the fat councillor who sat next to Bern raised his arm. There was another short wait before the final vote needed was raised. With the vote decided the remaining councillor abstained.

"Now that it is decided we are going to help your cause it is time to talk about compensation." Redwor was not finished yet. The idea had just come to him when he realised he had lost. "I am sure that King Unwin plans on compensating us for our generosity." A broad smile came across Redwor's face when he saw the expression on Sorrell's.

Bern also noticed the expression on Sorrell's face and jumped in before he had a chance to speak. "Let us see how much of that list you can supply and then we shall speak about compensation. I am sure that King Unwin does not have a problem paying his loyal subjects, or do you not believe this councillor?"

"That is exactly my point. If you spoke on behalf of King Unwin then you would be able to guarantee compensation. I doubt very much the King even knows you are here." Redwor was starting to get the attention of his supporters again.

"Of course the King doesn't know that they are here," to everyone's surprise it was Medwin who spoke. "The letter is a general rights note. King Unwin has signed and sealed it so they do speak on his behalf. The council has voted and we have agreed to help. If compensation was going to be a problem then you should have brought it up before we voted. I am sure when this is all said and done the King will do what he sees fit. Now that the purpose of this meeting is completed I am sure we all have more important matters to deal with. This is a long list and it will take a while to take stock." Medwin's voice took on a commanding tone. There could be no doubt in his authority. Even Redwor seemed surprised.

"Do you think you will be able to get everything to us by first light?" Sorrell's voice was calm now. Medwin's words had obviously appeased him.

"We will work throughout the night to try and get you on the road." Medwin stood as he spoke. "Now let us get to work."

Chapter 21: A New Surprise

The wagons started reaching the campsite two hours after dusk. The sight was welcomed by everyone in the army, but none more so than the cooks. They had been watering down all the food to try and make it carry further until they started to run out of water. The new supplies meant the cooks could properly feed the soldiers again.

Along with the wagons of food and water there were also more men for the army. Medwin had managed to find two hundred soldiers to bolster the ranks. He had taken quite a few men from the city watch. It was purely designed to annoy Redwor. He also knew that Redwor could fill his ranks from the regular soldiers. A number of tradesmen were also supplied, but not as many as had been asked for, but Sorrell had not expected to receive any at all.

The supplies continued to arrive throughout the night. Medwin had not lied when he told them they would do everything possible to get them on the road at first light. They didn't need all the supplies to start moving the army. It was more for peace of mind that they were going to receive what they had asked for. The soldiers would be on the march before everyone else and the wagons would have more than enough time to catch up.

The command group had convened in the command tent when they returned from the city. Sorrell had stayed behind at the palace to make sure that nothing untoward happened, but there was no point in everyone else staying. Medwin had suggested that they take rooms inside the palace for the night, but they had all preferred to get back to the main camp. Captain Aimon would need to know the result of the meeting and they did not want to leave the army alone for too long.

"I am glad to hear you were successful. I was somewhat doubtful we would get what we wanted," Aimon replied when he heard the result of their meeting.

"It seems we will get over half of what we asked for. That should be enough to keep the army on their feet for almost a month," Hadar said.

Bern had returned to his malaise, which indicated to everyone that the entity had disappeared. It was becoming harder to tell when it was happening and it wasn't obvious until the entity had gone.

"That is very fortunate. Where do we go from here?" Aimon asked.

All eyes moved to Bern, who was sitting at the back of the tent with Jarwe. Everyone had been so concerned about restocking their supplies that no one questioned their next move. It was clear to all that

Bern was in no state to make a decision, but unfortunately they needed to know. The army would be preparing to move in less than twelve hours.

"I don't know." Bern looked up from where he sat. His eyes were sunken and he looked years beyond his age. His voice was weak as he tried to speak. "I have no feelings at all."

"Why don't you go and lie down?" Hadar spoke softly. "You look near death. I am sure once you are rested you will have a better idea."

Aimon seemed annoyed with Hadar's suggestion. He wanted to know what their next move was. Although he had never been a General, Aimon had always had a certain amount of power within the Entero Royal Army. Now he had to wait on the advice of a farmer. They called him a General, but he had really done nothing to prove his place. Sure enough he had led them through the fog curtain, but that was pure luck. There had been no military tactics involved in his charge. Now he was considered, at least within the command circle, as the leader of the army.

Bern slowly got to his feet. His body ached from head to foot. His eyes flickered at the thought of sleep and he almost fell where he stood. He wavered on his feet for a moment before he started on his way. He could hear the others talking as he walked passed, but he could not make out what they were saying. It was as if he was walking in a dream.

He didn't know how he managed to find his tent or how long it took him to get there. He was sure there would have been a number of servants following him, just in case he needed something, but he did not notice them.

It was early in the morning when Bern woke again. He didn't know how long he had been asleep. He couldn't remember lying down on his bedroll or falling asleep. All he knew was that he felt much better for the rest. His body no longer ached and he felt as good as he ever had.

Outside his tent the campsite was still a hive of activity. The sky was still dark and the moon was covered by clouds so he couldn't gauge what time it was.

The command group was due to meet again before the army was ready to move. They still needed a direction to travel and after much discussion they had decided to continue in a southerly direction.

Sorrell had recently returned to the campsite from the city and found Bern wandering through the tents. The large man looked tired, although he still had all his strength about him. He smiled when he saw Bern walking towards him.

"How goes it General?" Sorrell greeted Bern warmly.

"Better now, General." Bern replied just as warmly.

The two men walked towards the command tent. It would still be too early for the meeting, but there was a chill in the night air and the tent would be much warmer.

"Do we know where we are heading from here?" Sorrell asked.

Bern still had no feeling on which direction they should travel. The pressure on him to decide was more frustrating than not knowing himself. They all knew he didn't control the feelings he felt. They came and left unbidden. All he knew was that he had to go where his instincts told him.

"I do not know. I have no indication on the direction we should be travelling. I just hope the others have decided." Bern spoke honestly, if a little downcast.

"Never mind. I am sure you will tell us what to do when the time is right. I think our course will lead us south. That is the direction we have been heading in and until you tell us otherwise that will be the course that we take. To be honest with you I wouldn't mind checking in on King Unwin. There was something Redwor said that has been disturbing me. I have asked a few people whilst I was in the city and they have all told me the same thing," Sorrell paused.

"What is it?"

"There is something wrong with King Unwin. Now these are only rumours, but there are only so many times you can hear something before you start to take it seriously. The first rumour is that King Unwin has himself a new advisor. It seems he is calling the shots in the palace and that is very disturbing. Unwin has always been a commanding leader and would not submit his control to another. It seems that Unwin has ordered some strange new laws. I don't know any specifics, but it seems that the citizens of Kiarome are struggling, at least those who do not bow down to this new advisor," Sorrell's voice was thick with concern.

"That is indeed disturbing, but I do not see what we can do to help. I don't think it would be a wise idea to take the army into Kiarome. If the King is under the spell of this new advisor I don't believe there is anything we can do." Bern's words were not what Sorrell wanted to hear.

To emphasise his point Sorrell banged his fist on the table. "I know that you're right. There will be nothing to gain if we try and invade the city. Without solid evidence that there is foul play at hand we should take things slowly. I guess either way we need to stay on whatever course we are on, but if it leads us past Kiarome then I will be paying a personal visit to the palace."

Bern simply nodded. He knew what Sorrell must be thinking. He was the most patriotic man he knew. He loved his King and Kingdom. For someone to come and cause havoc must be tearing him up inside. The fact there was nothing he could do about it made matters even worse.

He felt for the General, but he knew he must stay the course. If one city was to fall in the course of their mission then that was a cost he was willing to pay. If one kingdom fell it would be sad, but again it would be a necessary loss if they were to win the war. Cities and Kingdoms could be regained, but if they lost the war then all the Kingdoms would fall.

Before they had a chance to continue their conversation the tent flap was opened and a skinny, young serving man entered. When he saw the two sitting at the table he jumped with surprise. He looked around the tent for somewhere to hide.

"Come in lad," Sorrell's voice was soft, yet still commanding.

"Sorry, my Lord. I was instructed to start preparing things for your breakfast an hour before dawn. I will come back when you are finished," the boy stammered.

"Don't be silly. We are just passing the time away. You do what you have to do." Sorrell smiled at the young boy. As much as he wanted to continue his conversation with Bern he knew the others would be joining them soon and the young man would be in great peril if did not have the tent ready for them.

Over the next few minutes a number of young men and women came and went. They fussed over their own little tasks, fresh linen was placed over the table and a multitude of platters and jugs were lined up. It was Captain Aimon who had organised their breakfast. It was more extravagant than Sorrell and Bern would have expected. They both knew they had just replenished their supplies, but they also knew that it would not be long before those supplies would start running out again.

Both Bern and Sorrell restrained themselves until the others arrived. Neither of them touched the food, although they did treat themselves to a mug of tea. It was too tempting for them to wait and it also gave them a reason to avoid the conversation.

"It is good to see everyone here." Sorrell took the chair for their meeting when everyone had arrived and they were all settled.

"Where is it we are heading this morning?" Aimon asked the same question he had asked the night before.

"We continue on our southerly course," even though all eyes were on Bern it was Sorrell who gave the answer.

Aimon didn't look pleased. No one watched his reaction or else they would have questioned him. There was no good reason why he shouldn't want the army to move south. He quickly looked around the table to see if anyone had noticed his reaction. When he knew that he was safe he returned to his regular demeanour.

Since it was the direction they were already planning on travelling no one questioned their motives. They all assumed that Bern had made up his mind and told Sorrell before they arrived. Everyone was happy to except the fact that sometimes Bern differed control to Sorrell, considering it was his home Kingdom.

"Do we have a plan of attack or are we just wandering around aimlessly again?" Captain Aimon snapped when no spoke.

"What's wrong Aimon?" asked Hadar, who was sitting next to the Captain.

"I'm sorry. I much prefer to know where I'm travelling and who I'm fighting. I know there is some dissention within the troops. They need to know what we are doing. There is only so long before the aura of Bern's victory in Avalon wears away." Aimon tried to keep his voice level.

"You make a valid point Aimon, but until we know what we are doing the troops will just have to trust our judgement. We are not going to gain anything by giving them false information and we are definitely not going to gain anything by telling them the truth. The soldiers will just have to do their job and take their instructions from us. Once we know more then we will be able to give them more information," Bern's words were followed by some slow nodding by the others.

Once they had all eaten their fill they all made their way out of the tent. A soft grey light filled the sky, indicating the sun was about rise. The soldiers had already packed up their small tents and were starting to assemble. The remaining tents would be broken down and put on the wagons by the functionaries. Those in the command, the cooks and the other tradesmen all had people to help pack down and set up their tents and equipment.

"Will we lead them along the highway or should we take them another route?" Sorrell asked Bern when they were mounted at the front of the line.

Bern gave Sorrell a sour look.

"Sorry. I think we should lead them to the west of the highway. Generally the highway will be too busy to lead an army along. The ground to the west is a lot smoother than that to the east." Sorrell knew the land well and was hoping he might have an idea of what was ahead of them.

The entire army was waiting for one of two people to start them. There were those who still followed General Jarwe and those who followed General Bern. Jarwe, who was riding at the front with the rest of the command group, waited for Bern to give the command. As soon as Bern slowly kicked his horse into action and Jarwe followed, the entire army began to grind into action.

As they started around to the western side of the city wall they could still see wagons coming from the city. It was a promising sign that they were getting what they needed. They could receive supplies to the camp up until midday and they would still catch up with the soldiers by the end of the day. Hadar and the two dwarves stayed behind to make sure nothing untoward happened. Someone would have to sign off on the list to appease Redwor that they would be compensated.

The army moved at a quick pace with an extended break for the midday meal. Morale was better with the prospect of getting closer to their destination. No one knew exactly where they were going, but they knew what waited for them at the end. The victory in Avalon, even though it wasn't a great battle, was still thick in their minds and they were all confident they could do it again. Whether they followed General Bern or General Jarwe the army believed they were being led towards victory.

By the end of the day they had made it to a large clear field about two hours from King's Rest. The field was owned by an old farmer and his family and by rights the army didn't need to ask permission to camp there, but as a matter of courtesy to a fellow farmer Bern ordered that they must first receive permission.

Bern, Sorrell, Jarwe, Aimon and Pernian rode along the small dirt track that led to the farmer's house. The old man, who had just returned from his day in the fields, was surprised to see the small group approach. He was even more surprised when he looked to the north and saw the army approaching from the top of a hill. The setting sun made it difficult to see exactly how many soldiers were approaching, but either way the farmer was less than pleased to see them.

"What… What do you want?" The farmer stammered from just outside the front door.

Hearing their father speak brought the attention of his twin sons. Both the young men came out to the front of the house to see who it was. When they saw the four armed men on horseback they retreated back inside. The shock was so great that they didn't even notice one of the men was in fact an elf.

"Relax, my friend." Bern used his most calming voice. He had once had a visit from a small group of soldiers when he was younger. He had felt very nervous when he saw the swords hanging from their sides. The last thing he wanted to do was make this farmer fear for his life. By the reaction of his sons he figured he was already too late. "We are not here to hurt you."

Before Bern could continue the farmer's twin sons returned. One was brandishing a pitchfork whilst the other was holding a scythe. They both looked scared and determined. They would defend their family's farm to the death.

"Get out of here. We aren't afraid of you and your fancy…" the son holding the pitchfork spoke. He was doing alright until he noticed the army approaching over the hill.

"Please, we mean you no harm," Bern said again.

"Frane, Hane, go inside and help you mother with dinner. This is none of your concern," the farmer snapped.

"But father," they both said in unison.

"Go, the both of you before I clip you over the ears."

The twins lowered their heads and walked back into the house. They were both relieved that they didn't have to fight. They could defend their flock of sheep from stray wolves, but they would not stand a chance against trained soldiers.

"Sorry about my sons. They are still very young and do not understand the ways of adults," the farmer apologised. "Now what is it that I can do for you?"

"We only ask that we use your paddock for our campsite. We will be gone at first light." Bern got straight to the point.

"Well!" The farmer made a sign of scratching his chin. "You see that paddock," he paused again for thought. "I need to move my sheep in there later on tonight." Bern knew that it was a blatant lie. No farmer moved livestock during the night, unless they were on their way to market. It was obvious that the farmer was trying to barter some price in return for the paddock.

"I am sure that you will be able to wait a day before you move your animals," Sorrell jumped in before Bern had a chance to speak. He was not about to be blackmailed by a farmer.

"That is true, but what will the paddock look like when your soldiers have finished with it?" The farmer would not be dissuaded.

"What would you consider proper compensation for use of your land?" Bern spoke before Sorrell had a chance to go any further.

The farmer thought for a moment, or at least he made a sign that he was. "Two royal crowns should cover it." There was a hopeful look on his face.

Sorrell nearly started laughing at the request. Two gold coins in return for the use of the land was a joke. Bern looked towards Sorrell who winked at him. The farmer missed the entire exchange. He was too excited about the thought of the coins.

"You drive a hard bargain, farmer. As it seems we have no other choice we accept your offer," as he spoke Sorrell produced two golden coins from his money pouch. The army's treasuries were not great, but two coins were not a problem.

The farmer quickly took the coins from Sorrell. He flicked them over in his hand to make sure they were real, or at least make it look like he was. He had never seen Darshivallian gold crowns before so he wouldn't know if they were real or not. Once he was satisfied he was not being taken advantage of he looked up at the others.

"Be sure that you are gone by morning," the farmer quickly retreated back into the farmhouse before the soldiers changed their minds.

"You have a strange way of doing things," Sorrell spoke to Bern as they made their way back towards the army.

"I was a farmer once, in a different life. I figured that it was better to ask the man instead of just taking from him. He will tell his friends and I am sure that it will be better for our reputation in the future." Bern looked out at the approaching army as he spoke.

"I guess that makes sense," Sorrell shrugged his shoulders.

Aimon scoffed to himself as he rode behind. He quickly looked around to see if anyone had heard him. No one seemed to be taking any notice of him. He didn't like the way Bern did things. He was definitely no General. It could be a good thing, but it could also be really bad. The man could lead the army anywhere and that was not a good sign. He wanted to know where they were going, more than anything else.

The army made camp just before the sun set. Only half the tents were set as they would have to be on the move again early in the morning.

The command group gathered for the evening meal, but since there was nothing to report they didn't stay for long. Aimon left to check on the state of the Enteroite army, to make sure they were doing the right thing. Hadar went to check with the Captain of the Hondinian army. Sorrell checked on the Darshivallian army and Pernian checked on the elves. The remaining members of the Remidian army and the dwarven army had formed their own group. They were known as the Truth Fighters and were led by a lieutenant from Remidia.

They had seen what Bern had done in Avalon and had sworn fealty to him. Since Bern really had no idea of how to check on soldiers he let the lieutenant run things. Both Hulkan and Dorn checked in to make sure they towed the line. They liked spending time with their fellow dwarves, those who had remained showed no ill feelings towards Hulkan.

Bern was again left to his own devices. Or at least he was left alone with General Jarwe. He would much prefer it if Jarwe would regain control of the Alliance.

"How are you feeling General?"

Jarwe was staring at the back of the tent. He didn't seem to notice Bern at all. Bern wasn't sure he wanted to disturb the General, but he really needed to speak with him.

"I know you are in there somewhere. This is getting ridiculous. I know you were afraid once we reached the fog curtain, but that was the whole idea of it. It was nothing to do with your character. It was all to do with the spell that was being cast. There was nothing you could have done about it." Bern tried to be caring yet forceful.

There was silence for a moment and then Jarwe moved so he was facing Bern. He looked at the man, as if for the first time. There was a sudden look of recognition on his face, but was gone before Bern could guarantee it was there.

"I am sorry Bern." It was the first words that Jarwe had spoken all day.

"What did you say?" Bern was shocked that Jarwe had actually spoken.

"I didn't mean to leave you with the responsibility of the army, but I figured that they would accept you as the new leader if they thought I was incapable of leading myself. I thought it would be easier this way. I knew the others would help you as best they could." Jarwe chose his words carefully.

"So you have never been catatonic like everyone had thought?"

"I am afraid not. It was all been part of my plan. You see when I saw you lead the army into battle when I was incapacitated I knew it was time for me to hand down my command. I was never here to lead the army passed Avalon." A smile grew on Jarwe's face.

"So now that you are back what will happen?" Bern asked.

"I am afraid the army is not ready for my return. I will have to continue on as I am until I know the army will take your lead without me. Once that is done then I can return to normal." Jarwe was deadly serious. "You cannot tell anyone about this. The plan will only work if everyone thinks that I am completely useless.

Bern nodded his agreement. He didn't like the ruse, but it did make sense. Before Bern had a chance to ask any questions Jarwe returned to his catatonic state. The man did it so seamlessly Bern wasn't even sure if he had actually spoken at all. As much as Bern wanted Jarwe to return to power he knew the man had a point. At some stage in the future Bern would need the power to control the army and he would need to be able to do it on his own. If half the lieutenants were looking to Jarwe for orders then it wouldn't work. He only wished he could tell the others.

In the morning they were on the move again at first light. Again at the breakfast table the others asked if Bern knew where they were going. Again there had been no change. There was nothing that felt any different. There was nothing pulling him in any direction. It was frustrating because everyone was looking towards him for advice.

The weather remained fine for the day. There were a few clouds in the sky that threatened rain, but none came. All in all it was a pleasant day for a walk or a casual ride. Of course no one noticed the weather as they marched towards their impending doom. The army was in good spirits regardless. The men sang as they marched.

They passed to the west of King's Rest early in the morning. The only sign the villages received was a dull rumble in the distance. The sound was somewhat disturbing to the locals. The rumours of the approaching army had already reached the village, but since there was no sign of them nearing they soon returned to what they were doing.

The open paddocks made travelling away from the highway not such a bad option. Occasionally they came by a stone fence, marking the boundary of the many farmers' properties. They were more of a nuisance than anything else. Having over three thousand soldiers climb over a fence ate a lot of time. Not only that, but all the wagons would have to traverse the fence until they came across a gate.

The further they travelled away from the village the larger the paddocks became and the stone fences became less and less. They camped before dusk, but it was still nightfall by the time the wagons reached them. They had not travelled nearly as far as they would have liked.

"Do you think we should move towards the highway?" Hadar asked Sorrell as they ate their evening meal.

"I don't think that will gain us anything, we will soon reach the forest and the highway is too narrow for us to march the army through. The army will have to move around the west of the forest," Sorrell explained.

"I am sure we will move faster along the highway?" Aimon's spoke with a full mouth. "These fences are becoming very annoying."

"We are over a good hour's march away from the highway. By the time we march to the highway and then march back again we will lose any time we would make up," Sorrell was getting tired of Aimon.

Bern spoke again before anyone else could argue. "We shall follow our course," was all he said before returning to his meal.

With those words the conversation was over. Bern was sick of the arguments within the group, partly because he could do nothing to help. Until he received his next feeling or the entity took over outright there was nothing he could do. The only comfort he had was that he thought they were heading in the right direction.

The night passed without incident and in the morning everyone woke refreshed and ready to march again.

It was late on the fourth day since they left Bellarome when they could see the fringe of the forest. The trees loomed up on the horizon. Bern sat on his horse, atop a small hill, staring out. Both he and Sorrell had moved on ahead of the army to survey what was ahead of them. There was something very alluring about the forest. It was as if the trees themselves were calling to him. There was also something frightening about the prospect. The forest was dark and the fading light couldn't penetrate the thick canopy.

"What is it?" Sorrell asked after they had been stopped for almost ten minutes.

"There is something in the forest. I don't know what it is, but I have a feeling that we have to find out." Bern kept his gaze on the trees as he spoke.

"We cannot take the soldiers through. It will take too long." Sorrell sounded somewhat surprised at Bern's suggestion.

"Sorry, I didn't mean to take the army through. I think that you and I should go alone." Bern looked at Sorrell.

Although Sorrell wasn't happy with his answer he knew better than to question Bern further. There was a good relationship growing between the two and Sorrell was as understanding as he could be with what was happening to Bern. He was happy to do his bit and it helped that they were in his land. He knew the terrain and the people. He knew what they could and could not get away with.

Bern respected Sorrell more so than anyone else in the group. He appreciated the fact that Sorrell deferred all decision to him, but helped where he could. When Bern didn't know what to do Sorrell would make the decision and yet still make it seem as though it was Bern's idea. That is why he knew he needed to take Sorrell with him into the forest. The decision he had to make was who he was going to leave in charge while they were away. He would love it if Jarwe could reclaim his original position, but he knew it was not a possibility. Aimon was the next in rank, but he didn't trust him. He didn't know what it was, but there was something about him that just didn't sit right. The next obvious choice was Hadar, but that came with its own kettle of fish.

"The others will be here soon," Sorrel broke the silence. "We should decide on where we should camp tonight."

The decision was fairly obvious. It was wide and flat at the base of the hill making it a perfect place to camp.

"We shall camp closer to the hill. There is evil in those trees and we should stay away from them tonight." Sorrell watched Bern closely. There was something in his voice that told him not to question what he had said. He didn't know if it was the entity or Bern.

There was still light in the sky when they made camp. The soldiers were nervous with their early stop. They could have easily marched for another hour and didn't understand the reasoning from the leaders. It was a restless night.

Chapter 22: New Allies

The decision was made late in the night after much discussion. Both Bern and Sorrell had disliked it, but they had agreed for the sake of peace. Aimon was less than impressed when it was suggested that Hadar be left in charge. He was rightly disgusted being the next in line. Hadar didn't have a problem with Aimon being in command and wondered why they had overlooked him in the first place.

Bern and Sorrell left an hour before first light. They wanted to be gone before the army was on the move. If the soldiers saw their two commanders riding away it would do nothing for morale.

"I am worried about Aimon," Bern spoke to Sorrell as the two of them approached the forest.

"I am sure he will be fine. The others will keep an eye on him," Sorrell tried to reassure him.

"It's not just that. There is something not quite right about him. I haven't been able to put my finger on it, but I know it's there." Bern spoke again.

"I know what you mean. I suppose we shall just have to keep an eye on him when we return to the army. Until he does something obvious we can hardly accuse him of any wrong doing," Sorrell's words made sense.

The sun crept over the horizon as they reached the highway. They were still a gentle fifteen minute ride from the edge of the forest. Bern had kept a watchful eye, even though without the sunlight he couldn't see anything in the forest. Ever since it had come into view he had been receiving bad feelings.

As they approached the forest the feelings of dread increased. It was a worry. Normally his feelings were very accurate, but the bad feelings were almost enough to overwhelm him. He almost told Sorrell to turn around. Regardless of the feeling he knew he had to enter and carry on. He didn't know what he had to do once he was inside. He only knew they he could not back down.

Once they had crossed over into the forest the feeling of dread suddenly disappeared. The shock of it nearly knocked Bern from his horse. It took him a moment to settle himself and he was glad Sorrell had been concentrating on the trees around him and had not noticed.

They continued into the forest for about an hour. Sorrell kept a watchful eye on the trees. He well knew that the forest was full of bandits. He would have much preferred to have travelled with the army. He had gone along with Bern when he had suggested the idea, but he was starting to doubt his decision. It was only a matter of time before they were accosted.

Bern slowly reined his horse to a stop. There was something tugging at him out to the side of the road. Even his horse could feel it. Sorrell travelled a few paces further before he realised that Bern had stopped. He just sat in his saddle and stared into the forest.

"What is it?" Sorrell was almost afraid to ask.

"There is something in there." Bern raised his arm and pointed into the forest. The tone of his voice sent a chill down Sorrell's spine. "We have to go."

Bern kicked the flanks of his horse. The brown mare shook her head once and then started walking in the darkness. Sorrell watched the exchange with interest. As much as he didn't think Bern was doing the right thing there was nothing he could do about it. The last thing he wanted to do was let the General wander through the forest by himself.

The part of the forest was darker than usual. Sorrell didn't know whether it was due to the extra cloud cover or if the trees were deliberately hiding the sun. Bern seemed to be able to pick his way through without much light and Sorrell just let his bay follow behind.

They had not been travelling for long before they were stopped by a slender looking fellow who stood in a small clearing. He aimed a bow and arrow at Bern.

"This is not the place for men to travel lightly," there was no humour in the bandit's voice. "These are troubled times and it would be safer to shoot you and take your money instead of letting you run free."

The threat had no affect on Bern who had moved into the light coming through the trees. Sorrell wanted to move up beside Bern to help, but there was no room. Bern had deliberately blocked the view of Sorrell from the bandit. He was sure there were more bandits somewhere in the trees, but until they showed themselves he was happy to assume there was just one.

"I am here to see your leader." Bern ignored the threat and went straight to the point.

The bandit took a step back. He wasn't sure how to take the man before him. Most people were so scared that they would be throwing their money pouches and any valuables in his direction before begging for their lives. Instead the man just ignored his threat and made a demand of his own.

"What makes you think that I will not shoot you on the spot?" The question seemed legitimate enough.

"I do not have time for games. Now I am sure you are not foolish enough to come out here by yourself." Bern watched the bandit closely who shied away from the accusation.

"I see you're alone. That is very interesting indeed. Now if you don't drop me with the first arrow, you would want to be very quick in notching the next two. Now I would be willing to wager that I would be able to dismount and run you through before you were able to get another shot away." The stone cold tone made him believe every word. "Now I think you should tell me what you are doing out here by yourself?"

The bandit looked to his left and then to his right on the off chance that someone was to walk by and help him. He knew there was not going to be any assistance. Slowly he lowered his bow. There was no point keeping up the ruse unless he was going to follow through and slowly he lowered his bow and looked at the man before him.

"I am recruiting," he said softly, almost to himself.

"What are you recruiting for?" Bern was intrigued by the bandit's answer.

"I don't think I should say any more. If you want to see our chief then I will take you. I should warn you that you may not get the response you are looking for," the bandit said with a wry grin on his face.

"You just worry about getting us there."

The bandit thought about saying something, but then thought better of it. He eyed Bern before turning his back on the two men. He started picking his way through the undergrowth, making his way toward the camp. He made sure to pick the hardest track to make it harder for his two captors. It was not long before they both had to dismount and lead their horses. The bandit laughed quietly to himself when they did.

It took almost an hour for them to reach the hideout. The campsite was a hive of activity. Both Bern and Sorrell were surprised to see so many people moving around. They were also not being very quiet. Bern would have assumed that a bandit's hideout was a place to keep secret.

"What's going on here?" Bern asked as they walked through the crowd.

The other surprising thing was that no one seemed to notice them. When two strangers came to such a secretive site Bern assumed they would look out of place. The situation was very perplexing and not at all like what he was expecting.

"I think it would be best if you speak to our leader." The bandit didn't seem interested at all.

Bern and Sorrell were led towards the largest of the timber huts. Standing out the front of the hut was a woman. She was watching the hubbub closely and Bern assumed that she was the chieftain's wife. They walked up to the woman and stopped.

"What is it Riocard? I am very busy and don't have time for your rubbish." The woman dismissed the man without even looking at his companions.

"I am sorry, chief. These two have demanded an audience with you," the man's voice was shaky.

"They have, have they?" The women turned to face them for the first time. When she saw them she took a step backwards. "These are not bandits. They have the look of mercenaries about them. What are you doing bringing them here?" There was a mixture of anger and fear in her voice.

"I had no choice. I was by myself and they..."

"Run along. There is nothing you can do now." She dismissed Riocard with a wave of her hand. "You better tell me your names and your business. As you can see there are a lot more of us then there is of you, so choose your words carefully."

"My name is Bern and this is Sorrell." Bern paused after he made the introductions, deliberately avoiding their titles. "Why are there so many people around?"

"Well Bern and Sorrell, my name is Rolanda and I am the Chieftain. Here I ask the questions and you answer them. If I like your answers then I will not have you killed."

"Very well then. We are General's in a nearby army. We are here to recruit."

The words carried inside the hut. As soon as Bern had finished speaking a man appeared. He looked at Bern as if he was looking at a long lost friend. This made Bern even more curious. He had a feeling that his arrival was not completely unknown.

"You are friends with Dyrk, sorry I mean Alaric?" Delbert spoke with awe.

Bern's attention was piqued at the mention of Alaric's name. It was the first true sign they knew he was alive. A renewed hope filled his body. He felt as though things were finally starting to work out.

"That's right. We are the army that fights for him and everyone else in the Seven Kingdoms."

Delbert looked at his wife and smiled warmly. Rolanda returned the smile, but then motioned for him to return inside the hut. He tried to protest, but she was firm with him.

"Well it seems that my husband has a problem keeping his mouth shut." Rolanda started to speak, but was interrupted by Bern before she could continue.

"Where is Alaric? How long ago was he here? Did he leave a message for me?" Bern asked the questions so quickly Rolanda didn't have a chance to answer.

"Slow down Bern," Sorrell spoke. "One thing at a time. We can speak about Alaric later. What we need to know now is what is happening here?"

"As you can see there are a lot of people in our camp," she said, looking around. "We have been working on gathering the gangs of bandits in the forest to join your army. Alaric told us that you would be passing through and would need our help."

"That is very good, but are they soldiers?" Sorrell didn't sound impressed.

"No they're not soldiers, but they have had to fight their entire lives. Life in the forest is hard. Not only do you have to fight off the guards hired to protect the goods being transported, but you also have to fight off other bandits for your share of the bounty. The men I am gathering with be able to fight for you and hold their own in battle. It won't be a formal standard of fighting, but I think that may come in handy." Rolanda brimmed with pride as she spoke of her brethren.

"I will not deny that we are short on men, but I am still doubtful your men will be suitable," scoffed Sorrell.

"How many men do you have?" Bern spoke before Rolanda had a chance to reply.

"We have about fifty at the moment, but we have only been recruiting for a day and a half." She faced Bern and tried to ignore Sorrell as much as she could.

"In four days the army will be arriving just west of Lord's Wait. You will need to have as many people as you can gather by then."

"That should be fine. I can start moving the first few now. It will take a while to locate everyone in the forest. It's not like we know where everyone's campsite is. I estimate we should have about five hundred men ready to go." Bern was surprised at the number of bandits in the forest. He could certainly understand why Sorrell was sceptical of them entering. "It is a little difficult to convince the other chieftains that this is right thing for them to do. Some will come across easier than others. I don't know why, but so far they have all come across. It is strange. When Alaric first told us what we had to do I didn't think we had a chance, but he did so much for me and my husband that I had to try." Rolanda reflected a moment. "Now I assume you will need accommodation for the night and I am sure you would like to see the army I have been gathering for you."

"That sounds like a very good idea. Now if you don't mind I would like to speak to your husband about his encounter with Alaric."

"That's fine. I have quite a bit to do. I will make sure that there is a hut available for you. As you can guess we are tight for accommodation, but I am sure it will be fine."

"Thank you." Bern half bowed before he left.

Once they were inside the hut Delbert was almost overwhelmed to see them. He had prepared a small meal in the hope they would be staying. He was like a small child on the eve of a celebration.

"Welcome to my house. Come in, come in. I have made a small meal. Please, sit down and relax." Delbert hurried around until they were settled. "Now what is it I can help you with?" He spoke again once he was seated.

"Can you tell me where Alaric was headed?" It was the first question, of many, that came to mind.

"He was travelling to Kiarome. He was with two other men. One was Lord Richmond and the other was a man named Tancred. They were travelling incognito, for whatever reason. I travelled with them for a short while, but they did not confide in me. I gathered a little information, but not much." Delbert pre-empted a couple of questions.

"How long ago do they leave?"

"Late in the day two days ago. I would estimate by now they would be in the city. From there I don't know where they were travelling. I don't know why they were travelling to Kiarome either. All I know is that they were well when they left. They did seem very concerned about something. They thought at one stage I was an assassin. I don't know why, but I think that someone was trying to kill your friend. It is strange that they thought it was me. In fact there was a lot about the situation that was strange."

Bern looked at Sorrell. There was concern written all over his face. He didn't want any comfort from Sorrell, he just didn't want Delbert to see his reaction. He needed more information and he knew Delbert would not continue if he thought he was worrying Bern. He took a moment before he returned his gaze to Delbert.

"Did he leave any messages for me?" Bern asked a question that seemed strange to everyone else.

"I thought it was strange when he told me that you were coming. I didn't believe it until I saw the two of you walking in. He described the both of you perfectly." His last comment surprised both Bern and Sorrell. "What did I say?" Delbert asked when he noticed their reactions.

"Nothing, please continue," Bern spoke quickly before Sorrell could say anything.

"Anyway, he told me to tell you... Now what was it?" Delbert looked towards the roof of the hut, as if the answer would be written there. "That's right. He said that you must wait in Lord's Wait. If you wait at the local inn there will be a man coming to find you. His name is..." again he looked for answers on the roof. "Tancred. His name is Tancred."

"What are you talking about? Isn't that Lord Richmond's advisor?" Sorrell asked the question before Bern could speak.

"Yes, I think you're right," Delbert seemed surprised.

"Why would Tancred be meeting us in Lord's Rest? He should be with the others inside the capital by now." Bern was starting to get irritated with Sorrell speaking out of turn.

"I have no idea." Delbert was really excited with the extra attention. "He only told me to pass on that message. I am sorry I can be of no more assistance." He paused for a moment. "If there is anything else I can help you with all you have to do is ask."

Sorrell was about to speak, but Bern cut him off. "No, thank you. If something comes up we will certainly come and find you. Now if you would have someone show us to our accommodation I would like to rest for a moment."

Delbert jumped to action at Bern's request. Sorrell wanted to gather some more information, but Bern had heard enough. He ushered Sorrell out of the hut before he had a chance to speak. It wasn't long before they were sitting inside a small private hut. The General was almost fuming at being dismissed.

"What were you thinking Bern? There is so much more information we could gather from this man. He was begging to divulge all the information that he knew." Sorrell stormed around the small hut, waiting for a response.

Bern remained calm. Sorrell was a threatening man and in his current state would be enough to scare the most hardened of men, but Bern didn't flinch. Not answering only made Sorrell angrier. Bern wanted him to get it out of his system before he spoke. When it was clear that was not going to happen he decided it was time to calm him.

"We received all the relevant information from Delbert." Before he had a chance to qualify his statement Sorrell interrupted him.

"How do you know that he didn't have anything else to say?" As soon as Sorrell asked the question he already knew the answer. The realisation caused him to relax and sit down.

"The question you should be asking is how Alaric knew we were going to be here?" Bern raised his hand to stop Sorrell from answering. "That is not even the real question, although it would be nice to know for sure, but I have a fair idea. What I want to know is why Tancred is supposed to be meeting us in Lord's Wait? If Alaric wanted to give us another message then why wouldn't he give it to Delbert?"

"Maybe he didn't trust the man enough to give us the message," Sorrell shrugged his shoulders as he spoke. He had interrupted Bern again and not even noticed.

"Then why would Alaric not just leave Tancred here?" Sorrell was about to answer, but again Bern had to silence him with a wave of his hand. "I have a bad feeling now. Something isn't right, but I don't think we will get any answers until we reach Lord's Wait."

"I still think that we should question Delbert further," Sorrell sounded more sulky than anything else. "But if we are to meet at Lord's Rest then I think we should leave now. There is no point in hanging around here." Sorrell was starting to become agitated again.

"We will wait here and leave in the morning. We have time to kill at the moment. It will take a while for the army to travel around the forest and I do not believe that Tancred is waiting for us yet. Don't forget that Rolanda is gathering men together to join the army. I would certainly like to see some of them before we leave," Bern remained calm as he sat.

"But there is still plenty of daylight left. We could be through the forest before nightfall," Sorrell protested.

"I know, but I think we should stay here for the night." Bern had a nagging feeling that it wasn't time to leave and he knew not to try and fight it.

"Very well. If you insist on staying then I am going for a look around the campsite." Sorrell stood.

Bern grunted in Sorrell's direction. The General had been getting on his nerves. He was glad to be able to have some time to himself.

Bern had closed his eyes whilst he sat in the chair. A wave of sleep washed over him, but soon there was a knock on the door. The rapping was enough to wake him from his half slumber. He was still drowsy, but he was happy to see a woman holding a plate of food.

"It is not much, but I hope you will like it." She blushed slightly as she handed him the plate.

"Thank you." He was feeling rather strange after his sleep. He didn't think he had slept for long, but he couldn't be sure. "What time is it?" He asked, still a little hazy.

"Just past dusk, my Lord." She blushed again as she answered. When it was clear he wasn't going to ask any more questions she left.

He was hungry enough to finish his meal quickly. It was not the greatest meal he had ever eaten, but it was enough to satisfy him. He wondered where Sorrell was and what he was doing and once he had finished his meal he left the hut.

There were many fires lit around the campsite giving it an eerie glow. Bern started walking, not really knowing where he was going. He just wanted to find Sorrell and make sure that he was not causing any trouble.

It was difficult for him to recognise anyone's face as he walked passed. The light from the fire cast many shadows. The only advantage he had was that Sorrell was larger than most of the people. He was surprised that there were not more people around the fires. It was not that it was cold, but they seemed to be the easiest place to meet. To his disappointment he couldn't find his friend. He thought about going back to the chieftain's hut. There was something about Delbert that didn't sit right with him. He knew he was no threat, but he was a little too eager to help. He decided again it and went back to his own hut.

He found his hut empty of people. What he did notice was that their packs had been removed from their horses and left there. Bern couldn't guarantee the bags had not been placed there when he had been sleeping. He looked around the room for any other signs of movement. When his eyes saw the bed they didn't move. He couldn't remember the last time he slept in a bed. He had to admit that he found his bedroll suitable, but when he sat on the mattress he remembered what he was missing.

The mattress was straw, which wasn't nearly as comfortable as the last bed he had slept on, the soft down mattresses in the palace at Lel Dinion. Any thoughts of chasing after Sorrell were gone. His eyes flickered as he approached the bed. The thought of sleep almost overwhelmed him. He just managed to pull his boots off and crawl onto the bed before he fell asleep.

Bern's dreams were disturbed. He was caught in a deep sleep and didn't wake when Sorrell entered the room close to midnight. He woke in the morning feeling as though he had not slept at all. The dreams which had kept him from relaxing where just a distant memory as soon as he woke. He tried his hardest, as he lay on his bed, to remember, but he could not recall anything.

"Good to see you awake." Sorrell bustled in the room, followed by a ray of sunlight.

The light hit Bern square in the face, hurting his eyes, making him cover them with his hand. He didn't know why but he felt terrible.

"You don't look so good." Sorrell moved closer. "What did you get up to last night?"

"Huh, what? Nothing. I don't know." Bern murmured a few words before trying to rise. His head ached and he felt sick.

"You really don't look that good. I think that you should stay in bed," Sorrell sounded somewhat concerned. "I think I should see if there is a healer in the camp."

"No, don't fuss. I don't have time to be sick. I am sure it is just something temporary." Bern struggled to his feet. He was glad that he didn't have to dress.

Once they were outside Bern felt a little better. He was hoping his condition was just to do with his uncomfortable sleep. They were too close to action for him to be getting ill. His best bet was to reach Lord's Rest and then see the village's healer. He doubted very much that there would be a healer in the camp of bandits.

"I need to have a look at the men first." Bern puffed slightly trying to hide it behind a yawn.

"Last night I asked Rolanda to have them assembled this morning. It shouldn't take them long to be ready." Sorrell signalled a man he recognised when he finished speaking. "You should have something to eat while we wait. I will have someone get you something."

"I have enough food in my saddlebags. We should not dwindle their supplies any more than we have." Bern was right. The bandits would need to bring their own food, water and other supplies. The army would not be able to survive with the influx of people.

After they had eaten a miserly breakfast of hard bread and salted meat they made their way to where Rolanda was gathering the bandits. Bern felt a little better again after eating and walking, but he still didn't feel quite right. He had a bad feeling that something was wrong. The feeling was coming from the south and was quite uncomfortable. He felt as though he should be on the road again. Something was drawing him out of the forest, but he ignored it as much as possible.

The bandits were standing in a muddled group of what Bern assumed was a meeting square. They looked neither organised nor interested. He had been in the army for long enough to notice trained soldiers, and these were anything but. He was sure they would be able to handle themselves in a small skirmish, but that was not what they would be required to do. He was starting to doubt very much whether it was a good idea. He had to trust that Alaric knew what he was doing.

Bern stood on a box at the front of the crowd so everyone could get a better view of him. "Thank you for gathering here," Bern felt a slight flutter as he started to address the group. Most of the men were watching Bern, but there was still a quiet murmur coming from those who were not interested. "I am General Bern of the Alliance Army. I come to you in a grave time. We are marching towards a war that will define the world forever." The group was suddenly silenced when he continued to speak. "We need your help."

"Why should we help? No one has ever helped us before. No one cares about us. We are safe in the forest. Why should we help you?" A man called from somewhere towards the back of the crowd. Many agreements could be heard from the other bandits. The crowd became a rabble again.

Bern waited a moment. When it was clear they were not going to settle on their own he spoke again. "Of course you have lived as outlaws for all or most of your lives. The rest of the world has shunned you." His words regained their attention. "What you must understand is that you are anything but safe within the forest. The army we will face is not interested in gaining land or gaining power. Their sole purpose is to completely destroy everything. They will hunt you down, even if you are the last people left in the world," Bern's words boomed throughout the camp. Even those who were not assembled could hear his words and they touched everyone. "What we do is for the good of everyone and everyone has to do their job. I will not lie to you. Many of you and perhaps all of you may die, but if you do nothing then you will definitely die and all who you love will die." Bern paused and waited for what he told them to sink in. "We are building the largest army the Seven Kingdoms has ever seen. We will not fail. If we all work together then we will be victorious." His voice grew as he continued. It was starting to have its effect. He could see hope in their faces, which he had previously taken away. "We move to make this world a better place. Are you with me?"

There were cheers from the bandits standing before him. Bern stood down from the box. His head was spinning. He remembered his speech, but he had his doubts whether they were his words. He had done what he had come to do. There was nothing more he could say. It was up to Rolanda to make sure they arrived on time. She quickly took the box when Bern stepped down and ordered them back to work.

"Thank you Rolanda," Bern spoke softly. "I will not forget what you have done."

"That is alright. What your friend did for my husband and me I can never do enough to repay him." Her features turned soft for a moment. Bern imagined that in another lifetime she would have been very attractive. He could only image how hard she had to be to control her bandits. Not to mention the other bandits she was enlisting for his army.

"We have to leave now. Time is again starting to creep away on us. You have been very gracious. I will be sure to let Alaric know when I see him next." Bern bowed before walking away.

"Do you think we will see Alaric again?" Sorrell asked quietly as they led their horses away from the campsite.

"I have no doubt we will see him again. I am sure that it will be sooner rather than later. I do not think he is very far away at all," Bern also kept his voice low.

"How do you know that? Alaric already has a good head start and with the army we have been travelling slower than he has." Again the question came out of his mouth before he thought about it.

Bern didn't answer the question. They didn't speak again until they reached the highway.

Chapter 23: Bad News

Bern and Sorrell made it safely to Lord's Wait only to find the village in complete disarray. Their leading citizen and owner of almost all the village's services had been found dead. A farmer out with his dog had found the body in a shallow grave. The discovery had shaken the entire village. It was obvious to all who had seen the body that he had not died of natural causes.

Not only was the man loved by everyone, he had died without an heir. The villagers didn't know what to do with his businesses. At first everyone was in shock, but as reality sunk in the village folk became feral. Each had their own claim to Emil's possessions which none of them had any real right to. The village was starting to tear itself apart. People who were once the best of friends were no longer speaking to each other, those who had never spoken before were fighting in the street.

The blacksmith was fighting with a local farmer on the rights to the smithy. The blacksmith's claim was obvious. He had worked there for the last twenty five years. He was the only blacksmith in village and there was no one else who worked the smithy with him. He had a wife and children and it was his sole means of income. The farmer claimed he had been Emil's best client and he had spent a lot of money over the years buying his goods, having his wagons fixed and having his horses' hooves reshoed. He claimed that the amount of money he spent gave him the right of claim. He offered to let the blacksmith keep his job, which sent the blacksmith into a rage. Both were large men, working physical jobs their entire lives and no one was prepared to try and break them up.

When Bern and Sorrell arrived at the village the physical fighting had just begun. They were both surprised to see the two men fighting in the street and other people watching were also threatening each other. Bern was happy to let Sorrell take the lead. They were his countrymen and he thought that they would respond to him.

"What's going on here?" Sorrell boomed from his horse.

The villagers stopped what they were doing to see who had spoken. The two men continued to fight, not hearing the words.

Sorrell dismounted and stood around the fighting men waiting for his opportunity to step in. They were both large and a stray fist or elbow could really hurt. He waited for the right moment before he grabbed the farmer by his shirt and dragged him off the blacksmith. In doing so he gave the blacksmith the advantage who took a big swing, hitting the farmer across the chin.

The cheap shot enraged Sorrell and he threw the farmer to one side, which was no easy task, before moving towards the blacksmith. When the blacksmith saw who it was he took a step away. He didn't know

Sorrell, but he could see the anger in his eyes. Sorrell wasn't going to let him get away with the cheap shot. He advanced on him and when he was close enough punched him in the face. He controlled himself enough not to break anything and the blacksmith fell to the ground.

"What in the Gods' names is going on here?" Sorrell's voice boomed again, his face red.

Both men stood and watched the man before them. The crowd had spread out watching and waiting to see what would happen. Sorrell looked from one man to the other. Neither of them wanted to speak, even if it meant gaining the upper hand.

"If one of you doesn't start talking then I think both of you will spend some times in the stocks. Now I don't care who speaks, but I want answers, now!"

"Erhard, Meyer, I am sure you two have better things to be doing than brawling in the street. Now be gone with you before I send for the King's soldiers," a man barked as he approached the group. He had been standing in the crowd. "Everyone! Back to work. There is nothing more to see here." He addressed the crowd once the two men had started to move. "I am sorry for them," he spoke to Sorrell. "The village is normally a lot quieter than this, but be assured guests are always welcome."

"Who are you?" None of the edge had left Sorrell's voice. Bern was still quite content to watch everything from his horse.

"My name is Onfré. I think it would be better if we go inside. The day is getting late and the weather is turning." Onfré motioned towards the inn.

He was right. It was past mid-afternoon. Clouds had rolled across the sky just before lunch, threatening rain. After Onfré had finished speaking Sorrell felt a drop of rain hit his cheek. There was no doubt the rain was about to come down. Onfré had succeeded in getting Sorrell to forget about his rage.

Onfré led them towards the inn named the Lord's Wanderer. He had been the manager whilst Emil had been alive. He had continued doing his duties after his death. Not only had he worked for Emil, but he was also his best friend. He was one of the only people in the village who was not trying to claim anything for himself and he was probably the only one who deserved something for himself.

At the inn Onfré ordered the stableboy to stable the horses and have their bags taken to a room. He then led Bern and Sorrell into the tavern. He wanted to make the men as comfortable as possible. He recognised them as soldiers and thought if he treated them right they might be able to solve the problem of who owns what.

"What were those two men fighting about?" Sorrell had calmed down since he entered the inn. The chilled mug of ale didn't do anything to hurt.

"Things are in disarray in Lord's Wait at the moment. The man who owned this inn and most of the other businesses in village was murdered recently. He was found in a shallow grave not far from the village. No one knows who did it or why. Besides the obvious problem he died without an heir. Now everyone is trying to claim ownership of little bits and pieces around village. As you might have already guessed those two men were trying to claim rights on one business," Onfré explained.

"Isn't there anyone in village who can settle the disputes? There has to be a magistrate or someone like that?" Sorrell asked.

Onfré started to laugh, although it was from the irony more so than the humour. "That is correct. The only problem is that Emil was what you would call the local magistrate. If any problems arose within the village then they would come to him to settle things. As you can imagine with his untimely death there hasn't been any time to find a replacement."

"Are there any suspects to his murder?"

"Yes and no. No one and everyone. That is also the problem. Until we find the person in charge we will not know the real reason for his death." Onfré seemed happy to divulge the information.

"There must have been some people who didn't like Emil. Someone with so much in such a small place there would have to be people who were jealous of his success?" Sorrell pondered.

"I assume you're right, although no one comes to minds and no one openly voiced that opinion. He was well loved in the village. He was a very generous man. I really can't see anyone trying to kill him. There is no reason why they would. I mean if Emil had left them anything in case of his death then it would make sense, but now everything is in chaos. The villagers have been bickering all day. I hate to think what things are going to be like in a week's time if nothing is resolved," Onfré sounded sad.

"I suppose I could ask around. Guilty people generally don't do well under interrogation. If I get the right people I could get them to crack in under an hour," Sorrell spoke to himself.

"I wouldn't waste your time." Bern spoke for the first time. "The murderer has already left the village."

Both men turned and looked at Bern. It was the first time that Sorrell didn't instantly ask the obvious question, but he could do nothing to stop Onfré asking it. The inn keeper looked strangely at Bern trying to gauge why Bern would say such a thing.

"How do you know? There haven't been that many travellers in the last week. Now that you mention it though there was a group of three men who were here about three days ago, I think. It was around the last time anyone saw Emil alive. They left in a hurry in the morning. There is a chance it could have been them. Now that I think about it they were acting very suspiciously." Onfré tapped his chin.

Bern knew he was talking about Alaric and his new companions. He also knew that it wasn't they who had murdered Emil. It didn't change the fact, however, that the villagers were still at each others' throats.

"What are you going to do about the rest of the village?" Sorrell changed the subject before they got any further.

"What can I do? I was Emil's best friend, but he didn't entrust me with his possessions. Emil had control of the village and that was the way everyone liked it. No one had any plans to usurp control from him. Everyone was happy with the way things were running. You see Emil never really told anyone how to run their life. He offered advice to everyone and everyone knew the village would run just fine," Onfré explained. "There is nothing that I can do. I have no power. Now if you excuse me I have to serve these people." There was a small group who just entered the bar.

"What do you make of all of this?" Sorrell asked when they were alone.

"I don't know. I can feel the touch of the Evil One. Things have the potential to get much worse. I think that we have to do something to help the village," Bern spoke softly.

"That is all well and good, but we are supposed to be meeting someone here. Isn't that what Alaric's message said. Once Tancred arrives we will need to be on the road again." Sorrell had more important things to worry about.

"That is true, but don't forget we still have to wait for the army to arrive. We are here for a little while and I think that is where we are supposed to be. There is nothing pulling me in any direction and I don't think it will again until we sort this situation out."

There was something else that was disturbing Bern. Ever since they had left the forest he had been getting a really bad feeling. Sorrell had not noticed and Bern was not about to tell him. The feeling had come on so suddenly and almost made him physically sick. He had almost recovered from his restless night when it happened. The feeling came and went, but each time it came it was much worse. He had managed to keep it from Sorrell, but he didn't know how long that was going to last. The feelings had stopped once he reached the village and Bern hoped that it was something drawing him to Lord's Wait. Deep down he knew it wasn't true. It was something else that was causing the pain inside him. He also knew he wouldn't be able to do anything about it until he solved the problem in the village.

"Well we probably need to gain some information then. We don't know when Tancred is going to arrive, but we do know the army will be here. In three more days the army should be assembled to the west. From there we have to be ready to march, regardless of where we are heading." Sorrell's words made sense, but there was still nothing Bern could do. When it was time to go he would know.

***

The army had been marching hard. The forest which had started to the south of them and then loomed to the east worried the men. They sensed something evil. It was purely ignorance, but it made them move all the same. The sooner they were away from the forest the happier they would be. They kept the pace quick and that was all that the commanders could hope for.

It was day seven since they had left Bellarome and two days since the two Generals had left. The optimistic feeling in the command group had waned. There was something about the way Aimon commanded that didn't sit right with them and Jarwe just sat and listened.

"This is getting ridiculous." Aimon complained when they were camped for the night. "The men are starting to ask questions about Bern and Sorrell. They know that something is up."

"And all you have to say is that everything is alright and all they have to do is keep marching. It's simple. The soldiers will do what they are told. That is the way it is and that is the way it is going to stay." Hadar was starting to get upset with Aimon. He was beginning to wish that he had agreed to take control of the army when it was offered to him. Aimon had been making rash decisions that he was sure that no one else would make.

"That doesn't change the fact that morale amongst the soldiers is down. Soldiers get their strength of character from their commanders. At the moment we are wandering around without any direction. How do you think the soldiers are going to feel? If we do not do something then we are going to have a revolution on our hands. All I am saying is that we need to do something before all hell breaks loose," Aimon insisted.

"I don't know what you are talking about. I know the soldiers are a little skittish about being near the forest, but that is it. There doesn't seem to be any discourse amongst the men," Hulkan spoke.

"Well I guess that all depends on who you are." Aimon knew he couldn't keep up his argument with Hulkan. "The fact remains that my subordinates are telling me that there is dissention in the ranks."

Aimon was not going to be talked around. No matter who said what, he would not be swayed. He had his mind set that something was wrong. Now they had to wait to see what he planned on doing about it.

"We can argue about this all night, but the fact remains that we are on our course and nothing can move us off it."

"Well that is not entirely true." Aimon did his best to stop from smiling. In the end there was just a small turn in the side of his mouth. The look disturbed the other commanders. "I am going to move the army to the east. We will march into Entero. Once we reach Jarrat I can speak to Queen Oriana. We will replenish our supplies and we can get the intelligence that we so desperately need."

"You cannot take this army off its course. We are to meet up with Sorrell and Bern outside of Lord's Wait." Hadar slammed his fist onto the table and rose from his chair.

"Calm yourself Duke Hadar." Aimon remained in his chair, but there was now a snarl on his face. "I am the commander of this army. I have been left in charge. If I feel that the direction we are marching in is wrong then it is up to me to change it. I have never trusted the decision made by the Remidian and Darshivallian. They have been pushing their own agenda since they usurped control from Jarwe. Now it is up to me to set the Alliance back on their true course."

"You do not have the authority. Bern left you in command to steer the army towards our meeting point. It is your job to keep the army on course, not to lead it away. What do you think you are doing?" Hadar was in shock.

"I am doing the right thing," Aimon spoke with a passion no one had heard from him before. "This entire affair has been a disgrace. From the minute the Alliance was conceived we have been led in the wrong direction. Now we are wandering around aimlessly waiting for some mysterious spirit to give us all the answers. Think about it for a moment. When you do you will realise that it is the most ridiculous thing you have ever done. It is up to me to try and regain some sort of sanity. This army has a great battle to fight. If we do not reach the battlefield soon then the fight will be over. We have already lost most of the Remidian army. We can ill afford to lose the rest." Aimon's words were convincing.

Hadar returned to his seat. He had to admit that Aimon had a very good point. It was the same reason that King Lisle IV had not committed troops originally. It was not until Alaric came to visit that Lisle was convinced, as well as the insurgence of the Evil One's spies. The original plan had seemed crazy, but it was widely accepted. With Aimon speaking aloud all of a sudden things didn't quite make sense. All he did know was that he couldn't let Aimon lead the army away from Bern and Sorrell. Wherever they were going they needed those two with them.

"Now is the time to start doing something right. We need more information or else we are going to be marching this army all over the Seven Kingdoms. By the time we are finished everything will be destroyed." He continued to plead his case when no one responded.

"What you say makes sense," Hadar started to reply. "It still doesn't change the fact that you have to keep the army on its course."

"I didn't want it to come to this," there was something different in Aimon's voice now. It was cold and calculating. "I really wanted you all to be on board with this, but I have been left in command of the army and it is my decision on what we do. I will let everyone know that in the morning we will be setting a course for Jarrat." Aimon stood from the table.

It seemed that Aimon had already made his decision before he had even sat at the table. Hadar was sure that he didn't have to power to move the direction the army was taking. He looked towards Wojtek. He figured if anyone knew it would be Sorrell's advisor. The man simply shrugged his shoulders. It was clear that he was not going to be any help. There was no way that Hadar could let him get away with it.

"Lord Pernian." The elf was sitting closest to Aimon. He was also in the best place to block his exit. "Restrain the Captain."

Pernian stood and made a move towards Aimon. The Captain quickly drew his sword and took a step backwards. No one normally wore their weapons during their meetings and no one had notice that Aimon was wearing his sword.

"Now I don't think that you will be able to stop me unarmed." Aimon didn't make a move to attack. He wanted to give the others enough chance to get out of his way.

"Send for the guards," Hadar suggested.

"I don't think so," Aimon refuted. "I have made it quite clear to men loyal to me that if I don't come out tonight, or if I come out in chains that they are to inform the army that there has been a revolt.

There was nothing they could do. They doubted Aimon currently had enough support to turn the army, but he had enough information that would aide him. If the true situation of the command was leaked to the army then there was no telling what would happen. The most important thing was to keep the army together. If they lost any more soldiers then the army would be little more than a gang of mercenaries.

"Stand down Pernian," Hadar sounded resigned to fact that Aimon had won.

Aimon started for the exit. He was almost out of the tent when he heard a voice from behind him. The sound was enough to make everyone stop and listen.

"Not so fast Aimon." It was the first time they had heard Jarwe speak for days. "You are not in command of this army. I am General Jarwe and that commission is mine. If anyone is going to make the decision it will be me." There was a sigh of relief from everyone in the tent, except for Aimon.

"What!" Was all that Aimon could say. He had planned everything to perfection. There had not been a single situation he had not run through his mind, except for one. Not once did he believe that Jarwe would recover and regain his rightful position.

"That is right Aimon. I am still the rightful General of the Alliance. If you attempt to change the direction of this army it will be you who ends up in chains." All the strength had returned to Jarwe's voice and his demeanour. There was no doubt that he was capable of returning to his position.

"Fine, General. I was just trying…" Aimon stammered, but he was not given an opportunity finish.

"I know what you were trying to do and you nearly got away with it. I think you should leave now before I have you placed in chains. I am sure that the rumours you were going to spread will not hold up once I address the army." Jarwe had a broad grin on his face. He had never really like the Enteroite. He had known the man for a long time and had always found him boring and unwholesome.

Aimon knew when he had been beaten and there was nothing he could do. If he stayed he had no doubt that Jarwe would have him arrested. It would not help his plan if he was imprisoned. He would retreat and live to fight another day. At least he was still in the army's command group. There would be another chance for him to take control.

Chapter 24: Another Hard Decision

It had been a difficult day trying to gather information from the villagers about the death of Emil. No one had a problem in pointing the finger, but they both knew it was not one of the villagers who had killed him. Their first step to try and regain control of the village. Besides the investigation they also had to break up another two brawls. One contained six villagers and was threatening to get completely out of control. The last thing they needed was another death in the village.

There was no doubt everyone was at boiling point. It wouldn't take much to tip the villagers over the edge. Sorrell and Bern had been speaking to them late into the night. At first they had to visit the various shops to speak to them, but once word got out that there were two soldiers investigating the murder everyone wanted to have their say. Onfré set them up with a small room to act as an office. The villagers waited outside for their chance to tell their story. They all wanted to profess their own innocence whilst suggesting the guilt of others. No one openly accused anyone of the murder, but it was clear which way their opinions were leading.

In the morning there was another long line of villagers waiting for them. Some were new, some were those who didn't get heard the night before, but most were those who had forgotten some important piece of information. Sorrell and Bern had not had an opportunity to discuss what they had learnt the night before and to make matters worse Bern woke up feeling much worse than he had the previous day. Whatever it was that was wrong with him seemed to be getting worse. Sorrell seemed more concerned, but Bern just told him that it was just a bad night sleep. He didn't have time to be sick.

They were in no hurry to see anyone nor had they managed to eat a decent meal the night before so they took the opportunity to speak whilst they ate.

"I don't think anything is going to be gained by listening to the villagers. All they want to do is place the blame on their neighbours and make themselves look better. To be honest I don't know if there is anything that we are going to be able to do," Sorrell sounded downcast.

There was a thick layer of sweat on Bern's face. He was pale and didn't look at all well. Sorrell was so caught up with the problems in the village that he didn't notice. It wasn't until Bern spoke that Sorrell heard the weakness in his voice.

"We have to do something. We cannot let the town tear itself to pieces."

"You don't look well," Sorrell started. "I don't think that you should be out of bed."

"That is all well and good, but there is too much work to be done here." Bern struggled to speak.

"Don't be ridiculous. I can handle the villages. Realistically we are just killing time until either Tancred or the Army arrives. If anything important happens then I will come and get you. Until then I think that you should return to bed."

"I suppose it wouldn't hurt if I lay down for a little while." Bern didn't sound as though he was going to be conscious for much longer.

He slowly stood, took two steps towards the door before he started to sway. Sorrell quickly raced to his side, but Bern pushed him away. He didn't want assistance. Admitting he needed help would mean that he was really sick.

"I'll be alright. Remember that if something happens then you must come and get me." Bern almost used up the last of his breath to speak.

"Of course I will," Sorrell lied. There was no way he was going to wake Bern. If he didn't get better soon then he didn't know what they would do. They couldn't stay in Lord's Wait for long. As soon as the army arrived they would have to keep moving. Not that he knew where they were going next. "Send in the next one," Sorrell called out. He really didn't want to see anyone, but at least it would take his mind off their current situation.

The door opened and a short, plump, bald man walked through the door. He had patches of flour on his face. Sorrell surmised that he was either the baker or the miller.

"Tell me what you know," Sorrell sounded somewhat disinterested.

"I am the local baker and have been for the last fourteen years. Now I wasn't born in Lord's Wait, but I have considered this my home ever since I moved here. Now Emil was a really good friend of mine," the last was a lie. The baker only knew Emil because he paid his wage. The men had very rarely spoken to each other, at least not on a personal level. "I am sure that everyone has told you that already though."

"I'm sure they have. Now if you wouldn't mind getting to the point I have a lot of people to see," Sorrell sounded even more disinterested.

"Of course. I wanted to come in yesterday, but I didn't get a chance." The man fiddled with his apron.

"Just tell me who you think did it and why and then we can move on." Sorrell was starting to become irritated.

"Well that's just the thing. I don't know the man. I don't know if he killed Emil. All I know is that it was very strange. It was late in the evening and I was on my way home. I saw Emil speaking to someone, or at least I thought I saw Emil talking to someone. Well I walked a little further and I passed Emil in the street. Now I am not a smart man, but I know that there was no way he could have got ahead of me. I thought it was strange at the time, but then I thought my aging eyes might be playing tricks on me." The baker's words suddenly gained Sorrell's full attention. "The next time I spoke to Emil he seemed somewhat different. I can't explain it, but there was definitely something different about him. I wasn't sure whether I should come, but since everyone else has been helping I thought I better share this information."

"Indeed. I believe that there is something to what you have said." Sorrell looked pensive. At last there was clue towards Emil's death. It wasn't much of a clue, but it was a start.

Sorrell saw another half a dozen people after the baker before he became too frustrated. He simply informed the rest of the long line that he would no longer be speaking to anyone. He told them that he had enough information to make a decision on the murder. They all seemed somewhat disappointed.

Once he was done with the interviewing he went outside to think. As he left the inn he saw someone arrive on horseback. Both the man and the beast were covered in sweat. The man looked as though he was going to collapse, but the white stallion looked more determined to keep going. Sorrell watched him lift himself down off his horse. He took a moment to steady himself before he started walking. Whatever he wanted he didn't want to get involved. He had enough of listening to other peoples worries.

There was a cool breeze in the air and the ground was still wet from the previous night's rain. Sorrell looked around the town. It seemed as though the villagers were returning to their normal day-to-day lives. There didn't seem to be any signs of arguing. More to the point there wasn't anyone brawling in the streets. It seemed that what they had been doing was having a positive effect. Maybe that was the answer they had been looking for. Maybe it was just being there that was helping the people regain their sanity. He hoped that was the case because he still believed there was nothing they were going to be able to do to help. He didn't have the authority to distribute Emil's wealth. He didn't know the villagers well enough to make a final decision. As he walked through the streets he hoped that they would be able to find a solution.

***

Tancred had ridden hard since he had left the city. His quick departure had been noticed by the guards, but no one bothered to chase him. No one else was chasing him so they assumed he had done nothing wrong. The guards were too busy trying to control the flow of traffic into the city to worry about one man on horseback. It was a while before he was able to get Tormenta into a gallop. Even when he was outside the city walls the traffic was still bad. There were a lot of people on the road and more people were trying to get into the city than there were trying to leave.

Once he was on the highway he was able to travel at the speed he wanted to. He didn't have to command the white stallion into a gallop. Tormenta could sense the urgency of his rider. He could sense that there was something wrong and he knew that wherever they were going they needed to get there quickly.

Tancred was surprised how fast and how long the white stallion galloped. He had never ridden a horse that could keep up such a pace for so long. Tancred had to rein Tormenta to a trot after a while. He couldn't keep the pace up himself and was beginning to waver in the saddle. He had to slow down for fear of falling off.

As soon as they arrived at Lord's Wait they made their way straight to the Lord's Wanderer. Alaric had told him that he would meet someone at the inn. He didn't know how or why, but there was nothing else he could do. He knew Alaric and Richmond had been taken prisoner. He wished he knew what the situation was inside the palace. King Unwin had always been a strong ruler and he couldn't understand why he was no longer in control. He knew there was powerful magic at work, but he couldn't image Unwin being anyone's thrall. He had to admit he never really understood magic. He had heard about court magicians, but there had never been one in Bellarome. He had seen one in Kiarome when he was visiting the palace and he didn't look anything special and he had not done anything magical. All he could gather was that the man was just and old advisor to the King. Despite Tancred's inability to understand magic he had an uncanny knack of knowing when someone was casting a spell. He always felt a twinge at the back of his neck. At least he did before he met Alaric. He had managed to mask the spell he used in the tower and that was very disturbing.

Once Tancred was sure the stableboy was going to give Tormenta some extra attention he made his way into the inn. He didn't know what would happen once he was inside. He knew that Emil had been murdered and the assassin had taken his place, but he didn't know if the town knew that Emil was dead. He hoped that was not the case.

Once inside the inn he was greeted by Onfré. The innkeeper looked at Tancred with a strange expression as if he was trying to place him from a long time ago. A look of realisation came across his face, but was gone before Tancred could notice it.

"How can I help?" There was an edge to Onfré's voice that Tancred picked up on. He wondered the reason behind it.

"I am supposed to meet a friend of mine here?" he thought the lie would make things easier, he was wrong.

"What is your friend's name?" Onfré sounded suspicious.

Tancred looked somewhat embarrassed. "I don't actually know."

"Hmm, I see. Do you know what your friend looks like?"

Tancred looked around the inn. There was no one else in the room. "Well here's the thing…"

Onfré cut in before Tancred had a chance to answer. "So you don't know what your friend looks like either? What sort of a friend are you?"

"He's not exactly a friend. He is more a friend of a friend. He would have arrived only in the last day or two. He would be someone who you wouldn't recognise. Have you seen anyone like this?" Tancred hoped the man didn't question his integrity again. With the state of play in Kiarome he didn't think that he could control himself.

Onfré knew exactly who he was talking about. He also knew that Tancred was in the group of people who he suspected of murdering Emil. They were the last people seen with him and the stableboy said that they were chasing after him when he left in the middle of the night. He liked Bern and Sorrell, they were trying to help the town. He didn't know Tancred, but he knew the man was no good. If he didn't know either of the men by look or by name then he was not going to help.

"Lots of people pass through this town. I don't keep track of them. There were a couple of groups passing through yesterday. They were all heading towards the north," the lie came out smoothly.

Tancred knew he was lying or at least he wasn't telling the truth. The person or people he was looking for would be heading towards Kiarome. He knew that, even if Alaric had not told him. He wasn't sure why the innkeeper was being so obtuse.

"That's alright. I have been riding hard and this will give me a chance to relax for a while. I am sure they will be along shortly. In the mean time I think I would like a room."

Onfré thought about telling Tancred there was no room at the inn, but he didn't think that would perturb him. If he found out that Onfré was lying then there might be trouble. He needed more information and until he was sure he would treat Tancred like he would any other traveller.

"I am sure I can find you something. In the mean time would you like something to eat or drink? I'm pretty sure the kitchen is open." Onfré knew full well the kitchen was open and the offer of food would keep Tancred around.

"That would be nice." Tancred had not eaten that day and the talk of food made him ravenously hungry. The idea also meant that he could speak with Onfré further.

Tancred was happy when a buxom serving woman brought a steaming plate of food. She also had a cold mug of ale. Tancred normally didn't drink so early in the day, but since he could do nothing until he met Alaric's friend he thought he would. His hunger was stronger than his thirst so he polished off his lunch before he started on his ale. Onfré returned to the table.

"Did you enjoy your meal?" There was nothing genuine about his words. Tancred didn't hear it though as he was busy thinking up his own ruse.

"Thank you, that was just what I needed." Onfré picked up on the duplicity in his voice. "I don't mean to be rude." Tancred had thought carefully on what he was going to say next. "It seems to be quiet in here today. Is there a reason why you don't have many patrons?"

Onfré thought for a moment. He knew the answer, but he was deciding on whether he should be offended with the question or not. He thought he would still play it nicely. "The owner was murdered recently. He was well loved in the village. People are still mourning over his death."

Tancred couldn't help, but smile. He was lucky that Onfré wasn't looking. The man would be enraged at the expression on his face. The only reason why he smiled was because he thought that it would be harder for him to gain the information that he required. He thought that maybe he had misjudged the innkeeper. He may have been obtuse due to the fact that Emil had been murdered, but he could understand why the man wasn't being friendly. Then he realised when the fake Emil was fleeing the village Tancred was one of the men chasing him. If Onfré knew who he was then he may think that he was involved in the murder. The realisation cast an entirely new light on the situation. Tancred would indeed have to be careful. There was every chance that the man he was supposed to meet was already in the village. He didn't think it would be prudent to openly state that he did not murder Emil. He had seen enough criminals on trial to know that all guilty men said that they didn't do it.

"I am sorry to hear that." Tancred paused for a moment, out of respect for the dead. "Do you know who did it?"

Onfré also thought for a moment. "No, we don't know who it was. We do have a few leads though. We believe that it is someone from out of town." He watched Tancred who flinched slightly. It was not enough to confirm his suspicions, but it was enough to keep going.

"That will make it hard to catch the guilty party," Tancred didn't look up as he spoke. He stared into his mug. He knew that it was making him look guilty, but he didn't want to look the man in the eye.

"I believe in the old saying. 'The guilty always return to the scene of their crime.' I believe that the person who murdered Emil will come back to witness the chaos he has created."

Tancred knew that he was losing the conversation. It was only a matter of time before Onfré openly accused him. Either way he wasn't getting the information that he needed. He thought that he would be able to outsmart the innkeeper, but he was wrong. The man was sharp on his feet and he was keeping the conversation right where he wanted.

"I think that I might go and rest now. Could you let me know if my friend comes along? He knows that I'm staying here so I am sure he will ask for me." Tancred drained his mug and stood from the table.

"I will let you know," Onfré nodded. He thought if he was able to push a little further he might be able to get Tancred to confess, but he couldn't make it too obvious. There was no good reason why he should keep the man from his room. He would have to wait for another opportunity to interrogate him.

Tancred was glad to get away from the innkeeper. He knew the man would not let up. He wished Alaric had given him a name or a description. It would have made his life so much easier. It would also mean that they could already be on the way back to Kiarome. He hated to think what was happening to Richmond and Alaric.

***

Sorrell returned to the inn later that afternoon. He had asked Onfré to check in on Bern every once in a while. Bern did not look good and he didn't want to leave him alone. There was something very strange about his illness. One moment he looked fine and then the next he looked on his death bed.

Sorrell had managed to speak to the least amount of people as possible. He didn't want to speak to anyone, but unfortunately what he was doing was all over town. Everyone knew he was investigating the murder, but they didn't know who Sorrell was. The rumour was that he was either and important noble or someone from King Unwin's court sent to settle the matter. They also thought that he was sent to settle the inheritance.

He was glad to be back at the inn. He knew he was going to have to speak to Onfré, but at least the man was honest. He didn't have any secret agendas. All he wanted to know was who killed his best friend and get the village back to normal. He wanted to help Onfré, but he had more important things to be worrying about. In less than two days the army would be assembled and ready to march. He estimated they would pass by the west of the village shortly after midday. They would need to be ready to leave by then.

"How is Bern?" Sorrell asked quietly once he was inside the inn.

"I haven't checked on him in a while. Last time I checked he was sound asleep," Onfré almost apologised as he spoke.

"I better go and check on him then." Sorrell started walking towards the room.

"Very good, let me know if you need anything," Onfré called after him.

Sorrell thought the exchange was odd. There was something different about the innkeeper. It was almost like he was trying to get rid of him. He didn't have time to stay and he needed to check on Bern before he did anything else. If Bern was truly sick then he would have to locate the town healer, something he was sure would be a complete nightmare.

He found Bern sleeping soundly inside their room. There was a small trail of sweat across his forehead and his face was a little paler than usual. That was the only sign that he was ill. Sorrell thought it was a good sign. With a little bed rest he was sure that Bern would be back on his feet. There didn't seem to be anything for him to do so he refilled the glass of water on the bedside table before he left.

There was something very strange about his condition. Sorrell thought that it seemed as though Bern became sick when things had started getting difficult. He shook his head. He had seen Bern under stress and he didn't think that was the complete reason for his illness.

The inn's common room was starting to fill with people coming in for the evening meal. Sorrell looked around, hoping to find the man they were supposed to meet. Sorrell could recognise the locals from the visitors. Unfortunately there was nothing to tell him which man was the one he was looking for. There was nothing for it except to get something to eat and wait.

It was not long before Onfré saw that Sorrell had returned. He was eager to speak to him again.

"Good to see you again Sorrell," Onfré greeted him warmly. "Are you ready to eat? We have a nicely roasted deer for dinner. It was caught only today, so it's nice and fresh."

"Thank you that would be nice. Oh and by the way has anyone asked after me or Bern?"

Onfré thought for a moment. He trusted Sorrell and he didn't want to lie. Then a thought came to him. "No. There was no one looking for you or Bern." Onfré kept his back to Sorrell as he spoke. Tancred had never asked for Bern or Sorrell by name. He was only led to assume that it was the man they were supposed to meet.

Once Onfré had walked away Sorrell sat back to survey the rest of the room. He knew the man he was looking for was in the village and if he was in the village he would have to be staying at the inn. It was still early and there would be many more people entering before the night was over. Until he was sure, there was nothing he could do except wait.

It was not long before Onfré returned with two plates of food. It was clear that the innkeeper was planning on joining him. As much as he didn't want to talk to him the company would be nice and he would look less conspicuous if he was talking to someone.

"Did you have any luck today?" Onfré was dying to ask the question.

It was the last thing Sorrell wanted to talk about. He had much more important things to be worrying about.

"Sit down." Sorrell offered as Onfré placed his plate of food on the table in front of him. "I have come to a decision. After speaking to most of the villagers, at least once, and thinking about it closely I have decided that the murder was done by someone else. I don't think any of the villagers could have murdered Emil. No one had a motive. If he left all his possessions to someone I could understand, but there is no reason for one of the villagers to murder him."

"I am glad to hear that." Onfré also tried to sound like he did not already know it to be fact and his suspicions of Tancred increased. He made it clear in his mind that he could not tell Sorrell that the man was looking for him. If he could keep the two apart for long enough then they might not meet and he would have more chance of catching Tancred. "I must admit that I didn't think that any of them did it. I think that I may have a lead on the murderer."

Onfré paused after his revelation. He wanted Sorrell to ask the question, but Sorrell had been busy eating and not paying much attention.

"Who is it?" Sorrell asked lazily.

"I don't want to say too much as this point. I have my suspicions, but I don't want to say anything until I am sure. Hopefully I will have an answer soon and you will be able to arrest him for me," Onfré sounded excited.

Sorrell knew that whoever it was Onfré thought was the murderer was not correct. He knew that the murderer was in Kiarome. He wished he could tell Onfré the truth so he didn't accuse an innocent man, but Sorrell knew he couldn't say anything. It would draw more attention to himself and he had already done more than enough of that.

"Just be careful. Whoever did this is obviously an evil and sadistic man. If you are not careful you could end up the same as Emil. I think you should leave the investigating to me," Sorrell hoped he could talk

Onfré out of whatever he was planning. "Tell me who it is and I can talk to them."

"Thank you for your concern, but I have things under control. Emil would want me to help find his killer. It's the least that I can do for my old friend."

Sorrell returned to eating his meal. He had to think of a way of stopping Onfré. He was going to upset at least one person if he started accusing people of murder. Not to mention the fact that he could end up seriously hurt. Then he noticed there was someone else in the common room. It was someone he had not seen before. He wasn't sure but he thought that before he looked over the man had been staring at him. The feeling made him uncomfortable. He turned back to his food. As soon as he did he felt the man's eyes on him. He shook the feeling off, silently scolding himself for being stupid.

"What is it Sorrell? You look out of sorts."

"Nothing," Sorrell grumbled into his food. He scolded himself again for letting his emotions show so easily.

Onfré looked over to where Sorrell had been looking. The man in question was hidden behind a small group. Onfré tried to look through, but he could not see who or what it was that Sorrell had been looking at. Not being one to accept being pushed aside he continued his line of questioning.

"If there is someone bothering you than please let me know. I will make sure that they are thrown out," Onfré pushed a little harder.

Sorrell looked up and he saw the man staring at him. This time he caught the man in the act. There was something about the way he was watching him that made Sorrell very uncomfortable. It was as if the man was trying to size him up. He thought about taking Onfré up on his offer, but there was something telling him to do otherwise.

"Do you know who that man is?" Sorrell nodded in the direction of the man who had been staring at him.

Onfré looked over. As soon as he saw him he looked back down at the table. At least the man didn't see him. That was Onfré's only saving grace. It was now Sorrell's turn to push Onfré.

"What is it Onfré? Do you know who it is?"

Onfré scraped his plate and put the remaining food into his mouth. He didn't want to answer the question and would do anything to delay his response.

Chapter 25: A New Destination

Tancred had sat in his room for long enough. He could no longer sit and wait. His Lord and friend was sitting in a prison cell, at least that is what he thought even if he didn't know completely, and he had to find the mystery person he was supposed to meet. He doubted very much if the innkeeper would come and get him. There was something about his attitude that made Tancred believe he didn't like him.

The common room was much busier and there were many visitors mixed in with the locals. It was going to make things very difficult to find the person he was looking for. Short of going up to each person in turn he did not know what else he could do. He decided to sit and see how everyone acted. There was no point in announcing what he was doing, especially with the village in such turmoil.

He ordered a mug of ale before finding a seat at a small table. It was the last free table in the common room and it was as if the other people were leaving it there for him. Tancred almost laughed at the thought. He had seen enough strange coincidences recently to not discount it completely. The thought warmed his spirits. If he was meant to have the table then maybe he was meant to find Alaric's friend.

It was not long before he noticed a strange man across the room. There was someone sitting at a table with the innkeeper. He looked different to everyone else. There was no doubt in Tancred's mind that the man had once been in the army, if he was not still a soldier. Not only that the man looked like a commander, or at least he had commanded other soldiers in the past. He had a strength of presence that was rare among men. He wondered if this was indeed the man he was sent to find.

Before he could judge him further he had to look away. The man looked straight at him. It was not long before the man's attention returned to Onfré and Tancred returned his gaze. A group of people stood in front of them and he was glad to have a little anonymity, even if it was only for a moment. It gave him time to think. He was sure the man on the table with Onfré was the man he was looking for and he didn't know why Onfré had not told him. For now he had to speak to the soldier and hopefully get some answers.

When he had made his decision the people had moved giving him a better view. The man began looking back at him as he spoke to Onfré briefly who also turned to look. The innkeeper quickly turned away and looked at his food. Tancred was surprised at Onfré's reaction. The innkeeper was definitely hiding something. He was not going to wonder what it was anymore. If the man was not who he thought he was then at least he would have figured out what Onfré was up to.

As Tancred approached the table the innkeeper came to his feet. He looked as though he was going to block Tancred's passage, but a word from the soldier made him stop. There was a look of fear on Onfré's face. He didn't know what he had said to Onfré, but the words had their effect.

"Excuse me," it seemed as though it was the most appropriate way to start the conversation. "I don't mean to bother you."

Onfré thought he should try and regain his standing, he didn't want to be blamed for any delay. "General Sorrell, may I present Tancred."

"You may indeed, leave us now," barked Sorrell. There was no doubt they were destined to meet each other and there was also no doubt that Onfré had been keeping them apart. General Sorrell dismissed the innkeeper before he had a chance to explain. Onfré knew when to leave well enough alone. As much as he wanted to explain he knew he had better leave. "Please, have a seat."

Once Tancred was seated the General spoke again. "I must admit when Bern said we were going to meet someone here I had my doubts, but here we are."

"I know what you mean. When Alaric told me the same thing I didn't think there was a chance I would find you. There was nothing else that I could do. I had to take his word," there was a broad grin on Tancred's face.

"So now what do we do?" Sorrell asked.

"We need to get back to Kiarome. Alaric and Richmond have been taken prisoner."

"Why would King Unwin take Alaric and Richmond prisoner?" Sorrell seemed confused.

"Because it's not Unwin who is calling the shots anymore."

Both men looked up from the table at the sudden new voice in their conversation. Bern had taken both men by surprise. Tancred, because they had never met him before and Sorrell, because he thought he should still be in bed. Now Bern looked as though he was as fit as he ever had been.

"Bern, what are you doing up?" Sorrell's voice was full of surprise.

"I am feeling much better. Now I think it would be polite if you introduced me to your new friend.

"Yes, of course. This is Tancred. He is a friend of Alaric's."

"Very good. We have been waiting for you. Do you have word from Alaric?" Bern seemed excited.

"As I said, both he and Richmond have been taken prisoner. The last thing that Alaric said to me was that I had to find you. He said you must lead the army to Kiarome." Tancred was trying to get everything out at once and hoped that he was making some sense.

"Yes, you are right. I can see now that we must continue our journey to the south. We must free Kiarome from the Evil One's minions," the command had returned to Bern's voice.

"What are you talking about?" His words had caught Tancred off guard. "How do you know that it is the Evil One who has imprisoned Alaric and Richmond? All I have told you is that he is in Unwin's prison."

"Trust me. It is better if you don't ask. It is less confusing that way. All you need to know it that when Bern says something you have to take notice." Sorrell shrugged. "But for my sake could you tell us what happened Tancred.

"Okay." Tancred looked at them both suspiciously. "I will let that go for a minute," he continued to explain what had happened. "Now we need to work out how we are going to rescue the two. Alaric said to me that you were in charge of the Alliance, is that correct?"

"That is correct. The army is on the march and should be just to the west by mid to late morning," Sorrell confirmed.

"Good, then we need to lead the army against Kiarome," the words came out of Tancred's mouth before he had a chance to think.

"Just wait a minute. Let's not be so quick to attack Kiarome. Let's remember that it is only his advisor who is evil, not King Unwin himself. I am sure there is a better way to regain control of the city." Sorrell was still not happy with the idea of invading his home city. "What you are suggesting could lead to its total destruction."

"Be that as it may, it is something that we need to consider. I would rather see our capital burn than to fall in the hands of the Evil One. If his followers have control of the king then they also have control of his army. We may have no other choice than to take the city by force."

What Tancred said made sense, but Sorrell still didn't want to contemplate what he was saying. There had to be another way to free Alaric and Richmond and save King Unwin. He was a master General, tactics was his strong point and yet he couldn't think of anything. It was really frustrating him.

"Let's not think about that just yet. I am sure it won't come down to that. What we need is more information on the location of Alaric and Richmond," Sorrell turned to Tancred as he spoke.

"I left before they were captured. I can only assume they are in the royal dungeons, but that is all I can say. In truth they could be anywhere," Tancred sighed.

"Well I think we are safe to assume they are in the dungeons. I don't think Alaric would have sent you to find me if he was not in danger.

We have to make a plan to get us into the palace." Bern was trying to be as positive as he could.

The three of them stayed up well into the night trying devise up with a plan. Each time they came up with an idea they came up with a number of ways it wasn't going to work. In the end they were too tired to come up with any new ideas. They went to bed without a decent plan. No matter what they thought up with the best plan remained a full frontal attack of the city.

In the morning they met in the common room. They had a little time to kill before the army arrived. The problem of how to get into the palace without an assault was put on the backburner when Onfré saw them. He seemed to have recovered from the day before and was in full flight.

"Good morning. I hope that you all slept well. Now we need to come to a decision on Emil's estate." Onfré knew that they would be leaving soon and he needed them to create a peaceful environment within the village.

Tancred looked questioning at Sorrell who in turn shook his head. "It so happens that we are coming up with a solution as we speak. If you would give us some breakfast and a little time, we shall have a solution for you." It was the best Sorrell could come up with.

"What is that all about?" Tancred asked.

"The town is tearing itself apart trying to wrestle control of Emil's certain businesses. We said we would help the situation, although I am at a loss to know how," Sorrell explained.

Bern continued to go into more detail on the situation. He figured that if anyone knew the best way to resolve the situation it would be Tancred.

"Well it seems to me that we need to appoint an executor to his estate. It needs to be someone who Emil trusted and someone who will see that the appropriate people get what they deserve. Now normally that person would be Emil himself. It seems as though the assassin's choice was the most destructive person to murder and assume his identity," Tancred spoke the last softer than the rest, as if he was talking to himself.

"So what we need to do is find the person next in line to Emil. The person the villagers respect, someone who Emil respected and someone who won't take all the power," Bern surmised.

"It could take us a long time to find the right person and we don't have more than a few hours." Tancred wasn't helping.

"I don't think that is going to be a problem," Sorrell spoke as a serving woman brought their meals to the table. No one seemed to notice her until she placed the food down. "There is one man who fits the bill. Now I have been speaking to a lot of the villagers over the last few days and this man has more respect than anyone else. He was a good friend to Emil and I think he is worthy of the job."

"Who?" Tancred asked when he finished swallowing his mouthful.

"Onfré. He was Emil's best friend. He hasn't made a claim on anything, even the inn he has worked most of his life in. The villagers all respect him and I think they would trust his judgement. I think all it would take is a decree from General Sorrell and they will take it on board."

"Well I think that solves that problem," Bern spoke between mouthfuls.

"I hate to disagree, but I have found the man to be quite disagreeable," Tancred said.

Sorrell laughed, but Bern didn't see the funny side. When he stopped laughing he explained the joke to the others. "It seems that Onfré thinks that you are the one who murdered Emil. That is the reason why he has been so standoffish with you." Bern also started laughing when he realised what had happened.

"Fair enough. I suppose that he is as good a choice as any in the short time that we have. With that taken care of we can start for the city." Tancred was keen to keep moving.

"We still have to wait for the army to arrive. Someone will come for us when it is here," Sorrell advised. "In the mean time I think I shall have the villagers assembled. I shall announce that the murderer has left the village and that we will bring him to justice," the statement was true in one sense. "Then I will announce that I am handing over power of attorney to Onfré. That should be enough to settle things down in the village. The rest will be up to him."

It was mid-morning when the villagers were finally assembled. Everyone met outside the front of the inn. Even some people who didn't live in the village gathered around to see what was happening. Sorrell looked over the crowd. All eyes were on him in anticipation.

"Thank you for coming. As some of you may know I have been investigating the murder of Emil. I have come to some interesting conclusions. I will start with the murder... I have surmised that the murderer is someone from out of town. His motives are not clear to me." The crowd stood breathlessly. "It seems the murderer has a love for chaos. He figured that the death of Emil would cause the village to tear itself apart. By my reckoning he had done a very good job." The villagers dropped their heads as Sorrell spoke. "Nevertheless the criminal mastermind is no match for my team of specialists." Bern groaned at the blatant pandering to the crowd, but he kept his mouth shut. "We have discovered that once he knew we were on to him he fled to Kiarome. It is only since my detective returned yesterday that I know for sure who the murderer is. You can all rest assured we know his location and he will be brought to justice very shortly," Sorrell paused as there were a number of cheers from the crowd. Now that he had the villagers on his side the next revelation wouldn't be as painful.

"Now it comes to the sad duty I have of deciding on the fate of Emil's estate. I have done a lot of thinking and I believe that there is only one solution to the problem. I am giving Onfré power of attorney over the estate. To this charge there are a number of conditions. The first condition is that Onfré will now have ownership of the inn and all that is related to its running." His words brought a few comments from the villagers. "The second is that Onfré cannot take control of any of the other businesses within the estate. He is allowed a property and a certain amount of money. The other businesses and assets he shall divide up amongst the villagers in whatever way he sees fit. Another condition is that no villager shall possess more than one business. It is also permissible for Onfré to split a business amongst two or more villagers. As General of the King's Royal Army I speak on his behalf and therefore such is stated as law. There shall be no further discussion brought into the matter. Anyone who goes against this edict shall be charged with treason and treated accordingly." Sorrell was pleased with the result of his meeting. The villagers were not cheering anymore, but at least they seemed to accept what he had said.

When he finished speaking a number of horse hooves could be heard approaching. Sorrell breathed a sigh of relief. The distraction was welcome and he was also glad to see Hadar at the front of the small group of mounted soldiers. Sorrell had done all that he could to settle the unrest in the village. Now it was up to Onfré to do the rest. He knew he had done the right thing. Onfré was the only one who would respect the memory of Emil.

"Now you can go back to your regular business. I am sure Onfré will have an answer for you all shortly," Sorrell turned his back on the crowd.

"What was that all about?" Hadar asked when he finally made his way through the crowd.

"It's a long story. Right now I just want to leave the village. Tell me what has been going on," Sorrell sounded exhausted.

"Well I don't think it is as exciting as you, but there have still been some interesting developments," Hadar's words made Sorrell seem more interested.

When Bern and Tancred joined them, and the introductions were complete, Hadar explained the situation with Aimon and Jarwe returning to power. They continued the discussion on the way to the stables.

"I knew that Aimon was keen on power. He is the highest ranking officer from Entero in the Alliance, but he is still far behind the rest of us." Bern included himself in the comparison. He was considered a General, at least within the Alliance, which no matter how long he had been so he still outranked Aimon. "It is a little disturbing that he tried to usurp the army. That is taking things a little too far. What have you done about reprimanding him?"

"Jarwe has done nothing yet. He wanted to wait for your return, but he still feels that we have to tread very carefully. He still holds sway amongst the Enteroite soldiers. You remember what happened when Prince Hawthorne decided the take his soldiers away from the army? We almost lost half of our soldiers. We can ill afford to have the same thing happen with Aimon," Hadar explained and Sorrell nodded his agreement.

"We will definitely have to tread lightly where Aimon is concerned. He will not be happy once Bern is back in the army. We also have to face Jarwe who is back in command."

"I don't even know who is in charge," Hadar said. "Jarwe never officially gave up control, at least I don't recall him ever doing it." He looked at Bern for advice when he finished speaking.

"I think that it will bring stability back into the soldiers' minds if they see Jarwe back in command," Bern spoke.

"That is completely up to him," Hadar spoke again. "By the way he has been speaking it seems he is under the impression that he is just in command until Bern returns. I think the only reason why he came back was to make sure that Aimon didn't steal the army."

Bern knew what Hadar said was true. Jarwe was going to want to return control to him. This time he would be able to do it officially, but the situation had changed. With the impending siege on Kiarome he would need Jarwe in command. He knew nothing about sieges and he couldn't rely on the entity returning to help. He also had a feeling that he would have to leave the army at some point. That would not be good for morale if the commanding officer left before the battle had been won.

The army was not far from the village. It took them less than half an hour on horseback to reach them. The soldiers looked restless as they lined up, waiting for instructions. They had been waiting for over an hour and although they were still regimented they looked as though they were starting to waver.

"What's our plan General?" Jarwe asked when they had arrived.

"We head towards Kiarome," Bern began. "I also think for now you should retain your status as the commander of the army."

"Whatever you say General, but why?"

"I will explain later. For now we need to get the army moving."

"Why are we travelling towards Kiarome? I would have thought that was the last place to lead the army," Aimon asked, somewhat rattled.

"I will explain later," Bern turned his back on the group and started riding.

"That's not good enough," Aimon yelled after him as he kicked his horse into action.

Bern continued until Aimon reached him. Eventually Bern reined in his horse and turned towards him.

"You need to explain to us what is happening. We are all part of the command group and we deserve answers," Aimon continued to yell.

"I will tell you in good time. For now we need to keep moving," Bern spoke through clenched teeth. He was less than impressed with Aimon trying to steal his army.

Bern again turned his back on Aimon. This only infuriated the captain even more. Bern started his horse again whilst Aimon sat and watched. Before Aimon had a chance to chase after him Jarwe grabbed the reins of his horse.

"I am the General of this army, until Bern wishes to reclaim his rightful role. All you need to know is if I say the army moves south then the army moves south. Now I think you should go and relay these orders to your troops." Jarwe was a much more imposing figure than Bern and Aimon knew it.

There was nothing more that Aimon could say. He was not going to get any information out of them. He sniggered to himself as he rode away. He knew that he would have the last laugh when it was all said and done.

Bern rode the rest of the day at the front of the army. Everyone knew that he wanted to be alone and no one tried to approach him since his confrontation with Aimon. There was something driving him on. It was as if there was a voice calling to him on the wind. He knew he was being drawn towards Alaric. Alaric was in danger and it was up to him to save him. The only problem was that he didn't know if he was capable. Without the entity he was still just a farmer from Remidia. Sure he had learned many new skills, but he knew that he could not confront Alaric's captors.

Bern made the army march right up until dusk. It was only at Hadar's insistence that he called for a halt. Jarwe was still happy to let Bern set the pace, but gave the others a feeling of unrest. They were happy with the situation whilst Jarwe was somewhat catatonic, but with him was back in control they felt that he should lead. There was a lot they needed to discuss that evening.

"Let's get to the bottom of this," Aimon started when he joined the others. He didn't care what they had previously been talking about. He was going to be appeased. "I demand to know what we are doing."

"You do not come in here making demands, Captain. Sit down and maybe you will learn what you want to know." Jarwe almost spat the words at him. It was all he could do to keep from yelling.

Aimon sat down at the table like a sullen child. He looked as though he was about to say something, but then thought better of it. When it was clear he was not going to speak the others returned to what they were doing. They were still waiting on Duke Hadar to arrive before they discussed anything further. It was obvious that Aimon was not happy with the small talk.

Duke Hadar apologised for his lateness as he entered the tent.

"Now that we are all here I am sure you are waiting for some much needed information." Sorrell took the floor. Before he continued he formally introduced Tancred to everyone in the room. "Now there have been some disturbing developments," Sorrell opened the floor for Bern to speak.

Bern thought for a moment. He hoped the entity would arrive and speak on his behalf, but he knew it wasn't going to happen. He also knew what he had to say. He was slowly starting to learn how to be a General. "Tancred has brought word from Kiarome. Alaric, the Chosen One, has been taken prisoner." Everyone in the room gasped. The news was more than a little disturbing. "We don't have a great deal of information, but we believe he is imprisoned in the royal dungeons with Lord Richmond. We also believe that King Unwin is in the thrall of the Evil One's minions. We do not know the full extent, but we know enough to tread lightly." Bern thought for a moment. He could feel the entity in the back of his mind. He wasn't sure he should share the information that was coming to him, but he knew in the end that the entity would take over if he didn't volunteer the information. As much as it would be easier for him he really didn't want that to happen. "I believe there is a least one Dark Knight in the city." The revelation brought more gasps from the group. "I also believe that it is a another Dark Knight who is controlling King Unwin."

"If this is true then is there any hope for us. I have seen a Dark Knight at work before and I have an idea what they are capable of," Hulkan said.

"This comes down to the crux of the situation. There is very little doubt that we will have to take the city by force. If a Dark Knight controls Unwin then he also controls his army," Bern explained.

"A good portion of the Alliance is made up of Unwin's soldiers. How are we going to convince them to attack their own capital city?"

Hadar was unsettled by what he was hearing. It was the first time Bern had seen him lose his confidence.

"The soldiers will do as they are told. Unwin might be their King, but I am their General. They will do what I order them to do. They know they are part of the Alliance now and that's all that matters," Sorrell reassured them.

"This is insane. Are we seriously talking about a siege? This army is not prepared for that action. This army was designed for ground warfare. If we attack the city then we are doomed to fail," Aimon sulked.

"Then what do you have in mind?" Wojtek spoke before Sorrell had a chance to answer.

"I think that we need to know what we are up against. We need to infiltrate the city. We need to get into the palace and get a first hand view of the situation."

"That is easier said than done," added Tancred. "That is how the other two were captured. We were trying to infiltrate the palace. We got inside the palace grounds and that is when Alaric told me to find you. The theory is solid, but I don't think that it will work in practice. We had to sneak into the palace. There was no other way for us to gain access."

Aimon laughed before he starting speaking again. "I don't mean to be offensive, but I am sure that I will be able to get in the palace. I have had quite a lot of experience in espionage. I do not think that it will be all that difficult." Aimon looked smug.

Tancred was about to speak, but Bern silenced him with a raise of his arm. "I think that is worth a shot. It will be a dangerous mission, but if you think that you can do it then I think you should. If we can gather some intelligence from inside the city and it means we do not have to attack then I think that it is worth the risk."

"But what about if he gets caught?" Hadar rebutted. "At the moment we have the advantage of surprise. If he gets caught and gives away our plans then it will be much worse. At least Unwin, or whoever is in control of the city at the moment, doesn't have time to fortify."

"Hadar makes a very good point Bern," Tancred had to agree with the Duke's thinking.

"I can assure you that I won't get caught and if I do then I will be able to hold out until you come to rescue me," Aimon looked even smugger.

They threw around more ideas for and against Aimon's suggestion. Eventually Bern was sick of the bickering and he threw up his hands.

"I think there is only one way to settle this argument. We are a command group and I think we should start acting like one. I think we should have a vote on whether we send Aimon into Kiarome or not," Bern sounded somewhat exhausted.

"I think that is a very good idea," Jarwe agreed and was followed by more murmured agreements.

"Okay those who are for sending Aimon in Kiarome raise your hand now," Bern adjudicated the vote.

The hands were quick to be raised. Aimon was obviously the first. He followed shortly by Bern, Sorrell, Wojtek and Pernian. The five votes were enough to win. Both Jarwe and Hadar didn't look happy with the result. The two dwarves didn't seem to have an opinion. If Jarwe wanted to he could have overridden the decision, but since Bern was for the motion he decided against it. If he wanted Bern to take control of the army then he couldn't override him.

"It is settled then. Aimon will infiltrate the palace and then report back to us. You have a day. We will be in range of the city by noon in two days. By then we will need to have a plan," Jarwe kept his voice level.

"I will need a small group to enter the city. I will pose as a merchant with a small band of soldiers. I will be able to enter the city without being noticed that way. I will need a covered wagon and maybe some valuables, just in case I get checked," Aimon rubbed his hands as he spoke. Only Hadar noticed it and it did nothing to reassure his doubts.

"Very good then. You can leave first thing in the morning," Sorrell was happy with anything that meant he would not have to attack his own countrymen. This clouded his otherwise impeccable judgement.

"No," the group was about to leave the table when Aimon spoke. "I will leave tonight. If I leave as soon as possible then I can reach the city by mid-morning. I will need that time to get in and out."

"It will look suspicious if you arrive too early. Even if you push hard you would not reach the city from Lord's Wait before lunch with a wagon load of goods," Hadar rebuked his theory.

"You leave that to me," was all Aimon said, although there was a look in his eyes that made everyone nervous.

Chapter 26: A Dangerous Deceit

The army was on the march at first light, as usual. Word had gone down the ranks that they were heading towards Kiarome. That was all the information that the soldiers were given. The reason for travelling to Kiarome was kept purely within the command group. Aimon had left during the night with a number of handpicked men, but their absence in the morning went unnoticed.

The army would march hard for the rest of the day to try and make as much distance as they could. If they were going to besiege Kiarome then they would need time for the army to rest. There was no telling what would happen once they reached the city and they had to be prepared for all outcomes.

Bern rode at the front of the army again. The pull towards Kiarome was still ever present. He had started the day riding with the rest of the command group, with Jarwe in the lead. He didn't feel comfortable riding with the others and it wasn't until he was in the lead did the bad feeling abate. It remained just a tug leading him in the right direction.

The countryside passed throughout the day. At mid-morning they passed a small grove of trees to the west. There was something disturbing about it and Bern had to keep looking around and over his shoulder towards the trees. He had a feeling that he should investigate them closer, but the pull towards the city was stronger. Once they were well past the grove the feeling disappeared and Bern thought nothing more about it.

Although their course ever led them further to the east, they stayed out of sight of the highway. If anyone saw them on the road then it would not be long before the rumours were all over the city and then the palace would know they were approaching. If that happened then no matter what sort of intelligence Aimon gained they would still have to assault the city walls. They did not want to attack the city, but there was no telling how long it would take before they could penetrate the outer walls. Some sieges had lasted for over a year with no result.

They camped for the night far enough away from the city to be able to light fires. The night air had turned bitterly cold and they were grateful for the small mercy. If anyone had been travelling along the highway then they would have seen the fire, but the chances that someone would be on the road during the night was less than likely.

The command group gathered in their tent once the army had settled. The braziers blazed at the back corners and the table had been laden with food. As per their instructions their meals were not much better than those of the regular army as their supplies would only last for so long. If they couldn't get into the city and gain support from Unwin within a month then all would be lost. The army would have to disband and find their own way home.

"Do you think Aimon will have any luck in the city?" Jarwe asked when they had all finished their meals.

"There is something about that man that doesn't sit right," Hadar replied. "I don't know what it is, but I don't trust him. I don't believe that he will help our cause whilst he's there."

"Then why would he suggest risking his life like that?" Hulkan wasn't convinced.

"That I don't know. All I know is the feeling in my stomach and there is nothing there to say 'trust him'."

"There is nothing we can do about Aimon now. All we can do is hope that he will do the right thing." Bern also doubted that Aimon was true to their cause, but he also knew that he had to send the man in. He hated the little titbits the entity was tossing his way. He knew he was making the right decision, but he didn't know why and it was even more frustrating that he couldn't explain it to the others. "What we need to concentrate on is what we are going to do once we reach Kiarome. I hope that Aimon will succeed in his mission, but I doubt he will."

They sat in silence for a moment whilst Bern's words sunk in. No one really wanted to think about the impending battle, but they all knew it was inevitable.

"Do you think you could gain entrance to the city with some of your soldiers?" Hadar asked Sorrell.

Sorrell shrugged his shoulders and looked towards Wojtek. "It is possible, I guess. There should be no problems with you taking Darshivallian soldiers into the city. That is a very good idea Hadar," Wojtek sounded somewhat surprised with the Duke's insight.

"If we can get inside the city then we would be able to secure the gate before they knew they were under attack," Hadar continued, with a little more enthusiasm.

"Your theory is sound, but will the Darshivallian army attack their own city?" Lord Pernian spoke for the first time that evening.

"They will do what I command them to do, but I will have to tell them the reasoning behind it. It will make their decision a lot easier," Sorrell spoke confidently.

"Very good then. I think this should be our first plan, but I don't think we can rely on it succeeding. We need at least one more," Jarwe suggested.

"I don't think there is going to be any other way to get into the city without fighting," Wojtek said.

"Then we need to prepare ourselves for a siege. There is nothing else we can do," Jarwe's voice was grave. "I trust that you know the city well enough to know where the best place to attack?"

Sorrell and Wojtek looked at each other. "There's no point in travelling to the eastern side of the city. That is where the palace is situated and the walls are three times as thick. We could be there for a decade," Wojtek explained.

"That is good to know, but it still doesn't help. We need to know how we can enter the city, not how we can't!"

"If you wait I am getting there," Wojtek didn't appreciate being interrupted. "Kiarome was built with one purpose in mind and that was protecting the palace. The remainder of the city walls were built as an afterthought. As long as we don't go directly for the palace we should be alright. Now that said it will not be easy breaching the outer walls. The city walls are thick and well protected. Even in times of peace the walls are guarded. I would imagine that there are going to be archers posted all along the wall too and that would be the very best scenario. Depending on how paranoid this 'advisor' is there could be any number of nasty surprises waiting for us."

His last statement brought silence again to the command tent. The thought of what they had to do didn't settle anyone's nerves. The siege was going to be a more daunting task than they thought.

"We have no siege engines," was all Hadar could say.

"It will take too long to build the equipment we need to destroy the walls," added Lord Pernian.

"There are a number of carpenters and engineers in the army. I don't think it would take too long to design and build something to knock the walls down," General Jarwe sounded more optimistic.

"We need to start cutting down trees and collecting the wood. There are not a lot of trees near the city," Wojtek explained.

"There was a grove not too far back. There looked as though there was some good timber back there," Bern blurted out the words.

"We are already going to lose enough time as it is. There are plenty of small groves and the likes between here and the city. I don't think there is any need to back track," Wojtek explained.

"What are we going to tell the soldiers?" Hulkan asked. "They are going to be suspicious if we are just randomly chopping trees. The men aren't stupid and will put two and two together."

Again silence hit the tent. With each different problem they needed time to think about a solution.

"We could always tell them that we are building a small village outside of Kiarome," Lord Pernian suggested.

"That's an interesting idea, but why would we be building a village? We might be able to fool the dumber of the soldiers, but I don't think it will fool everyone," Hadar refuted.

"I agree with Hadar. I don't think many will believe it and then when we reach Kiarome and start building siege engines they will know that we lied to them. The army is on tenterhooks as it is and this ruse could tip it over the precipice," Wojtek had to agree.

"Then I suppose we should just tell the soldiers what were are doing." The elf was a little put out with his idea being shot down so quickly.

"Then we have the problem of explaining to the Darshivallian soldiers the reason for entering the city. If they think that we are preparing for a siege then they will figure out that they are not just simply returning home," Wojtek interjected.

"Then what are we going to do? We have to act quickly if we are going to be able to free Kiarome from the tyranny that controls it." Dorn didn't have any great ideas.

"We have to be honest with the army. There is nothing we can do about that. We can't trick them into thinking we are not prepared to attack the city," Sorrell spoke. "It doesn't leave us many options."

"The only way I can see it working is if we separate the army first thing in the morning. If we can get the Darshivallian army to believe that they are just returning to their capital then we can explain what we are doing to the rest. That way we will be able continue without upsetting anyone, or at least not upsetting them more than we have to," Bern mused.

There was a moment whilst everyone processed Bern's words. They were all looking for a flaw in his idea, but they could not find one.

"That is a great idea," Wojtek congratulated Bern. "It should keep everyone happy, or at least as happy as they can be."

"So who will go into the city and who will stay with the remainder of the army?" Pernian asked.

Wojtek was about to answer, but Bern cut him off. "Wojtek, Sorrell and myself will lead the soldiers into the city. The rest of you must keep the army under control. It will be hard without all the commanders here, but I am sure you will be able to handle it. The Enteroites will be the most difficult, with Aimon disappearing, but as I understand it I don't think you will have a problem with them attacking Kiarome."

Bern was right. There had been many battles fought across the border between Entero and Darshival over the years. The borders had changed in both directions many times. Once an Enteroite army marched all the way to Kiarome and they besieged the city for over a year before they returned home, unsuccessful.

"That sounds like a very good plan. I think that we should ready the Darshivallian army to march at first light. We will find an excuse to keep the remainder of the army here. I don't think that should be too hard. I am sure that most of the soldiers will be glad to be going home and won't question why." Jarwe liked the plan and there was a certain amount of excitement in his voice.

Everyone was happy that Jarwe's normal strength of character had returned. He held his commanding presence, even though he deferred as many decisions as possible to Bern, he still reassured the rest of the command group and his return would increase the soldier's morale.

Both Wojtek and Sorrell moved to make sure the Darshivallian army knew what the next day held for them. They neglected to tell them that they had to secure the Northern gate and wall. They would leave that to the very last minute. It would be hard to convince them that it was the right thing to do, but they were confident that when the soldiers knew their reasoning they would agree.

Whilst they were preparing the Darshivallians the others were thinking up reasons why the rest of the army was staying behind. In the end they decided that it was to allow Kiarome to prepare for their arrival. It would be quite a shock to the citizens to see such an army arriving on their doorstep. It was a weak idea, but it was the best they could do.

In the morning Bern, Sorrell and Wojtek all rode at the front of the Darshivallian component of the Alliance. Tancred, although not officially part of the command group, also joined them. The four of them were glad that they were able to start in the morning with the minimum of fuss. Everyone accepted their orders without question. The soldiers were too glad to be returning home, to worry too much about the reason.

The morning sky was completely clear of clouds and there was a thin layer of dew on the ground. There was no wind to speak of and it was looking as though it was going to be a hot day. It was not a bad day for battle, as long as the heat didn't get too intense. They estimated that they would reach the city shortly after noon.

They explained their reasoning to the soldiers during the midday meal and they took the news better than expected. They were prepared to do what they could, but they were not happy with the thought of having to kill their brethren, but if their King was in danger then that is what they would do.

They ate a quick lunch before they were on the move again. Nerves were starting to get to them and it would not be long before they had to try and get into the city. What they were doing was a pivotal part in their plan to avoid bloodshed. The soldiers didn't understand the true role they were playing, but they were still nervous nevertheless.

They had been marching for an hour before the city finally came into view looming up on the horizon. It looked larger than Sorrell remembered. Something caught in his throat as he thought about what they were about to do. The idea of invading his home city wasn't worth thinking about. The thought of besieging his city was even worse.

"Do you think there is something strange happening here?" Wojtek asked as they slowly made their way towards the city.

"What do you mean?" Bern asked.

"I know what you are talking about," Sorrell's voice was ominous. "There is no one on the highway. In fact there is no one moving outside of the city at all."

"What does that mean?" Bern asked.

Before Sorrell or Wojtek had a chance to answer a sudden movement caught all of them by surprise. They reined their horses to a stop and motioned for the army to do the same. Coming towards them at a great speed was a horse and rider. No one was going to move until they figured out who it was. Bern had a bad feeling that he already knew.

***

Aimon had snuck away shortly after midnight. He took with him a covered wagon and half dozen soldiers. Originally he was going to pose as a merchant, but he decided that he felt more comfortable on horseback. He made one of the soldiers dress up like a merchant instead. Although the man complained in the end he did as he was told. The look on Aimon's face told him that he had already pushed his luck by complaining in the first place.

He chose soldiers in no particular manner. The only reason he took them was because they were lowly ranked and would not be missed. He didn't need to trust the men he was taking with him.

It was not long after they started that they passed a small grove of trees. To the soldiers surprise Aimon suggested that they should take a rest. He had pushed the soldiers so relentlessly hard early in their journey that his sudden chance of mind came as a great surprise. None of the soldiers were willing to say anything. They had marched all day and although they were on horseback they were still extremely tired.

It was not long before Aimon's true plan was revealed to them. One by one the soldiers were slaughtered, followed shortly after by their terrified horses. One of Aimon's, or more so Argoz's, favourite pastimes was feasting on human flesh. He had not managed to find a chance to do so whilst he was involved in the Alliance. There had been some opportunities, but the risk of getting caught was too great. He could hardly contain himself at the meeting when the others had voted to let him go. It had taken all of his will power to control himself. He had waited long enough and the grove of trees had given him the perfect opportunity to hide the evidence.

Once he had finished feasting on the soldier's flesh he dragged their bodies into the middle of the grove. He then did the same with the horses and finally he destroyed the wagon and hid that as well. He had left his horse alive, he would need it to reach the city in time.

He had considered not warning Fenaroz of the army's plan to attack the city. It would be better for him if his brother would just disappear. He had done very well for himself in what he had done so far. He knew that it would please the Great Lord to see the King of Darshival under the control of Fenaroz. It was more than he had achieved. All he had managed to do is gather information. He had not been able to affect the movement of the army at all. In the mind of the Great Lord that would be a failure and failure resulted in death. At least he could warn Fenaroz and then it would seem as though he had at least a little success. That might save his life if he couldn't do anything else.

The main problem was Bern. He knew that something wasn't right with him. It wasn't just pure luck that kept him in the right direction, he was different to the other men he had known. They had spoken about an 'entity' that was taking over his body, but Argoz knew it was something else. Either way he would have to get rid of him if he was going to take control of the army. Jarwe's recovery had been unfortunate, but Argoz was confident that he could control Jarwe once Bern had been disposed of.

He wondered, as he rode, how Bern was able to penetrate the trap that had been set in Avalon. There should have been no one in the army that was able to see through the magic. The man had more power than anyone gave him credit for. Luckily Bern didn't even realise the power that resided inside him.

Argoz ignored the advice of the others and rode towards the gate as the sun bridged the horizon. Without the wagon and the other soldiers he was able to set his own pace. He did not care if he rode his horse to death. He was sure he would be given another one when he reached the palace.

He was stopped at the main gate by an elderly looking guard. There was no one else around and Argoz thought about killing him. It wouldn't be long before the body was found though and that could cause him some unwanted attention. He could use magic to control the man's mind, but that would announce his arrival. Masking a mind control spell was fine once the spell had been cast, but in casting the spell there was no one alive, not even the Great Lord himself, who could mask the residual effect. He had to use his guile to gain entrance into the city.

"Halt!" Even though the guard looked aged there was strength in his voice. "No one is allowed into the city without the appropriate papers."

"Good sir," the words almost stuck in his throat. "I have an important message for," Argoz paused, he didn't know what pseudonym Fenaroz was using. He knew one thing for sure and that was that he wouldn't be using his real name. "The King's advisor," it was the only name he could think of that wouldn't give anything away. "It is of the utmost urgency that I see him."

"That is all well and good, but no one is admitted into the palace now, regardless of their reasoning. Now if you don't have papers I ask that you return from wherever you came from." The guard seemed disinterested.

Argoz sat on his horse and thought. He wondered if there was any other way he could gain entrance into the city. Then it came to him. He might actually try to tell the truth.

"I am part of the Alliance. I have come here with a message from General Sorrell. I understand there are some issues that need resolving. I am sure that both King Unwin and his advisor will be less than impressed if you delay me any longer."

"Then why has General Sorrell sent you and not come himself?" The guard was less sure of himself now.

"Why would the General come himself? He has sent me as his messenger," Argoz was starting to become irritated, although he was able to keep his anger in check.

"That makes sense, but I ask you this. Why would he send an Enteroite and not a Darshival soldier?" The guard seemed somewhat smug.

"Because I am a Captain and this message cannot be entrusted to a mere soldier," Argoz thought about going through his rank, but he thought he would wait for the guard's response.

The guard was completely unsure of himself. Every word the man in front of him made sense. He knew the General, not personally, but by reputation, and he did not want to get on the man's bad side. When the war was over he would rather be remembered for helping the General and his staff, not for hindering them. There was nothing else that he could do but to allow the man into the city. Whether he was allowed into the palace was another story, but that was not his problem.

"Very well. Move along. I don't want to see you loitering in the street anymore." The guard tried to regain his composure, but it didn't work.

Argoz moved his horse through the gates. It would be harder for him to gain entrance into the palace, he knew that from the start. At worst he could announce his arrival once he was at the palace gates. Once he was there he didn't care who knew he had arrived. At the very worst Fenaroz would be forced to come out and see who was making such a racket. He couldn't leave someone with so much strength left unchecked in his city.

At first he had to ask directions towards the palace. The buildings loomed up around him and he didn't know which way he needed to go. The citizens who he asked looked at him as though he were a leper. There was nothing more in the world he wanted to do than to strike them down, but he had to resist the urge and continue on his path.

As he expected he was stopped once he reached the palace gates. There were more guards on duty then he had expected. There were a dozen heavily armed men in front of the gate and on the other side were another dozen. He could also see a number them standing guard on the wall. It was going to be even more difficult to gain entrance than what he had initially thought.

"I am here with a message for the King's advisor. It comes from General Sorrell."

"Very good. You are expected," it seemed that the guard on the Northern Gate had sent word of his arrival. At least that is what Argoz was hoping.

Argoz dismounted and led his horse through the gate. He looked around at the soldiers nervously. Fenaroz was very paranoid to have so many guards. That was not a good sign. His brother had always been the most nervous of the seven. He never trusted anyone and that could be very dangerous.

A young serving woman and a page boy met him at the main doors. There were also a number of soldiers standing on either side. The page boy took his horse whilst the woman waited for him at the top of the stairs. There was something about the woman that disturbed him. He didn't know what it was. There were women in the army, cooks, servants and the likes, but none as young as the one standing before him. Whatever it was that he was feeling inside he didn't like it.

"Take to me to the King," Argoz snapped at the woman.

"Yes, my lord," she spoke nervously. "I have been instructed to give you anything you wish." She looked at the ground as she spoke.

Argoz didn't know what the woman meant. She was irritating him. There was nothing that he wanted from such a disgusting creature, yet there was still something inside him. He shook the feeling off again as they walked down a highly decorated corridor. Thankfully for Argoz the journey was not too long. The woman kept giving him a strange look. She didn't look happy. Argoz couldn't work out what she was doing.

Inside the throne room Argoz felt a little more comfortable. He could see his brother standing next to the throne where King Unwin was sitting looking drawn and defeated. The woman stood at his side for a moment before she spoke.

"If there is anything you need then just call out," she made a point of not giving him her name. Her voice was sweet, but there was something underlying that Argoz couldn't put his finger on.

Instead of answering Argoz just grunted. He had more important things on his mind. Even though they were on the same side there was nothing that told him he should trust Fenaroz. He knew as well as any of his brothers that they were in a competition for the Great Lord's adulation. He would kill Fenaroz if he had a chance and it would be fortuitous as much as he knew his brother would kill him. He had to make sure that Fenaroz realised that he was better alive than dead.

"Come in brother, don't be shy. We are all friends here," there was nothing warm in Feranoz's tone.

"Of course," Argoz tried to be as friendly as he could as he walked towards the throne. "Are we safe to speak here?" Argoz nodded at King Unwin.

"There is nothing to hide here, brother." The voice sent a chill down Argoz's spine.

The man who stepped out from behind the stage was someone Argoz had never seen before. The face was unknown, but there was no denying the voice. "Don't look so surprised brother," Na'garoz spoke as Fenaroz laughed.

With the new revelation he didn't know what to think. His animosity towards Na'garoz dated to back so long Argoz didn't know why he hated him, but he knew that it was something he could not forgive. He looked at his two brothers trying to gauge the situation. It was not a good sign that the two were already together. He was beginning to regret his decision to help.

"What are you doing here?" He spoke through clenched teeth.

"That is none of your business. What we would like to know is why you are here? Have you failed your charge already and need our support?" Na'garoz's smugness annoyed Argoz and he wanted nothing more than to draw his sword and strike him down. He must have made it obvious because Na'garoz knew what he was thinking. "If you think you are up to it by all means give it a try, but I don't think that you are strong enough to defeat both of us."

"That's enough Emil," Fenaroz used Na'garoz's pseudonym for the first time. It was good that Argoz knew that name. If he let his true name slip then it would be disastrous for all of them. "You can call me

Gearalt brother and what name shall I use for you, or would you prefer if I just made one up." There was nothing soft in his words.

"Call me Captain Aimon," Argoz made sure to use his title, as if it meant something to the other two.

"Very well, Aimon. What is it that brings you to my doorstep?"

Na'garoz stood on the left hand side of the throne. He was swinging backwards and forwards like a child waiting to be told what to do. Argoz watched him closely. He attained that he was not there as Fenaroz's equal. Na'garoz was there on his brother's whim and that made things more favourable.

"I understand that you have captured the Cursed One?" Argoz started.

"I don't see how that is any of your business." Na'garoz broke in before he had a chance to continue.

"Well if you don't want the information that I have then I will continue on my way, but don't blame me when you are hanging from the gallows." Argoz turned to walk away.

Fenaroz took notice. Na'garoz was about to say something derogative, but was silenced before he had a chance. Argoz's heart started to race as he took a step to the door. If he failed then the Great Lord would not be happy. His only saving grace was that he tried, not that it meant anything in the eyes of their master.

"Okay, let us talk. There is no need for all this animosity. We are all on the same side." Argoz stopped and turned around. Fenaroz was hoping he would speak, but when he didn't it was obvious that he had to confirm his previous statement. "Yes, it is true that I have been able to capture the Cursed One."

"Then why have you not killed him?" Argoz knew the answer, but he wanted to hear it from his brother.

"You know as well as I do that it is the Great Lord's pleasure to kill the Cursed One. I am just keeping him here until I get word to him," that piece of information was more valuable than Fenaroz realised.

"I see. Well you may have to take matters into your own hands. There is an army on its way here. It will be here tomorrow afternoon. If you don't prepare yourself you will be overrun before you know what hit you," Argoz warned.

"Don't be silly," Na'garoz laughed as Fenaroz spoke. "All we have to do a shut the gates and then there will be no chance of them gaining entrance."

"Don't be so sure. The city walls are not impenetrable. There is one who travels with the army. He knows things. He knows things that he should not. You need to prepare yourself,"

"And what is it that you want in return for this information? I suppose that you want to hide out here for a while?" Fenaroz sounded suspicious.

"No, that's alright. It seems as though your house is already full," he looked at Na'garoz as he spoke. "All I want you to do is let the Great Lord know what I did when you speak to him next."

There was no way that Fenaroz could lie to the Great Lord, but he could omit certain details that made him look better. Since Argoz had asked him he had to keep his word. There was nothing else he could do. Still it was only a small ask for what he had risked.

"Very well. I will do as you say, but I am sure there is something else I could do for you," he wanted to know now if he was going to have to do anything for Argoz. He didn't want a surprise further down the track.

"No, that's about it. All I ask is that I can stay here until tomorrow. Then I will return to the army. From there I will do my best to make sure that they do not gain entrance to the city. Until the Great Lord can come for the Cursed One you have to hold out." Argoz knew that he had the upper hand. There was so much more information that he wanted, but he could not push his luck. He had achieved what he had come for and that was enough.

"You shall have a room until you need to go. I wouldn't advise staying here for longer than necessary. You have helped me so in turn I will spare your life, but my mercy only lasts so long. Now be off with you I have more important things to deal with." There was not a hint of gratitude in his voice, not that Argoz expected there to be any. The threat was all the thanks that he needed. He knew that Fenaroz was thankful and that was all that mattered.

For the rest of his stay in Kiarome he stayed in his room in the palace. There was nothing else he needed to achieve in the city so he thought he would relax. He thought about visiting the Cursed One, just to poke fun at him, but then he thought better of it. All he could do was to wait for the right time to leave. He had to make it look like he only just escaped with his life. Before he left the throne room Fenaroz had agreed to help him until he returned to the army. Once he was back in the army they were on different sides of the battlefield and there would be no quarter shown. Argoz had to laugh at the threat. He was sure that he was on the stronger side of the battle. In the end it would be Fenaroz who needed to be careful.

Chapter 27: A Terrible Siege

It was clear that the man on the horse was fleeing the city. From their vantage point they could see the arrows being fired from atop the city walls. There was nothing they could do to help. If they moved they would risk getting shot themselves.

When the rider approached they saw it was a dishevelled Aimon. The horse looked didn't look much better. They were glad to see that Aimon had returned safely, but the manner of his return did nothing to decrease their scepticism. They were, however, excited to hear what he had, but it was obviously not going to be good news.

"Are you alright Aimon?" Bern asked, just to be polite.

"Well I only just escaped with my life, but besides that all is fine," he replied somewhat sarcastically.

"Where are the others who went with you?" Sorrell asked, his voice harsher than he intended.

"They didn't escape with their lives. There was nothing I could do to save them." Aimon almost started drooling as he thought about how he murdered and devoured the soldiers.

They were all quiet for a moment. They were the first soldiers who had been killed serving the Alliance and it was the first time that Bern had sent anyone to their death.

"Well I think that you should tell us what happened?" Sorrell said.

"I managed to get into the palace. It's true that Alaric is trapped inside the dungeons. I didn't see him myself, but I heard that he is still alive," Aimon decided to hedge his bets. If he could get the army to kill his two brethren then it would be two more he didn't have to compete against. "There is a Dark Knight in the palace and he has King Unwin under his control." Aimon couldn't feed them the information quick enough.

"So it is as we feared," Wojtek sighed. "We have no option but to attack the city."

"We need to try and speak with someone. Maybe then we won't have to attack," Bern spoke.

"It's no good. The Dark Knight will not treat with you. He will see you dead before he follows the rules of combat," Aimon warned. "There is nothing we can do. If we want to rescue Alaric then we will have to breach the walls. The only problem is that they know we are coming."

"How do they know that?" Wojtek glared at Aimon.

"It's a little hard to hide an entire army. I think we were kidding ourselves if we believed we could sneak a hostile army on a city the size of

Kiarome," Aimon explained as if he was speaking to the dimmest of students.

"But we are not a hostile army. There is no reason why they should be concerned with our movements," Sorrell was not happy with Aimon's explanation.

"Remember that the advisor is a Dark Knight and has kidnapped Alaric. To him we are a hostile army and he is the one who is in control of the city." Aimon had an answer for every question.

"This is getting us nowhere. When it is said and done it doesn't matter how they found out we're coming. The most important thing is what we are going to do now." Bern stopped the bickering.

"The rest of the Alliance should only be an hour or so behind us now. We need to make camp far enough away so they can not attack us. From there we will draw up plans for an attack. We need to breach the walls as soon as possible."

***

It had taken them almost five days to plan and organise, but they were finally ready for their attack. The timber they had collected was used to build their siege engines, but they realised there was a lack of large rocks for ammunition. They did, however, come across a number of small stone farmhouses. With the approaching army the houses were completely vacant. Sorrell didn't like the idea of destroying someone's home, but they had no other option.

There had been no threat of attack from the city. They had been watching the guards pacing on top the wall, waiting for a sign. The Alliance was not going to attack before it was ready, but time was getting away from them. If they did not start soon then it would be too late.

"I still think we should try and speak to whoever is in command," Sorrell had continued to argue his point every day and each day he had been given the same answer.

"It doesn't matter who you speak to. The Dark Knight has King Unwin under his thrall. Whoever is on the wall will think he is taking orders from the King himself. I am almost positive they would have been given instructions to shoot anyone who approaches," Aimon continued to give him the same response, which they all had to agree to.

Bern had no great urge to approach the city. If he was supposed to bargain with the city guards then he was sure he would know it. The enemy held the city and they had to get it back.

"There is nothing else we can do. We have to breach the walls and take back the city," Bern didn't sound excited at the prospect.

"How long before the siege engines are ready?" Jarwe asked.

"They are ready to go now. All we have to do is move them into position. We have almost completed collecting ammunition," Hulkan explained.

"Then I don't think there is anything else for it. Have the soldiers move the engines into place," Bern sounded dejected.

"I guess this is it then. May the Gods have mercy on us all?" Sorrell was still against the idea of attacking the city, but he knew there were no other options.

There was a morose feeling throughout the entire army. It was clear to most there was no other option. Those who didn't agree with the decision kept their mouths shut. They couldn't come up with a better solution so they knew that it was better to stay quiet.

It was late in the afternoon when the siege engines were in place. The light was starting to fade as the ammunition was brought up to the engines. There was not a lot of time left for their attack. And it was debated on whether they should start or wait until the morning.

"There is no point in starting tonight." Sorrell was still trying to avoid the confrontation.

"I think we can at least get our aim in tonight. We won't breach their walls, so there is no risk of battle," Jarwe suggested.

"We wait until the morning. There is nothing to be gained by sighting the weapons tonight. They have made no move against us yet and I would like to leave it that way," the words sounded strange coming from Bern. His demeanour was the same, so it was impossible to tell if the entity had returned.

"Very well, but I want everything ready at first light. The more time that passes the more advantage the opposition has." Jarwe deferred to Bern again.

"Doesn't the city have its own projectile weapons?" Hadar asked Sorrell once the decision had been made.

"That's what is strange," Wojtek answered. "Although we are well out of range I would have thought they would have tried to send some rocks in our direction."

"Are the siege engines in danger of being destroyed?" Hadar scratched his head.

"They are out of reach for the moment. In the morning they will have to be moved into range. That is one of the reasons we needn't attack tonight," Sorrell glared at Jarwe as he replied. "If they know our weapons were in range I would imagine that they would all be destroyed come morning."

"I wasn't planning on leaving them within range over night. It would be just as simple to mark them and then bring them back," Jarwe didn't like what Sorrell was insinuating.

"This is getting us nowhere. In the morning we will start our attack. There is still much to be done so I say we should get back to it." Bern didn't like the bickering or the rising tension in the room.

There was an air of anticipation as dawn broke. The entire army knew they were going to start their attack. The commanders found themselves a place atop a small hill to watch the bombardment. Although the engineers were fairly precise with their measurements there was still the matter of sighting the machines. The first few shots would be to calibrate the engines.

On Jarwe's signal the test firing started. The first load crashed into the wall close to the bottom. All it managed to do was create a loud bang. At least the people inside the wall would have been given a mighty fright, but the stones did no damage whatsoever. The pieces of stone cut from the many farmhouses shattered against the city wall. The second test fell almost twenty feet short with the third sailing over the top. It was the third short that sent a chill down Sorrell's spine. There was no telling who or what might have been hit. The last thing they wanted to do was kill innocent people.

With the machines calibrated they waited for the word to attack. There had still been no retaliation from the city and that was indeed strange. They were out of range of the archers, but not by much. It would have been worth firing a shot or two to see what distance they could get.

Everyone expected a rain of rocks and stone to come crashing down around them, but there was nothing but silence coming from the other side of the wall. There were not even the shouts of angry soldiers.

"I don't like this," Bern said as they waited to give the order to attack.

"I know what you mean. This should have prompted some kind of response," Sorrell agreed.

"Well I don't care what their reasoning is. If they are not going to attack that is their own bad management. We will not make the same mistake. Fire!" Jarwe wasn't going to wait for anyone to agree with him. He recognised the opportunity to strike and he took advantage of it.

Everyone looked at Jarwe with a surprise expression on their faces, but no one said anything. Deep down they were just glad that Jarwe had made the decision. Eventually they were going to have to assault the walls, but no one wanted to be the one to give the order.

There was a moment, as the engines were being loaded, that time seemed to stand still. There was not a breath of wind. It seemed as though the world was holding its breath, waiting to see what was going to happen.

Everyone who wasn't feverishly working on loading the war machines were watching carefully. Once the loads were fired there was no way to bring them back.

When the machines were loaded there was no waiting to fire them. One after another they were released. As the large pieces of stone arched towards the wall the world seemed to hold its breath. Bern could hear the blood racing around his body.

After what seemed to take an age the first load stuck the wall, about half way up to the right of the Northern gate. Shortly after, the remaining projectiles also hit the wall. Dust and rubble flew into the air and it was impossible to see the result of their first bombardment. Once the debris had cleared they could see what they had done. From where they were positioned it looked as though the stones had done absolutely nothing. The wall remained intact and there didn't seem to be any damage at all. Up close there were a few cracks starting to open up, but nothing like what they had been hoping.

"Fire again," Jarwe's voice soared throughout the army.

There was another delay as the siege engines were reloaded. The engineers were also adjusting the weapons to make their attacks more efficient. There was still no response from inside the city so there was no urgency to their work. Once each weapon was loaded it was fired immediately. Once the rubble cleared there was a cry of success from the army. A small hole, no bigger than a man's head, could be seen near the top of the wall next to the gate.

"I think this is going to take a while," Sorrell spoke after the second attack. "I don't think we need to watch this." He was more upset than what he had thought he would be.

The rest of the command group agreed, except for Jarwe, who insisted that he stay and watched the men. There was still danger about and he wanted to make sure that something didn't creep up on them.

"How long do you think it will take to breach the wall?" Bern asked when they were back in the command tent.

"I would be very surprised if we break in today," Wojtek had more faith in the city's defences than the others.

"More to the point do we have enough ammunition to breach it?" Hadar didn't sound happy. "We took apart all the farmhouses in the vicinity. We did not leave a single scrap."

"There should be enough to last. I estimate that we will have enough ammunition for a two day campaign. If we focus on one section of the wall and don't waste any more shots we should be able to breach the wall with what we have," Wojtek explained.

"That still isn't going to make life easy for us. If we only focus on one area of the wall then they know where we are going to attack. They will be able to place all their resources in the one place. We will create a bottle neck that we can't possibly use to our advantage." As much as Sorrell didn't want to attack the city he also didn't want to lose. There was a lot more riding on their success than just their lives.

"I don't see how we have any other choice. There simply isn't enough ammunition around for a proper campaign. We just aren't set up for a siege. There is nothing we can do about that. All we can do is fight with what we have been given," Wojtek explained to his General. "I know that it isn't ideal, but I don't think that we have a choice."

They all sat in silence for a moment as they thought of a better plan. No matter what they came up with there was no chance it was going to work. They kept thinking until Bern finally spoke.

"I believe we are doing the right thing. All we have to do is breach the walls. Once we have done that then we can work out how we get into the city."

"So that is the reason they are not fighting back," Dorn spoke when he realised no one else was going to respond. "Why waste his resources when he knows we can only attack at one place?"

"But how do they know that we don't have the infrastructure for a long siege?" Hulkan continued on Dorn's line of questioning. All eyes moved to Aimon when he finished speaking.

"I didn't tell them anything," Aimon was rightfully defensive. All eyes looked at him in accusingly. "It wouldn't be hard for them to guess. They know that the army was built to fight a war in Avalon. There is no reason for the army to have anything for a siege. They will know this because it is true."

Aimon's words made perfect sense. It wouldn't take a master tactician to realise that this was a last resort attack. There was no reason to think that Aimon had revealed any information to the enemy. No one apologised for their unspoken accusations. It didn't matter if his words made sense they still did not trust him. It would take a while after he tried to usurp the army to regain their trust.

"We need to think about what to do once we have breached the wall," Hadar was quick to change the subject.

"I don't think that we have any other option than a full frontal attack," Hulkan sounded aggressive.

"Well that is not exactly true," Pernian spoke for the first time. He was seated at the end of the table. "We can play this situation to our advantage. If they think we are going to place all our efforts against the Northern gate then that is not what we should be doing."

"Well that is obvious Lord Pernian, but it still doesn't help the situation. We do not have the facilities to attack another section of wall," Hulkan refuted the elf's words.

"That is true master dwarf, but I am not talking about assaulting the wall," Pernian paused to add to the anticipation. "During the night we should move men around to different areas of the wall. There is a chance if we build ladders that we will be able to get soldiers into the city without them knowing about it," Pernian seemed pleased with himself.

"That is all well and good, but I doubt they would leave the rest of their walls unguarded," Wojtek didn't sound impressed.

"I have to agree with Wojtek. There is no way they could be that stupid as to not guard the rest of the wall," Sorrell agreed with his advisor.

"Maybe not now, but I think the idea might work. Once we have breached the wall they will be more concerned with our frontal assault. Once we start our attack it would be the perfect time to climb the walls and gain entrance to the city. If we can get the Northern gates open then we will be able to hold the outer city," Hadar added.

"That does have merit, but it is still hard to know what the enemy is thinking. I have no doubt that if we send all our troops into the breach then we will lose more men than we should. I think that we should at least build the ladders, even if we do not use them. There is more than enough left over wood."

Bern called the meeting to a halt. Although he didn't direct it as an order the others took as one. They left the meeting with the plan in mind. The first problem was making the ladders. That, unfortunately, was the easy part. It also gave them an excuse the leave the tent. The tension was starting to grow as the thunder of the attack could be heard in the distance.

Jarwe had remained on the hill for the entire day. It was late in the afternoon when Bern joined him. They both stood there, silently, for a while before Bern finally spoke.

"How goes it, General?" he asked.

"The hole is getting bigger, but I don't think that it is getting big enough." He stared off into the distance.

After he spoke there came another crash into the wall. At the start of the day the siege engines were being fired one after the other. As the day lengthened they were being fired individually as they were loaded and then recalibrated. The time between crashes was becoming longer and longer making the attack far less efficient.

"Cease fire!" Jarwe screamed out at the top of his lungs.

The soldiers attending the weapons all looked at where the sound had come from. Jarwe had not spoken to the soldiers since his initial order to fire. Once they saw who had voiced the command they all knew that their day was done.

"It was a strange day," Jarwe said as he gazed at the city. "Now let's head back. I think that I need something to eat and more to the point something to drink. I think it would be a good idea to crack a number of barrels of ale." Jarwe turned around and started back towards the camp. He didn't look at Bern at all.

They walked back to the campsite in silence. Jarwe made a point to remain a step ahead of Bern. He didn't know if Jarwe was doing it to avoid conversation or whether he was in a hurry. In Jarwe's mind it was a little of both. What he had seen during the day was disturbing and he wanted to discuss it with everyone. He knew if he didn't hurry he would be forced to divulge the information to Bern and he didn't want to relive it twice.

Back in the command tent Jarwe was quick to organise himself an ale. He didn't bother with offering anyone else a drink. He figured that if they wanted one then they could organise it themselves. He took a long drink before sitting at the table. The table was only half filled. The two dwarves, Pernian and Wojtek were still out with the army.

"How is it on the frontline?" Aimon asked when they were all seated.

"There is something disturbing at play," Jarwe spoke mysteriously before taking another long draught that emptied his mug.

"Well don't leave us in suspense," Hadar said.

Jarwe was not going to divulge any information until he was ready. A serving woman quickly grabbed his mug as he lifted it from the table. He waited for her to return and took another drink before he continued. It was clear that something had happened to disturb him. Everyone was waiting to hear what he had to say. The wait was excruciating.

"Now are you going to tell us what is wrong?" Hadar almost sounded annoyed as he asked the question.

Jarwe waited a moment before he spoke. "There is something wrong with this situation." It was again a leading opening.

"We know that something is wrong. The entire situation is wrong. Now if you don't have something more to add to the conversation then we really need to start planning tomorrow," Aimon barked at Jarwe.

Jarwe glared at the captain from Entero. He didn't like the tone in his voice, but he could not blame him. He wasn't deliberately trying to be annoying, but he couldn't think of the words to explain. "There is something even more disturbing and I am not sure how to say this."

"Just take your time. We are in no hurry." It was not true, but Bern knew Jarwe needed some reassurance. That made the situation even more disturbing.

"Thank you Bern, I will try my best. For starters you need to cast your minds back to the wall of fog back in Avalon." They all remembered the fear they felt when they approached the wall. If it wasn't for Bern then they would have all run away screaming. "What I felt today and what I saw today was similar to that."

"That is impossible." Aimon almost hit himself after his outburst.

"What do you mean?" Hadar was the one who asked the question that was on the tip of everyone else's tongue.

Aimon had to think quickly not to give away his true intentions. "In Avalon there were a number of spell-casters to create the spell. When I was in the palace I only saw the one Dark Knight. I don't believe that one knight could create something so powerful." He knew that it was possible, but he couldn't let the others know.

"I see," Jarwe continued, although he didn't completely trust Aimon. "I don't think it's the same as what we came up against in Avalon, but I know magic at play. I think there is something stopping us from seeing what is happening in the city. I also think that there is something blocking the true damage we are doing to the wall."

"What makes you say that?" Bern was worried by what he was hearing, more so than anyone else.

"I can't be exactly sure, but enough to bet my life on it. I saw some damage in the wall seemingly repair itself and then later I saw damage where no stone had struck. Someone is playing with reality and I don't like it," Jarwe explained.

Bern thought for a moment. He, or at least the entity, had been able to see through the magic at Avalon. He had not been on top of the hill for long, but when he had been there he had not noticed anything. He couldn't say for sure that Jarwe was incorrect, but he was sure that if something untoward was happening then he would know about it. He thought about mentioning it, but Jarwe seemed so sure.

"I have a feeling that is the reason it has seemed no one has been doing anything to stop us. If I am right, and I am sure I am, that means we have no idea what the enemy is doing," Jarwe continued to explain.

Aimon had to admit to himself it did make sense. He hadn't felt any magic, but then he had been busy and it would have been cast so far away. The more he thought about it the more he thought it could be true. He silently scolded himself for not seeing it earlier, not that he would have been able to tell the others anyway. He thought about blocking the spell, but he was happy enough that Jarwe had discovered the ruse. He was sure he would not have to do anything.

"So if this is true then it changes everything. We cannot simply walk up to the wall and assume everything is as it seems," Hadar voiced the obvious.

"So what do we do now?" Aimon asked.

"That is a very good question," Jarwe replied. "I can't see how we can do anything until the enemy reveals itself."

There was silence, yet again, as they all thought about what Jarwe was saying. It was not the answer that anyone wanted to hear. Sitting and waiting was the one thing that they couldn't do. They did not have the time.

"No!" All eyes turned to Bern. There was an edge to his voice that made everyone pay attention. "We continue the bombardment as planned."

"But what is the point if we cannot see what we have destroyed?" Jarwe was trying to understand what Bern was saying.

"If we stop the bombardment then they will know that we are onto them. Our only advantage at the moment is that we know something is not right and they don't. It does make things a lot more difficult, but I am sure we can figure out what they are doing."

Chapter 28: Enemies Revealed

The command group spent most of the night trying to work out their next plan of action. Without knowing exactly what the enemy was doing it was almost an impossible task. They all looked to Bern for advice. It was him who had seen through the enemy's ruse at Avalon, but unfortunately the entity did not make an appearance.

In the end sleep overcame them and all they had decided on was that they were going to continue with the bombardment. The only thing they could agree on was to meet again before dawn. There was a morose feeling throughout the group as they left the tent.

"So the key is to work out the most likely plan of attack by the enemy," Wojtek started the conversation when they all arrived in the tent.

"If it was me I would wait inside the walls, occasionally sending volleys of my own attacks," Jarwe answered.

"What we have to remember is that the enemy doesn't necessarily want to keep the city intact. If he feels as though his back is against the wall then there is no reason why he wouldn't send his soldiers out to attack us. Either way he wins. He will cause deaths on both sides." Bern's words made perfect sense. It was a view that had not been discussed before.

"Do you think he will send the army out to attack us?" Sorrell asked, unhappy with the prospect.

"That's what I would do," Aimon added. The idea made sense to him. If he was going to lose anyway he may as well send a few men to their deaths. With a battle at the Northern gate it would give him a chance to escape to the south.

Suspicious eyes turned to Aimon. The comment was innocent enough, but no one trusted him anymore. They were sure that something had happened when he was in the city. They weren't sure if he was in league with the enemy, but they were sure he had given them certain information about the Alliance.

"Whilst he causes havoc to the north then he would be able to escape to the south or the west," Wojtek pondered.

"Then we should post soldiers near the other gates and make sure that no one gets through," Aimon didn't want his brothers to escape. Things were looking more positive for him every day. The Great Lord would not be happy with their deaths, but he had done all that he could to prevent it.

"That's a good idea, but won't it be dangerous for simple soldiers to approach a Dark Knight," Hulkan remembered the confrontation they had outside of Lel Dinion with Morgoz.

"If there are enough soldiers they would be able to subdue a Dark Knight," Aimon replied.

"How do you know?" Hulkan replied. "Have you ever faced a Dark Knight?"

"No, but I am sure that they are not invincible," Aimon chose his words carefully. "If they were then I am sure we would all be dead by now."

"So we think that the attack will come from the Northern gate?" Jarwe brought the conversation back.

"I can't see it happening any other way," Bern replied.

"Well when do we think that it will happen?" Jarwe asked.

"I think the attack will come sooner rather than later," Bern suggested. "There is no telling how much longer the wall will hold or even if we have already breached it. Either way I don't think he will be able to keep up his ruse forever. If he thinks we are almost ready to attack he will want to be one step ahead of us." It was clear to all that it wasn't Bern speaking. At long last the entity had returned. "He will attack today at some stage. I don't know whether it will be morning or afternoon, but we need to be ready. Whilst we continue the bombardment we need to have the troops ready to attack."

"What about this Dark Knight?" Sorrell asked. "I am loathed to let him get away after he has caused this much trouble."

"He will not get away. I can assure you of that. I don't think we need to post soldiers by the gates," Bern's words were mysterious and it was clear he was not going to justify them.

"It's decided then. We prepare for battle." Jarwe stood from the table. "Now we should all leave and ready ourselves."

Outside the sun was starting to rise. A soft light glowed throughout the campsite and there was a fresh smell in the air. Bern thought it felt like the start of a new day. He couldn't remember what he had just said, but he knew that he had spoken and he knew that it was the entity. He had been remembering more and more when the entity had taken over, but this time there was nothing.

Once the sun was clear in the sky the bombardment started again. The men working the engines were told to keep their attacks slow and constant. Each attack would not be as effective, but that was not the plan. It was about being as crafty as their enemy. If they were able to prolong their attacks then it would seem that they had more ammunition than they really had.

It was almost noon when the army had assembled about half a league from the Northern gate. They looked out at the gate as if they were waiting for something to happen. They all knew what they were looking at was not real. Every now and again the scenery in front of them seemed to shimmer.

"What do we do now?" Jarwe asked as he watched the façade in front of him.

"We wait. The enemy will reveal itself soon," Bern also kept his gaze straight ahead.

There was nothing in the empty space in front of them. There was something very disturbing about the scene. The gate remained shut and there was no movement on top of the walls. It was as if the land in front of them was suspended in time. Bern felt that it was necessary to speak to the soldiers.

"Hold men!" He yelled at the top of his voice. "The enemy will reveal itself soon. Your strength of character will bring you victory this day." His words were followed by another attack on the wall.

After the crash Bern saw a shimmer. The scene he saw behind the veil nearly made him fall off his horse. He looked at the others who still sat stalwart and it was obvious they had not seen the same vision. With the magical veil gone, if only for a second, Bern could see the Northern gate was open and soldiers were assembling outside. They were not advancing, but it would only be a matter of time before they did. He didn't know whether he should tell the others or not. He figured that it was better they knew straight away instead of waiting for the impending shock.

"There is an army assembling in front of us." Bern kept his view out in front, just in case there was another vision.

"I figured as much. I don't know what it is, but I can feel the men out there." Bern was surprised at Jarwe's response. "Do you think they will reveal themselves before they attack or do you think that we will be fighting ghosts?"

"I doubt that whoever it is behind this ruse will be strong enough to keep it up whilst they attack, at least I hope so. If he is then I don't think there will be any of us alive at the end of the day." The revelation was grim, but true.

"I guess we just wait then. We'll know when they are going to attack one way or another," Jarwe sounded just as morose as Bern.

They didn't have to wait long before the army was revealed. It happened all at once. Bern had thought the scene would evolve slowly when it happened, but he was wrong. One moment there was a peaceful, albeit disturbing, scene and the next the land was almost in ruin. In front of them stood an army lined up and regimented. The land around them was not as calm it was and around the siege engines were a number of boulders and a scattering of arrows. It was clear they had been trying to destroy the weapons.

The Alliance soldiers had been warned that there might be an army suddenly appearing in front of them, but no one had truly believed it. The initial shock took them all by surprise, but they were quick to recover. They were ready for battle, even though none of them wanted to fight the soldiers from Kiarome.

The opposing soldiers also seemed dazed and confused. It was as if they were seeing things for the first time. It was as if they were seeing the Alliance army for the first time. They stood still and made no move to attack.

"Hold strong men," Jarwe yelled to the soldiers, keeping his gaze on the opposing army. "We let them make the first move."

Almost as one the opposing army drew their weapons. The sound of steel being unsheathed rang out across the makeshift battlefield. The sound sent a chill down Bern's back. He thought he would be able to avoid conflict with Kiarome. What happened next surprised everyone.

Shortly after the soldiers drew their weapons they all dropped them on the ground and took a step backwards. It was clearly a sign of deference. For a moment Bern's hopes returned. The thought that they may not have to fight returned to his mind, but he quickly shook it off. It was more than possible that this was a trap.

Once the army was unarmed two soldiers starting riding towards the command group. One was holding the banner of the King, the other looked as though he was a commanding officer. As they approached Sorrell recognised one of the men. The soldier was a good man and a reasonable leader. He didn't know what he was going to ask. The thought that they were surrendering entered his mind. He hoped, more than anything else, it was the case.

***

"The bombardment has started again," there was fear in Na'garoz's voice.

Fenaroz almost spat in the direction of his brother. The snivelling little worm was really getting on his nerves. He wished he could dispose of him, but unfortunately he wasn't strong enough to accomplish everything on his own. He was stretched to his limit as it was. With each passing day he could feel his strength waning. At least he would be able to release one of his spells that was taking up so much of his energy. He laughed to himself as he thought of the shock the others would get when they saw an army suddenly appear in front of them.

"This isn't funny," Na'garoz almost screamed as the sound of another crash could be heard in the distance.

"Of course it is. They can attack the walls as much as they like. They will never be ready for the surprise I have in store for them," Fenaroz gloated as he sat in the throne.

King Unwin was still in bed. He had been sleeping more and more as time wore on. Fenaroz knew it was to do with the spell he was under. Eventually the spell would drain all of the King's life force, but Fenaroz didn't care. He knew his time at Kiarome was nearly up. Once the Great Lord came to collect his prize they would both march triumphantly into the home land.

"I don't know. Argoz had some interesting insights into their army. I don't think that they are as simple as you think they are."

"Your limited ability of faith is somewhat disturbing. Remember that you are only alive because of me. I could have you killed at a whim." Fenaroz wasn't impressed with Na'garoz.

Na'garoz had to bite his tongue. Sure enough he had come looking for help, but now he knew that Fenaroz wasn't as smart as he thought. The power of his position was getting to his head. The thought of failure hadn't occurred to him and that was dangerous. Fenaroz hadn't survived so far by thinking he was better than everyone else. In fact he was exactly where he was due to the fact that he thought he wasn't better than everyone else.

"Your power is waning brother. With each passing moment your strength is fading. I can see it in your eyes. You are losing brother and I will not go down with your sinking ship," the words flew out of Na'garoz's mouth. He knew what he was saying was true and he was safe from any reprisal.

"How dare you speak to me that way? You came to me for help and I offered it to you without question. Now you turn on me?" Fenaroz was hot with rage.

"You only kept me here because it suited you. You needed someone to keep your prisoner in check whilst you continued your madness. I won't be a part of it anymore. There is nothing left here but utter destruction."

"You know if you leave the Great Lord will scorn you forever." It was the only threat Fenaroz had left. He didn't have the strength to fight with his brother.

"We shall see who the Great Lord scorns. I guarantee it will not be me. I will live to fight another day whilst you stay here and be destroyed," Na'garoz was being spiteful. He finally, at long last, had the upper hand and he was going to make the most of it.

Before Fenaroz could reply there came another crash from the north wall. The sound rattled Na'garoz again and again he looked afraid. It was a chance for Fenaroz to regain control. He hated to admit it, but he needed Na'garoz to complete his plan. Without him it would be very difficult for him to succeed. All he needed was for him to continue to block the power of the Cursed One. It was an easy task. All he had to do was to remain in the palace.

"Don't fear brother. We are safe in the palace. The two armies will tear each other apart long before they reach us. Go back to your room and relax. This will all be over soon enough."

"Yes, of course brother." The revised fear put Na'garoz back in his place. He used the change in his demeanour as an opportunity to leave the throne room. He couldn't believe his luck when Fenaroz suggested he do the very same thing. Now he would take his chance on the road. Hopefully he would have enough time to escape and get far enough away. He knew that he would not be safe whilst he had *the Prophecy of the Stone*, but he could not leave it behind. He needed to find the Great Lord. The Great Lord would protect him once he showed him what he had found.

He left the room before he gave away what he was thinking. He looked back at his brother and saw a glazed look in his eyes as he sat on the throne. He was already dreaming of his success. It was then that he realised Fenaroz was doomed. If he stayed then his fate would be the same.

King Unwin entered shortly after and Fenaroz stood from the throne. His ego didn't stand so far as to block out his intelligence. Whilst Unwin was still on the throne the people would still listen to what Fenaroz had to say.

"It looks like we go to war today King," Fenaroz snarled at Unwin. He despised the King. He didn't understand how someone so weak could rule a Kingdom. It had been all too easy to take over his mind and yet everyone did as he commanded. In trust it had not been as easy as he made out, but he would never admit it.

Unwin mumbled some words back at him. Within the past day Unwin had lost all coherence. There was a chance that the spell would have a constant effect and he would never regain his previous strength. That was the last thing on the Dark Knight's mind. Once the enemy's army had been defeated he doubted he would need Unwin anymore. The king could rot in the dungeon with the Cursed One for all he cared.

The crashes continued throughout the morning and each time there was a hit Fenaroz laughed. They were continuing to attack whilst he was preparing for battle. The army would have no idea what hit them. He couldn't hide the soldiers once they started, but it would be enough to hide them until then. There was a chance he could keep them concealed if he didn't keep his spell over Unwin, but he didn't want to risk losing control of the King. It wouldn't be long before the soldiers were in position. They had been moving out of the Northern gate all morning.

Suddenly there was a flutter in the environment. It was subtle, but it was definitely there. At first he brushed it off. He had more important things to worry about. He had to make sure that his spell remained secure over the army. The distraction had caused him to lose control. It had only been for a second, but it was enough to annoy him. He knew that no one would have noticed. They would have to be looking directly at the army to have any chance of seeing them appear.

It wasn't long before Fenaroz realised what it was and he cursed himself for not taking more notice. He cursed his brother for leaving him and breaking the spell around the Cursed One. There was nothing he could do now. He had to let the spell around the army go so he could dampen the Cursed One's power. With a cry of anguish Fenaroz let the veil spell drop from around the army.

***

Na'garoz was relieved once he had left the city. It had been difficult to leave through the Western gate. He still kept up the spell on the Cursed One, so Fenaroz would not know he had left the palace. He could try and mess with the psyche of the guards, but it would be a weak spell. He would also have to rely on the guards being of weak mind. It would also drain a lot of his energy which he needed for the journey ahead. It would not be long before the Cursed One was free and he would be chased. *The Prophecy of the Stone* would be a beacon towards his location. The further away he got the weaker the beacon would be. With any luck he would be far enough way that the Cursed One would not be able to find him.

In the end he did not have to play with the guards' minds. He was able to talk his way into being let out. There was no imminent threat to the Western gate so there was no real excuse to keep him inside, at least that was the way he played it. He did have to use some subtle magic, but not enough to drain any energy.

Once he was outside the city he felt more relaxed. As he had expected the countryside was clear. He jumped as he walked when he heard the sound of yet another loud crash and he laughed silently to himself. Maybe his brother was right, maybe the soldiers were too stupid to realise what was happening, but what Fenaroz didn't realise was that he had *the Prophecy of the Stone* in his possession.

He could feel the prophecy in the back of his pack. He knew it would also be calling to the Cursed One. He needed to get far away and then find the Great Lord. With a present like *the Prophecy of the Stone* he would be treated in high regard. He might even be considered his favourite of all the Chosen.

The thought of being considered the best of all his brothers made him smile as he walked. He hated walking, but it was better than trying to ride one of the worms' creatures. He missed his horseling. Those animals were pure malevolence. The other creatures, called horses, were too unpredictable. He never felt right sitting on top of one and they never felt right underneath him. He was much happier to be on foot.

He didn't know where he was heading. He knew that the Great Lord was no longer in Jarrat, if he had ever been there in the first place. He had heard a rumour that his brother Ra'naroz was there. The last thing the he wanted to do was to get mixed up with another one of his brothers. It was bad enough that he had to go to Fenaroz for help and it was mistake that he would never make again. The next time he saw his brothers they would be bowing down next to him.

Out of all the seven Dark Knights Na'garoz and Ra'naroz hated each other the most. He had no doubt Ra'naroz would try and kill him. Either way he was not going to take the risk. What he had in his possession was too great to risk losing.

The sun was shining as he walked, which annoyed him no end. He would much prefer to be travelling under the cover of darkness. At the very least he wanted some clouds to cover the sun. He had no choice, but to carry on. He knew it would not be long before the Cursed One would escape his prison. Without the spell cloaking his ability there would be nothing stopping him from killing Fenaroz.

Na'garoz had to smile when he thought about his brother being killed. Fenaroz had always thought he was better than him, at least going back for over a thousand years. The loss of Fenaroz would do nothing to spoil the Great Lord's plan. It would also serve to increase his standing and soon he would be at his rightful place by the Great Lord's side.

It was mid-afternoon when he stopped by a small grove of trees. There was one last thing he had to do before he continued. There were too many who knew what he looked like. His current disguise was not going to be good enough. Although he had not seen anyone else since he had left the highway he still wanted the cover of the trees to make his change.

The transition was slow and painful. If he hadn't change so many time recently it would have been possible to make the change instantaneously, but the resulting pain would be almost unbearable. The prolonged pain was something he would have to endure and he had the privacy to do it. His energy had almost been completely drained. His brother had used up more of his strength than he realised.

As he sat in the grove he thought about who or what he was going to change into next. If he changed into an animal then he would able to remain more anonymous. The only problem was the risk of being shot by hunters or captured by farmers. The safest bet was staying in man form. He was able to choose his own design since he was going somewhere where no one needed to know who he was. It was always risky when he chose his own identity. He normally liked to copy. That way he could be sure that he was putting everything in the right place.

He remained in the grove until after the sun had set. His normal appearance would disturb anyone he passed on his travels. Even though he was travelling through open country there was still a chance he would see someone. If someone saw him then he would have to murder the creature, which normally he would not have a problem with, but he was trying to stay incognito and the last thing he wanted to do was leave a trail for anyone to follow.

He was still weary when he continued. The night sky definitely made things a lot easier for him. He soaked in the darkness like he was taking a bath. When the sun rose over the horizon he was dead tired. He didn't know where he was headed, but he knew he had to rest. Again he found another grove of trees. They would give him the cover he needed until the sun set and he was able to move again.

Chapter 29: Freedom for All

They had been in prison for ten days. They had been treated like every other prisoner... and that is to say not very well. At first Richmond's spirits were relatively high compared to Alaric's, but then the beatings started. Once a day someone would come in and take each of them in turn. They would be beaten for almost ten minutes before being returned to their cell. Sometimes it would be first thing in the morning and sometimes last thing at night.

Since Alaric couldn't harness the energy around him he had slipped into a malaise. During the day he curled up into a small ball in the corner of the cell. He didn't even seem too worried when the guard came to beat him. Richmond tried to talk to him, tried to lift his spirits, but his words weren't getting through. Alaric's sombre mood was starting to rub off and Richmond started to fall into a deep depression.

On the morning of the tenth day Richmond had given up all hope of being rescued. Alaric was still curled up in a ball and he knew that it was only a matter of time before he was beaten again. He thought about trying to escape when the guard came and receiving a sword through the belly for his effort. Death would be a relief from the daily pain he was suffering.

All of a sudden there was a dull rumble. It came from somewhere outside. In the depth of the palace dungeon it was almost unheard, but it was enough to raise Alaric from his reverie. He sprung up so quickly that Richmond thought that he was having a seizure. The sudden movement made Richmond jump up from where he was sitting causing the two to nearly bump into each other.

"By the Gods Alaric, what are you doing?"

Alaric held his finger up indicating for Richmond to be quiet. He lowered his head as if he was listening to something. Richmond watched him with interest, but did as he was told and kept quiet. When Alaric's head rose again there was a broad grin on his face.

"What is it?" Richmond asked, his interest piqued.

"You can't hear that?" Alaric motioned for him to be quiet again. When Richmond shook his head Alaric continued to speak. "The Alliance is here. They have started bombarding the city walls. It should not be long now before we are free. I would say by lunchtime tomorrow, if not by the end of the day. Once they are in the city it will not be long before they enter the palace."

"Is that a good thing? If they are coming to rescue us wouldn't it make sense for the Dark Knights to execute us? That's what I would do," Richmond didn't sound as hopeful.

"I would dare say that they are going to be too busy worrying about the army to worry about us." Even with the bruises on his face Alaric looked suddenly revitalised. It was as if he had a new lease on life.

"I wish I had your confidence. I'm not happy with this situation. I think that we will have to be on our feet. When the guard comes to get us today I don't think that we will be coming back," Richmond was starting to become anxious.

"Then I guess we better not let them take us," there was a playfulness in Alaric's voice that had not been there for a long time.

Alaric remained standing for most of the day. He stood facing the door, as if he was waiting for someone to enter. Every now and again he would cock his head and listen. Each time his head lifted there was a smile on his face. Richmond was glad that he was no longer stuck in his reverie. Alaric's mood gave him some hope.

The guards did not come to beat them that day. There was no explanation why, but they were not going to argue. It was a good sign, a sign that something had changed. Richmond slept relatively easy that night for the first time since they had been captured.

Alaric, on the other hand, did not sleep at all. He had been noticing that he was surviving on less and less sleep. In his mind he knew it was not right for him to remain awake for so long, but there was no sign of fatigue. Throughout the night the feeling that things were getting better grew stronger.

In the morning things were quieter than usual in the prison.

"Something is wrong," Richmond spoke once he had woken. "It has not been this quiet since we arrived. I have a bad feeling."

"You can have a bad feeling, but it is not for us. They are starting to realise they are in trouble. You will see soon enough. It will not be long," he said with confidence.

It was mid-morning when Alaric sat bolt upright. All of a sudden Alaric could feel the energy, not just feel it, but touch it. The feeling only lasted for a moment before it disappeared again, but it was enough to tell him that things were about to get interesting.

"Something has changed. It will not be long now. I don't think that it will be easy to escape, so we will have to be prepared to fight our way out and without our weapons it will be even more difficult," Alaric explained.

"I'm ready," Richmond didn't look or sound like he was ready.

It was not long before they heard the lock open on their cell door. There was the sound of muffled voices before the door was heaved open. Standing in the doorway was the same large man who had come for them nearly every day. He had a club in his hand and he looked as though he was ready to use it. He took a step into the room. He was at least a head taller than Alaric.

"Come on scum. Today is your last day," the guard's voice was deep and cracked.

Alaric remained seated on the bed between the guard and Richmond. There was no point making his move too early. He could see the guard was on edge. Alaric wanted to make him feel comfortable.

"What's going on?" Alaric asked, in a friendly tone.

"Standard war rules. As soon as the city comes under attack all prisoners are to be executed." The guard thought for a moment. "I suppose we could have one last beating before we kill you," the guard sounded smug. "Now are you going come quietly or do I get to tenderise you a little before we get started?"

Alaric came to his feet and the guard reached out to grab him, as he did every time he came to get him. Alaric quickly grabbed the man's arm and twisted his wrist. The guard was caught by surprise and dropped to his left knee, crying out in pain. Once he was down Alaric struck him across the side of his face.

Another guard came rushing in to see what the commotion was about. He didn't see the first guard lying in the doorway and tripped over him as he rushed into the cell.

Alaric moved into action. He was not going to wait for the man to recover. He saw his advantage and kicked the guard on the back of his head. The guard went limp on top of the other one. The first guard struggled to get out, but the dead weight was too much for him to move. Alaric slowly stepped over the two guards, picking up the club as he did.

Once he was sure there was no immediate threat he stood over the two men. "Now isn't this a fortuitous situation?" Richmond stayed in the cell. He could see the look in Alaric's eyes. He knew what was about to happen. As much as he wanted retribution he didn't want to be the one to administer it. He didn't have the stomach for that sort of thing.

Alaric brought the club down on the first guards arm and he cried out in pain. "Well it looks like someone can give, but can't receive." Alaric looked the guard in the eyes, even though he was speaking to Richmond.

"Please, let me go. I will do anything that you want," the guard sobbed.

"Too little, too late. Compassion is only as good as the person receiving it." Alaric brought the club down hard on the arm again. This time there was an audible snap. "That's the sound I wanted to hear." The guard screamed out in pain again, but Alaric was not about to show any mercy.

"Get that tubby guard off him," Alaric barked at Richmond, harsher than he meant.

Richmond did as he was told. There was not a lot of room to drag the guard back into the cell and it took all of Richmond's strength to move him. When he did the first guard was able to move again, but he chose to remain on the floor.

"On your feet," Alaric snarled.

"No, please," the guard repeated a number of times before Alaric kicked him across the side of his face.

"On your feet now!" Alaric commanded.

The guard slowly did as what he told, his left arm hanging limply by his side. He could only hope that he made it out with his life.

"Turn around and walk into the cell."

The guard did as he told. Once he was inside enough for Alaric to shut the door Alaric walked over and struck him on the back of the head sending him to the ground. As much as Alaric wanted to man to suffer he was not willing to continue the punishment. Richmond was glad to see him stop. The situation was threatening to break out of control. Once the guard was down Alaric shut and locked the cell door. If all went to plan they would be down there for a long time.

"What do we do now?" Richmond asked. "We are still greatly outnumbered."

"Come on." Alaric motioned for him to follow. There were still more guards, but it seemed as though they were busy elsewhere. The guards had been there before the Dark Knights had taken over; they were just a part of city life. Alaric wasn't about to pay out justice to all of them.

They walked carefully through the maze of the dungeon system. There were many different cells, each designed to separate the different types of prisoners. They didn't see any guards at all when they reached the stairs leading up into the palace. At the top of the stairs there was a large oak door, reinforced with a number of iron straps. It was also locked up tight.

"How are we going to get out now?" Richmond asked when he tried to open the door. "There is nothing around to even try and pick the lock."

"It's okay. Just wait. It won't be long." Alaric remained calm.

They returned to the bottom of the stairs where there was more room. The only thing that stopped Richmond from crying out in anguish was the fact Alaric remained calm. He simply stood at the bottom of the stairs and looked up at the door. It was as if he was waiting for someone to open it. Richmond paced backwards and forwards. He knew that it was only a matter of time before one of the guards came.

"What are we waiting for?" Richmond didn't know how much time had passed, but it felt like it had been hours.

"You will know," Alaric didn't take his eyes off the door as he spoke. "You will know." It was almost like he was talking to himself.

More time passed and still nothing happened. All of a sudden Alaric dropped to his knees. The spell that had been blocking him suddenly disappeared. It happened so suddenly that it was like someone had poured iced water down his back and he drank in the energy that surrounded him. His first spell was to prevent anyone from blocking him again. He tied the spell off just in time. He could feel someone probing for him.

"Let's get out of here. We have work to do as well." Richmond was starting to become annoyed with Alaric's mysterious words.

"But…"

Alaric moved quickly up the stairs. Before he reached the top the door simply swung open. Richmond was still at the bottom looking on in awe. He didn't understand what had just happened. He looked to see if there was anyone on the other side, but he couldn't see anything.

"Hurry up," Alaric called down the stairs when he saw that Richmond still hadn't moved.

Richmond still didn't move. It wasn't that he didn't want to leave the dungeons; it was just that his legs wouldn't move. Slowly one leg lifted shortly followed by the other. It seemed to take forever, but he was grateful when they reached the top. He took a deep breath when he felt the cool air on his skin. The air in the dungeons had been hot and stagnate, but the air in the palace was cool and sweet.

"Now where do we go?" Richmond asked.

The hallway was empty, but there was something in the air. It was almost like there was fear in the palace walls themselves. Alaric looked to the left and then to the right. There was nothing that gave him any indication of which way he should go. He looked at Richmond who just shrugged his shoulders.

"I have never been to the dungeons before. I don't know which way we should go." Richmond was still in shock.

Alaric looked left and right again. In the end he figured right was as good as any. He had to find the throne room and free Unwin before it was too late. He knew that the Alliance was about to be attacked and the army was moving by disguise. He didn't know how he knew and he really didn't care. He also knew what would happen if he was not successful and that wasn't worth thinking about.

The hallways were empty. It was like the palace had been evacuated. If someone had been there then they would have been able to ask for directions. As they rounded a corner they ran into a small group of soldiers standing in front of an ornate wooden door. Alaric still had the club in his hand, but that was the only weapon he had. The six soldiers all had swords hanging at their hips and didn't look happy when they saw Alaric and Richmond approaching.

The soldiers looked as though they were part of the King's Royal guard. Richmond was loathed to attack the soldiers and not just because he didn't have a weapon. He didn't want to hurt them. They were obviously loyal to King Unwin and were only doing what they were told.

"What's this all about?" Alaric asked before the soldiers had a chance to speak.

"No one is allowed into the throne room." One of the soldiers stepped forward. He didn't look as though he was a superior officer. He just looked as though he was their designated spokesman.

"Is that Unwin's order or are you taking orders from his advisor?" Alaric snarled.

"We take orders from the King," the soldier didn't sound impressed with Alaric.

"Then you know he is under the thrall of one of the Evil One's Generals?" Richmond said.

"There is still nothing we can do. We take orders from the King and we do not question his motives." The soldier remained strong, unfortunately the other soldiers didn't feel the same. They all fidgeted and looked to the ground.

"I think that you should check with your fellow soldiers before you speak too soon. It seems that they don't share the same opinion."

The soldier glanced at his companions. There was something different in the look on his face.

"I am sure that you are being looked after a lot better than these other men. What has he promised you? A share of the booty when the war is over? All the women of your dreams? Power?" Alaric asked, the words were having their effect. The other soldiers looked at their spokesman like they had never seen him before.

"That's not true," he stumbled. "This man is the enemy. Remember, we were warned that there would be two men trying to get into the throne room. We were told that they would try and sweet talk us into letting them in." The soldier was trying to regain control, but his words were having little effect. He was in danger of having a mutiny on his hands.

"You know what is right in your hearts. You know that your land in under the veil of the Evil One. There is only one way to set it free."

The rogue soldier drew his sword and charged towards Alaric and Richmond. He was too quick for the other soldiers and there was nothing they could do. Before the soldier came within striking distance he seemed to trip over his own boots. As he landed his sword kicked up and stabbed him in the chest. Alaric couldn't keep the smile from his face as the others looked on in horror. The sword point had sliced through his heart, killing him instantly.

"I don't think anyone will miss him," Alaric spoke to Richmond. "He had sold his soul to the Evil One." He didn't make any move closer to the door. As much as the other soldiers seemed to be on their side he didn't want to take any risks. "Now is the time to make things right. There is a battle about to take place outside the Northern gate. You need to tell the commanding officers that the battle is over. You need to tell them not to fight the army that is outside these walls."

"But if the city is under attack we need to defend it," one of the soldiers spoke.

"The army is set to liberate the city, not to attack it. They are doing what is necessary to free the city from the yolk of the Evil One. If the two armies meet in battle then the Evil One will be the only one who wins." Alaric watched their faces, trying to gauge their reaction.

It seemed as though they believed him. His words were making some sense. They knew that the new advisor was controlling their King, but they didn't know if the man was evil. The fact remained if there was a hostile army outside of the city and they were supporting it then there was a chance that they were there to cause trouble.

"I am Lord Richmond, from Bellarome. What this man says is the truth. We, as are the army, are here to help you." Richmond tried his best to help.

"I can eliminate the Dark Knight who has power over your King, but you have to stop the battle that is building outside. We all have our parts to play and this is yours."

The soldiers looked at each other. They all wanted to help, but none of them wanted to make a decision. Alaric was about to burst with the waiting, but he could see that they were slowly agreeing. They looked at each questioningly, but also nodding at the same time. Finally one of the soldiers stepped forward.

"Okay, Lord Richmond, we will trust that you are doing the right thing." He looked at the others who were urging him to say something else. He clearly didn't want to, but the others would not leave without it. "If you are not who you say you are you can be sure that we will be back and we will bring the rest of the army with us."

Alaric let out a sigh of relief. "You can be assured that we will do the right thing."

The soldiers seemed happy with their answer. As one they started walking away from the door. Richmond and Alaric moved out of the way to give them free passage. They left the fallen soldier on the floor. The man had betrayed them and didn't deserve any respect. None of them looked back as they made their way towards the barracks.

Alaric stepped over the fallen man without taking notice of him. Before he reached the door to the throne room Richmond yelled out to him.

"Do you want the sword from this soldier?" Richmond had rolled the body over, but was yet to remove the sword.

"No, thank you. The sword has been tainted with the blood of the fallen. I will not take it in the same room as a Dark Knight. Anyway the steel will be no use against him. This battle will be fought on a different scale," Alaric's words were again mysterious, but Richmond was just as happy to leave the blooded blade where it was.

Alaric waited for Richmond to get a little closer before he opened the door. His heart was pounding and he could feel the blood pumping through his head. He could feel the presence of the Dark Knight inside the throne room, but only one. If there was only one Dark Knight then his chances of winning just doubled.

He pushed the door open and moved quickly into the room. The sight in front of him was better than he had expected. King Unwin was sitting on the throne. His head was lowered and there was drool in the corner of his mouth. He didn't seem to notice them enter. His appearance was dishevelled and it looked as though he had not bathed or changed his clothes in over a week.

Standing over the king was the Dark Knight. Alaric recognised him instantly. There was a broad grin on his face. He looked as though he knew something that Alaric did not. The expression made him somewhat nervous.

"It is about time. We have been waiting for you," the Knight spoke.

Chapter 30: One Battle

Alaric moved further into the room. Lord Richmond was a little slower to react. His heart stopped when he saw the condition of King Unwin. He wanted to rush to his aide, but knew that would only cause his death. He didn't know if he could do anything to help.

"Give me your name worm," Alaric sneered at the Knight.

"I am the Chosen of the Great Lord, but you may call me Fenaroz. It will be the last name that you will hear before you die. You can bow down before me now or you can bow down later, but you will bow down." Fenaroz kept all the venom in his voice.

Alaric moved further into the room until he was standing in front of the throne. He motioned for Richmond to remain near the door when he saw him starting to follow. He had tried to keep it secret, but Fenaroz saw the movement. He looked over and saw Richmond for the first time. The smile on his face sent a shiver down Alaric's spine. He should have kept Richmond out of the room. He just hoped he would stay out of the fight. It would be the only chance for him to stay alive.

"I see that you have brought a pet along. That is alright I have my pet here," he motioned at King Unwin as he spoke. Once he was done he stepped down from the small dais until he was standing in front of Alaric. "Now that we are on an even keel I am sure that we can discuss this... situation."

Before Alaric could speak there was the sound of another crash into the city wall. The sound and the reaction on Fenaroz's face brought a smile to Alaric's. The army was getting close and he knew it. He also knew that if he didn't fix the situation then it would not be long before the remainder of the Darshivallian army would be fighting with the Alliance.

"It seems that the noose is closing around your neck," Alaric's words were sharp.

The comment caused Fenaroz to laugh, although there was something nervous about it. He was not about to let Alaric think he had the upper hand. He was also not going to give up without a fight. "It is not over yet. I have a little surprise in store for your friends. They won't know what hit them."

All of a sudden Alaric felt something brush past his shoulders. He knew that no one was there and he was not about to flinch. He saw see one of Fenaroz's eyebrows twitch and the sight caused Alaric to laugh. He saw his advantage. He knew that he was not going to be able to talk Fenaroz into submission. He was going to have to fight him, but if he could rattle him into making mistakes then that was only going to help.

"It looks as though your power is waning," Alaric kept the smile on his face. "I didn't think the Great Lord rewarded weakness."

Fenaroz stormed forward for a couple of paces before he stopped. "The Great Lord will reward me for striking down his enemies. If I let you crawl out of here you will find that all your friends have been killed. You see it doesn't matter which side wins the battle. Either way I win," his voice was calm, but Alaric could see the anger in his eyes.

"I know something that you don't," Alaric deliberately sounded cocky.

Both sides knew that it would not be long before they were fighting. Fenaroz was slowly losing his confidence. He knew he had already drawn a lot of his energy to cast the spells that were in motion. He didn't think that Alaric was going to be much competition, but he still had to be careful. There would be no second place. The loser would never walk out of the throne room.

"And what might that be?" Fenaroz asked when Alaric didn't continue his statement.

"You will find out soon enough, but for now all you need to know is that you won't like it."

The two stared at each other. Fenaroz was trying to work out if Alaric was bluffing. Alaric was not about to give anything away. He just stared at Fenaroz with a blank look on his face. He knew that if he dropped his gaze n the Knight would attack.

"Well I don't think this talk is getting us anywhere. You obviously are set on killing yourself. I am sure that the Great Lord was looking forward to burning you himself, but I guess I'm going to have to do it for him," Fenaroz snarled.

"I will see you grovel at my feet before you die," Alaric kept his voice level.

The last threat was the last straw. Fenaroz, even in his own sick, twisted mind knew that he had lost the verbal battle. Most of the wormlike creatures folded in the first five minutes of his berating. This one was stronger. The Great Lord was right to warn them. Then he noticed something had changed. There was a spark in Alaric's eyes that he had not seen before. For the first time he was unsure of himself. He quickly shook that thought away. He was a much stronger being. There was no way he could lose to a simple man.

Alaric stood and watched. He knew he couldn't make the first move. If the Dark Knight realised his full power then what he was planning wouldn't work. He would have to wait for Fenaroz to attack.

The attack came sooner rather than Alaric had expected. Time was running against both of them, but it was Fenaroz who struck the first blow. A ripple in the air slowly moved towards Alaric. The closer it got the faster it moved. Alaric simply braced himself and as soon as the ripple hit him it pushed him backwards a few inches before disappearing.

Fenaroz looked a little surprised to see Alaric still standing before him. He knew he had hit him with all the energy, that wasn't still being used in his other spells. The force should have thrown him across the room.

Time was still not right for Alaric to counterattack. The blow sent by Fenaroz hardly touched the surface. Alaric wasn't expecting the Dark Knight's most powerful attack, but he had expected more than he had received. He could not give up such a perfect opportunity to provoke him even more.

"I haven't received a weak attack like that, well... ever. I don't think that would have knocked a baby over," in truth the attack would have come close to killing most people.

"It seems that I have gone too easy on you this time. I can assure you that I will not make the same mistake twice. Let's see if you can block this," Fenaroz snarled before closing his eyes. The strain was obvious on his face.

Alaric couldn't believe how easy Fenaroz was making it for him. The Dark Knight didn't even realise that he was playing right into his hands. He knew that he had to be careful. Just because the Dark Knight was being predictable it didn't mean he couldn't change. One mistake and Alaric could easily lose his life.

Fenaroz's next attack was a little more obvious to the two men watching, even Unwin, who still looked catatonic, could see it. The Dark Knight reached out with both his arms, palms facing each other and slowly a swirling ball of yellow light started to grow. The light gave an eerie glow across the entire room. Alaric simply stood and waited for the attack. He was glad that the Dark Knight had forgotten about Richmond. He was confident he could save himself, but he was unsure if he would be quick enough to save Richmond as well. Fenaroz had no intention of wasting the deadly ball of light on someone as insignificant as Richmond. When the ball had grown to be about a foot in diameter he tossed it up and down in his right hand. Without warning he threw the ball in Alaric's direction.

The ball of light sizzled in the air as it approached, moving faster than the throw had indicated. Alaric saw it in slow motion, even though it was travelling almost too fast for Richmond to see. Richmond gasped and Fenaroz cackled when the ball of light consumed Alaric. For a moment there was no man there, only the light. Richmond would have run to his aide if he had known what to do. After a few seconds the light disappeared and Alaric remained, unharmed. Both Richmond and Fenaroz couldn't believe what they were seeing. Their reactions were completely opposite, but they both thought Alaric had been destroyed.

"A little better," Alaric still had not finished his agitating the Dark Knight. "But I still think that you can do better. If this is all that you are going to do you may as well give up now."

Alaric's taunts were really starting to annoy Fenaroz. The Dark Knight had obviously used all the energy he could muster with his last attack and he would have to drop one of his spells to continue. The result of doing so was the last thing on his mind. He was full of rage and there was nothing that was going to stop him from killing Alaric.

Alaric felt a rush of energy come into the room. It was obvious to him that Fenaroz had dropped at least one of his spells. He looked towards Unwin still slumped on his throne. The only other spell that could have caused such an effect was the one that was affecting the army. Alaric relaxed a little. Things were starting to move into place. If he was right then he just avoided the two armies from attacking each other. Things had just become more deadly for himself, but he was happy he had avoided the senseless deaths of his allies.

"Now you will see the true power of the Chosen." The strain was again obvious on the Dark Knight's face. Whatever he had in store was not going to be pleasant.

Even Richmond and Unwin could feel the power that Fenaroz was drawing from the room. Alaric knew full well what was happening. He could feel the energy rushing around him. Whatever was going to happen was going to be big.

"I wish you would hurry up," Alaric tried to sound bored. "You know that you are not strong enough to defeat me."

Fenaroz ignored the jibe. If he spoke then he would lose his concentration. The taunt did distract him though, but not enough to completely ruin the spell. His face had turned a dark shade of red under the strain as Richmond watched on in awe.

Slowly the throne room started to rumble. It took Alaric a moment to realise what was happening and as he did Fenaroz started to laugh.

"I will bring this palace down on top of you," he boomed at the top of his voice.

Cracks started to appear in the ceiling. The spell was stronger than anything Alaric had experienced since Nyrra changed the weather in Nostiria. A large grin appeared on Fenaroz's face as the first piece of stone started to fall. In his mind he knew he was about to win. The spell he had cast was too strong for the Cursed One. It would not be long before he was covered in rubble.

The first piece of stone crashed onto the floor within six feet of where Alaric was standing. If the first strike had been on target there was a chance it would have killed him. Now he had a chance to counter the spell. The palace continued to rattle and the ceiling started to collapse. Alaric quickly released a spell of his own. When the pieces of ceiling started to fall they would suddenly stop before they hit the floor. Some came closer than others. The pieces remained, frozen in space, only for a short period of time before they started to rise back into the ceiling. With each failed attack Fenaroz was even more determined to bring the entire roof down on top of him.

The strain had returned to Fenaroz's face. As Alaric secured the pieces of broken ceiling Fenaroz strained to bring them down again. As time continued the pieces of stone remained in place for longer. The falling pieces became less and less until Fenaroz could only muster the strength to bring down one at a time. Finally he did not have the energy to continue his attack. His breathing was laboured and as he looked around the chaos he had created was completely gone. There was not a single scrap of rubble left on the floor.

"Well that was much better," Alaric said. He himself was feeling the strain, but he was not letting anyone see it. "I'll give you one more chance. As much as I am enjoying myself I really have other things to do." The pure arrogance of Alaric's words was enough to push Fenaroz over the edge.

The Dark Knight had one more trick up his sleeve and Alaric knew it. The last spell Fenaroz was holding was his control over King Unwin. It was the only thing that Fenaroz could do to gain enough power to destroy Alaric. Even though he had already expended a lot of energy with his initial attacks his rage had taken control. He could no longer think of the repercussions of his actions.

It was obvious when Fenaroz relinquished the spell. Slowly Unwin raised his head. He looked around the throne room as if he was seeing it for the first time. He wiped the drool from the corner of his mouth as he looked around the room again trying to work out who the people were in front of him. His eyes locked on Fenaroz and for a moment it looked as though he remembered.

"I can see that I have been too easy on you worm." Fenaroz was frothing at the mouth. "Now I will not be so easy." Richmond thought he was preparing another spell, but Alaric knew his strength had not yet returned. It was the perfect opportunity for Alaric to strike, but he knew if he failed he would not have the strength to defend another attack.

"You will now drop to your knees and beg for forgiveness," Fenaroz was puffing as he spoke. "You will know the pain of a thousand lives."

Slowly Alaric stumbled backwards. The fatigue was starting to get to him. He didn't want to show Fenaroz that he was starting to waver, but his body overtook his willpower. He only stumbled for a moment, but it was enough to give the Dark Knight the confidence he needed to continue. Slowly Alaric could feel him draw more energy. Alaric didn't know if he had enough energy to defend himself, but he would not stop trying.

"Ha, ha, ha. I will burn you to the ground. There is nothing that you will be able to do about it." The strength had returned to Fenaroz's voice. "The Great Lord will empower me beyond your wildest dreams. I will..." Suddenly his voice cut off as sword protruded from his stomach.

The look of surprise on Fenaroz's face was almost enough to make Alaric start laughing. His plan was finally coming to fruition. The blow was not enough to kill the Dark Knight, but it was enough to distract him. He couldn't believe that King Unwin had turned against him. In his own twisted mind he believed that Unwin did what he did because he was loyal. He didn't think for a moment that when he released the spell that Unwin would turn on him.

"What in the Great Lord's name do you think that you are doing?" Fenaroz took a stumbled step forward.

Unwin had retreated back towards his throne giving him a good half a dozen paces between him and the Dark Knight. The small short sword dripped with a black liquid that was Fenaroz's blood. Unwin had taken the sword from its hiding place under the throne. A small cabinet was opened under the throne where Unwin kept his secret weapon. Even if Fenaroz had known the sword was hidden there he would never have assumed that his life was in danger.

"I am taking back my life, my city and my Kingdom," Unwin still looked a little confused, but there was nothing but strength in his voice. "You will no longer have control over me."

There was a gnarled expression of Fenaroz's face. The skin started to peel away from his face as he was unable to contain the spell that changed his appearance, the spell that took no energy to contain. It was the rage inside him that caused the disintegration. The hole in his stomach continued to ooze the sticky black liquid. Fenaroz looked at it and wiped some away.

"I will not need to have control over you anymore," he took another step forward as he spoke. "You will bend down and prey to the Great Lord or you will be visiting him very soon." There was malice dripping from his threat.

King Unwin took another step back up onto the dais. His only move from there was to sit back down on the throne. He didn't know what he should do. He had thought his original attack would have killed the Knight. He looked at the sword in his hand and knew that it was now no good to him, so he let it slip from his hands.

"On your knees now," the Dark Knight screamed at him.

Unwin knew that he had no choice. It was do as he was told or die. At that moment he saw Lord Richmond out of the corner of his eye. The man stood defiantly to one side, even though he was paralysed with fear. Unwin did not know that as Richmond nodded to him. The move was enough to give Unwin the strength to continue.

"You will never enslave me or my people again."

"Very well then, it looks as though you have made your decision. I will look forward to killing you." A smile appeared on Fenaroz's grotesque, disfigured face.

The distraction was enough to give Alaric the advantage. The rage that had been building inside Fenaroz had caused him to forget about the main threat. All his attention was locked on King Unwin. As the Dark Knight approached the King, Alaric finished off the spell he had been working on. The only thing he needed to do was to get him away from Unwin.

"Forget about him, you piece of rat dung." The derogatory comment was enough to get Fenaroz's attention back. It was just in the nick of time. Neither of them would know how close Unwin had come to death. When Fenaroz was facing Alaric he continued with his taunts. "Come and fight me. I am the one that you want."

Fenaroz took a step forward before stopping. For the first time he stopped to think about the situation. There was no reason why Alaric should have diverted his attention. If he was going to kill him then it would have been easier for him to do so when his back was turned. He looked over his shoulder at King Unwin. He remained where he was, just in front of the throne. He didn't know what was happening, but he knew he had to be careful. The rage still burned deep inside.

"This fight is between you and me. Leave the others out of this."

"Maybe I should keep the others involved. It seems as though they want to be part of the action." Fenaroz stepped away from Unwin so he could keep everyone in sight. The move was exactly what Alaric had wanted.

"Okay then, let's see how you handle this." Alaric was finished talking.

Slowly he stretched out his arms in Fenaroz's direction. Suddenly bolts of electricity shot out from his fingers. The attack was a surprise to Fenaroz. The only way he could defend himself was by placing his arms in front of his face. The electricity struck Fenaroz up and down his body and he screamed out in pain. There was nothing he could do. He was already caught in Alaric's trap. The smell of burning flesh filled in the throne room.

Sweat poured from Alaric's face. It was his turn to turn red. His muscles twitched as he strained to contain the spell. If he lost concentration then there was no telling who the electricity might strike. He used up the last amount of energy he had stored and threw it at Fenaroz before collapsing to the ground.

When the final blast cleared they could all see the result of Alaric's attack. All that was left of the Dark Knight was a smouldering corpse. Richmond and Unwin both looked at each other in awe. They couldn't believe it was over. They still expected the charred remains of Fenaroz to stand up and attack. Neither of them moved.

Slowly Alaric came to his feet. The colour had completely drained from his face. Sweat still coated his pale skin and he wobbled on his feet. He looked at the other two men and a smile appeared on his face. Neither of them noticed it as they were still staring at the corpse.

"It is alright. He is gone now. There is nothing he can do." Alaric's voice was weak, but confident.

The sudden sound snapped the two men out of their reverie. It was Richmond who came to Alaric's aide as Unwin sank down in his throne. He still didn't fully understand the situation. He knew that there was something not right about his advisor, but he didn't know what it was. He had gone on instinct when he skewered the man with his sword, but now he wanted answers. Alaric could see it in the King's face.

"He is one of Nyrra's, I mean the Evil One's," Alaric corrected himself when he saw the shock on Unwin's face. "Dark Knights. He used some very intricate magic to gain control of your mind." He tried to choose his words carefully. "There was nothing that you could have done. He was very skilled in dark magic."

"I thought I had a strong will," Unwin lowered his head. "I didn't think that someone could take control of my mind so easily."

"Don't get so worried about it. It was a powerful spell. There was nothing that you could have done. The only thing you have to worry about now is fixing the situation. Your people need you now more than ever." Alaric could see that his words were having their desired effect. There was strength returning to Unwin's posture.

"You need to rest," Richmond spoke softly to Alaric as he held him upright.

"I will rest when this situation is finished." Alaric tried to move closer to the throne, but Richmond wouldn't let him.

"At least sit down. Stay here and I will get you a chair." Richmond was not going to be brushed aside. He knew that he had been no help when Alaric needed him the most. At least now he was able to do something.

Alaric did as he was told and remained where he was. He wobbled on his feet, but remained upright until Richmond returned with a chair. Alaric was grateful to be sitting down. Once Richmond was sure that he was alright he stepped away.

"I don't think you have been properly introduced yet," Richmond spoke to avoid silence. "King Unwin, may I present to you Alaric, the Chosen One," Richmond spoke in his most official voice.

"Thank you, Lord Richmond, but I don't think that we need to be all that formal at the moment." King Unwin was still trying to come to terms with what had happened. Everything since Fenaroz had clouded his mind seemed as though it was a dream. He knew he had let Fenaroz do some terrible things in his name. He didn't know how he was going to make it up to his subjects. When it came down to the crunch it was his fault everything had happened.

"You do not need to punish yourself for what happened. There was nothing you could have done about it." Alaric was trying his best to reassure Unwin.

"I think we need to organise our next move," Richmond said, trying to change the subject.

"That's right. We need to regain control of the city," Alaric agreed.

"I am still the King. My people will understand and will listen to what I have to say."

Alaric was almost completely drained of strength. His attack on Fenaroz took more from him then he was willing to admit. He could see that Unwin was starting to recover from his malaise. There was still a lot more to be done, but he needed to rest. Alaric noticed for the first time that the bombardment of the city walls had also stopped. He could only hope that he prevented the battle.

Richmond was pacing around the throne room. He didn't know what he needed to do. He looked at Alaric and then back to Unwin. Both men looked as though they were either physically or mentally drained. He knew they were not going to solve any problems until they got some rest.

"You two both need some rest. We won't achieve anything in this condition. I think I should have someone come in and clean up this mess. In the morning we can reconvene with rest of your council."

"I thank you for the offer, Lord Richmond, but I have a strange feeling that I dissolved the council," King Unwin replied.

"Well that will give me something to do for the rest of the day. I am sure that your council will not be far away. I will gather as many as I can, whilst you rest." Richmond was not going to be pushed aside.

Alaric didn't have the energy to argue. It was all he could do to stay upright in his chair. As much as he wanted to continue their conversation he knew he could not. The only thing that he was good for was sleep and he was in desperate need.

"Very well. We shall reconvene in the morning," Unwin didn't sound happy, but he sounded relieved. "I will make sure that you have rooms."

Unwin rang the bell pull that hung next to his throne. It had been a long time since he had rung the bell and it felt good. He was slowly regaining his strength, both in character and body. He looked towards the door as it slowly opened and a young serving boy entered the room. The boy looked at the three men before his eyes fell on the crusty corpse. The boy then started to gag when he realised what it was.

"Have rooms prepared for these two." Unwin paused for a moment. "The best rooms we have in the palace."

The pageboy was about to leave when Alaric called out.

"There is one more pressing matter." Alaric gasped for breath before he continued. "Hopefully your soldiers have been given the order to stand down. Just to be sure I think you should send word."

The pageboy looked at Unwin who simply nodded in return. He would have to find someone else to get the rooms ready whilst he raced towards the army.

Slowly Richmond helped Alaric to his feet. He no longer wanted to stay in the throne room. The stench of evil was still thick in the air, although it was slowly starting to dissipate. Alaric was a dead weight. He had little strength left to stand on his own feet making it a slow journey. Once they were outside Alaric felt slightly better. Although he still needed Richmond's assistance he was able to move a lot better.

Unwin waited behind after the others had left. The King looked around his throne room as if he was seeing for the first time. When his eyes fell on the burnt remains of Fenaroz he smiled. He was no longer under the Dark Knight's control and that thought was enough to keep him smiling all the way back to his royal bedchamber.

Chapter 31: A Fresh Day

The Alliance army stood in shock. No one knew what to make of the sudden appearance of the Darshivallian army. They knew that something wasn't right when they were assembled for battle, but no one could have guessed what it was.

The solider racing towards them was Captain Buhl, the leader of the Darshivallian army in the absence of General Sorrell. There was a strange expression on his face.

"General Sorrell," Buhl called out when he was within a few paces from the group.

"Captain Buhl, I see you have come to treat with us," Sorrell greeted him.

"Thank the Gods that you are here General." Buhl reined his horse in front of the group. "You could say that I am here to entreat with you, but a more accurate account would be that I have come to pass control of the Darshivallian army to you."

"What are you talking about?" Sorrell looked somewhat confused.

"You are the rightful commander of the army. You outrank me and therefore you should be in charge," Buhl spoke as though it was the most logical thing in the world.

"I guess that does make sense." Sorrell looked at Jarwe and then at Bern. "Why did you take the field if you were just going to surrender?"

"Here is not the place. Is there somewhere we can talk privately?" Buhl didn't want to speak in the middle of the battle zone.

"We have a command tent back at the campsite," Sorrell suggested.

"Good, I think we should meet there. Now what would you like me to do with your new soldiers Sorrell?" Buhl seemed pleased.

"We need to draw up plans to attack the palace. There is an agent of evil controlling King Unwin. For now I think it best if the soldiers were disarmed and kept under guard. Some of them may not agree with what we are about to do. I will have the Darshivallian component of the Alliance keep watch over them," Sorrell didn't sound happy about the prospect.

Sorrell didn't know what was more disturbing, the fact that they had to attack the palace or the fact that Buhl didn't argue. The Captain seemed more than willing to do whatever Sorrell commanded.

"See that the orders are passed on through the ranks. No one is to resist the arrest. Make sure that they know it is only a temporary arrangement," Buhl spoke to the standard bearer who in turn saluted and then turned his horse around.

"Make it known to our soldiers that the prisoners are not to be mistreated. Make sure they also know that this is a temporary arrangement," Sorrell spoke to his advisor.

"Yes sir," Wojtek said and also saluted before turning his horse around and riding back towards the army.

"Now that it is all over I think we should return to the tent. There is still much to be discussed," Sorrell looked at Buhl when he spoke.

The Captain agreed and the commanders made their way back towards the camp. No one could be happier that they did not have to fight. They all hoped their weight of numbers would force the palace guards to surrender.

Inside the tent there were a number of serving men and women rushing around, preparing for their victory feast. All the commanders had agreed not to do anything special. They protested that there had been no battle, so therefore there had been no victory, but it was only an excuse. They didn't want to waste the food. There was still no telling how long they would have to wait for more supplies.

"You didn't sound surprised when I told you that there was an agent of evil in the palace. Why is that?" Sorrell asked Buhl.

"I may be a loyal subject, but I am not an idiot. It is obvious that someone has taken control of the city. King Unwin would not do what he has done if he was in his right mind," Buhl replied.

"It is good to see that we are on the same page," Jarwe spoke for the first time. He had been content to let Sorrell speak to his countryman, but it was time Buhl realised who was in command of the army. "We need to work out the best way to attack the palace."

The abruptness of what Jarwe had said annoyed both Sorrell and Buhl. No one spoke after Jarwe's words. No one knew what to say.

"Bern, do you have any suggestions?" Jarwe asked when it was clear that no one was going to speak.

Bern thought for a moment, as all eyes moved to him, even the servants waited for him to speak. He looked around at the people sitting at the table. It was not the first time they had waited for his answer.

"There is no need to attack the palace," he said after an insufferable pause.

"What are you talking about?" Buhl said, obviously not understanding Bern's ability. "We have to take the palace by force. I don't think they will care that we have the rest of the army. I don't believe they are going to give up without a fight."

"I hate to agree with him," there was nothing malicious in Tancred's tone. "But don't forget that Richmond and Alaric are prisoners there. There is no telling how long they will be left alive once the Dark Knight finds out that he has lost."

"The wheels are in motion. There is nothing that we can do now." Bern was again being mysterious.

Buhl was about to speak again, but he was silenced by a wave of Sorrell's hand. He knew exactly what the captain was going to ask and there was no answer to his question.

"General Bern has a special ability. It is hard to explain, but when he gets 'one of his feelings' we all listen. There doesn't seem to be any pattern to it, but the information is always correct," Sorrell said, trying to find the words that would make sense to Buhl.

"I see," the Captain didn't sound convinced.

"Regardless of the reasons we listen to what he has to say." General Jarwe was starting to get annoyed with Buhl's attitude. "That is all you really need to know."

"Come now, gentlemen, this is getting us nowhere," surprisingly it was Captain Aimon who was the voice of reason. "We need to plan for our next move."

"Aimon is right," Hadar agreed.

"So what is it that you think we should do next," Buhl asked Bern.

"We wait until the morning. The day is already well past noon. Nothing will be achieved by moving into the city at night. Send your soldiers back to their barracks. There is nothing to be gained by keeping them here. We will have the Alliance set up a semi-permanent camp outside of the city. I don't know how long we are going to be here. At first light the command group will ride into the palace. I am sure by then all will be safe."

"That is a lot to bank our lives on," Buhl scoffed.

"And that is exactly what we shall do." Jarwe was again not happy with the disrespect from the Darshivallian Captain.

***

Richmond did his best to gather the councilmen who had worked for Unwin before he had been controlled by Fenaroz. He managed to gain some control over the household, but no one really knew who he was, even though he called himself Lord Richmond. They knew the advisor was dead and they were just happy that they were taking orders from someone who wasn't obviously evil.

It was harder for him to find someone willing to clean up the mess in the throne room. As much as they were all happy that the advisor was dead no one wanted to touch the body. They all felt they would be tainted by evil if they touched him. Eventually he managed to convince a small group of women that they would be well paid if they cleaned up the mess. The thought of gold was more powerful than the thought of hoodoo.

It was not long after Alaric and Unwin had gone to bed that word came that the armies had met outside the Northern gate. The two armies had met, but they had not fought. Richmond was glad that no blood had been shed. He was also hopeful that Tancred would be entering the palace soon. He missed his advisor and hoped that he had joined the army.

Richmond kept himself busy cleaning up and doing a few chores. The first was to make sure that the guards on the palace gates knew that Fenaroz was dead and Unwin was back in control again. That meant that anyone with legitimate business was allowed entrance into the palace allowing the flow of information to resume. Richmond needed all the information that he could gain if he was going to help bring things back to normal. Although the Dark Knight had not been there for long he had managed to create an enormous amount of chaos.

It was late in the night when Richmond finally made it to bed. Once word had gone through the palace that the King's advisor had been killed officials flooded to his chambers. He was pleased with what he had achieved. The city was already starting to heal from the pain that Fenaroz had caused.

The morning came around all too quickly for Richmond. As much as he enjoyed getting back into the politics of city life he did want to rest. The days spent in the dungeons had not been pleasant. He had been beaten every day, there was no room to exercise and when he did get to use the bed it was hard and uncomfortable. He knew he had to do his civic duty and continue with what he had started, but he hoped it would not be long before Tancred arrived.

He was met by a number of functionaries in the new office he had created. A light breakfast had been prepared for him as they all figured that he would not have time to sit and eat in his room. Richmond was grateful for the food, but still wished he had more time to relax. He didn't know when they were going to be on the move again. He didn't really have a choice until Unwin was ready to rule again and there was no telling when that was going to happen.

He continued with the duties from the day before. There had been no word overnight from the army outside the city walls. The Darshivallian army had returned to their barracks and the Alliance made no move on the city. It was as if they had all given up. Whatever their reasoning he hoped word had reached them that the Dark Knight was dead and the threat to the palace was gone. The last thing he needed was an invading army on his doorstep.

It was not long before word reached him that the soldiers had been released and were making their way back into the city. The Alliance had made no move to come any closer and Richmond was relieved that everything seemed to be working out. He also received word that the command group was planning on entering the palace to speak with Unwin. Neither the King nor Alaric had surfaced.

Both Unwin and Alaric arrived in the throne room for the midday meal. Resetting the room had been the palace staff's first priority. They knew that with the death of the advisor there would soon be a function to celebrate and they took great pleasure in preparing for such an occasion.

The command group arrived at the palace just as Unwin and Alaric took their seats in the throne room. Richmond greeted them in the palace foyer and was pleased to see that Tancred was with them. He introduced himself to the men he didn't know and offered for them to follow him to the throne room. There was a sudden air of excitement in the palace as the visiting dignitaries walked through the hallways.

Inside the room a lovely meal had been laid out on a large banquet table. Unwin was seated at the head of the table with Alaric on his right. On his left was his only child, a daughter named Princess Marina. She had long, wavy black hair that fell down around her shoulders. Her skin was fair and she had a quality about her that sent the young men in the palace crazy. Alaric could not see the resemblance between Marina and Unwin. He could only assume that she resembled her mother.

The three had been talking quietly. Unwin didn't want to speak about what had happened in front of Marina and he didn't know what else to discuss, so they talked about Marina to avoid an awkward silence. Her deep blue dress accentuated her full breasts and slender body, she was young and bubbly and had an inner strength that matched her beauty. Unwin had been lucky enough to shield Marina from the damage Fenaroz had created. As much as she had not been able to speak to her father she had also not seen the condition he had been in. She had known that something was not right, but she didn't know the full extent. She was just happy to have her father back and didn't care who knew.

"Welcome to my palace," Unwin stood as he spoke. "Alaric told me that you would be coming. Please have a seat and we can discuss everything."

They all bowed and murmured a quick greeting before sitting at the table. Richmond quickly found a seat next to his advisor, they had a lot to talk about. Although Bern sat next to Alaric he didn't want to speak to his old friend until they were alone. He did notice, however, that there was something very different about the man he had grown up with.

Everyone was relatively quiet as they ate. It had been a long time since they had eaten a good meal and they were enjoying it immensely.

"Now that the meal is over I suppose we should get down to business," King Unwin spoke jovially as their plates were being cleared.

The first part of the conversation brought everyone up to date. Unwin was not able to remember much of his ordeal with Fenaroz, but was interested to hear what the army had been doing. He was shocked to hear what had happened in Avalon and was relieved to hear their solution.

"So where do we go from here?" Jarwe asked when the discussion was over.

No one knew who the best person was to answer the question. They had previously looked towards Bern for all their tough answers, but with Alaric in the room they had another dilemma. They didn't know which man they should defer to. It was lucky they were seated next to each, so they could just look in their general direction.

Alaric looked at Bern who in turn looked back at him. For a moment Alaric thought he saw what it was that had changed in his old friend.

"For the moment we all stay put," said Alaric. The news that you bring from Avalon is very disturbing. We were due to fight a glorious battle and it wasn't to be. We can ill afford to make another move before we are sure where we must go."

"What about the prophecy? Can't you consult the prophecy?" Hulkan asked.

Alaric had not been expecting that question. He had known the exact moment that Na'garoz had left the city. He could feel it. He could still point to its exact location, but that would not last much longer. It would not be long before it was too far away. He also knew that he could not tell the others that the prophecy had been stolen. He only hoped Richmond and Tancred would keep their word.

"It is not as easy as it sounds. The words in the prophecy are twisted and hard to understand. We thought we knew what the prophecy said when we gathered at Avalon. It was only when it was too late did we understand that we were wrong. We must be very careful when we trust the ancient words. For now we must trust our own eyes and ears. When the time is right we will know where we must go, in that you must trust," Alaric's words were just as deceiving as Bern's. No one knew exactly what he said, but they knew there was no real answer.

"There is still much to be done here," Bern said when there had been a long silence. "Nyrra's evil has touched this place and it is our duty to remove all traces. Even though the Dark Knight has been destroyed there will still be agents in the city. We must root them all out and see if we can discover some of his secrets."

There was something in Bern's tone that Alaric found unusual. It was not at all like something his old friend would have said. He knew there was something different and it was just in the back of his mind, out of reach. There was something very familiar about the situation.

"Yes it is true that there is a lot of work to do, but for now it is a time of celebration. Tonight we shall have a large feast in your honour." King Unwin was sick of the depressing talk. "For the moment we are free and that is something that we should all be thankful for."

No one really agreed with Unwin, but they could see his point-of-view. The King had been enslaved for a long time and he would be taking responsibility for what had happened to the city and its people. They could not begrudge him a celebration, even if it meant putting their own concerns to one side.

Alaric remained silent for the rest of the meeting. He was still disturbed with Bern's condition. He also didn't want to speak as he had no answers for anyone. He knew, however, that Bern was right and the Alliance needed to remain where it was until things were back to normal. What he didn't know is what he was supposed to do. He could feel the prophecy moving further and further away. He wanted to go chasing after it, but there was something inside him saying that he should wait. He knew that there was something else he had to do in the city, but he didn't know what it was. The feeling was far more frustrating than it had been before.

Unwin organised for them to have rooms in the palace. As much as they dismissed the offer, saying that they should be with the army, Unwin insisted. There was still much to be discussed and they would only waste time moving between the army and the palace. Eventually they all agreed that it was the right thing to do. Jarwe was the only one who was to return to the Alliance. He much preferred to stay with the army and he was again happy to defer any decisions to Bern.

Captain Aimon protested the decision. He thought that Jarwe should be involved in the decision making and that he should be the one to look after the army, but after what had happened when he was in command no one agreed that it was a good idea.

Alaric watched the discussion carefully. There was something different about Aimon, something disturbing. Alaric could not figure out what it was and when the conversation ended he put it out of his mind. There were far more important matters to deal with.

The palace was alive with activity. When Fenaroz had been in control the palace staff had been afraid to walk through the corridors. The Dark Knight had been known to randomly take people from the staff and send them to the dungeons. The rumours of what was happening to the poor unfortunate souls were enough to scare them into staying put.

Whenever someone was summoned to do a job they would move as quickly as possible and then run back to their quarters. Now they were happy to be able to move about and do their jobs without fear of repercussions. It would take a while for the filth of the Evil One to wash away, but they were heading in the right direction. The more things returned to normal the easier the recovery process would be.

Alaric returned to his room, he wanted to spend the afternoon by himself. The change in Bern was still bothering him and with enough time he knew that he could crack the riddle. Unfortunately he was not given enough time alone to continue his train of thought. There was a steady flow of people coming and going from his room. Hadar was the first, he was looking forward to seeing Alaric. He had not seen him since he left Lel Dinion. He wanted to catch up on all the news. As well as the command group there were also a number of functionaries who came to see if Alaric was comfortable, a group of tailors to make him some new clothes for the evening's entertainments and a couple of chef's to ask what his favourite dishes were. By the time it came to leave for the banquet he felt exhausted.

The throne room was the largest room in the palace. It had completely changed since they had sat down for the midday meal. The room was now filled with tables and chairs and elegantly decorated. When Alaric arrived the room was half empty. He had been given a seat at the head table with King Unwin, Princess Marina and Lord Richmond. Unwin attributed his rescue to Richmond as much as it was Alaric. He still couldn't remember most of the details, but Richmond had been there when he came too so he assumed that he had been involved.

The command group sat on another table with some of the palace's more senior officials. They were still treated as special guests, but not as special Richmond and Alaric. Alaric had wanted to sit with Bern as much as Richmond had wanted to be seated with Tancred, but Unwin had insisted on the seating arrangements. Princess Marina was also happy to be seated next to Alaric. The man who saved her father was worthy of her attention.

King Unwin smiled when he saw Alaric approach the table. He stood as a sign of respect. Alaric could instantly see the strength was starting to return to his character. He no longer looked like a bedraggled, frail man. He had cleaned himself and had his hair cut. He was now dressed in clean clothes, a crimson shirt with a dark grey trim. On his left breast was his family crest, a golden eagle holding onto a fig branch. He chose to wear his family crest opposed to the royal crest as a sign of personal respect for his guests. He had also left his crown and his kingly gown behind so his guests would be more relaxed. His daughter was dressed in a fine, black gown as dark as her shiny raven hair. She wore a delicate, glass tiara on her head with a small sapphire that hung half way down her forehead. She also wore a gold necklace with a golden chain and a similarly small sapphire. She blushed slightly as Alaric walked by.

The room filled as Alaric watched on. He felt somewhat self-conscious being on the main table. He just wanted to hide in the background. The more people who knew who he was the more at risk his life was. King Unwin made small talk with his two guests to try and make them feel more comfortable. He spoke to them about the dignitaries as they entered the room. He told them who and what their functions were. If he knew any more information he also divulged. Richmond found the conversation interesting whilst Alaric found it utterly boring. He found himself staring at Marina as Unwin spoke.

Alaric was glad when the first course was served. He was grateful that Unwin was trying to keep them entertained, but he was sick of all the gossip. When everyone had eaten and the food been taken away the first of the entertainments began. A group of jugglers and tumblers cavorted around the room. There was a small space in front of the main table, but the performers chose to use the entire room. They moved around the tables with great skill not to bump into anyone. The crowd clapped and cheered.

When the jugglers and tumblers had finished their performance the main course was served. Those at the head table were served first followed by the table the command group sat at. Once they were served a group of musicians entered the room. They set up their instruments towards the back of the room leaving the space in front of the main table for people to dance. Of course no one would dare step onto the dance floor before the King gave permission and that would not happen before the main meal had been cleared.

Alaric relaxed a lot more as he ate the main meal. The mood of the room seemed to have lightened since the entertainment had started. It was customary for Unwin to make a speech between the first two courses, but he moved away from ceremony to help everyone relax. His plan seemed to be working, although he was going to have to make a speech at some point during the night. It was expected of him, but more so he wanted to try and shed some light on their current situation. Although the household was aware that something had changed Unwin would still have to choose his words carefully.

Unwin waited for the right moment before he stood and cleared his throat.

"My Lords, ladies and my very close friends," Unwin bellowed. It was the most informal start to his speech. "I welcome you all to this wondrous occasion. As most of you already know we have been under the yoke of a very evil man. Our lives and our city have been turned upside down. I myself now know the feeling of being a prisoner for the first time in my life. The two men on my right are two men who have set us all free." Unwin paused and there was a great cheer from the crowd. Richmond couldn't help but smile, even though he knew that he had nothing to do with the rescue. "We are now free again, but all is not back to normal." The revelation brought a hush around the room. "It is now time for us to help ourselves. The Evil One still has agents within the city and possibly within the palace itself. We will find these traitors and deal with them accordingly." Another cheer came from the crowd, but not as loud as before. "It is now time for us to work with the other Kingdoms to root out the Evil One's agents throughout the Seven Kingdoms. This is not just something that affects Darshival, this is something that affects everyone." Unwin continued his speech for almost fifteen minutes before he raised his glass in a toast to Richmond and Alaric. When he was finished the crowd was cheering and yelling.

When Unwin had finished speaking the musicians continued their revelry. The dance floor remained empty. Normally it was Unwin and Marina who stole the first dance, but this time the Princess had other ideas. She leant over until she could speak directly into Alaric's ear.

"Would you do me the honour of the first dance?" she whispered softly into his ear.

The offer took Alaric by surprise. He wasn't expecting her to speak so closely to him and the question was even more surprising. He could smell her soft perfume and it made his heart skip a beat. Her dark hair brushed against the back of his neck and he looked across to Unwin before he gave his answer.

"Don't look at me son. People think that I call the first dance, but in truth it is the princess who calls the shots." King Unwin had a broad grin on his face.

"Well, come on then," Marina's voice lifted as she grabbed Alaric by the wrist.

Alaric was surprised at the strength in the young woman. She looked very dainty, but she was still able to pull Alaric from the table, not that he resisted very hard. He had not danced for a long time and wasn't sure if he remembered how. The last thing he wanted to do was to look like an idiot in front of the entire room.

The music buzzed in his ear as he followed the princess onto the dance floor. He could feel the blood coursing through his body. He felt flushed as Marina moved him into position. Something changed inside him as she placed her left hand on his waist and her right hand on his shoulder. Alaric waited for a change in the beat and then moved into action. He surprised himself with how light he was on his feet. It was as if his body was moving on its own.

"Relax," Marina whispered in his ear. "Once this song is over the others will join us."

The princess' confidence helped Alaric to relax. Her scent filled his nose and he thought that it was more intoxicating than the wine. Her hair swished around as they moved as one around the floor. For a moment Alaric forgot all his problems. For a moment there was no one else in the room besides the two of them. When the music stopped Alaric suddenly remembered Alena. He remembered her touches and smells. He also remembered that she was Nyrra's prisoner. As the dance floor started to fill Alaric let his grip on Marina slip away. His hands brushed down her side as he did. He looked up and saw a warm smile on her face. The sight made his heart melt, but there was nothing he could do. He could not enjoy himself while his friends were still prisoners.

"I am sorry. I think I will retire for the night," Alaric apologised.

Marina lent in slowly to kiss him goodnight on the check. Before her lips could touch him he turned and walked away. Bern was the only one who noticed the exchange. He had been watching them closely. He watched Alaric leave the throne room. For a moment he thought his old friend looked happy. Bern thought about following him to his room, but in the end he thought that he would leave him alone until morning.

Chapter 32: A New Revelation

Alaric was greeted by Bern at first light. He knew that Unwin would have plans for Alaric that day. There had been rumours that there would be another ceremony and Bern really wanted to speak to his old friend alone. He didn't know if Alaric would have the answers he was looking for, but there was no one else to ask. At the very least he would be able to speak about old times.

Alaric was also glad to see Bern. When there was a knock on the door he cringed to think who it might be. He had not slept and all he could think about were his friends Eldred and Alena. He didn't know what Nyrra had in store for them, but he knew it would not be pleasant. The thought of Alena being tortured filled his mind and when he saw Bern he was happy for the distraction.

"It is good to see you again Alaric," Bern spoke warmly as he entered the room carrying a small platter of fruit. "I know it was a good meal last night, but I thought it couldn't hurt to eat something this morning."

Alaric rose from his bed. The two men sat down at a small table and started to pick at the platter. Neither of them knew where to start. They both had lots of questions. Alaric looked closely at his friend before he spoke. The difference that he had noticed the day before had gone and all he could see was his old friend. He did not know if that disturbed him more or less.

As they picked at the fruit they spoke about what they had been doing since Alaric had left Bern with the Alliance. Neither of them went into too much detail about what had been happening and Alaric continued to watch for a return to the difference in Bern, but nothing happened.

After they had been speaking for nearly two hours Bern could no longer contain himself. If he was going to get answers from Alaric then he was going to have to divulge more information. He didn't know why he had been waiting so long to ask considering he was his best friend. There was no one else who could answer his question.

"Something is happening to me Alaric," Bern started.

"I have to admit that I have noticed something. It is not there all the time, but I have seen it." Alaric blurted his words out as Bern broached the subject.

Bern continued to explain what had happened in Avalon. Alaric was interested in hearing about the wall of fog and the way it made everyone feel. He was amazed to hear how Bern was able to see through the ruse. Bern continued to tell Alaric about the strange feeling he had and how sometimes he would regain consciousness and not know where he was or what he had done. He remembered some things and forgotten others.

"That is indeed a mystery." Alaric didn't know what to think. It made a lot of sense, but until he could see the change again he didn't think he could work out what was wrong. He let his head drop in his hands as he tried to think.

"It's alright Alaric, I am sure the answer will come to you." There was something in Bern's voice that made Alaric look up.

Alaric looked at his friend and he saw the difference that he had noticed before. Suddenly the realisation came to him. "Heryion?" Alaric almost couldn't believe it.

"Yes. I was wondering how long it was going to take for you to realise." There was a smile on Bern's face, although Alaric knew it was not Bern.

"How? Why? I don't understand." Alaric was in shock. "Weren't you killed at the Cauldron Mountain?"

"When we were in the mountain I underestimated the strength of Nyrra. I didn't think that he would be strong enough to attack me as well as you. It is hard to explain without getting too deep." Alaric leaned in to listen. "For now I will try to explain it as best I can. My life essence was cut loose from my body when Nyrra attacked me. All I could do was float along on the wind. Where it would lead me I had no idea. I thought that my time in this tale was over, but then I was sucked into another body." Alaric felt as though there was something more important in his comment than what he was saying. "It was the first time that the spirit inside my new body remained. This is still a new situation for me. At first I was able to control Bern as much as I wanted to, but he is a lot stronger than I first thought. His conscious has been taking over more and more. I can still control him, as I am doing at the moment, but it takes more strength so I can't do it as often as I would like. On the other hand there is strength in Bern that will be very important when the time comes." Alaric was trying his best to follow Heryion.

"So what does all this mean?" Alaric was still in shock.

Heryion thought for a moment, the expression on Bern's face not revealing anything. "I don't really know. There's a reason why I am sharing this body with your friend, but I don't know what it is. Maybe it will be revealed to me in due course, but I think that it will just be played out without anyone truly knowing why."

"Okay." Alaric was starting to come to terms with the idea. "There are things that you need to know."

Heryion raised an eyebrow, but did not speak. He was curious to hear what Alaric had to say.

"There is a Dark Knight working against you in the Alliance."

"I know," Heryion's answer surprised Alaric.

"Then why haven't you destroyed him?"

"It is better to keep him where I can keep an eye on him. I have been suspicious of him for a while, but I set a trap that he fell into not long ago," Heryion seemed pleased with himself. "I can't guarantee that in this form I would be able to beat a Dark Knight, at least not while I don't have full control. If I uncovered him publicly and he escapes then there is no telling what he will do. Whilst I have control of the army there is not much he can do to undermine me. There is too much support for the Alliance for him to be successful with any ruse. Whilst he is in the command group I can gauge what Nyrra wants us to do by his reactions. It is much better to leave him where he is."

Alaric had to admit that Heryion made sense. Unless he was sure that he could destroy the Dark Knight there was no reason to scare him away. He was a lot happier knowing that his former companion was in control of the army. He had heard that Jarwe had all but given Bern command.

"What about Bern. Does he know what is happening?"

"He knows that there is something, helping him, but he doesn't know who or what it is. I think that for now it is better it stays that way. If he knew the true story then he might try and force me out." Heryion had more to say, but Alaric interrupted him.

"Wouldn't that be a good thing? Then you could find another body to take control over," Alaric sounded hopeful.

"Unfortunately it doesn't work like that. There was a reason why I entered Bern's body. There was a reason why this was meant to happen. If he forces me out then I don't know if I will be able to return. I can feel it myself. There is more that we have to accomplish together. If he remains unknowing to the true situation then there is less chance he will get upset. He knows that I am here to help him when he needs it and that's all that he needs to know. When the time is right I will reveal myself to him." Heryion was firm on his reasoning.

"So what are you going to do now?" Alaric asked.

Heryion shook his head. "I don't know. I was hoping that you might have some suggestions... Possibly in the prophecy?"

Alaric didn't want to tell him that he had lost the tome, but there was no point in lying. "There is a slight problem there. One of the Dark Knight's has stolen it."

Heryion took the news even worse than Alaric had expected. The expression on Bern's face showed his true feelings.

"Why haven't you gone to recover it?" Heryion barked. "In the wrong hands the prophecy could be just as deadly as one of the *Stones of Power*," his voice was thick with concern.

"There is more that I have to do here," Alaric was defensive in his response. "I can feel the prophecy. It is still not too far away. It is calling to me, trying to draw me too it."

"Then you should go to it. It's calling you for a reason. It doesn't want to be in the hands of the enemy. It wants you to come and get it." Heryion had become agitated.

"That is all well and good, but there is something that is telling me to stay in Kiarome. That is much more powerful than the draw towards the prophecy. I have to remain here until that feeling has been sated. Besides, the Dark Knight who has the prophecy, is weak-minded and not very powerful."

"Why do you say that?" The last statement had piqued Heryion's attention and brought it away from the missing text.

"When he stole the prophecy from me he had a chance to try and kill me again. After his failed attempt in Bellarome I would have thought he would have taken his new opportunity. Instead he stole the prophecy and brought it straight here to Fenaroz. The only reason he would have come here was for protection. Now as soon as things started getting tough the Dark Knight has fled the city. I don't think that he needed to do that. With both of them in the city there was a chance they could have held the Alliance at bay. I have no doubt that this Dark Knight is weak," Alaric explained.

"Then it must be Na'garoz. He was always the weakest of them all. He would always align himself with one of his brothers. He is crafty. I don't think we want him to have the prophecy for very long. I just don't know which of the Knight's he will try and align himself with now."

"I don't think he will try and meet up with another Knight. I think he will try and find Nyrra himself." The words brought another raised eyebrow from Heryion. This time Alaric was going to wait for him to answer.

"Why do you say that? I don't think that he would want to find Nyrra, not if he failed to assassinate you." Heryion wasn't convinced with Alaric's line of thinking.

"After what happened here in Kiarome I don't think that he will want to get mixed up with one of his brother's schemes. I think that he will try and find Nyrra, but I don't think that he will."

"Now you are being ambiguous. Why would you say something like that?" Heryion eyed Alaric closely.

"I guess there are just some things that cannot be explained." In truth he didn't know why he thought Na'garoz would be out looking for Nyrra, but he knew that it was true. He also didn't know why he didn't think the Dark Knight would find him.

Heryion wasn't overly happy with the response. He could not stay angry though. Alaric's words were a sign that he was growing. He had noticed there had been a change in Alaric just as Alaric had noticed the change in Bern. There was something different about him. There was more confidence in his posture.

Before they could continue their conversation there was a knock on the door. Alaric wasn't sure if he wanted to open it or not. There was still much to be discussed, but he was glad that Heryion could not question him further. Reluctantly he called for whoever it was to enter.

A young man entered the room. "King Unwin has requested that you join him in the throne room." The man seemed quite nervous.

"Very good. We will be along shortly," Alaric dismissed the man quickly. "Well. It seems as though we are required in the throne room," he spoke to Heryion when the door was shut.

"What's going on?" There was a confused look on Bern's face.

Alaric looked at him for a moment before he realised what had happened. Heryion had disappeared back to wherever it was that he went and Bern had returned. Alaric thought that he should tell his old friend the truth, but he didn't want to take the risk. There was something at play that he didn't completely understand. Until he did he was going to keep the revelation to himself.

"It seems that this entity of yours has surfaced. He has an interesting outlook on life." Alaric tried to keep the conversation light.

"What is it?" Bern was almost breathless as he asked the question.

"I don't know exactly what's happening," it was only a half lie, but Alaric still felt guilty. "Unwin has requested our presence in the throne room. I don't think we should keep him waiting."

Bern noticed the change in Alaric's demeanour. It was clear that he wasn't telling him the entire story. He thought about questioning him, but his friend had already risen and was making his way to the door. He didn't know if Alaric knew what was happening to him, but it was obvious that he knew more than he was letting on. Bern didn't know how long the entity had been in control, but there was a reason why it had been speaking to Alaric.

"Are you coming?" Alaric called back into the room when Bern remained seated.

"Yes, I'll be right there," Bern said as he slowly rose from the table.

The two of them walked in silence towards the throne room. Alaric tried to stay half a step in front to make conversation difficult. He was hoping that if enough time passed that Bern would forget.

The throne room had changed again since the night before. King Unwin sat on his throne at the head of the room and Princess Marina sat in the slightly smaller one to his left, normally reserved for the Queen. Since her mother had died Unwin liked it when Marina sat next to him at official functions. There was a large empty space in front of the dais and then rows and rows of chairs. The chairs were almost completely full. The front row had been reserved for the command group and a few select dignitaries. There were two vacant seats for Bern and Alaric.

Once the two men were seated a middle-aged man walked out into the vacant space in front of the thrones. He cleared his throat and then called out for the crowd to be quiet.

"Lords, ladies, gentlemen and honoured guests," his voice boomed. "It is my great pleasure to once again introduce to you the magnificent King Unwin." Normally the herald would continue on with a tirade of compliments, but Unwin had instructed him to be as brief as possible.

King Unwin stood and stepped down from the dais. He walked up and down in the space in front of him. The action was just a show to pique the crowds' excitement. His royal robes swished out behind him as he turned around. Finally he stopped in front of his throne.

"This is a momentous occasion," Unwin spoke to the audience. Unwin repeated his speech from the night before, adding a few more garnishes.

Alaric yawned in the front row. He was glad that he had been drawn away from the conversation with Bern, but he did not feel like sitting through a boring speech. He knew that he was right where he was supposed to be. For the first time he could not feel anything trying to pull him in any direction. Even the prophecy was no longer calling.

"Now this is the real reason why we are here." The words brought Alaric's attention back to the King.

A young page boy came out from the door behind the dais carrying a small wooden box. The box was made from mahogany and had a number of ornate patterns carved into the side of it. On the lid was a large J carved deep in the wood. The boy carried the box very carefully. It looked as though it was the proudest day of his life and it probably would be. He had been chosen out of all the page boys to take the box out to Unwin. It was the greatest honour that could be bestowed upon a page, at least it was in their world.

"Alaric," Unwin spoke directly to him once he had the box in his hand. "Come up here with me."

Whatever was in the box had everyone in the room on the edge of their seat. Alaric slowly made his way to the dais. He was very aware that all the eyes in the room were watching him. He looked up and saw that Marina was watching him as well. The warm smile on her face made him feel better.

When Alaric was standing next to him, Unwin slowly opened the lid. At the start Alaric was the only person who could see what was inside. He saw the green blade first and as he looked further he saw a golden hilt with a green stone inlaid. The stone was made out of jade as was the blade. It took Alaric a moment before he realised what it was. The temptation to reach out and grab it was almost overwhelming, but a soft voice in his head told him to wait.

"The dagger has been a sign of strength within the royal family for many generations. It has brought peace and prosperity to the land when all hope has been lost." Unwin was quoting the stories he had been told when he was a child. "The dagger has been uplifting in times of doubt," Unwin continued on with the rhetoric. "Now it is time to pass on the dagger, to someone who not only deserves it, but also needs it." There was a gasp in the crowd. "Let this blade guide you when you get lost. Let it be a beacon of glory in times of distress."

After Unwin had been speaking for almost five minutes Alaric quietly cleared his throat in an attempt to gain his attention. The King didn't hear him and continued with his speech. When Alaric was sure he wasn't going to stop he cleared his throat again. This time King Unwin turned to him.

"Now I will get to the point. Alaric, for the service you have given me and my Kingdom I present you with this dagger," Unwin handed Alaric the box.

Alaric held the box aloft so everyone could see what was inside. He didn't know why he did it, he just felt that it was the appropriate thing to do. As he did there came an all mighty roar from the audience. They started slow chanting. "Alaric, Alaric!" The feeling was something he had never felt before and he basked in the glory.

"Now I think it would be a good time for you to say something," Unwin whispered.

Alaric lowered the box and looked at the dagger. It looked as though the jewel in the hilt was gently glowing. There was something very compelling about the stone. If there had been any doubt in his mind before there was no doubt now. He was sure that this was the *Jade Stone of Power*. Slowly he wrapped his hands around the hilt and lifted the blade from its box. There came another great roar from the crowd. He held the blade out above his head so the crowd could get a better view. As he did the Jade Stone started to glow brighter. The sight brought a hush over the crowd and took Alaric by surprise.

"What is it that you want?" a voice spoke inside his head. The sound was such a shock that Alaric almost dropped the dagger. He quickly returned it to its box and shut the lid.

"I thank you for the gift." Alaric did his best to fill the silence. "I will do my best to uphold the honour you have bestowed upon me." The crowd cheered again. Alaric didn't want to be on the dais anymore. The feeling that had been tugging at his very fibre had returned. Now it was drawing him away from the throne room and it was more persistent than it had ever been. "I have to go now," he said as a thin layer of sweat appeared on his brow and the colour drained from his face.

"That's alright. It is not easy to speak in front of a crowd," Unwin thought that he was just nervous. "Just a few more minutes and we will be right to leave."

The feeling that Alaric had to leave the throne room was overpowering. The mahogany box felt almost too heavy to hold and his legs started to wobble. He didn't think he could remain upright much longer. Finally, before he lost consciousness, he left the dais towards the back of the throne room. There was a hushed murmur over the crowd as they watched him disappear out the back door.

Unwin wanted to go after him, but there was still more he had to do. He had to greet, thank and introduce the command group to the crowd. The citizens would be more relaxed about the army outside the city if they knew who was in control. He took one last look at the back door before he faced the crowd again. It took a moment for him to regain control, but once he did they all forgot about Alaric and his mysterious disappearance. Bern wanted to leave and go after Alaric, but in the absence of Jarwe he was to be recognised as the leader of the Alliance.

Alaric made his way back to his room feeling much better. The feeling drawing him away from the throne room was pulling him towards his room in the palace. He couldn't relax until he had safely closed the door behind him. He rushed to the table and placed down the wooden box before taking a step back. As he looked at the box he thought he could hear a faint tapping coming from inside. It was as if some small creature was trying to get out.

There was something very strange about the dagger, not that Alaric was expecting it to be normal. Nothing that involved one of the *Stones of Power* was going to be normal. Something wasn't right though and he felt as though it was pertinent to his situation. He couldn't bring himself to open the box, although there was something inside him telling him that was exactly what he should do. He moved towards it and sat down at the table. He placed his chin on his hands and stared at the intricate engravings.

It was in that position that Bern found him over an hour later. He was still staring at the box, listening to the gentle rapping that he wasn't even sure was real. He wasn't sure if he should let it out, whatever it was.

He didn't look up when his old friend entered the room. He was afraid that if he broke his gaze then something terrible would happen.

"Are you alright?" Bern asked. "You left the throne room in such a hurry. I would have come after you, but it was my turn to be embarrassed."

Slowly Alaric looked up from what he was doing. "Sorry, but I couldn't stay. I wouldn't have lasted another second."

"That's alright. Now let's have a look at the gift that Unwin gave you," Bern sounded excited.

"It is not as simple as that," Alaric made no move to open the lid. "The jewel inlaid in the hilt is the *Jade Stone of Power*. I think that it's calling to me." There was something in Alaric's voice that made Bern concerned. "If it remains in the case then it cannot harm anyone."

"I don't think the dagger wants to hurt anyone. If it did then it would have called out to Fenaroz," Alaric recognised Heryion's tone. "I think that this is all part of the prophecy."

Alaric sat back in his chair. The words made sense. There was no real reason why he should be afraid of the Jade stone. Slowly he let his hand come to rest on the top of the box. He let his fingers move over the J and a feeling of calm came over him. The thoughts of dread had completely left him as he slowly lifted the lid. Alaric thought he caught a glimmer of light from the stone, but when he looked closer the Jade was completely dull.

"It's magnificent." Heryion had moved around until he could see the dagger. "I had no idea that it has been here all this time."

"I think you are going to have to help me with some information." There was something in the back of Alaric's mind telling him that he already knew the answer to the question.

"As you know this is the *Jade Stone of Power*, attached to the hilt of this dagger. The ancient artefact has been missing for hundreds of years. I believe that it was the Jade stone that drew all of us to Kiarome. We are fortunate that one of the Dark Knights didn't get their hands on it," Heryion sounded excited.

"What is the significance of the dagger?" Alaric knew that there was an answer somewhere in the back of his mind, but he hoped Heryion could give him one.

"The dagger itself has no significance, or at least none that I really know. It's the stone," Heryion was enjoying himself. He bobbed up and down as he spoke. "You see the Jade stone is like the big brother of the stone family. It likes to keep track of what the other stones are up to." Suddenly it all made sense. He looked at the dagger with renewed interest. As he did Heryion continued to speak. "I wasn't sure exactly how the dagger would work, but your little demonstration has showed me. If you move the dagger around the stone will glow when it is pointing to one of the other stones."

"How do I know which one it is pointing to?"

"That I don't know. Maybe the colour of the Jade Stone changes, but I doubt it. I think that you will just have to trust that the stone knows where it will be sending you." The smile still remained on Bern's face.

"I don't like the sound of that. I don't have enough time to be chasing around the Seven Kingdoms on the whim of the stone."

"I don't see how you have time for anything else. Whilst the Ruby Stone is out in the open there is a risk that Nyrra will recover it. You must recover the other stones, one by one if you have to, until you find the Ruby Stone." The smile had left his face. The task ahead of Alaric would not be easy.

"Not only that but I still have to recover the prophecy from Na'garoz. There is no telling what sort of mischief he will get up to with it in his possession." The temptation to pick up the dagger was almost impossible to resist. He felt as though there was something calling to him in the back of his mind. Alaric did the only thing that would keep him sane. Slowly he closed the lid. Once the lid was closed the feeling disappeared.

"Unfortunately I can't help you with that decision. Time is against us and without the prophecy we are travelling blind." Heryion wasn't making Alaric feel any better.

Alaric let out a deep breath. The situation wasn't getting any better. He knew that he had a while to think about his next move. There was still much work to be done in Kiarome, even without the Dark Knight the agents of Nyrra still in the city could cause trouble. He could only hope that the right decision would come to him. He could still feel the prophecy in the distance. He knew that Na'garoz was off to the east, but he could no longer point to his exact location.

"Oh well. It doesn't look like we are going to be going anywhere in a hurry," Alaric wanted to fill the silence more than anything else.

"We shall see. There is no telling what will happen tomorrow," Alaric could see that Heryion had disappeared and Bern had returned. "Can I have another look at the dagger?" Bern asked. He didn't seem to notice that he had lost time.

"Sure," Alaric opened the case. The strange feeling in the back of his mind returned. He did his best to ignore it. He looked at the stone in the hilt. He knew that it marked the end of one journey and the start of another. He didn't know what was in store for him in the future, but he knew it was not going to be easy.

Epilogue: Pain and Suffering

Eldred sat in the corner of their cell. He wrapped his arms around his legs and let his head rest against his knees. He thought about rocking, but that would be admitting he had been broken. He could hear Alena whimpering in the far corner. It would have been the right thing for him to comfort her, but he had already done enough of that.

They had been in Jarrat for at least two weeks, Eldred was sure of that. He wasn't sure, however, exactly how long they had been trapped as the days had begun to merge together. Sometimes they would keep their prison dark for what seemed like days on end. There was also something different about the cell they were in. Eldred assumed they were kept apart from the other prisoners as there were no sounds of anyone else being tortured. That only posed more questions. If they were away from other prisoners then they were deeper in the dungeon system than he had originally thought. Their chance for escape became ever smaller.

Eldred felt his stomach churn. There was something in the water, he was sure of it. When they first were taken prisoner at Nostiria he felt the spell that blocked his powers. It had only happened to him once before, but the feeling was infuriating. Since they had been in the prison the spell had faded away, but he could still not draw on the power around him. If it was not in the water then it was in the food. It was certainly something he was consuming. Not only did it stop his magic it also made him feel sick. Occasionally he would retch, but whatever it was they were dosing him with remained in his body. It was strange. In all of Eldred's years of studying magic, and there were many, he had never come across any herb or poison that could block anyone's abilities. He could only surmise that it had come from the Northern Wastelands.

As he sat in the corner, listening to the gentle sobs of Alena, he thought back to the first day they had arrived in Jarrat. He had been somewhat relieved that they had reached their destination. The travelling has been hard and it was good to stop, but the feeling of relief didn't last long. Once they were in the palace the true hardship began.

"So what do we have here?" The voice was vaguely familiar.

Someone removed the black hood from Eldred's face. Bruises and dried blood had distorted his normal features. Eldred looked up from the chair his was bound to and saw a face that made his heart stop. The face had perfect features with short cropped, blonde hair. The man's physique was almost perfect. A soft, grey, silk shirt hung loosely over his shoulders with the top half buttons undone showing his smooth, lightly tanned chest. There was a magnificence in the man's appearance that Eldred knew was completely fake. Eldred did not know why Ra'naroz had chosen such a façade. There would have been a greater effect of fear if he showed his true features.

"I see the worm has crawled out from under the ground," Eldred tried his best to sound strong, but he could not hide the pain he had suffered.

Ra'naroz laughed out loud as he paced back and forth in front of the imprisoned wizard. His attention then turned to the she-elf who was bound and gagged. There was something sinister with the smile that appeared on his face when he saw her. He stood directly in front of her and gently caressed her face with his hand. Alena shook her head until his hand moved away.

"It seems the Great Lord's future bride has some strength to her," Ra'naroz said as he kept his gaze fixed on Alena.

Alena tried to speak, but it was just a muffled groan. She was almost in as much pain as Eldred, although no one could tell by looking at her. They all knew what would happen if Alena showed any outward signs of damage. Viper had been the one who had administered most of the torture. The serpentant now stood at the back of the room where neither of the two prisoners could see him.

"Leave her alone. It is me that you want," Eldred leaned as far forward as he could to try and look threatening.

Eldred's plan worked, but only for a moment. Ra'naroz moved away from Alena and returned his attention to the wizard. He looked at Eldred closely, as if he was studying him for the first time, or trying to place where he knew him from.

"Yes, you are right, but all good things come in time. For now you will tell me what you know about the one you call Alaric." Ra'naroz squatted down on his haunches so he was face to face with Eldred.

"There is nothing that I can tell you that you don't already know. In time you will face each other and he will destroy you." Eldred used the opportunity for a cheap blow.

Ra'naroz returned to his feet. He mused for a moment before he turned his back on him and took a number of steps away. "Viper, show our guests what we do to those who don't want to help."

The serpentant walked forward until he was within striking distance. The first blow struck Eldred across the side of his face. It was enough to open an existing wound which started to bleed. The next attack was a lot more subtle, yet much more painful. Viper took a step backwards and closed his eyes. A subtle flutter of his eyelids was the only sign of what was to come. A moment later Eldred let out a scream that echoed throughout the room. The sound was enough to make Alena start screaming, although it was again only a muffled noise.

When the screaming died down Ra'naroz turned to face him again. "Now, as I am sure that you know I can keep this up as long as you can."

"There is nothing that you can do," Eldred puffed his response, the pain obvious.

Ra'naroz nodded to the serpentant and it was not long before the screaming started again. It lasted a few seconds longer before it ceased. Eldred's body slumped in the chair, as much as his bonds would allow. The blood continued to flow from the cut on his face.

"Now let's start again." Ra'naroz walked closer to Eldred. "Tell me what you know about Alaric."

Eldred was breathing deeply. There was still a residue of pain coursing though his body making it hard for him to regain his composure. There was nothing he could do. He knew the pain would continue until he told Ra'naroz what he wanted to know. He also knew that he could not give anything away.

"Do your worst," Eldred did his best to sit up straight in a sign of defiance.

"Very well..." were the last words Eldred heard.

The screams came out of his mouth again for a moment before he went silent. It was at that point that Eldred woke with a start. He had not even realised that he had been unconscious, but he was glad he was alive. He could only imagine what they had done to Alena after he had passed out. He didn't have the heart to ask her and she didn't reveal anything to him.

The torture had continued for the next few days. Each time it ended in the same way. Eldred would lose consciousness before he revealed any information. Each time he would remain conscious a little longer and the pain lasted a lot longer. He knew that it would only be a matter of time before he died. His captors also knew that and had stopped the interrogations. The only other time the door opened was when someone threw down their food.

Eldred did not know how long he had been asleep. He could hear the gentle sound of Alena sleeping. It calmed him as it was the first time that she rested without screaming since they had arrived. There was something comforting in that thought. Eldred panicked when he heard the sound of the cell door swing open and saw a light shine in.

"It is time for you to speak," Eldred recognised the voice as Viper. "You have been strong up until now, but that time is over."

Eldred didn't respond. There was nothing he could say that would make any difference.

"Now come on, let's not go through this again." Viper was becoming bored with the charade.

"Why do you bow down to Nyrra?" Eldred asked as he got to his feet. "He has done nothing to help your kind. All he has done is made you his slave." There was a slim chance that Eldred could talk Viper into letting them go. It was the first time the serpentant had visited them alone.

"Don't you worry about me," Viper's said. "I know exactly what I am doing, do you?"

Eldred slowly made his way towards the door. He knew that there was nothing else he could do. He could try talking to Viper, but he didn't think there was much point. He only hoped that this time he would leave Alena alone. She was strong, but not nearly as strong as him. It was the first time she had slept peacefully for a long time.

"It's time to go for a little walk," Viper hissed.

As much as Eldred knew he was heading for more pain he knew the walk would be good for his legs. There wasn't much room to move in their prison cell and the exercise would do him good.

As he left the cell he could feel the brush of magic pass him. He knew that Viper was waking Alena. There was nothing he could do to stop him. He cursed at not being able to harness the energy that surrounded him. Without the power he could do nothing to help them escape.

It was no surprise to Eldred that there were no guards outside the cell. He also knew there was no chance of them overpowering Viper. It would just take a simple spell to put them both back in their place. Viper still wore his dark robe with the hood covering his head. Only his yellow eyes could be seen and occasionally his red, forked tongue as it flicked out.

He led the two of them along the dimly light tunnel towards the interrogation room. The questions would remain the same and so would the answers. The only thing that would vary would be the amount of pain they suffered. They had been given enough opportunity to recover from the first round of interrogations, but they were both still drained, physically and mentally.

Waiting for them in the interrogation room was a large man holding an evil looking leather whip. A smile appeared on his face when he saw the three of them enter. His pleasure disturbed Eldred.

"I am surprised that your master let you off your leash," Eldred said.

"Ra'naroz is not my master. There is more to this situation than you know." Viper paused before he gave away too much information. "Don't think that I am going to go easy on you. I have been left in charge of getting information from you and that is what I shall do." Viper's voice was dripping with arrogance. Eldred thought that it was for the torturer's benefit than any real emotion.

"No, I am just surprised that the Dark Knight would leave you in charge of such a thing," Eldred spoke casually as he walked towards the chair at the back of the room.

The words were hitting their mark. Viper was starting to become unsettled. Eldred wasn't entirely sure what he was trying to achieve, but he wanted to see how it played out.

"I know what you are trying to do." Viper reached out and grabbed Alena by the throat. "Such a pretty one," Viper flicked his tongue at her. "What's wrong Eldred? Got nothing to say now?"

Alena looked dead on her feet. She didn't seem to notice the grip Viper had on her. At least that was something. There was no pain on her face. Viper moved her to a wall with two shackles hanging down at head height. Without releasing his grip he used a small amount of power to chain her to the wall.

"Do what you like to us. We're not going to tell you anything." Eldred's eyes didn't leave Alena.

"Oh, I plan on it. You see it doesn't worry me in the slightest if you talk or not. My friend here is going to entertain you for a while. I'll return later in the day and see if you've changed your mind." Viper nodded at the torturer before he closed the door to the cell.

Eldred was securely tied to the chair at the far end of the cell, but it was Alena who the torturer set his attention. He sniggered as he ripped her shirt to reveal her skin.

"Leave her alone!" Eldred screamed, his emotions getting the better of him.

"Patience. It'll be your time soon," the torturer spoke with a drawl that was hard to understand.

Alena made no noise as the whip lashed against her back. That was the only saving grace. It seemed as though she had lost consciousness when Viper left the cell. Eldred closed his eyes. He couldn't bear to watch her being tortured, even if she couldn't feel anything. All he could do was wait for his own treatment and hope that someone would come and rescue them sooner rather than later.